GRAHAM
MASTERTON

TAKEN
FOR DEAD

HEAD
of ZEUS

First published in the UK in 2015 by Head of Zeus Ltd

9 7 5 3 1 2 4 6 8

A catalogue record for this book is available
from the British Library.

ISBN (HB) 9781781856802
ISBN (TPB) 9781781856819
ISBN (E) 9781781856796

Typeset by Ben Cracknell Studios, Norwich.

Printed in Germany
by GGP Media GmbH, Pössneck

Head of Zeus Ltd
Clerkenwell House
45–47 Clerkenwell Green
London EC1R 0HT

WWW.HEADOFZEUS.COM

For all the children of Dom Dziecka orphanage
in Górzec, Poland with affection and
best wishes for the future.

'Is i ding diféin a scoileann an dair'
'The oak is split by a wedge from its own wood'

One

'Congratulations and God's blessings on you both,' said Father Michael, coming up to Connor and Niamh and taking hold of their hands. 'What a wonderful, wonderful wedding! You'll be remembering this day for the rest of your lives!'

'It's all been perfect, father,' said Niamh, her cheeks flushed red. 'I loved what you said about Connor and me never forgetting to laugh, no matter how hard things might sometimes turn out.'

'Well, that's the secret of a lasting marriage,' said Father Michael. 'If there's one thing the devil can't bear, it's mockery.'

Niamh was so happy that her eyes were sparkling with tears, and her mascara was blotched. 'And I couldn't *believe* it – when Connor put the ring on my finger – the way the sun came shining all of a sudden through the stained-glass windows. It was like God Himself was pleased we were getting married.'

'I'm sure that He is, Niamh.'

'And none of the babies cried, did they, even when the organ played?'

'My mother cried, though,' put in Connor. 'She was honking like a seal.'

'Well, you know what they say,' smiled Father Michael. 'When a man gets married, a mother loses a son, but when a woman gets married, a father gains a feller to go fishing with!'

At that moment, Niamh's father came over, his rough cheeks even redder than Niamh's and his grey comb-over flying awry. 'It's time for the cutting of the cake, sweetheart! Everybody's ready!'

Connor took hold of Niamh's hand and they made their way through the guests gathered in the main function room. More than two hundred of them had been invited to the wedding ceilidh, and they could have invited more, because Connor's father was a popular city councillor, as well as owning O'Malley's Outfitters on Patrick Street, and Niamh's father was a partner in the Greenleaf Garden Centre up in Ballyvolane.

At the far end of the room, the Brendan Collins Boys had been playing 'The Coalminer's Reel' but now they stopped and the guests all applauded. Connor and Niamh had been blessed by the weather, even though it was October and chilly outside. The hotel stood on a high, steep hill overlooking the city, and down below the sun was gleaming on the River Lee so that its reflected light was flickering on the ceiling.

'Look,' said Niamh, pointing upwards. 'Even the angels are dancing.'

The wedding cake was composed of three large tiers, one on top of the other, frosted white, with sugar swags piped all the way around them. Miniature figures of the bride and groom stood on top. Niamh's father handed Connor and Niamh a large silver knife and said, 'Well done, the both of you. But you make sure you leave the biggest slice for me.'

Holding the knife together, Connor and Niamh started with the topmost cake, while cameras and iPhones flashed and everybody clapped and whistled. They easily cut through the first two cakes, because they were only sponge and vanilla cream, but they had only just started to cut down into the third and largest cake, at the bottom, when they stopped abruptly. They slowly withdrew the knife, frowning at each other.

'What the *feck* is that?' mouthed Connor. He prodded the point of the knife cautiously back into the side of the cake, but it wouldn't penetrate more than three inches.

'What's the matter, Conn?' called out one of his friends.

'There's something inside there,' he said. 'I don't know what it is, but it's pretty big, and it's *hard*.'

Connor's father came up, putting down his glass of champagne. He was a bulky, broad-shouldered man, with a high plume of white hair. He looked as if he would burst out of his tight grey morning suit at any moment. 'What do you mean, Conn, *hard*?'

'There is – there's something hard in there,' said Niamh. 'I felt it myself.'

'There can't be anything *hard* in there, girl! That's a sponge cake. Nothing but sponge. I ordered it myself from Crounan's.'

Connor's father took the knife and jabbed it into the cake. Like Connor, though, he could only manage to insert the blade two or three inches. He jabbed again, and then again, rotating the cake stand so that he could attack it all the way around, from every possible angle.

The guests were standing around with drinks in their hands, watching and chattering.

'Whatcha doing there, John?' called out one slurred voice, from the back. 'Trying to make sure it's dead?'

A few of the guests laughed, but when Connor's father looked up, most of them could see from his expression that something was badly wrong, and they fell silent. Connor and Niamh were now standing well back, by the windows that overlooked the city, and Niamh was biting her thumbnail.

Niamh's father and mother came up and said, 'What's wrong, John? What's going on?'

'There's something inside this cake, Barry. Something hard. I don't have any idea what, but we'll have to cut it apart and take a sconce at it.'

'What do you mean *something hard*?'

'I just told you, Barry. I haven't a clue.'

'What did I say?' snapped Niamh's mother. 'I said we should have ordered the cake ourselves! This had better not spoil things, John. This is Niamh's big day, and I'll not have it ruined because the two of you were too stingy to buy a proper cake from Bracken's.'

'I'll need a hand here, Connor,' said his father. 'I'm going to slice off the top two cakes so that we can find out just what the hell it is in the bottom one. It is big, you're right, and it is hard.'

'I can't believe this,' said Niamh's mother. '"Oh, we'll get the cake for free," you said, and now look. Too mean to part with a hundred euros, and there's poor Niamh almost in tears.'

As patiently as he could, Connor's father said, 'Anna – I admit Micky Crounan supplied me with this cake buckshee, as a favour, because I helped him to put through his planning application. But Crounan's is a first-class baker's and you know it.'

'So that's why you're cutting open my daughter's wedding cake to make sure it doesn't have a brick in it, or something? I've done that so often myself, like – accidentally dropped a brick in my cake mixture. Or a shoe. Or a cookery book. It's so easy done.'

'Anna,' said Niamh's father, and shook his head to indicate that she should keep her sarcasm to herself, at least for now.

Very carefully, Connor's father sliced off the top cake, which Connor set down on a plate; then the second cake. He was left with the bottom cake, with a circle of icing around the outside, and a sponge circle in the middle. By now the guests were clustering close to the table to see what he was doing.

'What's the story, John?' asked one of them.

'They told him there was euros baked into it,' said another. 'He couldn't bear the thought of anybody else getting a single one of them.'

Connor's father ignored this banter and picked up a dessert spoon. He started to scrape away at the sponge, little by little, his forehead furrowed in concentration, like an archaeologist scraping away the soil covering a Roman statue.

A small black lump appeared. It was soft and rubbery, and in colour and texture it resembled a blackcurrant pastille. He continued to scrape all around it and gradually two triangular holes appeared below it. To his horror, he realized that the

4

blackcurrant pastille wasn't a blackcurrant pastille at all, but the bulbous tip of somebody's nose. It was black because it had started to decompose.

At the same time, he became aware that a smell much stronger than vanilla was rising from the cake. It was sweet and it was fetid and his cousin had been an undertaker so he knew at once what it was. He retched, and then he stood up straight and flapped his hand at the guests gathered around him.

'Get back,' he managed to say, before he retched again. He pressed his knuckles to his lips for a moment to regain his composure, and then said, 'Please, folks, get right back. Somebody call the guards for me. Please. Tell them it's urgent.'

'In the name of Jesus, what *is* that?' asked Niamh's mother.

'Please . . . get back,' Connor's father told her.

'John? What's the matter?' asked Father Michael, making his way around the table and laying his hand on Connor's father's shoulder.

He peered short-sightedly down at the spooned-out remains of the wedding cake and said, 'What in God's name is *that* you've found in it? And what is that *smell*?' He took out his wire-rimmed spectacles and inspected the cake more closely.

'Holy Mary, Mother of God,' he said almost immediately, and crossed himself.

Connor's father turned around to Connor and said, 'Take Niamh off with you, Connor! Take her well away!'

'What is it, Dad? Tell me!'

'Just take Niamh away. Get yourselves changed for your honeymoon. I'm sorry, but the ceilidh's over.'

Niamh's mother elbowed her way past Father Michael. 'It's no good you telling me to get back, John, and not telling me the reason! This is my daughter's wedding ceilidh and we've paid thousands for it!'

The guests were milling around in confusion. The hotel's deputy manager was pushing his way through the crowd to find out what was wrong. The Brendan Collins band had set down their bodhrán and their flutes and their double bass and were looking bewildered.

Connor's father said, 'I'm not going to dig into it any further, but that's a man's nose there in the middle of that cake. I think there's somebody's head baked into it.'

Two

Michael Gerrety came down the courthouse steps, surrounded by an entourage that included his solicitor, James Moody, his wife, Carole, and three hard-looking men with shaven heads and black nylon windcheaters.

Halfway down, he stopped for a moment and looked across at Katie, and when he was sure that he had her attention, he gave her the sweetest of smiles. A very handsome man, Michael Gerrety, with his broad face and wavy chestnut hair. If Katie hadn't known what he had done, and what kind of a man he was, she could have found him quite attractive.

The media had all gone now, but Katie was still talking to Finola McFerren, the state solicitor for Cork City. She paused to smile back at him, although she knew what his smile really meant – *I told you I'd get away with it, you ineffectual bitch*. Her smile, in return, meant – *I'll nail you one day, you hypocritical scumbag, don't you have any doubt of it*.

'I *still* think we were right to go ahead and bring this in front of the court,' Finola was saying. She was a very tall young woman, with a beaky nose and a slight stoop, and there was always an air of tension about her, like a bird of prey that was just about to launch itself off a ledge to swoop down on a rabbit. 'It shows that we're determined to put an end to sex-trafficking, in spite of all the political and legal difficulties we're up against. But next time we prosecute Michael Gerrety, we *must* have much more conclusive evidence.'

'Well, I really thought we had more than enough dirt on him this time,' said Katie, still keeping her eyes on him. 'It didn't help that half of our witnesses didn't appear and the ones that did show up had suddenly developed amnesia. And his own witnesses didn't just say that the sun shone out of his arse. They seemed to think that we ought to get in touch with the Vatican and have him canonized.'

'You can't blame those girls for being frightened,' said Finola. 'Apart from sex work, what else are they going to do for a living? But come back to me whenever you like. You know that the courts will accept all kinds of covert surveillance these days.'

'You don't think we haven't bugged his sex shop, and his brothels? But he's a very cute hoor, is Michael Gerrety. I've never heard him once say anything on tape that might incriminate him. But I *will* get him. You wait and see.'

She watched with her lips pursed as Michael Gerrety climbed into his metallic-green Mercedes and drove away. The sun was so bright this morning that she was wearing her Ray-Bans but one of the nose pads had broken so that they were lopsided. Because of that, she was too dazzled to see Detective O'Donovan puffing up the steps until he had reached her. He was wearing a big ginger overcoat which matched his hair.

'I've been trying to ring you, ma'am,' he panted.

'What? Oh, it's you, Patrick! I've been in court all morning. Sorry, I haven't switched my phone back on.'

'Me neither,' said Finola. 'It's a blessed relief sometimes.'

'What's the story?' asked Katie. 'They haven't found Roisin Begley, have they?' Roisin Begley was the sixteen-year-old daughter of one of Cork's wealthiest property developers, and she had been missing now for more than forty-eight hours.

'No, no progress with that, I'm afraid. No – there's been an incident up at the Montenotte Hotel. You know that John O'Malley's son Connor was getting married today, didn't you?'

'Yes, to the Gallaghers' daughter. What's her name? Niamh. What's happened? Are they all right?'

'They're both grand altogether, don't worry. But it was during their wedding ceilidh. They were cutting the cake and they found something inside it that looks like a human head.'

'A *what* did you say? A human head?' Katie took off her sunglasses. 'You're codding me. Inside the wedding cake?'

'It seems like the bride and groom couldn't cut it all the way through so John O'Malley took it to pieces to find out what was in it. He came across a nose sticking out. After that he stopped digging and who can blame him? Nobody's touched the cake since.'

'Name of Jesus,' said Katie. 'Do they have any idea who the head belongs to? Or *used* to belong to?'

Detective O'Donovan shook his head. 'No idea. Horgan's up there with Dooley and they've cordoned off the main reception area. All we're doing now is waiting on the technical boys. They're down in Ballea at the moment because some feller got himself all caught up in a plough, but they've been notified, and they'll be up to Montenotte as soon as they've finished untangling him, like.'

'Okay,' said Katie. 'What about the wedding guests?'

'There were two hundred and seventeen of them altogether. Most of them are still there, but they're letting them go once they've been interviewed.'

'All right. Let's go up there, shall we? Finola – you'll send me your report on this fiasco, won't you? I have to go over it with Acting Chief Superintendent Molloy and I'm sure he'll be over the moon that Michael Gerrety got off. They'll probably go out to the Hayfield Manor tonight and crack open a bottle of champagne.'

Finola said nothing, but snapped her briefcase shut and raised her precisely pencilled eyebrows as if to say, We both know what's going on, but we'll just have to wait for the moment to present itself, won't we? Those rabbits may be gambolling today, but the time will come when we can swoop down on them.

***

When they arrived outside the Montenotte Hotel on the Middle Glanmire Road at least a hundred wedding guests were still assembled in the car park, most of the women with their partners' morning coats slung around their shoulders to keep them warm, and everybody blowing into their cupped hands and stamping their feet. Two Garda patrol cars were parked right outside the side entrance to the function room and three officers were standing around, stamping their feet like everybody else. Although it was such a sunny day, the front of the hotel was in shadow.

Katie went inside, and walked across to the long table by the window. The function room was silent and the decorative streamers and balloons pinned up around the ceiling only made it seem more abandoned. Every table was crowded with half-finished glasses of champagne.

Detectives Horgan and Dooley were standing by the wreckage of the wedding cake, along with the hotel's deputy manager and John O'Malley. Katie thought that the deputy manager looked very young, although his blond hair was thinning. As she approached he took a step back, and then another. It occurred to her that she must appear rather schoolmistressy in her long black overcoat and the light grey suit she had worn for her court appearance. She had recently had her hair cropped very short, which her sister Moirin said made her look too stern.

John O'Malley blurted out, 'I'm shocked, Katie. Totally devastated. This has ruined Connor and Niamh's day completely.'

Katie looked at the blackened nose protruding from the sponge. The ripe smell of rotting flesh and vanilla was enough to make her hold her hand over her face.

'Where did the cake come from?' she asked.

'Crounan's. I ordered it from Micky Crounan myself.'

'When did it arrive here?'

'Only this morning,' said the deputy manager. 'It came about a quarter to eleven.'

'Who brought it?'

'A van pulled up outside and two fellows in white overalls carried it in between them. They said they came from Crounan's, although there was no lettering on the van. It was just plain white. I signed for the cake myself and that was it.'

'Would you know these two men if you saw them again?'

The deputy manager shook his head. 'I doubt it very much. I was so busy at the time. I would say that one of them at least came from north Limerick, the way he said "G'luck teh yeh so" when he left. My grandpa always said that, in exactly that accent, and he came from Moyross Park.'

'All right,' said Katie. 'I expect the media will be here soon asking you questions about this. Can you please not make any comment to them until we let you know that it's okay for you to do so? And when you do, can you keep any speculation down to the minimum?'

The deputy manager blinked at her as if he didn't understand what she meant.

'For instance, can you please not tell the media that you think that somebody was deliberately trying to ruin this wedding ceilidh, or any other theory that might occur to you?'

'Oh, yes. No,' said the deputy manager.

Detective Horgan said, 'We've been interviewing every single guest, but we're not getting much out of them. The cake was already on display here when they arrived, so none of them could have tampered with it. The O'Malleys and the Gallaghers are both very popular, what with everything they do for charity and all, and not one of the guests can think of anyone who would want to spoil things for them.'

Katie turned to John O'Malley and said, 'You've had no arguments with anybody lately? No threats made against you, for any reason?'

'I voted against the Lower Lee flood barrier last week, and that didn't go down too well with some of the city-centre shopkeepers, but that's about all. Nothing that would justify an atrocity like this. If I've upset somebody this bad, why didn't they cut my head off and bake it into a cake, instead of whoever this is?'

'How about the hotel?' asked Katie. 'Have you had any trouble-some guests lately?'

'No more than usual,' said the deputy manager. 'You get some of them drinking too much and making a nuisance of themselves, or making too much noise in their rooms. We threw out one fellow last week for nearly burning the place down. He was so langered he couldn't work out how to turn up the heating, so he set fire to his mattress.'

***

It was another forty-five minutes before the technicians arrived. Three of them came rustling across the function room in their white Tyvek suits, as if they had just arrived from a space mission.

Katie said, 'How's your man in Ballea?'

'Oh, dead,' said the chief technician. '*Very* dead.' He was very grey, with short grey hair and a grey, lined face. Katie imagined that all the horrors he had witnessed in his career had gradually leached all the colour out of him, in the same way that people's hair was supposed to turn white when they encountered a ghost.

'Apparently the victim suffered from epilepsy,' he added. 'What-ever the cause might have been, he fell backwards out of the seat of his tractor into a double-direction disc plough.'

'Oh. *Ow*! Nasty.'

'We had the devil's own job getting him out of there, I can tell you. Have you ever got a lamb bone stuck in your mincer?'

'Thank you, Bill. I feel sick enough as it is. Look at the state of this. The bride and groom were cutting their cake when they felt there was something inside it. Mr O'Malley here took it apart and this is what he discovered.'

The chief technician leaned forward and examined the tip of the nose closely. 'Partly decomposed and partly *cooked*,' he said. 'We'll photograph this here, *in situ*, and then I think we'll take it with us back to the lab. We'll be able to scan it then with the ultrasound and test it for fingerprints and any other evidence before we cut it up any more. People often lick the spoon when they're icing a cake so we may be lucky and find some DNA.'

'I'll leave it with you, then,' said Katie. 'But please send me an image of the victim's face the minute you have one. The sooner we know who he is, the sooner we'll be able to track down our Demon Baker.'

Three

To Katie's relief, Acting Chief Superintendent Molloy had already left the station by the time she returned to Anglesea Street.

Katie's working relationship with Bryan Molloy had been growing steadily more scrappy ever since August when he had been shipped in from Limerick to take over from Chief Superintendent O'Driscoll. Unlike Dermot O'Driscoll, Molloy believed that women were nothing but a nuisance in the Garda. They weren't clubbable, like men, and they couldn't be trusted to close ranks if one of their fellow officers was found to have bent the rules a little.

Her phone rang even before she had taken off her coat. It was Detective Horgan, calling from just outside the Crounans' house on Alexander Place, up by St Luke's.

'We went to the bakery on Maylor Street but all the shutters were down. There's no sign on the door or anything, it's just closed. Now we're up at the Crounans' but there's nobody home and no cars outside or nothing.'

'Have you tried ringing them on their mobiles?'

'Of course, yeah. But Micky's is switched off and we couldn't get an answer from his missus.'

'What about the bakery staff? They must know why the bakery's closed and where the Crounans are.'

'Well, that's our next plan. But first of all we have to find out who the staff are, and how to get in touch with them. We're going to try asking at the shops next door, and some of the other bakers. Somebody at Scoozi's might know.'

'Okay, then. Keep me in touch.'

Katie began to leaf through the files that had been left on her desk, but almost at once there was a knock on her open office door and Inspector Liam Fennessy came in. With his circular spectacles and brush-cut hair and his tweed jacket with leather patches on the elbows he looked more like a lecturer in English from Cork University than a Garda inspector.

'We've had a sighting of Roisin Begley,' he said. 'One of her school friends saw her in a car driving along Pope's Quay less than an hour ago. She said that Roisin didn't appear to be distressed at all. In fact, she was laughing.'

'She was sure it was Roisin?'

'One hundred per cent. Blonde hair, red and white woolly hat. She says she waved to her, but either Roisin didn't see her, or else she didn't want to.'

'Who was with her?'

'Some man. The friend couldn't really describe him, because she was too busy trying to catch Roisin's attention. She thought he was wearing a blue tracksuit top because it had the two white stripes down the sleeves, but that was all she could remember.'

'At least Roisin's still alive, thank God. I thought we'd be after finding her drowned in the river. But if she was laughing, it sounds like she's run away, and that could make her much more difficult to find. I'll have the press office get in touch with the Begleys and see if they can't put out an appeal on the Six One News. You know – "Please come home, darling, we aren't cross with you at all, and Woofy misses you."'

'Woofy?' asked Inspector Fennessy.

'Well, you know, whatever they call the family dog.'

She told him about the wedding cake. He listened, shaking his head. 'Jesus. That's nearly as bad as that woman in Curraheen who fried her old feller in lard and fed him to her cats.'

'The technical boys are doing an ultrasound scan and maybe then we'll be able to see who it is.'

'How do you bake a head in a cake, for the love of God? And why would you?'

Katie closed the file in front of her and pushed her chair back. 'The day we can answer questions like that, Liam – that'll be the day that you and me are out of a job.'

***

She went home early that afternoon. This would have been her day off if she hadn't had to appear in court. She had planned to go shopping at Hickey's for new curtains and a new living-room carpet, but that would have to wait until the weekend now. She had almost finished redecorating her living room. All the Regency-style wallpaper that her late husband, Paul, had chosen had been stripped off and all the gilded furniture had gone. Maybe she would never be able to forget Paul's selfishness, and his unfaithfulness, and his self-pity, and how their marriage had gradually disintegrated, especially after the death of little Seamus – but at least she wouldn't have to live with his idea of luxury decor any more.

She lived on the west side of Cobh, overlooking the River Lee as it widened towards the harbour and the sea. The sun was still glittering on the water as she arrived home, but a chilly wind was rising and the trees along the roadside were dipping and thrashing as if they were irritated at being blown about.

When she turned her Focus into her driveway, she saw a man in a long grey raincoat standing in her porch. He turned around as soon as he heard her and raised his hand in greeting.

'Perfect timing,' he said, as she opened her car door.

She reached across to the passenger seat for her shopping bag, and then she said, 'You haven't come to sell me double-glazing, have you?'

He laughed and said, 'Nothing like that. We've just moved in next door and I came to say hello, that's all.'

16

'Oh, okay then. Hello. Welcome to Carrig View. Let me just open the door and put down this shopping.'

'Here,' he said, and took the bag from her.

She unlocked the front door, switched off the alarm and beckoned him inside. As soon as she opened the kitchen door, her Irish setter, Barney, came bustling out to greet her, wagging his tail.

'Well, now, there's a fine fellow,' the man said. 'And what's *your* name, boy?'

'That's Barney,' said Katie. 'Oh, just dump the shopping on the table, if you don't mind. Thanks. That's grand.'

The man held out his hand. 'I'm David ó Catháin, but most people call me David Kane. I'm a vet, so from next week you'll start to see a lot of people coming and going during the day with various animals. Dogs and cats mostly, and parrots, but I have had to treat the occasional alligator.'

'Katie Maguire,' said Katie.

She liked the look of David Kane. He reminded her a little of John, who had left her in the late summer to go back to live and work in America. He was tall, like John, and dark-curled, although his face was leaner, with a straight, sharp nose and a sharply squared jaw. He was thinner, too, but then John had built up his muscles working on his family farm, until Ireland's collapsing economy had forced him to sell it.

David Kane's voice was rich and confident and deep, but it was his eyes that appealed to her the most. Brown, and amused, as if he found it hard to take life seriously. Katie's day-to-day life was grim enough, and monotonous enough, and she appreciated anybody who could bring some laughter into it.

'The woman from the letting agency told me that you're with the Garda,' said David. 'We won't have to be worrying too much about security, then, with you next door.'

'Well, she really shouldn't have told you that, but yes.'

'Like, you're speeding around in a patrol car all day? That must be exciting.'

'No, nothing like that. Sitting behind a desk mostly, sorting out mountains of paperwork.'

'Oh. And what about your other half?'

'The only other half I have at the moment is Barney.'

'Oh, I'm sorry. It's just that the letting agent kept talking about "the couple next door".'

'I think I shall have to have a word with your letting agent and tell her to be a little more discreet.'

'Truly, Katie, I apologize,' said David. He took hold of her hand between both of his and gave her a look that would have melted chocolate, as Katie's grandmother used to say.

'Don't think anything of it,' said Katie. 'You would have found out anyway. There's not much happens here in Cobh without everybody knowing about it two minutes later. Sometimes I swear that they're gossiping about things even before they've happened. But why don't you and your wife come round tomorrow evening for a drink and we can get acquainted? I'd ask you tonight but I have a rake of work to catch up with. What's your wife's name?'

'Sorcha. She's not what you'd call the sociable sort, but I'll ask her.'

'Yes, please do. Around seven-thirty would be good.'

David suddenly seemed to realize that he was still holding Katie's hand. He let go of it and grinned, as if to say, *what am I like, holding on to your hand for so long?*

Katie showed him to the front door. As he turned to go, he said, 'Would it be too intrusive of me to ask you what you actually do, in the Garda?'

'Of course not. You'll probably see on the nine o'clock news in any case. Detective Superintendent.'

David raised his thick, dark eyebrows. 'Detective Superintendent? How about that, then? You're the *capo di tutti capi.*'

'Not quite. I still have a chief superintendent to answer to, and an assistant commissioner above him.'

'All the same, I'm impressed.'

18

'Good to meet you, David,' said Katie. 'And it's very good to know that if Barney ever gets sick, God forbid, I now have a vet living right next door.'

David paused, looking at Katie as if he were about to say something, but instead he turned around and walked off down her driveway, lifting his right hand in farewell, like Peter Falk in *Columbo*. Katie stood in her porch watching him until he had disappeared behind the hedge.

What an unusual, interesting man, she thought, as she closed the front door behind her. There was something about him that made her feel off-balance, or maybe it was just that she was missing John. But what had he meant about his wife Sorcha being 'not what you'd call the sociable sort'? That was strange.

She went back into the kitchen and started to unpack her shopping. Barney sat beside her as if he were guarding her, but more than likely he was simply waiting to be fed. *Just like the males of every species*, she thought. *You think they're protecting you, but all they have at heart is their own appetite.*

***

She dreamed that night that she and John were riding a tandem down Summerhill, on the north side of the city, at such a speed that she couldn't pedal fast enough to keep up.

John was sitting behind her, so that she couldn't see him, but she could hear him shouting at her over the wind that was blustering in her ears. She could tell that he was angry, really angry, but she couldn't make out what he was so angry about. The trouble was, she didn't dare to turn her head around because she might veer off the road.

She kept applying the brakes, and every time she did so the brake blocks gave a shrill, penetrating shriek, but they didn't slow the tandem down at all.

'John!' she cried out. 'John, please stop shouting! The brakes won't work! The *brakes* won't work!'

19

They jolted over the kerb and on to the pavement, heading directly for somebody's front gate, but at that moment Katie opened her eyes. She sat up in bed, panting and hot, as if she really had been careering down Summerhill. Her bedroom was completely dark except for the small red light of her television and the clock on her bedside table, which read 2.25 a.m.

The shouting, however, was still going on, and so was the intermittent shrieking. But it wasn't John shouting at her, and the shrieking wasn't the sound of bicycle brakes. The noise was coming from the house next door – a man who was obviously furious about something, and a woman who was screaming back at him.

Katie sat listening for a few seconds. It was impossible to tell what either of them was saying, but then she heard a loud crash and a clatter like saucepans falling on to a tiled kitchen floor. She climbed out of bed, went across to her bedroom window and opened the curtains.

Even through the beech hedge that separated the two properties, she could see that her neighbours' kitchen window was lit up. The man was shouting in short, sharp sentences now, almost like a fierce dog barking. The woman wailed *owww! owww!* three or four times, and then she started to cry. Her crying sounded so despairing and so sorrowful that Katie was tempted to get dressed and go next door to make sure she was all right.

It sounded as if the man had hit her, and if he had, it was Katie's duty as a peace police officer to ask her if she wanted to press charges against him.

She waited, undecided. The shouting had stopped now, and so had the shrieks, although she could still hear occasional sobs of misery.

After a long while, the sobbing stopped. Katie opened her window and listened intently. She could hear voices, much calmer now, but she still couldn't distinguish what they were saying. It was a damp, chilly night; the sky was so overcast that she couldn't even see the full moon. She gave a quick shiver and closed her window as quietly as she could. As she did so, the kitchen light next door was switched off.

She went through to her own kitchen, opened the fridge, and took a swig of fizzy Ballygowan water straight out of the bottle. She didn't know if she had just overheard an incident of domestic violence or not. Of course, all couples argued, and most of the time their arguments sounded much worse than they really were, even if they were hitting each other. Two years ago she had organized a campaign in Cork against wife-beating, called Gallchnó Crann, or the Walnut Tree, after the old rhyme 'a woman, a dog and a walnut tree, the more you beat them, the better they be'. But in so many cases the wives would refuse at the last moment to give evidence in court, even when they had suffered black eyes and split lips and broken ribs. They made the excuse that it had been their fault for provoking their husbands. 'I nag him something terrible sometimes, I don't blame him for lashing out at me.'

She climbed back into bed, although she didn't switch off her pink bedside lamp. She lay there, with her eyes open, thinking about what she had just heard. She thought about John, too, and wondered what he was doing now. For him, in San Francisco, it would only be 6.41 yesterday evening, and the sun must still be shining. She wondered if he were thinking about her, or if he was sitting in a bar laughing with some other woman.

Then she thought about David Kane, and tried to work out what it was about him that had made such an impression on her. Maybe it was something of the quality that made Michael Gerrety so charismatic – a sense that he was dangerous.

***

The next morning, when she was standing in the kitchen eating a bowl of muesli, she heard a car door slam next door. She went through to the living room in time to see David Kane driving away

21

in a silver Range Rover. He glanced at her house as he passed, but she was so far back from the window that she didn't think he could see her.

She got dressed, putting on her thick white cable-knit sweater and the bottle-green tweed suit that she had bought when she and John had taken a weekend away in Kenmare. It was less than six months ago that they had gone there together, and yet it seemed so remote now, almost as if it had happened to somebody else, or in some film that she had once seen.

Before she went to work she walked around to the Kanes' and rang the doorbell. They hadn't yet put up curtains in the living-room window and she could see cardboard boxes still stacked in there. She waited and waited, but there was no reply, so she rang the bell again.

She was just about to walk away when a woman's voice from inside the house said, 'Who is it?'

'It's Katie, from number forty-seven next door. Katie Maguire. I only came to say hello.'

'I'm not decent, I'm afraid.'

'Well, I did invite your husband and you to come around for a drink this evening.'

'I can't, not this evening. I still have so much unpacking.'

'How about tomorrow morning, then? I have the day off tomorrow, hopefully. Why don't you come round for coffee? Sorcha – it's Sorcha, isn't it?'

There was a very long pause, and then the woman said, 'I don't know. I have so much unpacking to do, and I have to make the place look liveable in. David's a bit of a stickler.'

Katie hesitated. She was very tempted to tell Sorcha that she had overheard her fight last night, but then she decided against it. If it became a regular occurrence, then maybe she would take some action, but it wasn't her job to intrude on other people's private lives. If she had arrested Paul every time he had shaken her or pushed her during an argument, he would have spent more time in prison than out of it.

'All right,' she called out. 'But the invitation's still open if you feel like coming around for a chat.'

'I will so. Thanks a million.'

Katie walked back to her own driveway and climbed into her car. She had just started up the engine when her iPhone played 'Banks of the Roses'. She took it out of her pocket and said, 'DS Maguire.'

'Hello? Hello? Oh! Good morning to you, ma'am! It's Bill Phinner here from the Technical Bureau!'

'Yes, Bill. I can hear you perfectly well. You don't have to shout.'

'Oh, sorry. I'm a little deaf myself and when I can't hear other people too distinctly I think that they must be deaf, too. Anyway, it's your wedding-cake man. Or your wedding-cake *head*, I should say – but it *is* a man, not a woman. We did the ultrasound scan and it's his whole head all right, severed a bit rough-like between C3 and C4. Hard to tell exactly what with until we completely spoon him out of there.'

'Any idea who he is?'

'Not one hundred per cent, but Neela thinks it could be Micky Crounan. She's always running to the baker's for doughnuts and she reckons from the ultrasound image that it's him. And after all, it was his bakery the cake came from.'

'All right, Bill. I'm just leaving now. I'll see you in twenty minutes or so, depending on the traffic. How about fingerprints and DNA?'

'No fingerprints. Not one. Whoever iced this cake was wearing latex gloves, I reckon. But we're testing a few samples for possible DNA.'

'Well, whoever did it, their motive completely escapes me,' said Katie. 'Why on earth would you cut off a baker's head and bake it into one of his own cakes?'

'I have no idea, like,' said Bill Phinner. 'But you know the proverb. "The most dangerous food in the whole world is wedding cake."'

Four

Acting Chief Superintendent Molloy had texted Katie to come and see him in his office as soon as she arrived at Anglesea Street. However, she knew that whatever he had to say to her would only make her irritable for the rest of the day, and so first she went up to the technical laboratory.

Bill Phinner, the chief technician, and two of his assistants were standing in their long white coats around one end of a stainless-steel autopsy table. The sun was shining in through the window and lighting them up like three angels from some medieval painting depicting a beheaded martyr. On the table in front of them, four large Tupperware containers had been filled with lumps of wedding cake, each numbered according to the quadrant of the cake from which they had been cut.

Still resting on the circular silver stand on which the cake had been carried into the wedding ceilidh was a man's severed head. He had wispy grey hair from which cake had been painstakingly cleaned, and a bushy grey moustache. His face was pale yellowish, the colour of good-quality smoked haddock, with the tip of his nose and his earlobes tinged black and dark brown. His eyes were closed as if he were peacefully sleeping, even though the rest his body was missing. Bill Phinner had been right: his neck had been cut through so raggedly that it looked as if he had been beheaded with a large cross-cut saw.

'Here's your man,' said Bill Phinner. 'We're certain now that it's Micky Crounan. We've found several photographs of him on

Google Images, at various business and charity functions, and it's unmistakably him.'

'He's such a strange colour,' said Katie.

'So would you be if you'd been dead for nearly a week and then baked in the oven for an hour and a half at 160 degrees.'

'He's been dead that long?'

'I'm sure the state pathologist can give us a more accurate estimate of when he was killed, but I'd hazard a guess at six or seven days ago, at least.'

'So why did nobody report him missing, I wonder?'

'Don't ask me, ma'am. It's not like he was some homeless tramp, was he, who nobody's going to miss? He had a wife and a family and a business to run, and he was on every council committee you could think of.'

'Yet he was murdered almost a week ago and nobody asked where he was?'

Bill Phinner shrugged. 'There must have been a reason for it. I'm glad it's not my job to find out what it was. But here, look, come and take a sconce of the pictures.'

He took her over to a laboratory bench on the opposite side of the room, under the window, and showed her the ultrasound scan that they had take of Micky Crounan's head while it was still inside the cake. A dark, shadowy face with its eyes closed, like a ghost from the TV series *Most Haunted*. Then he spread out a selection of pictures that they had taken as the sponge cake was gradually scraped away.

Finally, he laid out ten or eleven pictures that they had downloaded from Google Images, showing a smiling Micky Crounan shaking hands with various Cork dignitaries, and at the Fota Golf Club annual dinner, and showing off some of his soda bread loaves for a feature in the *Echo*.

'It's really hard to understand who would want to kill a man like that,' said Katie. 'It's not as if anybody has been in touch with us, or with the media, to take credit for it. Like, "We killed Micky Crounan for such and such a reason, and he deserved it."'

Katie went back across to the autopsy table and stared for a long time at Micky Crounan's head. Then she turned to Bill Phinner and said, 'Thanks,' and left the laboratory. She was ready now to talk to Acting Chief Superintendent Molloy.

**

'It's Micky Crounan,' she told him, as she entered his office. He was sitting at his desk, binding grip-tape around the handle of a golf club. He had one end of the tape wrapped around his five-iron and the other clenched between his teeth.

'Oh, and good morning to you, DS Maguire,' he said, without opening his teeth. 'I thought I asked you to report to me first thing.'

Katie didn't answer that but sat down opposite him, setting down on his desk the file she had received from Finola McFerren about Michael Gerrety's acquittal. On top of that she opened the folder containing the technicians' photographs and the ultrasound scan of Micky Crounan's head.

'Micky Crounan? Why would anybody want kill Micky Crounan?' said Acting Chief Superintendent Molloy. 'I knew Micky myself – not particularly well, but at least to say how-do to.'

'Well, that's for me to find out, isn't it?' Katie told him. 'At the moment Crounan's Bakery on Maylor Street is all shuttered up and the last time we called at the Crounan house there was nobody home. Bill Phinner estimates that he's been dead for nearly a week.'

Bryan Molloy finished binding the handle of his mashie and propped it up against the side of his desk. 'Somebody's trying to make a point, I'd say. We had a similar case in Limerick once, a restaurant owner who defaulted on his loan from one of the local sharks. They found his head in his own kitchen, in an Irish stew, simmering away with the carrots and the onions. Believe me, everybody else who owed that fellow money, they paid up quickly enough after that.'

'I don't know yet if Micky Crounan upset anybody, or had any serious debts,' said Katie. 'The first thing we have to do is find his wife, Mary. I have an officer keeping an eye on the family house for me, in case she comes home.'

'Very well,' said Bryan Molloy. 'I'll let you get on with it. But there's two other matters I want to discuss with you before you go.'

'I assume that Michael Gerrety is one of them.'

'He is, yes,' said Bryan Molloy. He paused for a moment, frowning, and then he said, 'Michael Gerrety was acquitted yesterday of all thirty-seven charges of sex-trafficking and brothel-keeping and reckless endangerment, and so far as I'm concerned there's an end to it. Finish. You will not pursue Michael Gerrety any further, and you will discontinue any surveillance on him or his employees or his premises. Any further investigation of Michael Gerrety would amount to harassment, and I don't want us being accused of hounding a perfectly innocent local businessman because some female officer has got a bee in her bonnet about young women being exploited for sex, which as far as I understand it they aren't. They're all doing it voluntarily, and they're enjoying it, and it gives them a standard of living far better than they could expect if they took some minimum-wage job stacking shelves at Tesco's.'

'I see,' said Katie. 'And what's the other matter you wanted to rant about?'

'Don't you speak to me like that, DS Maguire,' retorted Bryan Molloy. His eyes bulged and his face began to flush. 'Dermot O'Driscoll has gone now, and this station is going to be run with discipline, and strict observance of the chain of command.'

'I'm sorry,' said Katie. 'I should have said "complain", shouldn't I? Not "rant".'

Bryan Molloy took several deep breaths and rocked himself backwards and forwards in his chair. Katie had seen him do this before and realized that it must be his technique for calming himself down. Eventually, he said, 'One of your team has been asking questions about me. Questions related to financial transactions.'

'Oh, you mean like backhanders? Payments for services rendered?'

'Let me make this crystal-clear, Katie. I have never accepted any financial reward whatsoever for turning a blind eye to anybody's misdemeanours.'

'So you've done it as a favour, for free?'

'You're walking much too close to the edge now, girl. I don't know what you've heard, or what anybody's told you, but I have never taken a bribe of any kind, and if you continue to suggest that I have, or if any of your detectives continue to make inquiries into my personal affairs, then I shall lodge an official complaint against you.'

'Please do,' said Katie. 'That will give me a golden opportunity to present all of the evidence I have about you.'

'What evidence? You don't have any evidence. Evidence of what?'

Katie stood up, closing the folder of photographs of Micky Crounan. 'Lodge your official complaint, Bryan. Then you'll find out.'

Bryan Molloy stood up, too, his neck swelling in his tight white collar. 'Are you saying what I think you're saying?' he demanded.

'I don't know,' said Katie. 'I'm not a mind-reader, and if I wanted to read *your* mind I'd probably need to learn Braille.'

'You're threatening me, aren't you? You've been trying to undermine my authority ever since I arrived here, and you're threatening me.'

Katie looked at him steadily. Her heart was beating very fast underneath her sweater, but she wasn't going to allow Bryan Molloy to frighten her.

'Yes,' she said, 'I am. In the same way that you're trying to hinder me from carrying out my duty and you're threatening *me*. Look at the state of you. You look like you're going to explode at any moment.'

With that, she tucked the folder under her arm and walked towards the door.

'*Katie*,' said Bryan Molloy, as she put her hand on the door handle. She paused, and waited to hear what he had to say.

'You're going to regret this, Katie. I can tell you that for nothing.'

'Oh, that's good,' she replied, without turning around. 'At least I won't have to pay you for it, like everybody else has to.'

***

Before she reached her office, her iPhone played the first few bars of 'Banks of the Roses'. It was a cheerful folk tune, but she had chosen it because of the words at the end of the first verse: 'O Johnny, lovely Johnny, would you leave me?'

It was Garda Brenda McCracken calling her. 'It's Mary Crounan. She just came home, with two children and a dog.'

'Thanks a million,' said Katie. 'I'll be up there in ten minutes, tops. If she leaves before I get there, follow her.'

She went up to the squad room and found Detective Sergeant Ni Nuallán, who was busily typing with two fingers on her computer keyboard. She was frowning at the screen as if her words were coming out in a language that she didn't understand, and she didn't look up when Katie came in.

'Kyna,' said Katie. 'You can leave that for now. Come on, quick as you can. Mary Crounan's home, and we have to give her the news about Micky.'

'Oh God,' said Detective Sergeant Ni Nuallán, lifting down her coat. 'Of all the jobs we have to do, this is the one I hate most of all.'

Five

The front door of the Crounan house was opened by a pale, plump girl of about eleven, with blonde pigtails and a bright blue home-knitted jumper.

'Is your mother in?' asked Katie, showing the girl her badge. 'We're from the Garda. It's Detective Superintendent Maguire and Detective Sergeant Ni Nuallán.'

The girl blinked at them and then lisped, 'Just a second, please.'

She disappeared, leaving Katie and Detective Sergeant Ni Nuallán on the doorstep. They looked around the small front garden, which was showing signs of neglect. There were dead hydrangeas that needed cutting back, and weeds growing between the black and white tiles of the pathway that led to the gate.

The house itself was looking sad and damp and in need of repair – a four-bedroom semi-detached house off Alexandra Road, once painted lemon-yellow but now streaked with grey from overflowing gutters. There was a fine view of Cork City to the south, with the spires of Holy Trinity Church and St Fin Barre's Cathedral rising above the rooftops, and all of this locality around Military Hill was now one of the most expensive areas to buy a house. However, it looked as if the Crounans had been running short of money for some time. The car parked at the side of the house was a 2007 Honda Civic, with a large dent in the passenger door.

Mary Crounan appeared, wiping her hands on a tea towel. She was a small woman in her late forties with curly dyed-black hair, wearing a purple jumper and a purple skirt. Katie thought she must have been very pretty when she was younger, but she had one of those plump babyish faces that doesn't age well, and at the moment she looked tired and anxious.

'I'm Detective Superintendent Maguire, from Anglesea Street Garda station,' said Katie. 'This is Detective Sergeant Ni Nuallán.'

'Yes? What do you want?' she asked them. Before Katie could answer she glanced quickly up and down the street as if to make sure nobody was watching them.

'I think we'd better come in,' said Katie. 'This isn't really something we can talk about on the doorstep.'

'It's Micky, isn't it?' said Mary Crounan. 'Have you found him? Is he all right?'

'Please, let's just go inside,' said Katie.

Mary Crounan led them along the hallway to a large, chilly living room. The furniture was all baroque and enormous, which made Katie feel as if she were Alice and had drunk a potion that had made her shrink six inches. The Wonderland feeling was heightened by the immense mirror that hung over the marble fireplace.

'Why don't you sit down, Mary? said Katie.

'What's happened to him? He's not hurt, is he? They haven't hurt him?'

'The bakery's closed. Can you tell me the reason for that?'

'We tried to keep it running between us, me and Lenny O'Dowd, the manager, but in the end we couldn't cope. Where's Micky? Please, tell me Micky's all right.'

'I'm sorry, Mary. There's no other way to tell you this, but Micky's dead. Some remains were discovered yesterday and we're ninety-nine per cent certain that it's him. I'm really, really sorry.'

Mary Crounan nodded, and continued to nod, as if she had known all along that her husband had gone. At the same time, though, tears rolled down her cheeks and dropped on to her purple jumper, like a sparkly necklace. She clasped her hands in her lap, twisting her wedding ring around and around.

'Did he suffer?' she asked. 'They said they would hurt him. Please God, tell me that they didn't hurt him.'

'We don't know yet exactly how he died, Mary. But who was it who said that they were going to hurt him?'

'I can't tell you that. I can't.'

'Where has he been this past week? Did somebody abduct him?'

Mary Crounan stopped nodding and shook her head instead, very emphatically. 'I shouldn't even have said "they". There is no "they".'

'Mary,' said Katie, 'Micky didn't kill himself. Somebody did it and we need to find out who it was, and as quick as we can, in case they try to do it to somebody else.'

'When did you last see Micky?' asked Detective Sergeant Ni Nuallán. She was standing by the window, looking out. She had grown her blonde hair recently and braided it into a coronet, so that she looked almost Eastern European, especially since her grey overcoat was so square-shouldered.

'Last Friday morning,' said Mary Crounan. She took out a scrunched-up tissue and wiped her eyes. 'He was going to the bakery first and then for lunch with Donal Neely from the tourism committee. He went to the shop all right but about half past one Donal rang up and asked me where he was. He thought he might have forgotten their appointment, but Micky never forgot anything. He even remembered my mother's birthday, God bless him.'

'You must have tried ringing him yourself,' said Detective Sergeant Ni Nuallán.

'I did, of course. But his phone was switched off. I couldn't understand it. He never switched his phone off, ever.'

'So when did they call and tell you what had happened to him?'

Katie stayed quiet while Detective Sergeant Ni Nuallán questioned Mary. Kyna had such a quiet, persuasive voice, and a natural instinct for what people needed to say, even when they were reluctant to talk. She was taking Mary Crounan back in her mind to relive the moment when she had been told that her husband had been kidnapped.

'They said he was safe but they wanted a hundred thousand euros to let him go.'

'Did they let you talk to him?'

Mary Crounan nodded again, and fresh tears welled up in her eyes. 'He said that everything was grand and I shouldn't worry. But I shouldn't tell anybody, and not the cops most of all. If I did, they would hurt him.'

'How long did they give you to get the money together?' asked Katie.

'Three days, they said. A hundred thousand euros, in cash.'

'So where were you going to get that from? Business hasn't been going too well, has it? Come to that, it hasn't been going too well for anybody in Cork these days, except for the pay-day moneylenders.'

'Business has been a disaster for the past three years,' said Mary Crounan. 'Micky kept on smiling but we've been getting deeper and deeper in debt. We had to take Keela out of Regina Mundi and if Micky's father hadn't died and left us an inheritance I don't know what we would have done. Micky always used to make a joke about him being a baker and starving while everybody else was eating his bread. "Let me eat cake," he used to say. But it wasn't too far from the truth.'

'Did you raise the hundred thousand?'

'I managed to raise eighty-seven six hundred. I went down to the Patrick's Quay car park and found Micky's Mercedes and sold it. I sold all of my jewellery, too, even my eternity ring. We didn't have any savings left, and I couldn't cash in any more of Micky's pension.'

'Did you hand the money over?' Katie asked her.

Mary Crounan whispered, 'Yes.'

'Where? And who did you hand it to?'

'I shouldn't tell you. They promised that all kinds of terrible things would happen to me and my children if I told you.'

'Mary, your husband has been murdered. We have to catch the people who did it. Until we do, we can protect you. I mean that. We can make absolutely sure that you and your children are safe. But you *have* to help us. We can't let killers and extortionists go free.'

At that moment, the living-room door opened and Mary Crounan's daughter put her head around it and said, 'Ma? Is everything all right?'

'Yes, darling. I won't be very long and then I'll make you some lunch.'

'Can me and Donny have a biscuit?'

'Yes, of course you can. Take two each, if you want to.'

The door closed again and Mary Crounan looked at Katie with such an expression of grief that Katie went over and sat on the couch next to her and took hold of her hands. There was nothing she could say that would comfort her. Katie had experienced grief herself, more than once, and she knew that the pain was too great to be shared by anybody else.

Detective Sergeant Ni Nuallán turned away from the window and said, 'You left the money somewhere? Is that it?'

'Yes,' said Mary Crounan. 'I wrapped it in a shopping bag and left it under one of the settles in the Blair Inn at Cloghroe, on the way to Blarney. They had told me to buy myself a drink and sit there for ten minutes, so I wouldn't look suspicious to the bar staff. When I'd finished my drink I went directly back home and waited for a call, but it never came.'

'You didn't see anybody outside when you left the pub?'

'Only three or four cars parked there, that's all.'

'And that was the last you heard?' asked Detective Sergeant Ni Nuallán. 'They didn't even ring you and tell you that it wasn't enough?'

'They never rang me again. I didn't know what to do. I shut up the shop and when anybody called for Micky I just told them that he was visiting his mother in Galway.'

She let go of Katie's hands and wiped her eyes again. 'Can I see him?' she asked.

Katie looked across at Detective Sergeant Ni Nuallan. How was she going to tell Mary Crounan that all they had retrieved of her husband's body so far was his head, and that had been discovered in a wedding cake? Not only that, his head could only have reached such an advanced stage of decomposition if his abductors had killed him days ago. They had probably done it soon after he had last talked to her on the phone. No matter how much money she might have been able to raise, she would never have seen him alive again.

'I'm afraid the state pathologist will have to conduct a post-mortem first,' said Katie. 'But as soon as that's over . . .'

'What are you not telling me?' Mary Crounan demanded. 'There's something you're not telling me, isn't there?'

'Please, Mary. When somebody is murdered, we have to examine their remains very thoroughly, to see if we can establish the cause of death, and if there's any chance of working out who might have done it.'

'His body's in a state, isn't it? What did they do to him?'

'We simply don't know yet, and that's the truth.'

Mary Crounan stood up. 'You really can protect us? You swear it?'

Katie said, 'We can find you somewhere to stay far away from here, where nobody will know who you are, and you'll have officers to keep an eye on you twenty-four hours a day.'

Mary Crounan turned round and stared at herself in the mirror for almost twenty seconds, saying nothing. It looked as if she were consulting her mirror image about what she should do.

'You see that woman there?' she said to Katie, nodding at her reflection. 'She's a widow.'

Katie didn't answer, but waited for what she was going to say next.

'The fellow who spoke to me and demanded the money said that he was one of the High Kings of Erin. Don't ask me what he meant by that. He said that the High Kings of Erin had taken Micky because he was one of the businessmen who have brought ruin and shame on Ireland, and he had to be punished.'

'The High Kings of Erin? Was that all? They didn't give you any other names?'

'No,' said Mary Crounan. 'The High Kings of Erin. That was all. I hope they end up in hell.'

***

They stayed with Mary Crounan for over two hours while Katie comforted her and Detective Sergeant Ni Nuallán called the station to arrange for transport. There was a house in Redwood Park in Clonakilty which the Garda frequently used for witness protection; it was small and private and screened from the road, and nobody could approach it without being seen.

Once that had been arranged, Mary Crounan packed two suitcases for herself and the children and waited in her overcoat by the living-room window for the unmarked people carrier to arrive to take them away.

'Who could have imagined this, only a week ago?' she said. 'Our whole lives broken into pieces.'

'I'm so sorry for you,' said Katie.

'You will let me know as soon as I can see Micky, won't you? I have to set eyes on him just once more, before he's laid to rest.'

Katie nodded. She didn't know what she could say. Just then, though, Detective Sergeant Ni Nuallán came in from the hallway and said, 'They're here. I'll give you a hand with your cases.'

Mary Crounan held both of Katie's hands tight. 'You'll catch them, won't you? Promise me you'll catch them. I want to spit in their faces.'

On their way back to Anglesea Street, Detective Sergeant Ni Nuallán said, 'The High Kings of Erin? Strange thing to call themselves. We learned a bit about the High Kings of Erin in school. Some of them were real, weren't they, but most of the stories about them . . . well, they're just legends, with witches and fortune-tellers and talking trees and all that kind of nonsense?'

'That's right,' said Katie. 'But I remember our history teacher telling us that the High Kings were always fighting each other, and they were always cutting each other's heads off. They reckoned

36

that if a fellow didn't have a head, he couldn't wear a crown.'

'Well, fair play to them, you have to admire their logic,' said Detective Sergeant Ni Nuallán. 'You think there might be a connection with Micky Crounan having his head cut off like that?'

'I have no idea. Maybe it was just simple extortion by somebody with a very warped sense of humour. Maybe somebody had a serious grudge against him. If you can get Horgan and Dooley on to that aspect of things – get them to dig into his past and find out if anybody hated him enough to kill him. Even pillars of the community like Micky Crounan can have their shady secrets. Look at that bank manager, what was his name? Martin O'Shea. Having sex with his own daughters like that. No wonder they poured petrol through his letter box.'

'And then, of course, there's Michael Gerrety,' said Detective Sergeant Ni Nuallán.

'I detest any man who thinks he has a right to take advantage of vulnerable girls like that. It wouldn't be their heads I'd be cutting off first.'

Six

Back at the station, Katie called Dr O'Brien at the state pathologist's office in Dublin to arrange for a post-mortem examination of Micky Crounan's remains. Dr O'Brien was one of Ireland's two deputy pathologists, and Katie liked working with him. He was very rigorous, but he would often come up with a highly creative theory as to how and why the corpse he was examining had met its end.

Instead, she was put through to the state pathologist himself, Dr Owen Reidy.

'Oh, it's you, Detective Superintendent,' he said, grumpily. 'Can it not wait until later? I have a meeting with the commissioner in five minutes and I don't want to be gasping for breath when I get there.'

'Actually, I wanted to talk to Dr O'Brien if he's there,' said Katie.

'Dr O'Brien is in Horseleap, in Offaly. A woman's body has been dug out of a bog. She's almost perfectly preserved, so she could have been there for six months or sixteen hundred years, like Old Croghan Man.'

'That's interesting.'

'Interesting? It's highly annoying, I'll say that. Examining bog bodies is time-consuming and very expensive, as you're well aware, especially if we have to bring in a forensic archaeologist. It's only October and my budget is stretched to the limit already. But what did you want?'

'We have the severed head of a homicide victim here which needs examining.'

'Only the head? What about the rest of him?'

'The rest of him hasn't been found yet.'

'In that case, why don't you send us the head by courier? If you do that, I could have Dr Sanjay looking at it by tomorrow morning at the latest.'

Katie thought about Mary Crounan, tearfully pleading to see her husband one more time before his interment, and then thought about Micky Crounan's head being driven to Dublin in a cooler box by First Direct, and it was both absurd and tragic at the same time. But she needed every scrap of evidence that the pathologists could find.

'All right,' she said. 'I'll arrange it. You can expect it later today.'

**

Katie spent most of the afternoon with her five-strong drugs team, led by Detective Niall Brannigan, who was stocky and brown-haired and bristled like a bull terrier that has scented a hedgehog. He was planning a series of coordinated raids against premises in Blackpool and Farranree.

For the past three weeks the clubs and pubs in Cork had been flooded with crack cocaine and other controlled drugs like ecgonine and crystal meth. Recent tip-offs suggested high-quality rocks were being cooked up in almost industrial quantities in a house on Rathpeacon Road and a flat over a shop in Bóthar Chúrsa an Uisce.

Katie's detectives had discovered that there was a new and highly organized gang behind this new drug operation. What interested her was that they appeared to be Belgians, rather than the usual suspects from Lithuania or Romania or Somalia.

'So far as we can find out, the fellow behind it calls himself Necker, and he comes from Antwerp,' said Detective Brannigan. 'I checked with the cops there, though, and they laughed at me. They didn't know of any drug dealer by that name, and Necker just means "devil" in their language.'

'I don't care if he calls himself Santa Claus,' said Katie. 'Let's find him and stop him before half the young people in the city get addicted – the half that aren't addicted already.'

***

She went home early that evening – or what was early for her. It had started to rain by the time she parked outside her house in Cobh, a fine chilly rain that was almost a mist. In spite of that, she still had to take Barney for his walk, although she didn't go as far as she usually did, only up the hill to Rushbrooke Lawn Tennis Club and back.

Barney pattered on ahead of her, as always, but since John had left he had taken to turning around now and again, as if to reassure her that he would look after her now that she was alone.

'Go on, boy,' she told him. 'I'm okay.'

In reality, though, she didn't know if she was okay or not. She was still asking herself if she had made the right decision, staying in Cork when she could have gone with John to San Francisco and taken up the job that he had arranged for her with Pinkerton's detective agency. But here she was, walking through the wet streets in her black hooded raincoat, tired and hungry and, worst of all, lonely.

She had only just returned home and was hanging up her raincoat when the doorbell chimed. When she went to open it, she found David Kane from next door standing in the porch. He was holding a bottle of Prosecco in one hand and a bunch of orange roses in the other.

'Oh,' said Katie, and looked at him blankly.

'Don't tell me you've forgotten!' he smiled. 'Drinks, seven-thirty? Am I too early?'

'Oh my God, it totally slipped my mind,' said Katie. 'It's just been one of those days. Well, every day is one of those days. But come on in.'

As David stepped into the hallway, Barney came sniffing excitedly around his legs and wagging his tail.

'Barney – get down!' she said. 'Behave yourself!'

'He can probably smell the other dogs on me,' said David. 'I had my first two patients today – a German shepherd and a shih tzu. Well, a budgerigar too, but the poor old budgie had advanced polyoma so I had to put it down.'

Katie held the front door open and peered outside.

'You couldn't persuade your wife to come?'

'Sorcha? No, I'm afraid not. She said she wasn't in the mood for it. She's had a very hard day hanging up curtains and arranging furniture. She said she wanted an early bath and bed.'

David took the Prosecco and the roses into the kitchen and laid them on the table.

'You have some champagne glasses? I admit it's not real champagne, but we might as well pretend.'

'Of course, yes,' said Katie, and took two flutes from the cupboard over the sink. 'They're not very classy, I'm afraid. My husband got them free with petrol. My late husband, Paul.'

'They'll do fine. Better than drinking champagne out of a coffee mug. I did that the day I passed my MVB.'

He paused, and then added, in a mock-Italian accent, '*Medicina Veterinaria Baccalaureate*,' in case she didn't know what MVB stood for, although she did.

Katie went to the larder and took out a packet of peanuts and some chilli-flavoured crisps. The last thing she felt like doing was entertaining anybody for drinks, but she could hardly tell David to take his bottle of Prosecco and his orange roses and go back home.

David popped the cork and filled their glasses and then they went through to the living room and sat down.

'You'll have to excuse the decor,' said Katie. 'I haven't quite finished redecorating yet. It's almost impossible to find the time.'

David looked around at the plain, cream-painted walls and the three bold abstract prints that hung on the opposite side of the room. Katie had replaced almost all of the rococo-style furniture with a mint-green leather couch and two matching leather armchairs with chrome-plated legs. Now the only reminder of Paul was his silver-framed photograph on one of the glass-topped side tables, wearing the same unfocused smile that he always wore, as if his face was present but his mind was somewhere else. In Killarney, probably, in bed with somebody else's wife. It had occurred to Katie last week that she could no longer remember what his voice had sounded like.

'So, what heinous crime are you trying to solve at the moment?' asked David. He looked very relaxed, in a black roll-neck sweater and grey wool trousers, sitting in one of the armchairs with his legs crossed. But Katie was looking at the heavy gold signet ring on the third finger of his right hand and wondering if it had left an impression when he hit Sorcha last night – always supposing that he *had* hit her, of course.

'I can't possibly tell you that, I'm afraid,' said Katie. 'You'll have to wait until you see it on the news.'

'Oh, you can give me a hint, can't you? Is it a murder? Or is it a robbery? Fraud, is it? Or drug-dealing, or sex-trafficking?'

Katie smiled and shook her head. 'I have all of those to deal with, believe me, and more'

'More? What else is there?'

'You'd be amazed what people get up to.'

'Come on, don't keep me in suspense. I'm fascinated to know what you do all day. You can change the names to protect the innocent, if you like. That's what they used to say on TV, isn't it, at the beginning of those true-crime programmes?'

'*Slainte*,' said Katie, raising her glass. David raised his glass too, and looked her steadily in the eyes, saying nothing.

'Is that one of your treatments?' Katie asked him.

'What? Sorry?'

'Hypnosis. Is that one of the ways you cure your animals?

'Oh, was I staring? I apologize. I was just thinking to myself that you don't look very much like a detective superintendent. In fact, to be fair to you I wouldn't have had you down for a Garda officer at all.'

'No? What is a detective superintendent *supposed* to look like?'

'A female detective superintendent, like you? Much more butch, I'd say. Maybe just the faintest hint of a moustache on the upper lip. And *gruffer*. And certainly not wearing high-heeled boots. You're not like that at all. In fact, if I'd been introduced to you for the first time and I didn't know what you did for a living, I'd have said – '

'What?' said Katie.

'I'd have said TV news presenter. Or maybe the editor of a fashion magazine. Something professional, but very feminine. Something that takes brains but needs some glamour as well.'

Katie was thinking, *what a load of cat's malogian*. But at the same time, she couldn't deny that David was charming and persuasive, and it felt good to be flattered so profusely after such an abrasive day, even if she didn't believe a word of it. It had been emotionally draining, breaking the news to Mary Crounan that her husband had been killed, and her constant confrontations with Bryan Molloy had badly jolted her confidence in her own authority.

David had also been shrewd enough to say that he would have mistaken her for a woman who was not only attractive but clever, too. She appreciated that.

'Here,' he said, and got up from his chair to refill her glass.

'There's domestic violence, too,' she said, in a level voice, while he was still standing over her.

'Sorry? I don't follow you.'

'You asked me what more there could be, after murder and robbery and drug-running and sex crimes. I have to deal with more domestic violence than almost any other offence, especially on pay-day. I've even started up a group to help women who have been beaten or intimidated by their partners. It's called the Walnut Tree.'

David sat down again. He refilled his own glass, and then he said, 'Why do I have the feeling that you're trying to tell me something?'

Katie raised an eyebrow. 'Why do *I* have the feeling that you know exactly what I'm saying to you, but you can't decide if you want to discuss it?'

'You've seen Sorcha, is that it?'

'No. I haven't seen her. I went round to your house after you'd left this morning and knocked at the door but she wouldn't open it for me. But why would you think that I *had* seen her? Was it because I happened to mention domestic violence?'

'You're a very interesting woman, Katie. I'll give you that. The Walnut Tree, I get it. The woman, the dog, the walnut tree. Do you think that I've been beating Sorcha, is that it?'

'All right. Talking of beating, I won't beat around the bush. I heard you two in your kitchen last night. It sounded very much as if you were hitting her.'

'I slapped her, yes.'

'So you admit it?'

'Yes. I slapped her a couple of times. It was the only way I could get her out of it.'

'Get her out of what?'

'Her hysteria. It's impossible to know what to do with her when she's throwing a fit like that.'

'Can't you just restrain her?'

David stood up again, crossed his arms and lifted up his sweater. His torso was lean and muscular, with a thin line of dark hair running down to his navel. However, his chest and his stomach were criss-crossed with scores of crimson scratch marks. He looked as if he had been wrestling with a wildcat.

'She's bipolar,' he said, lowering his sweater and sitting down. 'Sometimes she's depressed and talks about committing suicide. Other times, she's so hyperactive that she rushes about the house screaming and smashing things, and if I try to stop her she'll attack me.'

'Has her doctor given her anything? You can get drugs, can't you, to stabilize people with manic depression?'

'She was on Seroquel for a while to control her mood cycles, and when she was taking that she didn't have so many highs and lows. The trouble was, it made her about as responsive as a zombie. I don't know whether I'd prefer to have a wife who's sobbing one minute and laughing like a lunatic the next, or one who sits staring at the TV for hours on end and hardly utters a word.'

Katie said, 'I'm sorry. I didn't mean to pry. It was just that when I heard you two shouting at each other last night it sounded like a classic domestic.'

'That's all right. I married Sorcha, didn't I, for better or for worse, in sickness and in health? That was the oath I took and I won't go back on it.'

'Well, if there's anything I can do to help – '

He sipped his Prosecco and shook his head. 'I have to grin and bear it, that's all. Sometimes fate deals you a really bad hand, but look at it from Sorcha's point of view. Fate has been pretty good to *her*, hasn't it, considering her condition, giving her me to look after her?'

Katie and David sat for almost half a minute looking at each other, saying nothing. Katie thought David was very attractive, and she was impressed by the way he had talked so openly about his wife, and about what had happened in their kitchen last night. He appeared to be relaxed, too, but she couldn't help feeling that it was a studied relaxation. She had sensed a similar tension in some of the criminals she had interviewed. They had smiled, they had joked, they had told her whatever she wanted to know – but she had always felt that they were spring-loaded, that the smallest provocation would make them explode.

She still wasn't one hundred per cent sure that David hadn't been beating Sorcha, even if the claw-marks on his chest and stomach seemed to bear out his story. However, she didn't question him about it any more. She was at home, after all, not in the interview room at Anglesea Street, and David was her new next-door neighbour, not a suspect.

They talked for another hour – mostly about life in Cobh, and which were the best pubs and restaurants, and about David's work as a vet. They finished the Prosecco and Katie brought a bottle of Pinot Grigio out of the fridge.

Eventually David looked at his watch and said, 'I have to go. I want to make sure that Sorcha's okay – hasn't drowned herself in the bath or tied a plastic bag over her head or anything stupid like that.'

Katie showed him to the front door. Before he left, he took hold of her hand and kissed her on both cheeks.

'You're a very unusual woman,' he told her. 'I'm really glad that I've met you. You see? It looks as if fate has dealt me at least one good card.'

'There's a word for that,' said Katie. 'My grannie would have called it *plámás*.'

She couldn't tell from the expression on his face whether he knew it was Gaelic for 'sweet-talk', or not, because all he did was smile and walk off into the darkness and the fine chilly rain.

Seven

Katie had only just sat down at her desk the next morning and prised the lid off her latte when Detective Sergeant Ni Nuallán appeared in her doorway, accompanied by a middle-aged woman in a brown fake-fur coat that had seen better days.

'Good morning, ma'am,' said Detective Sergeant Ni Nuallán. 'This is Mrs Shelagh Hagerty. I thought you'd want to see her directly.'

'Oh yes?'

Detective Sergeant Ni Nuallán came across the office holding up a jam jar. 'She found this on her front doorstep this morning. Come on in, Shelagh. This is Detective Superintendent Maguire.'

'How do you do?' said Shelagh Hagerty. She looked pale and puffy-eyed and she was holding her handbag tightly, as if she were afraid somebody might snatch it away from her.

Detective Sergeant Ni Nuallán set down the jam jar and Katie could see that it contained at least a dozen teeth, some of which were smeared with blood. She picked it up and examined it closely. They looked very much like human teeth.

'You found this on your doorstep? At what time? Was there any note with it?'

'About half past six. I was putting out the empty milk bottles because I'd forgotten to do it the night before. Well, the state I was in, like. There was no note with it but this fellow rang me almost as soon as I'd gone back inside.'

'Who was he? Do you know?'

'He's never told me his name. But he said that if I didn't have the money ready by midday Wednesday then he'd be sending me more of Derek piece by piece until there was nothing left of him at all.'

'Sit down, Shelagh,' said Katie. 'We need to go over this right from the very beginning. Who's Derek? Is he your husband?'

Detective Sergeant Ni Nuallán dragged over a chair for Shelagh Hagerty and she perched herself right on the edge of it, her hands clasped together, holding her handbag. 'That's right. Derek Hagerty of Hagerty's Autos on the Curraheen Road at Looney's Cross. Two nights ago he didn't come home and the same night I had a phone call. It was a man's voice but it was kind of muffled, like. He said that if I didn't raise two hundred and fifty thousand euros by Monday I would never see Derek alive again.'

She let out an extraordinary sob, as loud and as unexpected as the cry of a trumpeter swan, and her eyes filled up with tears. She tried to open her handbag to find a handkerchief, but Katie pulled a Kleenex out of the box on her desk and passed it over to her.

'He said that if I contacted the Garda or the newspapers or the TV, and he found out about it, that would be the end of Derek immediately. But I don't know how I'm going to raise two hundred and fifty thousand euros, even if I sell all my jewellery. We don't have anything else much of value. We used to own a caravan but we had to sell that when business started going downhill.'

Katie picked up the jam jar again. 'Do these look like your husband's teeth?'

'I don't know for sure. But I think so. There's one gold one in there and Derek has a gold one.'

'Who's your dentist?'

'Dr Michael Lynch, in Patrick Street.'

Katie stood up and gave the jam jar to Detective Sergeant Ni Nuallán. 'Kyna, take these to Bill Phinner in the technical lab, would you, please, and then ask Dooley to go round to Dr Lynch, fairly lively if he could, and ask for Derek Hagerty's dental records. He can explain that Derek Hagerty's missing and we urgently need to identify his teeth.'

'Supposing Dr Lynch won't release them? I mean, he's going to plead patient confidentiality, isn't he?'

'Have him call the Dental Protection people and discuss it with them. They should tell him that it's okay if they're required by a police officer. If he still won't let us have them, we'll have to apply for a warrant, but I don't want to waste time doing that if we can possibly help it.'

Once Detective Sergeant Ni Nuallán had left her office, Katie sat next to Shelagh Hagerty and took hold of her hand. 'You said that your business had been going badly, Shelagh. Does Derek owe anybody a lot of money?'

Shelagh Hagerty nodded. 'The bank most of all, AIB, but I think he's been borrowing money from his friends, too – right, left and centre. I told him almost a year ago that he should think about declaring himself bankrupt, but he wouldn't hear of it. Hagerty's Autos was started by his father and it's been going since the 1960s. "It's not a business," he always says, "it's a family tradition."'

'We'll need to see the company accounts, and the order books, too,' said Katie. 'They might give us some clues. But do you know if any of his creditors has been threatening him at all?'

'There's Sean O'Grady, who's one of his suppliers. He was all sweetness and light, Sean, when things were going well, but as soon as Derek was a month late with his payments he started to say he was going to take him to court. Worse than that, he spread it around that we were in the height of loberty, which wasn't at all true, but of course it made Derek's other suppliers very reluctant to give him any more credit.'

'And the man who called you – I know his voice was muffled – but there wasn't anything about it that you recognized?'

Shelagh Hagerty shook her head. 'The only thing I'd say is, he wasn't local, like. Tipp, I'd say, or Limerick maybe.'

'Well, we can check all your recent phone records,' said Katie. 'If your man knows what he's doing, though, he's probably calling you from a pre-paid mobile or one of those stealth phones that changes its identification number with every call.'

'Dear God, please find Derek and save him,' said Shelagh Hagerty. 'I know this fellow said that I shouldn't come to you, but what else could I do?'

'When did you last see Derek?' asked Katie.

'On Tuesday morning, around seven-thirty, when he left for work.'

'Did he appear at all worried about anything? Did he say anything that struck you as unusual?'

'All he said was, "I wouldn't mind chops for my tea." Oh – and he asked me to call Danny Rearden the plumber for him, because the upstairs toilet cistern's been leaking. Then he kissed me, and went.'

'Did he phone you at all during the day?'

'No . . . I tried to phone him myself to tell him that Danny couldn't come until Thursday, but his mobile was dead and when I called the workshop Fergal said that he'd gone to the bank.'

'And what time was that?'

'Three-thirty, four o'clock, something like that.'

'So what's happening at the workshop? Is it still open?'

'Fergal's running the business for now. He's the chief mechanic and he mostly runs it anyway these days. I told him that Derek had gone to Macroom for a few days to take care of his elderly ma because his pa's in hospital, may the Blessed Virgin forgive me for telling such a lie. His pa's been dead these five years but his ma . . . well, she's still tipping away like a small tractor.'

'Did your man say when he was going to ring you next, or how to get in touch with him if you managed to raise the money?'

'He said he would call me this evening, at six o'clock, to see how things were going.'

'All right, Shelagh, I want you to ring Fergal and tell him that you're sending an accountant to collect all of your books, because you've been asked to do an audit for the revenue commissioners. Actually it will be a plain-clothes detective, but we don't want him to know that.'

'You don't think Fergal's involved in this, do you?'

Katie shook her head. 'I'm not suggesting that at all, but it's better to be safe than sorry. When you've done that, I want you to go back home and carry on doing what you can to raise the money this man's asking for. We don't know what contacts he has and it's important that you look as if you're still trying to meet his demands. I'll be after sending Detective Horgan or Detective Dooley round to your house a little later, and also one of our technicians to record his voice when he calls you this evening, to see if we can't trace where he's calling from. I'll also be assigning two gardaí to keep your street under surveillance, but nobody will know that they're there.'

'Oh God, you will find Derek, won't you?' Shelagh begged her. 'I haven't made a terrible mistake, have I, coming here? Supposing they followed me here without my knowing?'

Katie laid a hand on her shoulder and said, 'Shelagh, you've been very brave coming here. It was the best thing you could have done. We'll do everything possible to get Derek back for you, safe and well.'

All the same, she couldn't help thinking about Micky Crounan and how his abductors had probably killed him even before his wife had begun to raise the ransom money. Derek Hagerty's kidnappers had sent only some of his teeth, not his head, but that was no guarantee at all that he was still alive. They could have been wrenched out of his jaw after he was dead.

'I bought the chops for his tea,' said Shelagh, dismally. 'I went to Coughlan's specially.'

Katie stood beside her for a while, until she had dabbed her eyes and recovered her composure. Then she said, 'It's all right. I'm grand altogether. Let me phone Fergal.'

**

When Shelagh Hagerty had made her call and left for home in a taxi, Katie walked along to Acting Chief Superintendent Molloy's office.

He was talking loudly on the phone, pacing up and down as he did so, and letting out bursts of his harsh, abrasive laughter. He beckoned Katie to come in and sit down, but she went over to the window and looked down at the rain-slicked car park. It was always interesting to see which officers spoke to each other in the car park, when they didn't think they were being watched or overheard. Katie could tell by their body language when they were sharing confidences, or affection.

'Well, okay, Ryan, you old langer, I'll let you go,' said Bryan Molloy. 'I'll see you on Saturday afternoon three o'clock at the Lee Valley Golf Club. I can't tell you how much I've been looking forward to beating the dust off you again!'

He put down the phone, sniffed loudly, looked at his watch, and then said, 'Well?'

'There's been another abduction,' said Katie. 'Derek Hagerty, the owner of Hagerty's Autos. He went missing two days ago and his wife Shelagh has received two phone calls demanding a quarter of a million euros for his safe return.'

'Jesus. They haven't sent her his head, have they?'

'No, but she found a jam jar on her doorstep this morning with teeth in it and she believes they might be his. I've sent Dooley to get hold of his dental records.'

'His *teeth*? That's a new one.'

'I didn't count them myself but I'd say there was at least ten, including one gold crown. Bill Phinner's looking at them now.'

'His *teeth*,' repeated Bryan Molloy. 'Gives me the shudders to think about it. I hate the dentist. Usually when some poor soul gets kidnapped they cut off an ear, or a pinkie, and send that along as proof that they've got him. Mind you, in Limerick, the Duggan gang once pulled out some fellow's toenails, all ten of them, with pliers, and send them to his missus in a Jiffy bag. Shows how stupid they were. They could have been anybody's toenails. How do you recognize your husband by his toenails?'

Katie said, 'I may be way off but I have a feeling that Derek

Hagerty could have been taken by the same people who killed Micky Crounan.'

'Have they allowed Mrs Hagerty to talk to her husband at all? Does she have any idea who might have snatched him, and why?'

'No. They haven't identified themselves in any way, although Shelagh Hagerty said that the man who called her had what sounded like a northside Limerick accent. The manager at the Montenotte Hotel who signed for the wedding cake said that the fellow who brought it also sounded like he came from Moyross.'

'That's almost a criminal offence in itself, talking with a Moyross accent.'

Katie came away from the window. 'I think the most effective way of dealing with this is for Shelagh Hagerty to tell the abductors that she's managed to raise the full ransom and arrange for a drop somewhere. So long as they don't suspect that she's contacted us, we should be in with a fair chance of putting a tail on them. It's our best hope for keeping Derek Hagerty alive, wouldn't you think? Always assuming that they haven't killed him already.'

Bryan Molloy sat down at his desk and pressed his hand over his mouth, as if he were trying to stop himself from saying something that he was going to regret. Katie stayed where she was, saying nothing, watching him. This was a complicated man – irascible, prejudiced, but not a fool.

After a few moments he took his hand away and nodded, and kept on nodding. He reminded her of a toy bulldog on the back shelf of a car. 'I agree with you,' he said.

'You do?' said Katie. 'Well, there's a first.'

'No, fair play to you, what you're saying makes absolute sense. We don't want this Hagerty fellow getting himself topped and, like you say, if we play our cards right we could nail these scummers. We'll have to plan it real careful, though. They'll be wanting to count the money before they let Hagerty go. We can't just jump on them as soon as they show up to collect it, and we can't palm them off with a bundle of cut-up newspaper.'

'That's what I thought,' said Katie. 'But that means we'll need to indent for two hundred and fifty thousand in real banknotes.'

'Let me sort that out. Jimmy O'Reilly's in Dublin at the moment but I'll give him a call and see how quick he can authorize it. As soon as he gives me the go-ahead I'll let you know, and you can contact Hagerty's wife. Meanwhile, if you can do whatever you can to confirm that those teeth really *do* belong to him.'

'Of course,' said Katie. She hesitated for a moment, and was tempted to say that maybe the two of them might be able to work together in harmony after all. But she knew that Bryan Molloy would immediately take that as a sign of female weakness. He would probably tell her that they would never be able to cooperate closely unless she kept her nose out of his private financial affairs, and joined his golf club, and the Masons, and grew a dark red beard – and a penis.

He picked up his phone and said, 'Get me the assistant commissioner, would you?' Then he looked up at Katie. 'Was there something else?'

She gave him the slightest shake of her head, and left. As she walked back to her own office, she smiled at herself for thinking that she and Bryan Molloy could conceivably find a way to rub along together. He had been so effective in his fight against the criminal gangs in Limerick because he understood completely how some people can detest each other for no rational reason at all except that they do, and he detested her.

Or then again, she thought, maybe he didn't.

Eight

She had finished all of her paperwork by five-thirty, so she left the station and drove to Tivoli Estate, which overlooked the River Lee to the east of the city, to see how Shelagh Hagerty was coping. It was on her way home to Cobh in any case.

The Hagerty house was hidden from the steeply sloping road behind a high beech hedge, but to avoid attracting attention she parked at the bottom of the hill and walked the rest of the way, letting herself into the garden by the side gate. She could see the white Ford van parked further up the road with *O'Keefe Double Glazing* emblazoned on the side. There were two armed gardaí sitting in it, allegedly keeping a watchful eye on the property, although from Katie's experience one of them was probably asleep and the other was likely to be reading the sports pages in the *Irish Sun.*

All the same, they must have noticed her and alerted Detective Horgan. As she came through the garden, he opened the kitchen door for her and said, 'Didn't expect to see you, ma'am.'

'I just thought I'd see how Mrs Hagerty was bearing up.'

'Well, she's trying to put a brave face on it so. But I think the strain is getting a bit much for her.'

Katie followed him through the kitchen into the living room. Shelagh Hagerty was standing by the tall French windows with a bunched-up handkerchief in her fist. Outside the clouds were growing darker, and the room was becoming gloomier and gloomier. A young technician with brushed-up Jedward hair and headphones around his neck was sitting beside the telephone, to which he had attached a Vidicode voice recorder. On the table beside him were two laptops loaded with spy software for tracking and listening in to mobile phone calls.

'Nobody rung yet, then?' asked Katie.

'One wrong number and one feller wanting to sell me double glazing.'

'Double glazing? That's ironic. His name wasn't O'Keefe, was it?'

Katie went over to Shelagh Hagerty. 'I won't ask you how you're feeling because I can guess,' she said. 'I just want you to know that the assistant commissioner has approved the release of the ransom money.'

Shelagh Hagerty nodded and tried to smile. 'Thank you, Super-intendent. What would we have done if he hadn't?'

'Oh, there was no question of that. Don't even think about it. Any road, the chances are very high that we'll get it all back.'

'Would you care for a cup of tea?' asked Shelagh Hagerty, but at that moment, the phone rang, and even Katie felt a tingle of shock. Shelagh Hagerty looked at her wide-eyed and said, 'What shall I tell him? I don't know what to tell him!'

'It's simple. All you have to do is tell him that you've managed to raise two hundred and fifty thousand euros.'

'Oh God, I'm so scared!'

'Please, Shelagh, try to keep calm. You have the money, so there's every chance that you can get Derek back safe and well. But try to keep your man on the line for as long as you possibly can.'

The phone kept on ringing and ringing. Eventually Shelagh Hagerty took a deep breath and picked it up.

'Hello?' she said, in a high, strangled voice. She listened for a moment, and then she covered the receiver with her hand and mouthed to Katie, '*It's him!*'

The young technician held up a pair of earphones and Katie plugged one of them into her left ear. She heard a man's voice with a slurry accent say, 'Hello there, Shelagh. What's the craic?'

She was sure that the caller would be using a stealth phone, or what was called a 'burner,' a throwaway phone that would make it impossible to trace his number. But the software would allow the technician to work out roughly where he was by triangulating between the radio towers that were carrying the call, and then use the signal strength to narrow down his location even further.

Detective Horgan was listening on earphones, too. He looked across at Katie and she thought she had never seen him so grim-faced. Usually he was cracking jokes and pulling faces, but she wondered if the job was beginning to get to him. She was always careful to watch her team for the first signs of stress – and herself, too.

Shelagh Hagerty said, 'I have the money. The two hundred and fifty thousand you asked for.'

'You have it? That's grand. It looks like you'll be seeing your precious Derek again, then, doesn't it?'

'It was very hard to raise it,' said Shelagh. 'I had to sell almost everything we own. I had to borrow some, too, and that wasn't easy, because I couldn't tell anybody what I wanted the money for.'

'Listen, Shelagh, I don't give a shite how hard it was to raise it. The only thing that matters is that you have it. All we have to do now is arrange for you to hand it over.'

'I need to see my Derek first. Or at least to talk to him on the phone. I have to know that he's still alive before I give you all this money.'

'Well, I'm sorry, but you'll just have to trust me, because he isn't here with me now. But I can tell you for sure that he's still living and breathing, and that as soon as I get the money he'll be free to go.'

Shelagh Hagerty didn't know what to say next, but Katie gave her a thumbs up and mouthed 'okay'.

'All right, then,' said Shelagh. 'Tell me what to do, and I'll do it.'

'You haven't been in touch with the shades, have you?'

'What do you think? My Derek's life is at stake.'

'Very sensible of you. Well, then, here's what to do. The money should all be in two-hundred and one-hundred-euro notes, just about half and half, all used, with non-sequential numbers.'

'Wait a minute, wait a minute,' said Shelagh Hagerty. 'Let me write that down.'

'Come on, Shelagh, lively now, I don't have all day. Wrap up the money in five bundles of fifty thousand euros each in cling film. You understand me, the ordinary cling film like you use in the kitchen. Put the bundles into the back of your car and park it on the second level of the Merchants Quay car park at two o'clock tomorrow afternoon. Leave the car unlocked with the keys and the parking ticket in the glove box and take a taxi back home. We'll call you when we've checked that you've given us everything we asked you for.'

'But what about Derek?'

'When we call you, we'll let you know where you can find your car, and we'll also let you know where you can find your husband.'

'He is alive, isn't he? You took out some of his teeth, didn't you, but you haven't hurt him any more than that, have you?'

Shelagh Hagerty was breathing hard, and Katie could tell that she was boiling to tell this man how angry she was, and how much she hated him, and what a monster he had been to pull out so many of Derek's teeth, but she managed to keep her anger under control.

'Have you traced his location yet?' Katie asked the technician.

The technician nodded. 'I'm getting there. He's calling from somewhere between the phone towers on the North Ring Road and Mayfield Industrial Estate, but he's much closer to Mayfield. I'm just checking the signal strength to narrow it down a bit.'

'I shall never forgive you if you've hurt him,' said Shelgah Hagerty.

'He's living and breathing, Shelagh, as God is my witness,' the man replied. 'If you do exactly as I've told you, and no funny business, you'll be seeing him again before you know it. Two o'clock on the dot tomorrow, second level, Merchants Quay car park. G'luck to you so.'

With that, he switched off his phone. Immediately, though, the technician said, 'He's less than a hundred and fifty metres away from Mayfield Shopping Centre. In fact, it's most likely that he's calling from the car park or somewhere right outside.' He swivelled one of his laptops around so that Katie could see the map on his screen, with a small red icon flashing. Mayfield Shopping Centre was less than five kilometres to the north-east of Cork City centre, and only six minutes north of Tivoli Estate, where they were now.

Detective Horgan said, 'I'll have Dooley go up there. I don't think we have much hope of catching this fellow without knowing what he looks like, or what kind of car he's driving, and he's more than likely driven off by now. But if we check out the shopping centre's CCTV we may be able to pick out somebody in the car park making a phone call at a time that tallies.'

'Well, you can try,' said Katie. 'These days it seems like everybody's walking around with a phone glued to their ear.'

'So what should I do?' asked Shelagh Hagerty. 'Do you really think they're going to let Derek go?'

'Do exactly what your man told you to do. We'll have the money ready for you by tomorrow morning and we'll bring it round here. Then just drive down to Merchants Quay and follow his instructions.'

'What will you do? Follow them? Supposing they see you?'

'I can't tell you what we're going to do, Shelagh, but I promise you that we won't take any action that might jeopardize your husband's life.'

'I'm trying very hard to believe that,' said Shelagh Hagerty. 'Right now, though, I'm wishing that I'd never told you. I could have raised that money somehow, and at least I'd be sure that Derek wouldn't be hurt any more.'

'Shelagh, there are never any guarantees with people like these. But if we let them get away with it once, they'll do it again and again, and you don't want another wife to suffer the way that you've been suffering, do you?'

'I don't know,' said Shelagh Hagerty. 'Right now, I don't care very much about anybody else.'

Nine

That night, she was woken at two-thirty by the sound of shouting and screaming from the Kanes' house next door. She turned over and covered her ears with her pillow, but the noise continued, as well as door-slamming and clattering and a sudden burst of loud pop music, as if a radio had been turned on full and then immediately turned off again.

At last, after more than twenty minutes, there was silence, but by now Katie was so wide awake that she climbed out of bed and went to the window. She pulled the curtains aside, but the Kanes' house was in darkness. She went back to bed, switched on her bedside lamp and picked up the crossword she had been trying to finish before she had grown too sleepy.

One of down clues was 'Together, the top and bottom of the world are manic'. The answer was 'bipolar'.

***

Next morning, as she came back with Barney from his early-morning walk, she found David Kane standing in her porch with the collar of his grey raincoat turned up. It was raining hard now and Barney had been stopping every few yards to shake himself.

'Good morning, Katie,' said David. 'That's the trouble with dogs, isn'it? You have to take them out to do the necessary, what-ever the weather.'

Katie lowered her umbrella and shook it. 'Don't you have a dog?' she asked him.

'No, I couldn't. If my patients smelled another dog in the house, whether they were dogs themselves or cats or whatever, they'd find it very disturbing.'

He stood close beside her as she unlocked her front door. 'Talking of disturbing, the reason I've come over is to apologize for all the racket we were making last night, Sorcha and me. Sorcha was having one of her episodes.'

Katie stepped into the hallway and Barney followed her. David stayed in the porch as she hung up her raincoat.

'Has she been back to her doctor?' she said.

'Several doctors. None of them seem able to make her any better.'

'Come in. I have to go to work in half an hour, but I was going to make myself a cup of coffee, if you'd like one.'

David came into the house and closed the front door behind him.

'Here, take off your coat,' said Katie.

'Are you sure? I feel like I'm imposing on you.'

'That's what I do for a living, David. It's my job to be imposed upon.'

'Yes, but by criminals. Not by your next-door neighbour.'

'My father used to be a Garda inspector. He always told me that some people are destined to take care of everybody else, whether they like it or not. "We're born to wipe the tears of the world," he used to say.'

'Oh, well, if you put it like that.'

They went through to the kitchen. Katie put on the kettle and spooned some ground espresso into her cafetière. While they waited for the kettle to boil, David sat down on one of the kitchen chairs and dry-washed his face with his hands.

'Have you thought of taking her to a psychotherapist?' asked Katie. 'We have a very good one who helps us when we interview suspects who have some kind of mental disturbance, Dr Gillian Murphy. She has a practice in Wilton.'

'She saw one psychiatrist in Dublin, but he was worse than useless. He put her on lithium and told her to watch comedy films if ever she felt badly depressed. Can you believe it? Comedy films!'

'You're going to have do something, David. You can't let things go on the way they are.'

'Well, no, you're absolutely right,' he said, watching as Katie poured him a mug of coffee. 'I'll try this psychotherapist of yours in Wilton if you can give me her number.'

He paused, and then he said, 'You have no idea what I would give, though, Katie, for a normal evening out with a normal woman. Just to go to a restaurant and not be constantly on a knife-edge in case she bursts into tears or starts screaming at the waiter or throwing her food all over the place. Just to have a few hours of inconsequential conversation about this and that and the other, if you know what I mean, and a bit of a laugh. I'm not trying to do Sorcha down, but she's wearing me out.'

Katie sat down opposite him. 'I don't know that there's anything more I can do to help you, David. Maybe I could have a talk with Sorcha myself. I have a lot of experience in dealing with depressive women. In fact, more than half of the women we arrest for violent crimes are suffering from what we used to call manic depression – most of it brought on by the men they've been living with, I might add.'

David shook his head. 'I can't see that it would make much difference. And if you started to give Sorcha sympathy she'd be ringing at your doorbell to bother you night and day. No – I'm only talking about a night off, to remind me that a relationship with a woman doesn't have to be non-stop tension and breaking plates.'

Katie knew what was coming next. It couldn't have been more obvious than the yellow-fronted 10.35 train slowly approaching Cork station from Dublin Heuston. David had been working up to this from the moment he had first appeared on her doorstep, especially with his flirtatious *plámás*. All the same, she said nothing and waited for him to come out with it.

63

'I understand, of course, that you must have very little free time, Katie. But I really enjoy talking to you and I was wondering if maybe I could take you out to dinner sometime soon. Even tonight, if you can make it. No strings attached. Just for the normality of it.'

Katie looked down and sideways to avoid his appealing eyes. 'I had an idea that you were building up to this. But you know what my answer has to be, don't you? You're a married man and I can't afford any scandal at all, no matter how unjustified it might be.'

'Katie – '

'No, David. If you and I went out to dinner together, the next thing I know there would be a front-page picture in the *Echo* with a headline saying something like "Who's The Mystery Man With Cork's Top Female 'Tec?" Besides, you're absolutely right, I do have very little free time. I'm right in the middle of a major homicide case at the moment, as well as a whole rake of other investigations. I scarcely have the time to open a tin of baked beans, let alone go out for dinner.'

David raised his eyebrows. 'You're absolutely sure I can't tempt you? I know it's selfish, but you'd be doing me a power of good.'

'Sorry, but I can't. Apart from me, what about Sorcha?'

'Sorcha wouldn't have to know. I wouldn't tell her, to be honest with you. It would only make her worse and she'd start breaking things. We have few enough dinner plates left as it is.'

'The answer's still no, David.'

'Oh well, I tried,' he said. 'But don't go mad if I ask you again.'

'I won't. But you'll get the same answer.'

David finished his coffee. He was about to say something else when Katie's iPhone rang.

'Yes, Kyna?'

'Bill Phinner's just called,' said Detective Sergeant Ni Nuallán. 'He came in early this morning to finish checking the teeth that Shelagh Hagerty brought in. He reconstructed them using the dental records that Dooley got hold of yesterday. He said there's no doubt about it, the teeth match Derek Hagerty's exactly. All from the front. Four incisors, three canines and one premolar crown, which was the gold one.'

'Well, I suppose that's some kind of relief,' said Katie. 'At least we can be sure now that it *is* him that we'll be paying for.' She was conscious now that David was listening to her, and so she said, 'Hold on a moment, Kyna.'

To David she said, 'Do you mind if you show yourself out, David? This is quite important. If you want to drop by this evening, I'll give you Dr Murphy's number, and there's another psycho-therapist I can think of who may be able to help you.'

'Thanks,' said David. He came up to her and kissed her on the right cheek. He would have kissed her on the other cheek if she hadn't lifted her iPhone back up to her ear and turned away from him. He gave her an awkward little finger-wave and a twinkly-eyed wink, and went back out to the hallway to collect his raincoat.

Katie heard the front door close. 'What about the money?' she asked Detective Sergeant Ni Nuallán.

'Two security guards from AIB brought it round about twenty minutes ago. Inspector Fennessy signed for it.'

'You've checked it?'

'It's all there. Two hundred thousand in two hundred euro notes and fifty thousand in hundreds. I was very tempted to stuff some into my pockets, but I resisted the temptation. To be fair, I don't know what I'd spend it on.'

'Shelagh Hagerty's car?'

'The technical boys fitted two GPS trackers last night. As soon as I take the money around to her house, we're all ready to go.'

'I'm just leaving home now,' said Katie. 'I know I've said it fifty times already, but it's absolutely critical that Derek Hagerty's abductors have no idea that Shelagh's contacted us, so there must be strictly no references to any of this on the radio apart from the code signals that we've agreed. I don't want some blabbermouth garda saying "We're in position at Merchants Quay" or anything like that.'

'I think that Bryan Molloy has already told his officers that. But I'll make doubly sure.'

'I want to catch these scumbags, Kyna, but most of all I want to see Derek Hagerty reunited with his wife and kids. Alive, like, and not in a box.'

Ten

They were still laughing when they left Tom's Tavern in McCurtain Street, in Fermoy, and climbed into Meryl's car. The two of them hadn't seen each other in five and a half years and they had so much catching up to do.

Their reunion had been painful as well as funny. Eoghan and Meryl had been childhood sweethearts ever since they had attended Carrigaline Community School together. Everybody had assumed that they would one day be married. They had always talked about it themselves, and what their children might look like.

'So long as our daughter isn't born with a hooter like yours,' Meryl used to say. 'And so long as our sons don't have my curly-wurly hair.'

But, as usual, fate had had different ideas, and after Eoghan had graduated from college he had been offered a job with Rank Audio in west London. It was an opportunity he had been unable to refuse, since there were no comparable jobs available in Cork. He had promised Meryl that when he had made enough money he would come back and marry her, but after seven months in England he had met Patsy and made her pregnant, and married her instead.

Meryl had eventually married the boss of the travel agency where she worked, Norman, who was twenty-two years older than she was, but considerate and kind and treated her well, although he was unable to give her children. Meryl still kept a photograph in her purse of herself and Eoghan, standing by the river's edge at Crosshaven. They were both smiling, but they looked as if they were cold.

'I'll drive you home the long way,' said Eoghan, as he started up the engine. 'The longer this afternoon lasts, the better. In fact, I wish it didn't have to end at all.'

Meryl laid her hand on his. It was his left hand, on which he wore his wedding ring. 'We can't turn back the clock, Eoghan. What's done is done.'

Eoghan closed his eyes for a moment and gripped the steering wheel tightly, as if he wished the car was a DeLorean and could transport them back to the past. But when he opened his eyes again, it was still the same day, and nothing had changed.

'Come on,' said Meryl gently. 'This afternoon can't last for ever. But you can take me back the long way if you like.'

They drove out of McCurtain Street and crossed the seven-arch stone bridge over the Blackwater River. The river was running fast and dark today, because the sky was so grey. Once they were over the bridge they turned left along the Mallow Road, although Eoghan wasn't planning to drive as far as Mallow – only as far as Ballyhooly, and then make his way back cross-country to Cork City. He just wanted to be alone for as long as possible with the fields and the trees and the crows and the distant hills, and Meryl.

'Will I see you again?' he asked her.

'I don't think that's a good idea, Eoghan.'

'But I have to go back to England first thing on Saturday morning, and God alone knows when I'll be able to come here next.'

He took the turning just before Ballyhooly which would take them back south over the Blackwater. The narrow road was completely deserted, with hedges or stone walls on either side. The only living things in sight were the cows grazing in the pastures by the side of the river and the crows perched along the telephone lines.

'I made a mistake, and I've paid for it,' said Eoghan. 'I'm still paying for it. I'm going to be paying for it for the rest of my life. Isn't there any way that – '

'What, Eoghan? Isn't there any way that what?'

He had to blink as he drove because there were tears in his eyes. 'Nothing,' he said. 'Absolutely nothing at all.'

They drove in silence for the next ten minutes. Meryl was tempted to lay her hand on his knee, just to reassure him that she was still fond of him, but she knew that he would probably take it the wrong way and it would only make matters worse. In Tom's Tavern he had already suggested that they take a room at the Grand Hotel for the rest of the afternoon, and he had only been half joking.

As they drove around the curve past Ballynoe, Meryl suddenly twisted around in her seat and said, 'Eoghan! Stop!'

'What? What is it?' he said, slowing down.

'Stop! Look – there's a man lying on the ground back there!'

Eoghan stopped the car and turned around to look back along the road.

'Is that a man? It looks more like a sack of potatoes to me.'

'It's a man, I saw his face! We can't just leave him there! Supposing he's hurt? Supposing he's dead?'

'Supposing he's dead drunk, more like.'

'Well, we can take a look, can't we? Just to make sure.'

Eoghan hesitated for a moment. Here he was, enjoying a few last minutes alone with Meryl, and now it was all going to be spoiled by this drunk lying sprawled by the side of the road. Whatever happened, the spell was going to be broken.

At that moment, though, his iPhone pinged. It was a message from Patsy. *Sammy's been sick twice going to take him to the doctor.* It was then that he realized that there really was no spell, except the spell that he was under. Meryl was right. This wasn't a good idea at all, because it would only lead to pain and suffering, and most of that pain and suffering would be his.

'Hold on two seconds,' he told Meryl, and he quickly tapped out a reply to Patsy, telling her to text him later, when she knew what was wrong. Then he backed the car up the lane to where the man was lying on the ground, and climbed out. Meryl climbed out, too, but stayed back while Eoghan went to take a closer look at him.

The man had resembled a bag of potatoes because he was wearing a light brown tweed suit of the same colour as sacking. The suit was soiled and dusty, and one of the sleeves had almost been ripped away at the shoulder. His shirt collar was stained dark brown with blood.

He was lying with his right cheek against the dirt track. His grey hair was tangled and filthy, and his face was so bruised that it was difficult for Eoghan to tell what he looked like, except that he had a bulbous nose and bushy grey eyebrows. His lips were grossly swollen, so that he appeared to be pouting.

Eoghan knelt down next to him and leaned over him, trying to hear if he was still breathing, but the bushes were rustling in the breeze and the trees were creaking so it was hard for him to be sure.

'Is he dead?' called out Meryl.

'I don't know. He's got blood on him but I don't know where it's from.'

'Try shaking him.'

'That's all right for you to say. Supposing he's dead?'

'Then he won't mind, will he?'

Eoghan cautiously reached out and laid his hand on the man's shoulder. He shook him three or four times, and said, 'Hey! Hey! Mister! Are you awake?'

The man opened one blue eye and stared at the ground. 'What?' he murmured.

'We thought you were dead,' said Eoghan.

'What?'

'We were driving past and we saw you lying on the ground here and we thought you were dead.'

The man raised his head and stared up at Eoghan in bewilderment. He tried to sit up, but didn't seem to have enough strength, so Eoghan took hold of his arm and helped him. He sat there, looking around him, blinking at the bright grey daylight.

'Where am I?' he asked, in a muffled, blubbery voice.

'You're about halfway between White Cross and Ballynoe.'

'How did I get here?'

'I wouldn't have any idea at all. You must have walked here, unless somebody threw you out of a car.'

Now Meryl came forward. 'State of you la,' she said, shaking her head. 'Did somebody give you a beating or something?'

The man thought about that, and then nodded. 'They beat me with, yes, with a metal bar. They pulled most of my front teeth out. They said they were going to cut bits off of me, first my fingers and then my toes, and after that my nose and my ears.'

'Holy Mary, Mother of God,' said Meryl. 'Who were they? Do you know who they were?'

'No. Never saw them before. You wouldn't have any water on you, would you? My throat feels like emery paper.'

'No, sorry,' said Eoghan. 'But look – I'll call for an ambulance for you, and the guards, too.'

'No, no, no, don't do that!' the man told him, suddenly agitated. 'They swore to track me down and kill me if I went to the guards. My family too. I was sure they would have killed me anyway, if I hadn't managed to escape.'

'You need medical attention, though,' said Eoghan. 'If they were beating you with a metal bar you could have internal injuries. And look how they've smashed up your mouth. Jesus. What did they use to take out your teeth? A hammer?'

'Don't call for an ambulance, please. If you call for an ambulance, the paramedics will have to tell the guards, they're obliged to. I know I look bad now, but once I've had a chance to clean myself up and once the bruising's settled down –'

'Well, we can't just leave you here,' Eoghan told him, although he was thinking to himself, I wish we could, you stink to high heaven and whatever happened to you, I don't want Meryl and me to be involved in it.

'What's your name?' Meryl asked him.

'Well, maybe it's better for you if you don't know.'

'I have to call you something, don't I?'

'Call me Denny if you like. That'll do.'

'Look, then, Denny, I'll take you home with me,' said Meryl. 'My husband will know what to do.'

The man frowned at Eoghan and said, 'Oh, so *he's* not – ?'

'No, he's just a friend. Do you think you can manage to stand up?'

'I'll try, if you give me a bit of help.'

Eoghan and Meryl took one of his hands each, and between them they managed to heave the man up on to his feet. He stood swaying for a moment, but then he took one shuffling step forward, and then another.

'What time is it?' he asked.

'Just gone one o'clock,' said Eoghan.

'Oh, right.' He thought about that, and then he said, 'What day is it?'

'You really don't know?'

They helped him into the back seat of Meryl's car. Before they climbed in themselves, Eoghan said, 'What the hell are you going to tell Norman?'

'I'm going to tell him the truth, what else? I bumped into an old friend by accident – although that's not quite the truth. We decided to go for a drink at one of our favourite old watering holes and have a catch-up, and on the way back to the city we came across this unfortunate fellow.'

'And you think he'll swallow that? He won't be asking you who this "old friend" was?'

Meryl took hold of Eoghan's hands. 'Eoghan, darling, even if he does, it's the truth, and the truth can't harm you. And nothing happened between us, did it?'

'Well, you're right, of course,' said Eoghan. 'I suppose I'm only wishing that Norman *did* have something to be jealous about. Here – '

He handed her back her car keys. 'You can drop me off anywhere you like. Anderson's Quay would be grand.'

They got back into the car. It now smelled strongly of body

odour and dried urine, mingled with the pine air-freshener that dangled from the rear-view mirror. The man's chin was resting on his chest and he was snoring, with a string of bloody dribble hanging from his lower lip.

Meryl said, 'Eoghan – ' but Eoghan said, 'No, Meryl, you're right. It's all too late, isn't it? It's all far, far too late.'

Eleven

At 1.53 that afternoon, Shelagh Hagerty drove her silver Renault Mégane into the multi-storey car park at the back of Dunne's Stores on Merchants Quay and parked it on the second level.

As she switched off the engine and took out the keys, a dark blue Ford Mondeo reversed into a parking space directly opposite her. A young blonde woman climbed out and opened the rear door so that she could unbuckle her baby from its car seat.

Katie was watching this from the main CCTV viewing room at the Garda station in Anglesea Street. Inspector Fennessy was sitting beside her with his hair sticking up at the back like a small boy and his tie loosened, looking weary, while Detective Sergeant Ni Nuallán was standing so close that Katie could smell her strong floral perfume.

Crime Prevention Officer Tony Brennan was there, too, ruddy-faced, noisily sipping a latte and keeping a proprietary eye on his thirty-six flickering TV screens, showing street scenes from all over the city.

The young woman in the blue Mondeo was Garda Brenda McCracken, the baby was a dummy, and the technical team had installed a camera behind the Mondeo's front grille so that they could see clearly whoever might turn up to drive Shelagh Hagerty's car away. The car park was already covered by CCTV and they were watching the feed from that, too, but the camera in the Mondeo was high-definition and less than fifteen feet from the back of the Renault Mégane.

Shelagh Hagerty walked to the lifts and Garda McCracken followed her, pushing her dummy baby in a buggy. She was a slim, willowy girl, and when she was in uniform her cap looked as if it were two sizes too big for her. Although she appeared so vulnerable, however, Katie had found her to be fearless and determined, and she had selected her as a decoy on several plain-clothes investigations.

When the lift doors opened, three people emerged, two women and an elderly man, all of them carrying bags of shopping. They had already been identified as 'no discernible threat' because Katie had posted two gardaí on the ground floor to keep an eye on the lifts, with instructions to send her a coded message if they saw anybody who looked at all suspicious.

They waited over an hour and a half. By 3.37 p.m., thirty-nine shoppers had come out of the lifts to collect their cars and drive away, but not one of them had approached Shelagh Hagerty's car.

'I doubt they'll be too much longer,' said Inspector Fennessy, glancing up at the clock. 'The car park closes at six-thirty so they'll want to be out of there before then. I can't see them leaving that amount of cash in the back of an unlocked car overnight. Apart from that, it'll cost them forty-eight euros if they do.'

Katie stretched. Her back hurt and her eyes were dry after staring so long at the TV screen. Detective Sergeant Ni Nuallán laid a hand on her shoulder and said, 'How about a coffee, ma'am, or a sandwich maybe?'

'No, I'm grand altogether, thanks. I wouldn't say no to a fresh bottle of water, though. There's something about watching CCTV that's very dehydrating.'

Just as Detective Sergeant Ni Nuallán turned to go, one of the gardaí watching the lifts on the ground floor said, '*Shatter.*' A few seconds later, a man in a black baseball cap and black windcheater came out of the lift, pushing his way past a middle-aged couple and their honey-coloured Labrador. The peak of his cap was pulled down low and a black scarf was wrapped around the lower part of his face, so that all Katie could see was the tip of his nose. He was carrying a large Dunne's shopping bag.

He walked slowly along one line of cars, then stopped and turned back. Then he stopped again.

'Hello,' said Officer Brennan, sitting up straight. 'Look at your man. He's foothering around like nobody's business. Most folks know exactly where they've left their car, and head straight to it. Either he's forgotten where he's parked or else he's trying to find Shelagh Hagerty's car.'

Katie watched with mounting tension as the man walked along the next line of cars. He reached Shelagh Hagerty's Renault Mégane, but for a moment she thought he was going to walk right past it. He stopped, however, and took a look around, and then he opened up the boot and lifted his shopping bag into it.

From the HD camera in the front of the Mondeo, she could see him hurriedly tipping out whatever it was that he had been carrying in his bag, and replacing it with the five bundles of banknotes wrapped up in cling film. Then he closed the boot and carried the bag around to the front of the car, opening up the driver's door and climbing in.

Inspector Fennessy said, 'Pole position,' into his radio. Less than fifty metres away from the car park exit in Parnell Place two gardaí were waiting in an unmarked car, and this signal alerted them that a suspect had taken Shelagh Hagerty's car and was about to drive away. Katie had instructed them not to follow him, but simply to make sure that he didn't switch cars as soon as he left the car park.

Two GPS trackers were concealed in the Renault's wheel arches and these would allow her team to follow the suspect's progress through the city streets. In addition, she had positioned five different unmarked cars at strategic points both north and south of the river to check on it visually, especially if it stopped for any unusual length of time. Even so, she was not going to give the go-ahead to close in for an arrest until she had heard that Derek Hagerty was alive and free – or proven beyond doubt to be dead.

'There he goes,' said Inspector Fennessy, as the Renault backed out of its parking space and headed towards the exit. It disappeared from sight down the ramp, and all they could see now was Garda McCracken walking quickly across the parking level, pushing her baby buggy in front of her. Two young mothers stared at her in astonishment as she picked up the dummy baby and perched it on the roof of her Mondeo while she folded up the buggy, then threw both the buggy and the baby into the boot.

She climbed behind the Mondeo's wheel, started the engine, and pulled out of her parking space with a squeal of tyres.

Katie could see a jiggling, jolting view from the camera in the front of Garda McCracken's car as she swerved left down the exit ramp. She had been instructed to stop at the bottom of the ramp, as if she had broken down, so that no other vehicles would be able to leave the car park for at least five minutes. This was just in case one of Derek Hagerty's abductors had been waiting somewhere in the car park in another car and tried to follow Shelagh Hagerty's Renault.

Garda McCracken had reached the first-floor level when Katie saw that the Renault had stopped halfway down the narrow exit ramp, blocking it completely. Garda McCracken pulled up close behind it, and called in, 'Callinan! Callinan!' That was the code word for 'unexpected development, what should I do now?'

'Tell her to back up, fast!' said Katie.

'What's the code for that?' asked Inspector Fennessy.

'Don't worry about that, just tell her to back up! Now! He could have decked that we're tailing him!'

If Derek Hagerty's abductors were capable of pulling a man's teeth out, Katie was quite sure that they wouldn't hesitate to take extreme measures to protect themselves. The man in the black baseball cap might well emerge from his car with a gun, and she wanted Garda McCracken out of harm's way as quickly as possible.

She was too late. The TV screen that was showing her the picture from the Mondeo's camera flashed blinding white, then immediately went blank.

A second later, they heard a muffled boom from the direction of Merchants Quay, which was only six hundred metres away to the north.

'Mother of God,' said Detective Sergeant Ni Nuallán.

Katie snatched up the headset that she had left lying on the desk in front of her, thumbing the earphones into her ears and twisting the microphone into position. 'Garda McCracken! Garda McCracken! Can you hear me, Garda McCracken? This is DS Maguire! Are you hurt at all? Come back to me, Garda McCracken!'

There was no answer, only a soft, thick hissing noise.

'Garda McCracken, can you hear me?' she repeated, but there was still no response.

'Oh, please, no,' said Detective Sergeant Ni Nuallán, and crossed herself.

Katie pushed her chair back and said, 'Liam – get me there, now! Kyna, call for the paramedics and the fire brigade and the bomb squad. And Bill Phinner and his technical boys, too. Then follow us over to Merchants Quay, lively as you can.

'Name of Jesus,' said Officer Brennan. 'Would you take a sconce at that?'

The CCTV camera opposite the car park was showing billows of thick grey smoke rolling out of the car park and across Parnell Place. They could see shoppers running in all directions, and their own unmarked squad car pulling up outside the entrance.

Katie and Inspector Fennessy left the CCTV room and hurried along the corridor. As they reached the lifts, one of the lift doors opened and Acting Chief Superintendent Molloy came bursting out, accompanied by Sergeant Keoghan.

'A bomb!' he said. 'They only blew the fecking car up! Why in the name of God would they do a thing like that?'

'I have no idea, sir,' Katie told him.

'It's fecking unbelievable! I just hope they didn't blow up the fecking money too! Jimmy O'Reilly's going to have my head on a stick if they blew up the fecking money!'

'It's Garda McCracken I'm worried about,' Katie told him. 'I tried to contact her immediately after the blast but I couldn't raise any response. She was right behind the suspect and I'm worried she might have been injured. I'm going there directly.'

'Well, I'll be there myself as quick as I can. I've already given orders for the street and the car park to be cordoned off and the store evacuated.'

They heard sirens from the fire station across the street. The building echoed with gardaí shouting to each other and clattering down the staircase. Inspector Fennessy was patiently holding the lift door open, so Katie said, 'I'll see you after, sir.'

'Yes, well, Katie, this a fecking disaster. You should have seen this coming.'

'I don't exactly know how I could have done that, sir.'

'You're a detective, aren't you? I thought that detectives were supposed to detect, or have I been living under some kind of misapprehension all these years?'

'I have to go,' said Katie, and stepped into the lift. Inspector Fennessy followed her and pressed the button for the ground floor. As they sank downwards, Katie could tell by his expression what he was thinking.

'Don't expect me to say anything, Liam,' she said. 'Men like Bryan Molloy have a way of self-destructing, sooner or later, without any assistance from anybody else. All you need is the patience of a saint.'

* * *

It took them less than five minutes to reach the entrance to the Merchants Quay car park. Gardaí had blocked off the street with squad cars, and four or five of them were standing at each end, keeping back the crowds of onlookers. Two fire engines had arrived, as well two ambulances, although there was no sign of the bomb squad yet because they would have to be called together and then driven down to the city centre from Collins Barracks.

Inspector Fennessy parked and he and Katie crossed the road to the car park entrance. One of the gardaí from the unmarked car was standing at the exit gate. He was only in his early twenties, with big red ears and a fuzzy blond moustache on his upper lip, more like a schoolboy than a police officer. He looked shocked and disorientated.

'Where's Garda McCracken?' asked Katie. 'She hasn't been hurt, has she?'

'She's – she's up there, ma'am, still in her car,' said the young garda. He kept furiously blinking and his teeth were chattering as if he were cold. 'I'll show you up there so.'

'No, you're grand,' said Katie. 'You just wait here and keep an eye on things.'

She and Inspector Fennessy walked to the bottom of the exit ramp, their shoes crunching on shattered glass. There was a strong smell in the air of burned plastic and rubber. Halfway up the ramp was a tangle of metal that had once been Shelagh Hagerty's Renault. It resembled a giant dead tarantula rather than a car, because the roof had been ripped apart to form angular legs, and the foam-filled seats were bulging like a furry black body.

There were no human remains inside it, and no fragments of banknotes scattered around. The suspect must have left the car before blowing it up, and taken the bag of money with him.

Close behind this wreck was Garda McCracken's Mondeo. Six or seven paramedics and firefighters were already clustered around it in their yellow high-visibility jackets. The windscreen had been blown out, and as Katie inched her way between the concrete wall and the jagged remains of the Renault, she could see Garda McCracken still sitting in the driver's seat, looking pale and bloody, with an oxygen mask over her face.

A grey-haired female paramedic had cut the right sleeve from Garda McCracken's pale green sweater and attached a colloid drip, holding up the bag of fluid as high as she could. Two of the firefighters were using a long crowbar to wrench open the rear nearside door, which had been wedged backwards by the explosion. The squeal of bending metal reminded Katie of a pig being slaughtered.

One of the paramedics stood back so that Katie could get up close to the car. The blast had torn off the Mondeo's bonnet, which was lying upside down at the top of the ramp. It had also forced the steering column back into the passenger compartment, so that the steering wheel had crushed Garda McCracken's collarbone and chest. At first sight, her injuries didn't look too serious, until Katie realized how deeply the wheel had impacted into her ribcage. She looked up over the oxygen mask with glazed, unfocused eyes, but it was miraculous that she was still conscious.

Katie smiled at her and said, 'Don't you worry, Brenda. We'll soon have you out of there. You have the very best people taking care of you.'

Garda McCracken nodded, although Katie wasn't sure that she had understood what she was saying.

She stepped away from the car and beckoned Inspector Fennessy over to the side of the ramp. 'Call Father Burney, would you, Liam?' she said, quietly. 'I don't think she's got too much longer.'

Inspector Fennessy took out his mobile phone. He looked at Katie with a grim face as he waited for Father Michael to answer. 'Why is it always the best ones?' he said. 'Never the useless collips sitting on their fat arses behind a desk all day, counting the hours till they can go and play golf.'

Katie went back to Garda McCracken. The firefighters had prised off the rear passenger door of the Mondeo and one of them was now lying sideways behind the driver's seat, loosening the bolts that fixed it to the floor. He was grunting with effort.

'We'll have to be very cautious now,' said the grey-haired paramedic. 'We don't know if the pressure of the steering wheel is keeping any of her main arteries constricted. If it is, we may cause catastrophic bleeding when we ease her away from it, and who knows what other damage we might do. I'd say that her sternum's split and all of her ribs have been broken and pushed inwards, and her right lung's collapsed. It's pure amazing that her heart's still beating so strong.'

Her heart may still have been beating, and she may still have been breathing, but Garda McCracken's eyes were now closed and her face was as white and greasy-looking as candle wax. The firefighter standing next to Katie said, 'We'll disengage her from the steering wheel and then we'll take the roof off with the cutters and lift her out. Can't say that I fancy her chances, though.'

The word 'disengage' gave Katie a chilly feeling down her back. 'What do you think?' she asked the firefighter. 'It looks like her airbag didn't work. That might have saved her from the worst of it.'

'Yes, no, you're right, but I don't have any idea why it didn't. It only takes one twenty-fifth of a second for an airbag to inflate fully from the moment of impact, but maybe the blast was faster, who knows?'

Now Detective Sergeant Ni Nuallán came climbing up the ramp, followed by three more firefighters carrying Holmatro hydraulic cutters, as well as a petrol-driven generator and hoses. She stopped for a moment to look into the spider-like wreckage of the Renault, then she joined Katie and Inspector Fennessy.

'How is she?' she asked. The firefighters had now freed Garda McCracken's seat from the floor of the Mondeo and two of them were slowly inching it backwards. Garda McCracken let out a muffled mewling sound behind her oxygen mask, but that was all.

'I'm praying for her,' said Katie. 'To be truthful, though, I'm not holding out much hope. Father Burney's on his way from Holy Trinity.'

'Oh, Jesus. That's so sad. She's always so happy out. And such a future ahead of her. I always thought she was going to be another you.'

'How's the surveillance going?' asked Katie. 'Did you see the suspect leave the shopping centre? That fellow in the black baseball cap, with the scarf around his face?'

Detective Sergeant Ni Nuallán shook her head. 'Tony Brennan's still watching out for any sign of him, and he's going to run through all of the recordings for Merchants Quay and Patrick Street immediately prior to the bomb going off, and immediately afterwards. But by the time I left we still hadn't spotted him, or anybody else carrying a bag big enough to fit all that money into.'

'Well, that's just grand,' said Katie. 'There's so many different ways he could have taken out of the building. He could have gone through Dunne's Stores, or Marks & Spencer, and there's a service door on Merchants Quay. It's likely that he changed his clothes, too, and that he had more than one accomplice to split up the money and carry it in smaller bags. We have no idea who he was, or what he looked like, or where he went.'

'There might be some forensics in the car,' said Detective Sergeant Ni Nuallán.

'We'll be able to find out what explosive he used, C-4 or Semtex probably, but that's about all. He took his own bag away with the money in it, so there won't be any traces of that. And he was wearing gloves.'

Katie was watching as Garda McCracken's seat was pulled back as far as it would go. Dark red blood was beginning to soak through the front of her sweater with alarming speed, and the paramedic took out a pair of surgical scissors to cut the fabric.

Detective Sergeant Ni Nuallán, though, was watching Katie and trying to read the expression on her face. 'What are you thinking?' she said.

'I think you know very well what I'm thinking,' said Katie, still without taking her eyes off Garda McCracken. 'I'm thinking that our abductors weren't just being wide about the possibility that we were keeping them under surveillance.'

'Somebody tipped them off?'

'It must have been more than just a tip-off. I think they knew exactly how we planned to keep track of them. If our suspect wasn't aware that Garda McCracken was following close behind him, why did he blow up Shelagh Hagerty's car? It doesn't make any sense otherwise. What would be the point?'

'But why blow it up at all?' asked Detective Sergeant Ni Nuallán. 'He could have just climbed out and hopped off.'

'No – I'll tell you something else about these characters,' said Katie. 'They're out to show us that they're highly dangerous and they're not to be messed with. And do you know why I think that is? I think they're planning to do this again.'

'Do you think they're the same people who killed Micky Crounan?'

'It wouldn't surprise me at all. And it wouldn't surprise me if we never saw Derek Hagerty alive again, either.'

Detective Sergeant Ni Nuallán said something in reply, but at that moment the Holmatro generator started up, and Katie couldn't hear what it was. Inside the Mondeo, Garda McCracken had been completely covered with a thick fawn blanket to protect her from debris and the firefighters had started to cut away the roof with their lobster-claw cutters.

The noise of the generator and the sound of tearing metal and plastic drowned out any possibility of conversation, and when Father Burney came puffing up the ramp Katie could do nothing but clasp his hand and point to Garda McCracken, hidden under her blanket as if she were already dead.

Twelve

It had started to rain again by the time Meryl turned into the driveway of her house on the Boreenmanna Road, south-east of Cork City. It was a large detached house almost completely hidden from the road. The rain crackling in the high hedges that surrounded it made them sound as if they had just caught fire.

As soon as she switched off the engine, the man in the back seat snuffled and opened his eyes and looked around him.

'Where are we?' he asked. 'Did I fall asleep?'

'Yes, Denny, you did for a while,' said Meryl. 'This is my house. I'm going to take you inside and you can clean yourself up and then we'll decide what to do with you.'

'You won't be calling the guards?'

'No, I promise you. But first you need to have a shower and change out of those filthy clothes. I'm sure Norman will have something to fit you.'

'That's your husband, yes?'

'That's right. Like I told you, the other fellow was just an old friend, that's all.'

She helped him to heave himself out of the car and up the steps to the porch. As they reached the front door, it suddenly opened and Meryl's husband appeared. He was stocky and bespectacled, with grey wings to his rust-coloured hair, and wearing a check shirt and beige trousers held up with bright green braces. In one hand he was holding a folded-up copy of the *Examiner*, with the cryptic crossword almost completed.

'Meryl!' he said. 'Where in the name of Jesus have you been all day? Who's this? My God, look at the condition of him!'

'This is Denny,' said Meryl. 'I'm really sorry I haven't been answering any of your calls, darling, but while I was shopping I met an old friend and we went for a little drive around for a catch-up. On the way back we saw Denny lying by the side of the road and we couldn't just leave him there.'

'For the love of God, Meryl, you could have called for an ambulance, couldn't you? What did you bring him home for?'

'Because she's a good Samaritan, your wife, sir,' said Denny, clearing his throat. 'She and her friend did not pass by on the other side of the road and leave me lying there.'

'What friend?' frowned Norman. 'Why did you have to drive around with her? You could have brought her back here, couldn't you? I've been worried.'

'Can't we get Denny inside, Norman?' asked Meryl. 'The poor fellow can barely stand up.'

Norman peered at Denny over his spectacles, his mouth puckered in distaste. 'I suppose we don't have much option, now that you've brought him here. But I think we should call for an ambulance. I don't see what we can possibly do to help him.'

Together, they helped Denny shuffle into the house. They took him through the hallway into the living room and Norman spread sheets from his newspaper over the red brocade sofa so that he could sit down. Denny looked around, blinking. Norman had owned the house before he and Meryl were married and the living room was decorated in 1970s style, with a red-brick fireplace, an oak cabinet with all of Norman's golf trophies inside it, and a large reproduction painting of Blackrock Castle on a stormy day.

A long-case clock ticked wearily in the corner, as if it were tired of life.

Meryl said, 'I was hoping that Denny could have a shower and maybe you could lend him something to wear. That old maroon sweater of yours and a pair of trousers.'

'That old maroon sweater is what I wear when I'm gardening,' Norman protested.

'Well, I'll buy you a *new* maroon sweater and you can do your gardening in that.'

'I'm going to call an ambulance,' said Norman.

'No, please, no,' Denny interjected, lifting his hand. 'I know you're not at all happy about taking me in like this, and believe me, I appreciate your Christian kindness more than I can tell you. But I wasn't knocked over, or involved in any kind of a road accident. I was taken hostage by a gang of criminals so that they could demand a ransom for my release.'

'You were *what*?'

'It's true. They snatched me and blindfolded me and took me somewhere near to Fermoy, as far as I can guess. Then they contacted my wife and said they wanted two hundred and fifty thousand euros or else they were going to kill me. And to prove they had me, they pulled out all of my front teeth, with no anaesthetic at all, and they sent them to my wife in a jam jar.'

Norman stared at him, then took off his spectacles and leaned forward and stared at his bloated lips even more closely. 'Holy Jesus.'

'They beat me, too,' said Denny, lifting up his shirt to show Norman and Meryl the angry crimson bruises on his ribs. 'They warned me that if my wife told the Garda what had happened to me, even after they let me go, they would kill us both. In fact, if we told anyone else about it, they would come after them, too. That's the reason I don't want to tell you too much. '

'So what happened?' asked Norman. 'Your wife paid the ransom and they let you go?'

Denny shook his head. 'I have no idea whether she's paid it or not, because I managed to escape. The last time they fed me I hid a spoon down my sock, and I used it to force the catch on the toilet window. It was a fifteen-foot drop down from the window to the garden and I think I cracked one of my ribs when I fell, but I ran off and I kept on running, and then walking. After that,

I don't really remember what happened until your wife and her friend came across me.'

'So who are they, this criminal gang? What name do they go by?'

'It's better that I tell you nothing at all. You know what they say – what you don't know can't knock on your door in the middle of the night.'

Norman looked across at Meryl with a mixture of exasperation and bewilderment. 'I don't know whether to believe any of this or not,' he said. 'Either you're telling us the truth here, Denny, or else you're stringing us along something rotten.'

'I swear to God,' said Denny. 'But I can't tell you any more for your own safety.'

Meryl said, 'Please, Norman. Just let him have a shower and a change of clothes and something to eat and drink if he wants it. Then I can drop him off wherever he wants to go to, and that'll be an end to it.'

Norman breathed in noisily through his nose. 'All right. But I don't like this one bit. And I'd still like to know what you were doing driving around with this friend of yours. And you've taken a drink, haven't you? I can smell it.'

'I'll talk to you after, Norman,' said Meryl. 'Meanwhile, why don't you take Denny upstairs to the bathroom and give the poor fellow a towel and something to wear.'

'I have that yellow sweater I've never worn, the one with the zig-zag stripes that your mother gave me.'

'All right, whatever. He only needs something to go home in.'

Norman turned to Denny. 'Do you think you can manage the stairs?'

'I think so. You don't know how grateful I am. You're a saint, sir, believe me.'

With Norman grasping his arm to support him, Denny climbed to his feet and stood between them swaying. 'You'll get your reward in heaven for this,' he told Meryl. 'The angels will be applauding you as you walk through the pearly gates.'

'Just come along,' said Norman testily, and guided him into the hallway.

Denny heaved himself very slowly up the stairs, clutching at the banister rail and wheezing with every step. Norman led him along the corridor to the bathroom.

'Be wide of that shower,' Norman cautioned him. 'Sometimes it runs ice-cold and then without any warning it starts to run boiling hot, so you may have to do a bit of adjusting if you don't want to get yourself scalded to death. If you hold on a second, I'll bring you a towel and some fresh clothes.'

Norman went to his dressing room to fetch the yellow sweater with the zig-zag stripes and an old pair of olive corduroy trousers that were now too tight around the waist. Then he went to the airing cupboard and took out a bath towel that he had stolen years ago from Ballybunion Golf Club. When he returned to the bathroom he found that Denny had completely undressed, apart from a droopy pair of Y-fronts stained with yellow and a single pale blue sock. He had bundled up his suit and his shirt and perched them on top of the clothes basket.

It was not only his ribs that were patterned with bruises. There were red and yellow and purple contusions on his shoulders and his arms and his legs, most of which looked as if they been inflicted with a thick stick or a metal bar.

'Jesus, they certainly gave you a clatter, didn't they?'

'They said I deserved it. They said that I was one of the worst examples of the bad businessmen who had brought Ireland to its knees. Borrowing too much, running into debt that I couldn't pay back.'

'Well, you weren't the only one, by any means,' said Norman. 'We all thought that the boom times were going to last for ever, didn't we? If your criminal pals manage to beat every businessman in Ireland who got himself involved in rash speculations in the Celtic Tiger days, I'd say that at least two thirds of the male population will be walking around in the same state as you.'

Denny patted his puffy, scab-encrusted lips with his fingertips. 'It makes no sense to me at all. Why did they think they could get so much money out of somebody who doesn't have a pot to piss in or a window to throw it out of? Like I told you, I don't even know if my poor wife's managed to raise that much. I hope to God she has or else our lives won't be worth a thrawneen.'

'Well, take your shower now and think about that later,' said Norman. The sight and smell of Denny was making him feel like going out into the garden, for all that it was teeming with rain, and taking a deep cold lungful of fresh air.

'Thanks again for doing this, sir,' said Denny. 'I know how rank I must look to you now, but you should see me when I'm all dickied up.'

Norman gave him a brittle smile. 'I'll leave you alone, then,' he said, although he was thinking, *I must make sure to throw that bar of soap in the bin after.*

***

'Would you like a cup of tea?' Meryl asked him when he came back downstairs. 'I've just brewed a pot.'

'Wouldn't you better off with a strong cup of coffee?' Norman demanded. 'You go out drinking with some anonymous friend and come back home bringing some stinking beaten-up tramp with you. I think you owe me an explanation, don't you?'

Meryl said, 'Very well. I won't lie to you, Norman. It was Eoghan.'

Norman stared at her in disbelief. '*Eoghan*? Eoghan Carroll, you mean? What in the name of God were you doing going out drinking with Eoghan Carroll of all people?'

'I told you. We were catching up, that's all.'

'I hope that was all you were doing. No wonder you didn't answer my calls. Eoghan Carroll, for Christ's sake. He's a married man now, just like you're a married woman.'

'We went for a drink and a laugh, that's all. I'm not your prisoner, Norman, and just because we're married that doesn't

mean I can't have an innocent conversation with a man who used
to be my boyfriend.'

'Jesus. I don't believe it. And to think I trusted you. And I've
only gone and left my phone upstairs in my dressing room.'

'Norman – '

'Oh, don't "Norman" me, girl. I thought we had a marriage
as solid as a rock.'

'We do, Norman! Eoghan wanted us to get a room in a hotel,
but I said no. I told him it was long over, me and him.'

'I'll kill him! I will personally strangle him, I swear it! I have
to get my phone.'

Norman went back upstairs, leaving Meryl in the living room
with her eyes filled with tears. The power-shower motor in the
attic was still rumbling, but as Norman passed the bathroom
door he could hear that the shower itself had stopped clattering,
so Denny must have finished washing himself.

He had taken only a few more steps along the corridor when
he heard Denny say something like, 'Yes, okay, that's grand.'

Norman tiptoed back to the bathroom door and inclined his
head towards it.

There was a moment's silence, and then Denny said, 'Okay,
yes. I have you. Yes. I'll see you at five at Michael's.'

His voice was gummy and indistinct, and he said 'yesh' instead
of 'yes' and 'shee' instead of 'see', but there was no doubt that
he was talking to somebody on a mobile phone, and that he was
making an arrangement to see them later.

For a while he said nothing but 'yesh' and 'yesh' and 'I deck
that, yesh'. But then he said, 'No, no question at all, they've
shwallowed it one hundred per cent. I should hope sho, any road.
The husband especially, Norman. He's really getting thick about
it, sho I think he will. Yesh. For sure, yesh. Okay. I'll shee you
after.'

Norman felt like bursting into the bathroom and demanding
to know who Denny had been talking to, and what he and Meryl
were supposed to have swallowed one hundred per cent. Instead,

though, he gently eased down the door handle and pushed the door a little way open so that he could see inside.

The bathroom was still humid from Denny's shower. Denny was standing in front of the washbasin with his back to the door, towelling his neck and his shoulders, but the mirror was steamed up so that he couldn't see Norman looking in at him. A black mobile phone was resting on the shelf next to Norman and Meryl's toothbrush mug.

Denny had been abducted, thought Norman, *and yet his abductors hadn't taken his mobile phone off him?* That made no sense at all. More remarkable than that, though, almost all of his bruises had disappeared. He still had a few faint red marks on his back, but all of the darker bruises had vanished completely. Norman could only conclude that they hadn't been real bruises at all, but make-up of some kind, and that Denny had soaped them off in the shower.

Tempted as he was to confront him, Norman quietly closed the door. He hurried to his dressing room to collect his phone and then went back downstairs. Meryl was standing by the window, looking miserable.

'I'm sorry, darling,' she said. 'I never should have gone with Eoghan for a drink. It was only for old times' sake.'

'Don't worry about that now,' said Norman. 'Your man upstairs is an impostor. He has a mobile phone up there with him, and all of those bruises he showed us, they've all washed off. He was talking to somebody about how he's managed to fool us, and he's arranged to meet them at five o'clock.'

Meryl stared at him. 'You're serious?'

'I heard him and I saw him for myself. With a bit of luck, though, I don't think he saw me.'

They heard the bathroom door open. Norman put his finger to his lips and whispered, 'The best thing we can do is act as if we don't suspect anything. He might turn violent if we let him know that we're on to him, or call his friends to come round here and give us a beating, or worse.'

'So what are we going to do?' Meryl whispered back.

'Act natural. Give him a cup of tea and then I'll drive him into the city. But I'll call the guards before I go so that they know all about him, and where I'm going to drop him off. I can't imagine what kind of a game he's playing, but it seems to me like it could be very dangerous.'

Denny appeared in Norman's yellow zig-zag sweater and his olive corduroy trousers, carrying his old clothes rolled up under his arm. He was smiling as much as his swollen lips would allow, although they were bleeding a little where the scabs had washed off and he had to keep dabbing them with a folded piece of toilet paper.

'Feeling better, Denny?' Meryl asked him, trying hard to sound natural.

'Grand altogether, thanks to the both of you. I'll never forget this.'

'Well, sit down and I'll pour you a cup of tea. Do you think you could manage some brack?'

'I don't know about that. My gums are fierce sore. But the tea would be welcome.'

'I'll drive you into the city after,' said Norman. 'Any place special you want me to drop you?'

'Grand Parade, right outside the old Capitol Cineplex, that would be perfect.'

'No problem at all,' said Norman. 'I'll go and get my car out. You take your time with your tea, Denny. After what you've been through, you need to take it easy.'

Thirteen

Katie was sitting in the waiting room outside the intensive care unit at Cork University Hospital when her iPhone rang.

Dr Owen Reidy was calling from his pathology laboratory in Dublin. He sounded unusually amiable, as if he might have taken a glass of wine with his lunch, or maybe two.

'We've finished examining your man's head, Detective Superintendent. So far as we can tell, it was severed with a chainsaw. It's impossible to say without the rest of his body whether this was done before or after life was extinct. Even if it was done before, it certainly would have been extinct after.'

The fluorescent light in the waiting room flickered and made a buzzing noise like a bluebottle, and the rain pattered sporadically against the windows.

'Any other marks or bruises?' Katie asked him. 'Presumably somebody must have held his head still while they cut it off, even if he was dead already.'

Detective Sergeant Ni Nuallán was sitting with her legs crossed on the opposite side of the room, flicking through a copy of *Hello!*, but she looked up when Katie said that.

Dr Reidy said, 'There are five distinct bruises to his temples which were probably caused by thumb and finger pressure, but we weren't able to lift any prints from them – not entirely surprising since his head was subsequently baked in a cake. However, he's missing three teeth from his lower left jaw – the second and third molars and second premolar.

94

Dr Reidy hesitated, but Katie could sense that he had something more to tell her, something critical. He always enjoyed disclosing his findings with dramatic pauses, and he always left his most important revelations until last.

'All three teeth were extracted at the same time, and I would say that they were taken out almost immediately prior to the victim's beheading, because the cavities hadn't even begun to heal. What's more, they weren't pulled out by any dentist, I can tell you that for certain. The gums were damaged in such a way that I would guess they were forcibly removed with pliers.'

'Ordinary DIY pliers, like you'd buy in Hickey's?'

'Exactly that. We found squarish contusions around the cavities which exactly match a pair of 125mm flat-nose linesman's pliers.'

'You'll send me your pictures?' said Katie.

'Of course. They should be coming through to you in the next few minutes. Full report to follow. Difficult to give you an exact date and time of death because of the effects of the baking process, but I've done my best.'

Katie said nothing to Dr Reidy about Derek Hagerty's teeth being sent in a jam jar to his wife. Those teeth, too, had been forcibly extracted, but so far she had no irrefutable proof that Micky Crounan and Derek Hagerty might have been abducted by the same offenders, even though each new piece of evidence seemed to be telling her that it was increasingly likely.

She told Detective Sergeant Ni Nuallán what Dr Reidy had said to her, and then she rang Inspector Fennessy and informed him, too.

'Jesus,' he said. 'It gives me the raging toothache just to think about it.'

'Have you heard from the bomb squad?'

'Not more than ten minutes ago. They searched the car park but they didn't find any more devices. I've just had a call from the technical boys, too. The bomb was definitely C-4, probably about twenty to twenty-five pounds of it, judging by the blast damage. It was detonated by a mobile phone.'

'Any indication who might have built it?'

'Bill Phinner says what's left of the wiring suggests that it might have been put together by Fergal ó Floinn. Either ó Floinn himself or somebody that he might have taught to put a bomb together.'

'Ó Floinn? That piece of work. He swore blind to me after that Cathedral Quarter bombing in Belfast that he would never touch an ounce of explosive again as long as he lived. Of course, that bombing was nothing at all to do with him. None of those bombings ever were.'

'Well, as I say, we can't be certain that it was him,' said Inspector Fennessy. 'I've asked Patrick to find out where he is, though, and we'll be having a word.'

'Okay. Good. But don't let him fob you off with his usual *buinneach*.'

'What's the news on Brenda McCracken?' asked Inspector Fennessy.

'She came out of surgery about an hour ago,' said Katie. 'They haven't told me anything except that she's critical.'

'We're all praying for her. She's one of the best. Fearless, absolutely fearless, that girl, and always ready with a laugh.'

'I'll call you as soon as I get an update so,' Katie told him. 'Right now, I think our prayers are probably the best chance she has.'

***

Katie sat in the waiting room for another twenty minutes, while Detective Sergeant Ni Nuallán repeatedly went out into the corridor to answer calls on her mobile phone and to send texts to the detectives who were making inquiries all over the city about the bombing in the Merchants Quay car park. They were also still looking for Micky Crounan's decapitated body. Three floaters had been fished out of the River Lee in the past four days, but one was a heavily pregnant Nigerian woman, and although the other two were both white and male and middle-aged, their heads were still attached.

Katie checked her watch, then she stood up and said, 'I'll have to go back to the station, Kyna. It's coming in from all sides and I need to take control. I don't want Bryan Molloy accusing me of neglecting my duty because I'm a sentimental woman.'

'With that feen you can't win either way,' said Detective Sergeant Ni Nuallán. 'I'll bet if you hadn't stayed here to see if Garda McCracken was going to pull through, he would have blamed you because you showed no compassion for the rank and file.'

Katie picked up her grey leather shoulder-bag, but as she did so one of the surgeons came into the waiting room. He was a thin Iranian with protuberant eyes and a hooked nose, and a small black pillow of hair on top of his head that might have been a wig.

'DS Maguire?' he asked. He spoke so softly that Katie could hardly hear him. 'My name is Saeed Akbari. I am the leading surgeon of the team that has been trying to save the life of your colleague.'

'How is she?' asked Katie.

'I regret to tell you that there is no more hope for her survival. She suffered catastrophic internal injuries and it was a miracle that her heart went on beating for as long as it did. She is still on life-support at the moment but she can never recover.'

'So there's no hope at all?'

Mr Akbari shook his head. 'None whatsoever, I am afraid. Without life-support she would have passed away already.'

'I understand,' said Katie. 'Can I go in and see her?'

'Of course. Her sister is there already, as well as Father Burney.'

He led Katie and Detective Sergeant Ni Nuallán along the corridor to the ward where Garda McCracken was lying behind curtains. Her curly-haired sister was sitting on the left-hand side of the bed, while Father Burney was standing on her right, his hands clasped together, holding a rosary. A plump bespectacled nurse was sitting next to him, busily filling in a form on a clipboard.

Brenda McCracken herself was lying with her eyes closed and an oxygen mask covering her face. Underneath the thin green cotton blanket that covered her, her chest was protected by a metal cage. The heart monitor beside the bed was tirelessly beeping, but it was only counting out the seconds that the respirator had allowed her to borrow. In reality, she was dead already.

Katie went up to the bed and laid her hand on Brenda's sister's shoulder. Her sister looked up and her eyes were red-rimmed and her mascara blotched.

'She was one of our very best,' said Katie. 'She was brave and she was confident and everybody was fond of her.'

The nurse finished filling in her form and stood up, taking off her glasses. Katie was unsettled to see that she looked the bulb off her own mother – same dark red hair, same sympathetic expression in her eyes, as if she completely understood how much everybody in this room was already grieving, even if she didn't share in their grief.

'I'm afraid it's time,' she said.

Brenda's sister started to sob and her shoulders shook. Father Burney stepped forward and made the sign of the cross.

Very quietly, he said, 'May the Lord support us all the day long, till the shades lengthen, and the evening comes, and the busy world is hushed, and the fever of life is over, and our work is done. There in His mercy may He give us a safe lodging, and a holy rest, and peace at the last. Amen.'

The nurse gently lifted the oxygen mask from Brenda's face. She looked so peaceful, like a young woman in a Pre-Raphaelite painting. It was difficult for Katie to believe that she wasn't simply sleeping a dreamless sleep, but dying.

After a few minutes the nurse checked her heart rate, and said, 'Brenda's passed away. I'm sorry.'

***

Katie walked so briskly out of the hospital that Detective Sergeant Ni Nuallán almost stumbled in her wedge-heeled shoes to keep up with her. She had felt angry many times before. The scummers she had to deal with every day were so cruel and stupid and thoughtless that it was very hard not to feel angry with them, although most of the time she was able to keep her temper under control. But she had never before fumed with such vengefulness as she did now. The inside of her head felt like a slow-motion car crash.

A precious young life had been taken away, for nothing more than a few thousand euros. She was determined to track down whoever was responsible, and against every principle that she had sworn to uphold when she joined An Garda Síochána, she even found herself hoping that the offenders would try to resist her when she came to arrest them, so that she would have an excuse to use deadly force.

As they reached Katie's car, Detective Sergeant Ni Nuallán's iPhone rang and before she climbed into the passenger seat she stopped with her door still open to answer it.

Katie heard her say, 'No' and '*No!*' and 'Come back to me?' and '*No*, you're codding!'

'Who was that?' Katie asked her, starting up her engine and backing out of the parking space.

'Patrick O'Donovan, and you're not going to believe this. We've just picked up Derek Hagerty, alive and reasonably well.'

'So, well, they actually let him go,' said Katie. 'I suppose that's something to be thankful for. Where did we find him?'

'Grand Parade. A member of the public tipped us off that he would be there. Some quite well-spoken fellow, that's what Patrick said.'

'Did he give us his name, this well-spoken fellow?' asked Katie. She was keeping her attention on the traffic as she pulled out into the Bishopstown Road.

'No. He wanted to remain anonymous. He said that his wife found Derek Hagerty lying in a very poor state by the side of the road up by Ballynoe. She brought him home because he told her he was afraid of what his kidnappers might do to him and his family if he contacted the Garda.'

'That was very Christian of her. Pure stupid, but very Christian. *Jesus* – you eejit! Pull out in front of me without making a signal, why don't you?'

Detective Sergeant Ni Nuallán waited while Katie put down her window and remonstrated with the van driver who had just cut her up. Then, as they drove on, she said, 'The caller said that he and his wife allowed Hagerty to take a shower and they also gave him a change of clothes.'

'More than most people would have done. Then what?'

'When Hagerty was in the bathroom, your man overheard him talking on a mobile phone and so he started to grow suspicious. Like – what kind of kidnappers would allow their hostage to keep his mobile phone? Not only that, Hagerty had shown this fellow and his wife that his body was covered in a mass of bruises. But when he sneaked a look at him in the bathroom, it looked like all of the bruises had washed off.'

'They'd washed off? Serious?'

'That's what your man told Patrick. He'd agreed to drive Hagerty into the city centre, but before he left his house he called us up and told us where Hagerty wanted to be dropped.'

'I don't understand this, Kyna. Why wasn't I told about this anonymous caller as soon as he rang?'

'I have no idea. According to Patrick, Molloy took charge of it personally, so if anybody should have told you, it was him.'

'What? *Molloy* took charge of it? He had absolutely no right to do that. This was my operation, and it still is, even if I have made a real hames of it.'

'You couldn't have known about the bomb. Nobody could have seen that coming.'

'It's my job, Kyna. I'm supposed to look after my team. That means I need to take precautions against every eventuality that I can think of, and a few more that I can't.'

'I know. But you can't blame yourself for what happened to Brenda McCracken.'

'I can, Kyna, and I do.'

'There's one more thing, though,' said Detective Sergeant Ni Nuallán as they stopped at the traffic lights at Victoria Cross. 'The caller said his wife found Derek Hagerty at approximately one-fifteen. He told her that he had escaped from his kidnappers by climbing out of a toilet window.'

Katie turned to frown at her. 'One-fifteen? That means that he managed to get free more than three quarters of an hour before the ransom was due to be paid. So there was no need for us to pay the ransom at all, and Brenda McCracken needn't have died. What time did this anonymous caller get in touch with us?'

'About twenty minutes ago, give or take. He didn't say where he was calling from.'

'Get in touch with Tony Brennan. Tell him I need to see today's CCTV footage from Grand Parade as soon as I get back to the station.'

'Anything else?'

'Yes. Make sure that Bryan Molloy is still in his office and hasn't sloped off to play golf. I'm going to have that man's mebs for earrings one day.'

Detective Sergeant Ni Nuallán looked at her and shook her head. 'Don't,' she said, very seriously. 'They wouldn't suit you.'

Fourteen

'I'm not saying that you're incompetent, Katie, not for a moment,' said Acting Chief Superintendent Molloy. 'I'm simply pointing out that you might have considered a different approach to handling the money drop . . . one that gave Derek Hagerty's abductors some credit for intelligence. They were bound to suspect that you were going to bug Mrs Hagerty's car.'

'I took that into account, of course,' said Katie. 'That's why Garda McCracken was following him, and that's why I had five other cars in position all around the city, just in case he swapped vehicles. I even had officers watching the Passover and all of the other pedestrian bridges in case he abandoned her car altogether and tried to get away on foot.'

'But it never occurred to you that they might blow the car up?'

'To be honest with you, no. But then I don't suppose it occurred to *you*, either.'

'Maybe not, Katie, and I can't deny that I gave this operation the go-ahead. But I wasn't in charge of the tactical details, was I? Perhaps if I had been, things might have turned out different. As it is, we've lost a young garda's life and a quarter of a million of taxpayers' euros, and all for nothing. No arrests, no leads, and to cap it all the hostage had already managed to escape before we handed over the ransom money. The very least damage it's done is to make us look like a bunch of clowns.'

'Bryan – I disagree with you entirely,' Katie told him. She was trying very hard to keep her temper, but her voice was strained.

'I think it shows how much dedication we put into this job. There was no possible way we could have foreseen that they were going to blow up Mrs Hagerty's car, or that Derek Hagerty would have got himself free. We're not psychic.'

Bryan Molloy looked at his Rolex. 'Oh well, I'm holding a media conference at five-fifteen. That's what I'll tell them, shall I? A garda was killed and two hundred and fifty thousand euros of public money has gone missing because we're not psychic?'

'Before you do that, I want to talk to Derek Hagerty myself.'

'If you think it'll do any good, go ahead. He's in the first-aid room on account of the leathering they gave him. So far he's refused to say anything at all. He won't even admit to being Derek Hagerty, even though we've had his wife in and she's identified him.'

Katie stood up. 'You say you're not blaming me, Bryan, but it sounds very much as if you are.'

'It was your operation, Katie. Your idea. You have to admit that.'

Bryan Molloy stared at her with those bulging eyes, one eyebrow suggestively raised. Katie was sorely tempted to tell him that the responsibility for what had happened at the Merchants Quay car park was ultimately his, and that Chief Superintendent O'Driscoll would have accepted that he was personally accountable even if he hadn't been involved in the finer points of planning the operation.

However, she kept her lips tightly closed. She was quite aware that Bryan Molloy was doing everything he could to undermine her – partly because she had made no secret of the fact that her detectives were looking into his political and financial connections, but mostly because she was a woman.

But it wasn't Bryan Molloy who concerned her the most. It was what appeared in the media that mattered most – that, and how Assistant Commissioner Jimmy O'Reilly would react. After all, it was Jimmy O'Reilly who had authorized the release of all that untraceable cash, and it was Jimmy O'Reilly who would have to explain to Phoenix Park how Katie had let Derek Hagerty's kidnappers get away with it.

She said, tautly, 'I'll see you before the media conference, after I've talked to Derek Hagerty.'

Bryan Molloy pulled a face, as if to say, Do whatever you want, girl, I don't give a fiddler's . . .

She left his office. While she waited for the lift at the end of the corridor, she took several deep breaths, as if she were about to dive deep underwater.

***

Detective O'Donovan was waiting for Katie outside the first-aid room. He was halfway through eating a Mars bar and when he saw her coming he quickly wrapped up the rest of it and dropped it into the pocket of his dark blue windcheater.

'I don't mind if you want to finish that, if you're hungry,' said Katie.

Detective O'Donovan wiped his mouth with the back of his hand. 'No, you're all right. I'm trying to lose weight anyway.'

'Well, don't blame me if it goes all melted. What's the story here?'

Through the circular window in the first-aid room door, Katie could see Derek Hagerty lying on one of the two recovery beds, still wearing the yellow zig-zag sweater and olive corduroy trousers that Norman had given him. His grey hair was neatly parted and his hands were pressed together over his chest like a figure on top of a tomb. His eyes were closed, but Katie had the feeling that he was not really asleep.

'Doctor Murphy came in about a half-hour ago and gave him a bit of a check-up,' said Detective O'Donovan.

'Oh yes? And what did the good Doctor Murphy have to say?'

'He's not in such a poor condition as he looks. His mouth's a total mess and he has a few minor bruises on him, but nothing's broken. As far as Doctor Murphy could tell, he's perfectly fit, apart from a fierce bad case of dhobie itch, and that's probably caused by stress and not being able to wash himself for a couple of days.'

'So, what with those fake bruises that your informant told you about, it looks like he's been after making out that he was much more seriously hurt than he really was?'

'Who knows?' said Detective O'Donovan. 'Until he starts talking to us, your guess is as good as mine.'

Katie pushed open the door and they went inside. A young garda was sitting in the opposite corner of the room. He stood up when Katie and Detective O'Donovan came in and put down the copy of *Irish Car + Travel* magazine that he had been reading.

'How is he?' asked Katie.

'Surviving, I'd say,' said the garda.

'He hasn't said anything?'

'Not a sausage.'

Katie went up to Derek Hagerty and stood over him. She could see his eyeballs darting from side to side under his eyelids, so he was either in REM sleep and dreaming or else he was awake.

'Derek,' she said, loudly. 'Derek, this is Detective Superintendent Maguire. I need to have a few words with you about your abduction.'

Derek Hagerty's eyelids remained closed, although his eyeballs continued to move.

'Derek, it's important that you talk to me. This isn't just a case of kidnap any more, it's a homicide investigation. A garda was killed by a bomb when your ransom was handed over.'

Derek Hagerty opened one eye, and when he saw Katie standing there he opened the other.

'*What*?' he blurted

'I think you heard what I said. A bomb was planted in your wife's car. When it went off, a young woman officer was fatally injured.'

'Oh, Jesus, no,' said Derek Hagerty. 'So that was what it was – that explosion?'

'You knew about it?'

'We heard about it on the car radio when we were driving into the city.'

'What – you and the fellow who dropped you off at Grand Parade?'

'That's right. There was a newsflash, like, about some kind of a detonation at Merchants Quay. They didn't say what had caused it, though, and they said nothing at all about anybody getting hurt. A bomb! Jesus, and in Shelagh's car!'

'I'm afraid it's true, Derek. A garda by the name of Brenda McCracken was caught in the blast, and she died about an hour ago.'

'That's terrible. That's truly terrible. Oh God.'

'That's why I need to talk to you, Derek. I need to know as many details as possible about who it was that abducted you, and how you got away from them, and who it was that rescued you. We're talking about murderers now, not just kidnappers and extortionists.'

'I don't know what to tell you,' said Derek Hagerty. 'I have no idea who they were.'

'You never saw them?'

'Only two of them, when they first grabbed me, and only for a few seconds even then. I was too scared and too confused to take a good look at them. They blindfolded me from the moment they first took me and I was kept locked up in a coal-black room for most of the time, except to go to the toilet. Even then they guided me there and back, and the window was painted over black so I couldn't see out.'

'Did they speak to you at all?'

'Oh yes, they spoke to me all right. They were always in and out, pounding my ears, but they wouldn't answer any of my questions. The first thing they told me was that they were asking a quarter of a million euros for my release. They said that if they didn't get it within seventy-two hours they were going to start cutting bits off me and sending them in the post to my wife.'

'As it is, they pulled out eight of your teeth. When did they do that?'

'I'm not sure. Like I say, it was dark all the time and they took away my watch so I didn't know whether it was day or night. But I'd say that it was less than twenty-four hours after they grabbed me.'

Katie was about to say, 'They let you keep your mobile phone, though?', but she decided to leave that question until later. For the moment, she didn't want Derek Hagerty to think that she suspected him of complicity in his own kidnapping. After all, his front teeth had been wrenched out, and not by a professional dentist, and she found it difficult to imagine that he had voluntarily agreed to anybody doing that.

'When did they snatch you?' she asked him.

'Tuesday afternoon it was, about twenty past three. I was on my way to the AIB in South Mall to lodge the previous week's takings, like, and to have a word with the manager.'

'What about?'

'What do you mean, what about?'

'What were you going to have a word with him about, your bank manager?'

'Oh, I don't know. Nothing specific, like. This and that.'

'So where did they snatch you?'

'I ordered a taxi from ABC. When it arrived I thought it was the genuine article, like, because it was yellow and it had the ABC light on the roof. But instead of taking me straight to South Mall, the driver went up Pana and over Patrick's Bridge. He said there was some kind of roadworks on Grand Parade so he had to take a diversion. He drove halfway down McCurtain Street and then he stopped and two other fellows got into the taxi, one on each side of me. They forced a pair of handcuffs on me, and then they tied a blindfold over my eyes.'

'Did they say anything to you?'

'I was protesting, like, and shouting at the driver to stop, but one of them said that I needed to shut the eff up or else he'd box my effing head.'

'So you stayed silent?'

'Yes,' said Derek Hagerty, 'I didn't want to beaten up, did I? And they might have had a knife or even a gun for all I knew.'

'Then what?'

107

'I stayed silent and so did they. I had the feeling we were driving uphill, so I guessed we were heading north. We drove pretty much straight for maybe half an hour, like, which made me guess that we were heading in the direction of Fermoy. After about half an hour we turned three or four times and then I heard shingle under the tyres and we stopped. I guessed then that we were in somebody's private driveway.'

It was at that moment that Detective Sergeant Ni Nuallán knocked at the door and came into the first-aid room. She said, 'Sorry to interrupt you, ma'am, but may I have a quick word with you?'

Katie left Derek Hagerty with Detective O'Donovan and went out into the corridor. Detective Sergeant Ni Nuallán held up a sheaf of bank statements in one hand and a maroon accounts ledger and a small green notebook in the other.

'We've just finished going through his books. Hagerty's Autos is over one hundred and seventy-five thousand euros in debt, most of it to the AIB and the tax commissioners. We've found a notebook, too, listing Derek Hagerty's debts to personal friends, and even to his mother, and they amount to well over sixty-five thousand.'

Katie took the bank statements and briefly leafed through them, shaking her head at page after page of O/D balances. Then she said, 'This doesn't make any sense at all, does it? If you're going to extort money out of people, you choose somebody who has some, like Denis O'Brien or Dermot Desmond or one of the O'Reilly family. You don't choose some bankrupt car mechanic from Bishopstown.'

'Not unless he's involved in it himself,' said Detective Sergeant Ni Nuallán.

'Well, you're right, and it's looking almost certain that he was. The only thing that I can't work out is why did he escape, or pretend to escape? I'm really beginning to wonder who's been fooling who. If he was part of a scam why didn't he just wait until the money had been paid over? And if something had gone wrong, and he'd fallen out with his alleged abductors, why didn't he just call for help? He still had his phone. And why did he cover himself in all of those pretend bruises?'

'There was no pretend about his teeth being pulled out.'

'Maybe that was done simply to throw us off. I don't know. Maybe he thought that having his front teeth pulled out with pliers was better than losing his livelihood. It's interesting that Micky Crounan had some of his teeth pulled out, too, although only the three of them.'

'Why don't you let me talk to him?' said Detective Sergeant Ni Nuallán, glancing in through the window. Derek Hagerty was sitting up now, and talking to Detective O'Donovan.

Katie thought about that for a moment. Kyna was relentless with her questioning – persistent and thorough – and if she believed that a suspect was guilty she never let them off the hook until she had persuaded them to confess. Quite often she had them breaking down in tears, and at the station they called her 'Sergeant O'Polygraph'. For now, however, Katie wanted Derek Hagerty to think that she completely believed his story that he had been nothing but an innocent victim.

Before they started to question him more aggressively, she wanted to trace the man who had driven him into the city, and talk to him and his wife. She was hopeful that Crime Prevention Officer Tony Brennan would be able to find CCTV footage of him dropping off Derek Hagerty at Grand Parade. There might even be footage of Derek Hagerty's abduction in McCurtain Street, if he was telling the truth about that.

'All right, then, understood,' said Detective Sergeant Ni Nuallán. 'I have to return these accounts to Detective Horgan, but maybe I could come back and sit in while you question him? I'd like to get a sense of the fellow.'

'I've no problem with that. Good idea.'

Katie went back into the first-aid room. 'How are you feeling now?' she asked Derek Hagerty,

'Fair to Midleton, except for my gob.'

'Yes, that's what I wanted to ask you about next. Did your abductors tell you *why* they were pulling out your teeth?'

'Partly to prove to Shelagh that they really had me, that's what they said, and partly to punish me.'

'Punish you for what, exactly?'

Derek Hagerty gave a lopsided shrug. 'They kept harping on about the economic crash, like. They said it was small businessmen like me who had borrowed far more money than they could ever pay back, and because of that we had brought down the whole Irish economy.'

Katie thought, *That's exactly what Micky Crounan's abductors had said to Mary Crounan.* Detective Sergeant Ni Nuallán glanced at her and she could tell by the expression on her face that she was thinking the same. *Almost word for word, the same justification for murdering her husband that had been given to her by the High Kings of Erin.*

Katie looked across at Detective O'Donovan, too, narrowing her eyes to signal to him that he shouldn't say anything. Detective O'Donovan gave her an almost imperceptible nod, to show that he understood.

'Did they mention the names of any other small businessmen who had done the same?' asked Katie. 'Anybody else they wanted to punish?'

'No, they didn't. But from the way they were talking, yes, they did give me the feeling that they were on some kind of crusade. Like it was revenge they were after, more than the money.'

'So, from what they said, you think they might do this again?'

'Couldn't say, like. Maybe.'

Detective O'Donovan said, 'The two fellers who grabbed you in the taxi. Could you describe them at all?'

'Like I told you, I was too shocked to notice much. One was wearing a black leather coat, the other some kind of khaki combat jacket. Mid-thirties, I would say, both of them, and both of them unshaven.'

'And when they were holding you hostage in that house, you're absolutely sure you never got a sconce at any of them? Not even a sneaky one?'

'No. Nothing at all. Like I say, they kept me blindfolded, and most of the time in total darkness. They even made me eat my meals wearing a blindfold, so I couldn't see what I was putting in my mouth. Soda bread and leek and potato soup they gave me, mainly. Well, after they'd pulled out my teeth I could only manage to eat the bread by sucking it until it was soft.'

'Did any of your abductors have a distinctive smell?' asked Katie. 'Aftershave, body odour, anything like that?'

Derek Hagerty shook his head. 'No – not that I can remember. One or two of them stunk of fags, and sometimes I could smell beer on their breath, but that was all.'

'When you say "one or two of them", how many of them do you think there were?'

'Three at the very least. Probably more like five.'

'How about their voices? Did you recognize any of them? Is it possible that one of them might have been somebody you knew?'

'No, I didn't reck any of them. I dare say I would, though, if I ever heard them again.'

'No distinctive accents? Kerry, Tipperary, Limerick, anything like that?'

'No. I would have said that they were all Corkonians, but I was under a whole lot of stress, as you can imagine. I was thinking more about my throbbing gums than anything else.'

'Southsiders? Norries?'

'Norries, I'd say. They definitely spoke with a bit of a Mayfield whine.'

'None of them ever called any of the others by name? Not even a nickname?'

'No.'

'Did you hear any other distinctive sounds when you were

being held hostage? The sound of a road, maybe, or cattle, or trains, or aircraft?'

'Crows I could hear, and sometimes a car on the shingle. A TV playing now and then, and voices, but that was all.'

'All right,' said Katie. 'Now I'm going to ask you how you managed to escape.'

Fifteen

Dabbing repeatedly at his lips, as if he were afraid that the scabs were about to flake off, Derek Hagerty explained to Katie how he had forced open the toilet window with a spoon, and climbed out.

'I was scared shitless, I can tell you. But I was seriously beginning to think that I wouldn't be coming out of that house alive.'

Katie nodded. She thought his story sounded plausible, but the flat tone of voice in which he recited it made her feel that he had rehearsed it – as if it hadn't really happened, but he was trying to remember every invented detail. She had interviewed enough liars in the course of her career to notice the way in which his eyes kept darting from side to side, as if he were reading from some memorized script.

The lip-dabbing allowed him to pause now and again to collect his thoughts, and possibly to make sure that he hadn't left out anything important.

'I'm surprised your kidnappers didn't come after you,' she told him. 'It couldn't have been too long before they began to wonder why you were spending so long in the toilet.'

Derek Hagerty shrugged. 'I climbed over a fence and into a field. I ran along a hedgerow, keeping my head well down, and then I went into a wood. They may have come looking for me for all I know, but they didn't find me, thank God. I'm sure they would have given me another beating, or worse.'

He stopped dabbing his lips and looked at Katie directly. 'Thinking about it now, I suppose it was a stupid thing to do.

Maybe I should have waited till I heard that the ransom was paid. On the other hand, I had no idea how Shelagh was going to be able to raise enough money for them to release me. I didn't want them to start cutting bits off me – as if having those teeth pulled out wasn't painful enough. You can get false teeth, but you can't get yourself an artificial mickey.'

'So, anyway, a woman found you lying by the side of the road and took you back to her house?'

'That's right. She was a saint. Well, she and her friend, they were both saints.'

'She had a friend with her?'

'Some feller. He wasn't her husband. They must have been out drinking somewhere, I could smell it.'

'What was her name?'

'I can't tell you that. I swore to those fellers who took me hostage that I wouldn't report any of this to the guards, and that I wouldn't say a word to the media, or anybody else at all for that matter. They swore that if I did they'd come after me. They said they'd come after my family, too, and that I'd sorely regret it. Not only that, they'd soften the cough of anybody else I told about it. So one way or another they need to know that *I* didn't report it to you. It wasn't me, for sure. Shit, I can only guess that Norman must have called you.'

'Norman?' asked Katie. 'Was that the woman's friend, or her husband?'

Derek Hagerty blinked and looked confused. 'I didn't say "Norman".'

'You did. You said that Norman must have called us. Who's Norman?'

'I can't tell you that.'

'Derek,' said Katie, leaning forward, 'this is a murder inquiry. You're not in any trouble yourself at the moment, because it appears that you were nothing but an innocent victim. But let me make this clear to you – if you refuse to answer my questions or obstruct our investigation in any way at all, then believe me, you will be.'

Derek Hagerty became suddenly angry. His nostrils flared and he spoke in gummy, barely intelligible honks. 'If it *was* Norman who called you – Jesus! he doesn't have the first idea what he's let us all in for! Not only me and my family, but himself and his wife! I mean what a fecking eejit! I specifically told him not to say anything to the cops, or to anybody else! I told him and I told him and he swore *blind* that he wouldn't! God alone knows what those people are going to do to us. They blew up Shelagh's car, didn't they, blew it up, for feck's sake, and killed that young garda? They'll murder us! I know they will! They'll only fecking murder us!'

Katie gripped his arm and tried to sound calm and reassuring. 'Derek, listen to me, we can protect Norman and his wife, and we can protect you and your family, too. But you have to tell us everything. There's no way that we can help you otherwise.'

Derek Hagerty stayed silent, staring at the floor and breathing hard. His lips had cracked and started bleeding again, so Detective Sergeant Ni Nuallán pulled a tissue out of the box by the bed so that he could wipe his mouth.

'Shelagh's here,' said Katie. 'What do you think Shelagh would say to you? The more information that you can give us, the sooner we can catch these scumbags, and the sooner you can go back to living a normal life. They won't be able to hurt you if they're inside.'

'Shelagh's here?'

'Yes, she identified you earlier, when you were asleep.' She was tempted to say 'pretending to be asleep', but she stopped herself. 'It was Shelagh who first informed us that you'd been taken hostage, well before Norman called us.'

'*Shelagh* told you?'

'Yes . . . she was very brave, but she also needed to find a way to raise the ransom money. She couldn't manage it on her own.'

'She was *warned* that she shouldn't! Jesus! This whole fecking thing's turning into a nightmare!'

'What "thing", Derek?'

'Nothing. Nothing at all. I said nothing.'

115

'I need to speak to this Norman and his wife,' said Katie. 'Do you have any idea where they live, or how I can contact them?'

Derek Hagerty stayed silent.

'Derek,' said Katie, gently. 'I badly need your help here. Don't make it necessary for me to arrest you.'

Derek Hagerty looked up at her. 'I'm absolutely shitting myself,' he said. 'You might say that you can protect us, but Holy Mary, Mother of God, you don't know what these people are like.'

'You're right, I don't know what they're like, not completely. But I do understand that they're ruthless and they don't care who they kill to get their money. But maybe you'd like to enlighten me.'

'I'm not saying any more,' Derek Hagerty told her. 'I've already said way too much. I'm a fool to myself.'

'Well, I'll give you some time to think about it,' said Katie. 'Meanwhile, I'll tell Shelagh that you're awake now. Maybe you'd like to discuss all this with her.'

'I'm telling you straight,' said Derek Hagerty, as Katie stood up to leave. 'They'll murder us. I mean it. You don't know what they're like. They'll fecking cut our heads off and piss down our necks.'

***

Less than five minutes after she had returned to her office, Katie's private phone rang.

She tucked the receiver under her chin so that she could prise the lid off her caffè macchiato. 'Yes?' she said.

The voice that answered was hoarse and throaty, with a distinctive slur on the letter 's'. 'Ah! Detective Superintendent Maguire! That is Detective Superintendent Kathleen Maguire?'

'Yes.'

'So glad to have caught you! I thought you might have been out somewhere, chasing bombers!'

'Who is this?' said Katie.

'Well now, who do you think?'

116

'I have no idea. Who are you and what do you want? How did you get this number?'

'Aha! Wouldn't you like to know that? This is one of the High Kings of Erin.'

'The High Kings of Erin?'

'That's correct.'

'Would that be the same High Kings of Erin who did for Micky Crounan?'

'"Did for" isn't quite the right way of putting it, Detective Superintendent. "Executed" is more like it.'

At that moment, Detective O'Donovan appeared in Katie's office doorway. Katie pressed her hand over the receiver and mouthed, 'Patrick! Have this call traced and recorded! It's on my private number!'

Almost as if he had heard her, the caller immediately said, 'By the way, don't trouble yourself trying to find out where I'm ringing you from. You won't be able to find me. In fact, you'll never find me, nor any of us. You'll just have to get used to the fact that we're back, after more than eight hundred years, and we're claiming our rightful place as the rulers of Ireland.'

'And that's how you're going to rule, is it, by cutting off the heads of local businessmen?'

'Micky Crounan wouldn't bend the knee so Micky Crounan got what was coming to him. Anybody else who defies us will suffer the same. Like Derek Hagerty.'

'It was you who took Derek Hagerty hostage?'

'I can't say that you're not cute! No wonder they put you in charge of all the detectives! Of course we took Derek Hagerty, and that's the whole reason I'm ringing you. The High Kings of Erin are claiming responsibility for the bomb at Merchants Quay.'

'So you murdered Garda Brenda McCracken?'

'That was tragic, I'll grant you. But we share the blame for that more or less equally, Detective Superintendent.'

'How can that be? You deliberately detonated a bomb in a public car park. It was a miracle that nobody else was killed.'

'Well, you say that, but if Shelagh Hagerty hadn't ignored our warning and squealed to you lot that her husband had been taken for ransom, we wouldn't have needed to plant a bomb at all. If the Garda had known nothing about it, everything would have gone off peaceful, and Derek Hagerty would be home by now in the bosom of his family.'

'There's nothing peaceful about extorting money with menaces,' said Katie.

'Micky Crounan and Derek Hagerty and dozens of others like them have brought nothing but shame to Ireland and they deserve to atone for what they did. The High Kings of Erin are going to restore this country's pride. If a few people get hurt in the process, it's a small price to pay. *Ch'an eil bàs fir gun ghràs fir.* There is no man's death without another man's gain.'

'That goes for women, too,' Katie retorted. 'You may believe that I won't be able to find you, but I will, you can count on it.'

'I'm not holding my breath, Detective Superintendent. Meantime, you'd better remind Derek Hagerty to keep his bake shut, otherwise we'll have to shut it for him. Him and his missus, and those eejits who told you where to find him.'

'I don't have any idea what you're talking about.'

'Oh, no? So how did you know where to pick him up, like? Saw it in your crystal ball, did you, Madame Maguire? Come on, I wasn't born last Thursday.'

Katie said, 'Whoever you are, and whatever kind of a game you think you're playing at, you've murdered two people already and injured a third, and I promise you now that I will have you. If you threaten one more person, or hurt them, or kill them, then you will suffer for it.'

'Good luck to you, Detective Superintendent,' said the caller. '*Éirinn go Brách.*' With that, he hung up.

Katie sat staring at the receiver for a moment, as if it could tell her who the caller was, but then she hung up, too. As she did so, Detective O'Donovan came to the door, shaking his head. 'We tried, but he wasn't talking for long enough, and he was using a stealth phone, and he was probably travelling in a car, too.'

'It was one of the High Kings of Erin again,' said Katie. 'The same psychos who decapitated Micky Crounan. He claimed the credit for kidnapping Derek Hagerty, and for killing Garda McCracken. He also gave me the impression that they would go after the people who found Derek Hagerty in the road and brought him into the city, as a punishment for tipping us off. The trouble is, Derek Hagerty won't tell us who they are. All he's let slip so far is that the husband's name is Norman.'

'Tony Brennan has the CCTV recording from Grand Parade, but it doesn't help much. There's no camera coverage of the exact spot where Hagerty was dropped off, right outside the old Capitol Cineplex. It's a blind spot, like.'

Katie stood up. 'Do you think Hagerty might have known that?'

'I don't know. I don't see how.'

'But there *is* some general footage of Grand Parade?'

'Yes, except that the camera's fixed to the wall of the Cineplex itself, facing Finn's Corner. So all you can see is the traffic going in and out of Washington Street and the pedestrians on the opposite side of the road.'

'Let's take a look at it anyway,' said Katie. She was surprised that her conversation with the so-called High King of Erin had unsettled her so much. Many criminals were boastful about what they had done, but it wasn't often that they took credit for their crimes with such obvious relish, and his slow, slurred voice had made her feel distinctly shivery, almost as though he had been breathing obscenities into her ear. At the same time, though, it had strengthened her determination to track him down, him and his fellow High Kings, and to see them standing in the dock, charged with murder.

As she followed Detective O'Donovan along the corridor, carrying her coffee, it occurred to her that this was why she hadn't been able to follow John to San Francisco. It was her duty to be here, protecting the people of Cork.

Sixteen

They watched the CCTV footage from Grand Parade five times over. They could see the two patrol cars arriving at speed to pick up Derek Hagerty. They slewed to a halt outside the Soho Restaurant opposite the old Capitol Cineplex, and eight gardaí ran across the road to the bottom of the screen, and out of the camera's field of vision. A few seconds later, the gardaí came back into view, two of them holding Derek Hagerty's arms. They pushed him into the back of one of the cars and drove off.

'Ah, this is useless,' said Detective Horgan. 'Look how many vehicles are passing up and down the street there. Hagerty could have been dropped off by any one of them.'

Katie leaned forward and frowned at the screen. 'Can you run it just once more?' she asked the spotty young garda who was controlling the playback. 'Take it back about four minutes before the patrol cars arrived.'

The garda ran the recording again and this time Katie said, 'There – see the fellow in that green Audi? He turns left into Washington Street. But only a couple of minutes later, here he is again, coming back *out* of Washington Street, turning right, heading the way he first came. We lose sight of him then because he's driving through the camera's blind spot. But there's another camera, isn't there, at the junction of South Mall and Princes Street? You must have caught him on that.'

It took the garda two or three minutes to find the recording from the South Mall camera, but Katie was right. The green Audi A3 appeared around the corner from Grand Parade and then turned right into Princes Street, heading south.

'It could be a coincidence,' said Katie. 'It might not be our man at all, but that's the only vehicle that appears twice in the time segment when Derek Hagerty might have been dropped off, coming and going.'

'He could just as easily have been dropped off by a vehicle coming into Grand Parade from Patrick Street,' Detective Horgan put in. 'Then we would have seen him only the once.'

'Not today he couldn't,' said Crime Prevention Officer Tony Brennan. 'Bord Gáis are digging up Pana just outside Tom Murphy's, so there's a diversion for westbound traffic.'

The garda froze the image of the green Audi and Detective Horgan made a note of its number plate. It began 132-C, followed by its number, which told them that it had been registered in Cork City in the latter half of 2013.

'Give me two minutes,' said Detective Horgan. Katie looked at her watch. It was five minutes to five now and she wanted to talk to Acting Chief Superintendent Molloy before the media conference at 5.15.

While they waited for Detective Horgan to trace the Audi's owner, the garda at the control desk followed the Audi's progress out of the city centre as far as he could, checking the recordings from CCTV cameras at every successive road junction. He had taken the South City Link Road as far as the Old Blackrock Road, but after that they lost him.

'He must have turned off somewhere,' said Tony Brennan. 'He could have taken the next turning for Ballintemple, or maybe the turning after that for Douglas, either one.'

'I would guess that he doesn't live too far away,' said Katie. 'Think about it, it was hardly more than twenty minutes between the phone call that tipped us off and Hagerty being picked up. Traffic's pretty slow in the city centre at the moment, what with all the roadworks, and it took your man at least four minutes to turn into Washington Street and then come back out again.

Considering what little time he had, I doubt he had to drive into the city more than two or three kilometres. Ballintemple is a very fair guess, I'd say.'

Detective Horgan came back, his cheeks flushed from hurrying, and read out what he had scribbled on a sheet of notepaper. 'Here you are, ma'am. The Audi is registered in the name of Norman Anthony Pearse, Ard na Fálta, Boreenmanna Road, Ballinlough. He's fifty-three years old and the manager of Faraway Travel, Marlboro Street. He's married to Meryl Saoirse Pearse, née Collins, thirty-one years old. She was formerly an assistant at Faraway Travel but now she's working in the stationery department at Eason's bookstore in Patrick Street. Pearse has one conviction for speeding, 1997, but there's nothing else recorded against him.'

'Right,' said Katie. 'I want you and DS Ni Nuallán to go out and question Mr and Mrs Pearse. Ask Mr Pearse why he drove into the city today, and why he turned into Washington Street and then immediately turned round and came back out again.'

'Okay, sure.'

'Ask Mrs Pearse if she was the one who found Derek Hagerty lying by the side of the road up at Ballynoe, and brought him back home. If she says yes, don't forget to ask her who was with her when she found him. Derek Hagerty said she had a friend with her, so this friend is another potential witness.'

She checked her watch again. 'I have a media conference now. It might still be going on by the time you get some answers out of them, but text me anyway.'

'Supposing the Pearses deny all knowledge?'

'I'll be asking Derek Hagerty some more questions later, so if it really *was* them who took him in, whatever they say, I think he'll probably come out with it in the end. He's trying his best not to tell me anything, but I think he knows that he and his family won't get any kind of realistic protection from anybody else except us. When it comes down to it, he doesn't really have a lot of choice.'

'If the Pearses admit it, though, we'll bring them straight in,' said Detective Sergeant Ni Nuallán.

'Of course, if only for their own safety. If these High Kings of Erin are anything like as murderous as they claim to be, the Pearses will be needing us to give them round-the-clock security, too. We may even have to hide them away for a while. Derek Hagerty called them saints, but they don't want to be joining the rest of the saints for a while yet.'

***

Acting Chief Superintendent Molloy was gathering his papers together to go to the media conference when Katie knocked at his open office door.

'Well?' he said, without looking up. 'Did you get anything more out of Hagerty?'

'Not much, but I think we may have identified the people who picked him up and drove him into the city. A travel agency manager called Norman Pearse and his wife. They live in Ballinlough.'

'You've sent some of your people out to interview them?'

'Of course. Detective Sergeant Ni Nuallán and Detective Horgan. We should be hearing from them very soon, with any luck.'

'That's good. At least I can tell the media that we're making some positive progress.'

'Wait, that's not the end of it by any means,' said Katie. 'I've just been called by a man representing the group that calls itself the High Kings of Erin – the same group who said they kidnapped Micky Crounan.'

Now, Bryan Molloy slowly lowered his clipboard and raised his head to stare at Katie with those bulging blue pit-bull eyes.

'Go on,' he said.

'He claimed that the High Kings of Erin were responsible for the bomb at Merchants Quay, and also for the kidnapping of Derek Hagerty, and for killing Micky Crounan, too.'

'Did you trace the call?'

Katie shook her head. 'We couldn't, no. He was using a stealth phone and he wasn't talking for long enough. But I'm ninety-nine

123

per cent convinced that it wasn't a hoax. For instance, he knew that Shelagh Hagerty had contacted us, although I can't think how. Our security has been ultra-tight. The media don't even know that Derek Hagerty was kidnapped yet, do they, let alone that he managed to escape? Or claims he did, anyhow.'

'Well, they're about to find out,' said Bryan Molloy, picking up his clipboard again and glancing at the clock on his office wall. 'We're going to need all the help we can get on this one. You may have had a call from the High Kings of Erin but I've had a call from Jimmy O'Reilly about the money.'

'I don't suppose he's exactly delighted with us.'

'Delighted? You're messing, aren't you? He'll be back from Dublin tomorrow, and if I had any choice in the matter, I think I'd rather go head to head with these High Kings of Erin or whatever they call themselves than Jimmy O'Reilly when he's throwing a sevener.'

'So what are you going to say to the media about all of this?'

'There's not much else I can say except to tell them the truth. I think you'll agree that we've made a bags of this and we're just going to have to admit it.'

'I'm not at all sure that we have made a bags of it, not yet. It's a bit early for us to be saying that we misread the situation at Merchants Quay. We may find out later it wasn't our fault at all. Sure, I think you can tell the media that Derek Hagerty appears to have been kidnapped but is now a free man, but I don't think you should give them much more than that. Come on, Bryan. We're not at all sure yet that his story rings true.'

Bryan Molloy took his uniform jacket off the hanger on the back of the door and shrugged himself into it. 'The media are going to want more details than that, Katie. Otherwise they're going to be thinking that we're hiding something.'

'Of course we're hiding something. We have to, for the time being. Listen, we don't yet know for certain that it was Mrs Pearse and her friend who picked Hagerty up, or that it was Mr Pearse who called us. And we can't yet be sure if there really is a gang of kidnappers called the High Kings of Erin, or whether somebody's just stringing us along. It's happened enough times before, God knows, people claiming credit for crimes they had nothing to do with. Even murders.'

'We'll be late,' said Bryan Molloy. With that, he stepped out into the corridor, leaving Katie to close the door behind her.

***

The conference room where the media were assembled was crowded with at least twenty reporters, as well as cameramen and sound technicians. It smelled of new carpet tiles and stale cigarette smoke and Lynx aftershave. As Katie sat down at the desk between Bryan Molloy and the Garda press officer, Tadhg McElvin, the TV lights were switched on and she had to shield her eyes with her hand.

After a fusillade of coughing and shuffling everybody settled down and Bryan Molloy said, 'We've called you all here this afternoon to give you some background into the cause of the bombing at Merchants Quay, and to bring you up to speed on our investigations.'

'Has anybody claimed responsibility?' asked Dan Keane from the *Examiner*. As usual, his hair was sticking up as if he had just got out of bed, and he had a cigarette tucked behind his right ear.

'I'll be taking questions later,' said Bryan Molloy. 'But the answer to your question is yes.'

'So was it political?' put in Fionnuala Sweeney, the pretty gingery-haired presenter from RTÉ. 'Or was there another motive behind it?'

'It was partly political and partly criminal. And we do have a fair idea why they did it.'

Katie leaned towards him and murmured, '*Bryan*, we don't know their motives, not for certain. Let's just stick to the basic facts, for the love of God.'

'You don't *have* any basic facts, do you?' Bryan Molloy muttered back, leaning his head close to her without turning to look at her.

125

'That's the whole fecking trouble. But this lot have to leave here this evening thinking that I'm well on top of it.'

'Oh, I thought you were going to admit that we'd messed it up.'

'*I* didn't mess it up, Katie. Not me. There was only one person in charge of organizing that farrago at Merchants Quay and that was you.'

Dan Keane raised his hand and asked, 'Excuse me, Chief Superintendent, I hate to interrupt, but is there some kind of an internal disagreement going on here?'

'Not at all,' said Bryan Molloy, picking up his clipboard and giving the assembled media his toothiest smile. 'Detective Superintendent Maguire here is simply filling me in on one or two operational details.'

'My apologies,' Dan Keane told him. 'Whatever happened at Merchants Quay, though – whoever set that bomb off – I gather that you're not very happy with the way the operation was handled?'

Bryan Molloy's neck reddened to the colour of tomato soup. 'I don't know what in the world gave you that idea, Dan. In retrospect, I believe we could have handled the situation with more professionalism than we actually did, and with considerably more foresight, but even our most experienced officers can't be expected to be psychic. We're all human, after all, like most of you here, and we all have our failings.'

When he said that, Katie felt like standing up and walking out. If she did that, however, she knew that she would only be making herself look temperamental, and incompetent, and even more culpable for Garda McCracken's death than she really was. It would also give Bryan Molloy the floor and allow him to carry on saying whatever he felt like, unchallenged.

Bryan Molloy looked directly into the TV cameras and furrowed his brow so that he looked almost comically serious. 'The responsibility for the bombing at Merchants Quay has been claimed by a group who call themselves the High Kings of Erin. On Tuesday last week they abducted Mr Derek Hagerty, the owner of Hagerty's Autos at Looney's Cross. They called his wife, Mrs Shelagh Hagerty, and demanded a quarter of a million euros for his safe release. She was warned not to notify anybody, especially the Garda.'

Now the conference room erupted into waving hands and shouted questions. 'Was the ransom paid, or not?' 'Have they let Derek Hagerty go yet?' 'Was he injured at all?' 'Why did they set a bomb off?' 'Why do they call themselves the High Kings of Erin?' 'Do you have any idea at all of their identity, sir, and what they're after?'

Katie sat with her fingertips pressed to her temples as if she were suffering from a headache, but she didn't speak. The very last thing she had wanted Bryan Molloy to tell the media was the name of the High Kings of Erin. Apart from the fact that she didn't yet know if they really were responsible, it was a highly emotional name from Ireland's medieval history, before the English claimed kingship, and it would give a gang of murderers and extortionists a nationalistic glamour that they didn't deserve.

Bryan Molloy waited until the hubbub had died down, then he said, 'I can confirm to you that the ransom has been paid in full. Mrs Hegarty herself was unable to raise the amount of money they were demanding, so she was assisted by the state. Detective Superintendent Maguire conceived a plan whereby the kidnappers would be tracked electronically once they had collected the cash and arrested once she was certain that Derek Hagerty had been released unharmed.'

'So what went wrong?' asked Fionnuala Sweeney. 'A bomb went off and a young female garda was killed. How could that have happened?' She was literally licking her lips as she waited for an answer, and Katie could imagine the rest of the reporters all salivating, too, as if the room were crowded with hungry dogs. There was nothing like a botched Garda operation to make front-page news, especially since it had led to a fatality.

In the simplest words she could find, Katie explained how she had planned to track the kidnappers until she was sure that

Derek Hagerty was either safe or dead, whichever it was, and then arrest them.

Dan Keane said, 'It sounds to me as if this gang *knew* that you were tracking them, like. So how exactly did they find out that Mrs Hagerty had been in touch with you, and that you'd be waiting for them?'

'Right now, I simply don't know,' Katie replied. 'We kept a very tight lid on this whole ransom payment right from the start, and even those officers directly involved on the ground knew only what they needed to know and nothing more. Only four of my detectives were aware that the kidnap victim was Derek Hagerty, and that was because they had to check on his background and any business problems he might have had.'

Now Bryan Molloy interrupted her. 'Unfortunately, and very regrettably, it turned out that there was no reason for the ransom to be handed over at all. Earlier in the day, Derek Hagerty had managed to escape from his abductors and he was discovered alive and reasonably well, lying by the roadside near Ballynoe. This was more than forty-five minutes before we gave the High Kings of Erin two hundred and fifty thousand euros in non-consecutive, non-traceable banknotes.'

'We weren't aware that he had escaped, of course,' said Katie. 'If we had been, the story would have been very different.'

'So he didn't call you and tell you that he had escaped?' asked Branna MacSuibhne, from the *Echo*. Katie noticed that young Branna had lost some weight and twisted her hair up into a ponytail, instead of her usual Jackie Kennedy bob.

'No, Branna, he didn't. He was frightened of what his abductors might do to him and his family.'

'So how did *you* find out that he had escaped?'

'We had a tip-off from the people who found him,' put in Bryan Molloy. 'We believe that they were a married couple from Ballinlough, but we have yet to confirm that, as I'm sure Detective Superintendent Maguire will tell you. She still has a fair amount of catching up to do, wouldn't you agree, Detective

Superintendent? But she's swimming as hard as she can against the tide.'

The media conference went on for another twenty minutes. Fionnuala Sweeney repeatedly asked if the bombing at Merchants Quay could have been averted by better Garda intelligence, or by setting up the handover at another location where nobody was likely to be injured or killed.

Katie emphatically shook her head. 'As police officers, Fionnuala, we demand a great deal from ourselves, more than most people ever realize. But we're not psychic, as Chief Superintendent Molloy has already admitted to you, and we don't have X-ray vision or super-hearing, and none of us can fly.'

She refused to speculate on the identity of the High Kings of Erin, or to give the media any more details about where Derek Hagerty was now and who had tipped them off about his escape. She was glad she hadn't. While Bryan Molloy was winding up with a speech about how he was going to improve Garda response times, and how he was going to bring in software updates for the PULSE and AFIS computer systems in Cork – almost as if he were going to do it single-handed – her iPhone rang.

It was Detective Sergeant Ni Nuallán. She sounded as if she were standing by a main road, with cars swishing past.

'We've just finished talking to the Pearses. They're adamant, both of them, that it wasn't them who picked up Hagerty and took him in. We separated them and talked to them individually, but both of them were insistent that they had never even heard of Derek Hagerty.'

'So what was Norman Pearse doing driving into Western Road and then back out again?'

'He says he was picking up a stationery order from Snap Printing down at Crawford House, some letterheads and some compliments slips.'

'Have you checked that with Snap?'

'They're closed now, but I can track down the manager at home.'

'All right, then. I'll see you after. We've almost wrapped up this media conference. More than a little shattering, if you get my meaning.'

Just as she dropped her iPhone back into the pocket of her jacket, Katie heard Bryan Molloy announcing that the High Kings of Erin had also claimed responsibility for abducting and beheading Micky Crounan.

She could only sit and listen with her head bowed as he answered the media's questions about Micky Crounan's abduction and murder. Bryan Molloy told them that he was sure now that they were looking for a ruthless gang who were pursuing a political agenda, restoring the glory of Ireland's native kingship, while at the same time enriching themselves with ransom money.

'Their motivation appears to be anger that our present-day politicians and businessmen have shown themselves to be so greedy and corrupt, and a determination to punish them financially for the economic crash. However, they're not above lining their own pockets with the proceeds of that punishment. I suppose you might say that we're dealing with a combination of Brian Boru and Robin Hood.'

Thank you, Bryan, thought Katie, as Bryan Molloy smiled smugly at his own turn of phrase. I love you, too. You have just made me appear to the media like an amateurish woman who bungled a highly sensitive operation, leading to the tragic and avoidable death of one of our own, while at the same time giving them the impression that you, the great Bryan Molloy, are close to having all of these cases efficiently wrapped up.

It didn't help that Bryan Molloy was still highly regarded for the way in which he had stamped out the worst of the rampant gang warfare in Limerick. That was one of the reasons he had been appointed to take over Chief Superintendent O'Driscoll's job here in Cork, if only on an interim basis. Katie, on the other hand, had failed in her efforts to bring Michael Gerrety to justice on thirty-seven charges of profiting from prostitution. The *Examiner*'s headline had been 'Gerrety, 37 – Garda, 0'.

***

As they went back up in the lift to their offices, Katie said, 'Well, Bryan, you haven't made my life any easier, have you?'

'Is that what I'm here for?' he retorted. He wasn't looking at her directly, but he was staring at her in the mirror in the back of the lift. 'I thought I was here to make sure you did your job properly. You're a detective superintendent, Katie, and it would be very gratifying if you did some actual detective superintending once in a while, instead of preening yourself. Perhaps if you spent more time going after criminals and less time nosing around in my bank accounts. You won't find anything of interest there, I can assure you of that.'

'Bryan, you shouldn't have mentioned the High Kings of Erin. For all we know they're nothing but spoofers. And we have no hard evidence at all to tell us who killed Micky Crounan. It might have been the High Kings of Erin, it might not.'

'Then it's up to you to prove it, girl, one way or another, wouldn't you say?'

He pushed his way out of the lift in front of Katie, which was something that Dermot O'Driscoll would never have done. Katie stepped out into the corridor after him and said, 'I'll prove it, Bryan, you can be sure of that. And it will give me great satisfaction to show you you're wrong.'

Bryan Molloy let out a bark of a laugh and marched off towards his office, his clipboard tucked under his right arm, his left arm swinging as if he were on parade at Dublin Castle.

Katie watched him go, and at that moment she badly missed Dermot O'Driscoll – and John, too, or anybody who could understand how isolated she felt, and how guilty, and how helpless. She could confide in Kyna Ni Nuallán, she knew that, but she had decided to keep her relationship with Kyna on a strictly formal footing, superintendent and sergeant. God alone knew where their mutual affection would lead if she allowed it, and her career was in more than enough trouble already.

Her iPhone rang. Detective Horgan was calling her from Mayfield.

'Sorry, ma'am, I haven't been able to contact the manager of Snap Printing yet. I went to his house but there's nobody home.'

'Leave it till the morning then. A few hours isn't going to make much difference.'

She stood alone in the corridor for a few moments, her eyes closed as if she were praying, but in fact she was only thinking how tired she felt. Then she went along to her own office to collect her raincoat.

Seventeen

It rained hard all the way home to Cobh and even when her wind-screen wipers were flapping at full speed Katie could hardly see the road ahead of her. It seemed to be raining even harder when she turned into her driveway, climbed out of the car and hurried to the front porch with her head down and collar turned up.

There was no question of taking Barney out for his evening walk – not unless the rain eased off, anyway. She let him out into the garden where he sat in the shelter of the patio awning, looking mournful. She sometimes wondered if he missed John as much as she did.

She went through to the spare bedroom that she still called the nursery, lifted her nickel-plated .38 Smith & Wesson revolver out of the flat TJS holster on her belt and placed both gun and holster in the top drawer of the chest that had once held Seamus's baby clothes, his Babygros and little blue cardigans.

Back in the living room, she poured herself a glass of Smirnoff Black Label and switched on the TV. There was news and sport on the first three channels and *Mrs Brown's Boys* on the fourth, so she pressed the remote to mute the sound and went through to the kitchen. She didn't feel like listening to news, and she didn't feel like laughing, either. She opened the freezer and stared at the shelves, trying to decide if she felt like a Marks & Spencer chicken casserole or salmon fishcakes or a pizza.

She was still making up her mind when the doorbell chimed. Barney heard it, too, because he barked and started scratching at the kitchen door. Katie said, 'Hold on a minute, Barns!' and went to the front door to see who it was.

Standing in the porch outside, wearing only a black cable-knit sweater and light grey trousers spotted with raindrops, was David Kane. She could immediately tell by his expression that he was distressed.

'David?' she said. 'What's wrong?'

'I'm sorry,' he told her. 'This is a terrible imposition, I know, but I was wondering if I could stay here in your house for maybe an hour or two. It's Sorcha. She's having one of her episodes and she's pretty much thrown me out. I thought it was better to leave straight away than try to fight it out with her.'

'All right, come on in,' said Katie. 'Is Sorcha okay? She doesn't need any medical attention, does she?'

'No, she's all right, really. She just needs some time to herself to calm down. Whatever I do or say, it only sets her off. If I try and be nice to her, she accuses me of lying, but if I try to be strict with her, that makes her really violent. That's when she starts hitting me and breaking things. The best alternative is for me to get out of there. I don't want to end up hurting her, for the love of God.'

'Do you want me to go round and talk to her?' Katie asked him.

'No, no. That would only make her even more aggressive. She'd accuse you of interfering and all sorts. It's best to leave her when she's like this. Her medication will start to kick in soon, and then she'll simply go to sleep and wake up the next morning without the faintest memory of what she was like the night before.'

Katie led him through into the living room. *Mrs Brown's Boys* was still on, so she switched the television off. 'Would you like a drink?' she asked him. 'I have whiskey, but I also have some Satz in the fridge if you'd rather.'

'A whiskey, please. I need it after the evening I've had, I can tell you.'

She lifted up a bottle from the drinks table, but it was nearly empty, so she picked up another one. 'At the moment I have only

Paddy's, I'm afraid. The last time my dad came over he must have finished off all of my Green Spot.'

'Paddy's is fine,' said David. She poured him a large glass and he sat down on the leather couch. '*Slainte*,' he said. 'You're a life-saver.'

'Isn't Sorcha getting any better?' asked Katie, sitting down beside him.

'Her doctor seems to think so, but her doctor isn't there when she's throwing one of her fits. I made up my mind a long time ago that it's just something I'll have to live with.'

Katie heard Barney mewling and scratching at the back door again, so she excused herself and went into the kitchen to let him in. He trotted inside, soaking wet, and shook himself violently in the middle of the kitchen floor.

'*Barns*! You could have waited for me to fetch your towel!'

She turned round and found David standing right behind her. 'Oh,' she said. 'I hope you didn't get showered.'

His face remained serious. 'I just wanted to tell you how grateful I am that you let me in.'

'Well, of course, don't be silly. It's lashing outside and you don't even have an umbrella.'

Katie rubbed Barney down with his frayed old bath towel and gave the kitchen floor a quick squeaky going-over with her sponge mop. Then she led David back into the living room and they both sat down on the couch again.

'I don't know,' said David. 'Sometimes I feel like there's no way out of it, and it's never going to end.'

'Well, you and me both,' Katie told him.

'What? You've had a bad day, too?'

'Oh, you don't want to hear all of my problems. Besides, I shouldn't really discuss them with anybody. It's mostly to do with an ongoing case I'm dealing with.'

David took another swallow of whiskey and then set down his glass. 'If it'll make you feel better to talk about it, go ahead. I won't tell a soul.' He paused, and then he said, 'I'm a doctor, remember.'

'Oh, yes, but you're only a dog and a cat and a budgerigar doctor! It can't be too difficult to maintain patient confidentiality when your patients can only tell you things in woofs and miaows and chirrups.'

David smiled, but his smile faded almost immediately. 'It's not what the animals tell me, Katie, it's their owners. Just because I'm wearing a white coat they think that they can unburden their souls. I had a woman from Coolamber come in the other day who told me that she hated dogs, *despised* them – couldn't stand the smell and the slobber and the clearing up after them. But taking her spaniel for a walk every evening gave her an excuse to visit her lover three streets away. The spaniel didn't get a whole lot of exercise, but she did.'

Katie thought for a moment, then she said, 'Well – this case that's giving me so much grief – you'll see it mentioned on the news tonight anyway, and in the papers tomorrow, so I don't suppose there's any harm in your knowing about it.'

She told him about Micky Crounan's kidnapping, and the ransom handover that had gone so disastrously wrong. She told him about the media conference, too, and how Bryan Molloy had damned her with faint praise in front of the press. She knew that she shouldn't discuss internal Garda affairs with civilians, but she felt so demoralized that she needed to talk to somebody about it. Six months ago she could have told her father, because he had been a Garda inspector for eleven years and would have understood, but ever since the tragic death of the woman he had been intending to marry he had closed himself off and spent most of his days staring out of his window at the rain, and the toing and froing of the Passage West ferry.

'David – you mustn't breathe a word of this to a single soul,' she said. 'I could really be goosed if you do.'

David smiled at her and laid his hand on top of hers. 'You don't have to worry, Katie. Heaven knows I have enough difficulties myself with Sorcha, and I shouldn't be telling anybody how mad she can behave sometimes. Mostly, yes, I can cope with it, as I'm sure you can cope with your friend Bryan Molloy. But, come on, it's a great relief to be able to share your problems with somebody who's prepared to listen, and who understands what you're going through, even if there's nothing else they can do to help – not in a practical way, anyhow.'

Unexpectedly, Katie found that David's words had made her feel very emotional, and her throat tightened. Part of the reason was that he reminded her so much physically of John – that dark, lean look, like some martyred medieval saint. Yet he also possessed an animal magnetism that John had never had. She almost felt that he understood everything that was upsetting her so much, that he was capable of showing her how to get her strength back, and her courage, although she was more than aware that she might have to pay a price for it.

She felt tears prickling in her eyes, so she said, 'You'll excuse me for a moment. I need to give Barney his supper.'

She got up and went into the kitchen – not only to open a can of Brandy's Chunks in Gravy for Barney, but also to take a few deep breaths and stare at her reflection in the window over the sink. The glass was jet-black and bejewelled with raindrops and there she was, a pale ghost looking back at herself from the yard outside. Barney was making a clattering noise pushing his bowl around the floor, but Katie could hear David talking on his mobile phone.

'Yes, that's grand. No problem at all. I'll see you tomorrow so.' 'Yes, me too.' 'Of course I do. I just can't say it at the moment.' 'Because I can't.'

She came back into the living room just as he was pushing his phone back into his trouser pocket. 'Everything all right?' she asked him. 'Would you like another drink?'

'Yes, go on, then, thank you,' he said, holding up his glass.

'You're a vet,' she said, 'so tell me something I've always wondered about. Do our pets really love us? Or do you think they only show us affection because we feed them and take care of them and make a fuss of them?'

David shook his head. 'Oh, I believe they genuinely love us, and in the same way that we humans love each other.'

'But how can you know that?'

'Because sometimes we humans hurt each other badly, don't we? But we still come back for more. In the same way you can whip a horse but it will still remain faithful to you, or you can thrash the living daylights out of a dog and it will still be devoted. Men and women can cause each other terrible pain sometimes, but that doesn't stop them from wanting and needing each other. After all, what else is there?'

They carried on talking for well over an hour. David was an attentive listener, and for the first time in her life Katie found herself describing to a stranger how she had only joined An Garda Síochána because none of her sisters were interested in becoming police officers and she hadn't wanted to let her father down. Midway through her training at Templemore she had almost quit because of the bullying and sexual harassment, even from other women trainees, and she had nearly resigned again when she had been assigned to Crosshaven Garda station, in Coastguard Cottages, Crosshaven, where there was hardly any crime except for bicycles having their wheels pinched or fishing nets being vandalized or drunken yachtsmen punching each other in the car park of Cronin's pub.

'I fought really hard to get where I am now,' she said. 'I lost my husband and the man I love. Now I'm beginning to wonder if I was a fool. I could be in San Francisco now, with a really good job at Pinkerton's, instead of living on my own, eating supermarket dinners-for-one, and worrying every day if I'm going to have the rug pulled out from under me.'

'Katie,' said David, 'you're unselfish, and you're loyal to the people who really need you. Those are very rare qualities. You'll get your reward, you'll see.'

'Where?' she retorted. 'In heaven?'

* * *

It was past eleven by the time David drained the last of his whiskey and stood up.

'I'd best be getting back to Sorcha,' he said. 'She'll be spark out by now. Thanks again for giving a poor pilgrim shelter in a storm.'

Katie stood up, too. 'Do you want to borrow an umbrella? It's still spilling out there.'

She lifted a red folding umbrella down from the coat hooks in the hallway and opened the front door for him. 'Sorry it's a bit gay, but it'll keep you dry.'

David shaded his eyes with his hand and made an exaggerated show of peering out into the darkness. 'That's okay. Not a soul in sight, thankfully. Wouldn't want to get mistaken for a steamer, would I?'

He laid his hand on her shoulder and kissed her on the right cheek, and then the left. For a few seconds he looked into her eyes as if he had seen something inside her mind but wasn't quite sure what it meant. Then he raised the red umbrella and said, 'See you,' and ducked out into the rain.

Katie closed the door and went back into the kitchen. Barney had retired to his basket now, although he wasn't asleep yet and he raised his eyes to look at her, as if to say, 'What's the story, mistress? Are you all right?'

'Yes, Barns,' said Katie, out loud. 'I'm all right, boy. Surviving.'

She thought of pouring herself another Smirnoff but decided against it. She would need to be pin-sharp in the morning to decide how to interview Derek Hagerty, and there was sure to be more questioning from the media about the High Kings of Erin. She would also have to work out a game plan for dealing with Acting Chief Superintendent Molloy. She couldn't allow him to continue second-guessing her. After Gardagate, in which Commissioner Martin Callinan had resigned, and the resignation of Justice Minister Alan Shatter, there was a mood for heads to roll in An Garda Síochána for almost any kind of corruption or incompetence, real or perceived, and she didn't want hers to be one of them.

She switched off the lights in the kitchen and the living room and went out into the hallway to switch on the alarm. As she raised the keypad towards the control box, however, the doorbell chimed. She hesitated, and then she went over to the front door and looked through the spyhole. All she could see was darkness.

'Who is it?' she called out.

'Me,' came the reply.

'David?'

'Yes.'

She opened the door. David was standing in the porch, holding her folded umbrella. His hair was wet and raindrops were clinging to his eyelashes. Behind him, rainwater was frantically clattering from an overflowing gutter.

'Did you forget something?' Katie asked him.

'Yes,' he said.

Without another word, he dropped the umbrella and stepped inside the hallway. He took Katie in his arms and pulled her close to him and kissed her on the lips.

She said, '*Mmmfff*!' and her first reaction was to grab his arms and wrestle herself free from him. But then he kissed her again, and again, and even though she was gripping the wet woollen sleeves of his sweater, she stopped trying to prise herself away and found that she was kissing him back.

No man had held her so tightly in his arms since John had left her, or kissed her with such passion, and it gave her a heady feeling of being wanted and desired which she had thought she might never experience again. Several of the officers at Anglesea Street had made it obvious that they found her attractive, and one or two of them were reasonably good-looking and very masculine, but it would have been impossible for her to have an affair with a man she outranked.

Not only was David arousing her, he was making her feel secure, too, as if she no longer had to protect herself, because he would make sure that she was safe from harm. She hadn't felt like that in a long time, either.

'The door,' she gasped.

He closed the front door behind him with his foot, and kept on kissing her. At last, however, she placed her hands flat against his chest to push him away. He had a mischievous smile on his face and his eyes were bright.

'What about Sorcha?' she asked him.

'Sorcha's dead to the world. Besides, this is nothing to do with Sorcha, or anybody else. This is me and you.'

'We can't.'

'And who says we can't? God?'

He took hold of her wrists and lifted her hands away from his chest so that he could lean forward and kiss her again. This was the moment when she could have said, *No, I really like you, David, I think you're a very handsome and charming man, but I'm not going to allow myself to get involved with you.* But his tongue slipped into her mouth, and she closed her eyes, and even though she was saying the words inside her head, she didn't want to stop kissing him and say them out loud.

She took hold of his hand and looked up at him with her eyes sparkling as if she were about to show a boy what she had bought him for Christmas. She led him along the hallway and into her bedroom. He waited by the door while she switched on the pink bedside lamps and drew the rose-coloured velvet curtains. The bed was still unmade from this morning; she had woken up late and hadn't had time to straighten it. The pink patchwork cover was thrown to one side and the impression of her head was still on the right-hand pillow.

'Let's get you out of these wet clothes,' she said, walking back to him and taking hold of his sweater. She tugged it upwards, but it wasn't easy because it was soaking from the rain and he was so much taller than she was. Eventually, though, she managed to drag it over his head and drop it on to the bedside rug. He laughed and brushed his wet hair back.

Next she unbuckled his braided brown leather belt. By now his erection was so hard and angular that she found it difficult to jerk down his zip. Underneath his trousers he was wearing blue pinstripe boxer shorts. She grasped his penis through the cotton, squeezing it and rubbing it up and down three or four times, and then she pulled his boxer shorts down to his knees. His penis reared up mauve-headed in front of her, and she was surprised and aroused to see that he was completely shaved, and had no pubic hair at all. The nakedness of his penis made it look even longer than it really was, giving it the appearance of a classical sculpture in dusky pink marble.

'Sit,' she ordered him, and he sat on the end of the bed while she took off his wet black socks, then finished taking off his trousers and boxer shorts.

Still sitting, he reached up and unbuttoned her dark green cardigan. When he had taken that off, though, he stood up to take off the lighter green sweater that she was wearing underneath, and while he did so she held his stiffened penis in her hand, as if she wasn't going to let it go. After he had lifted her sweater over her head, he ran his fingers into her tousled red hair and kissed her again.

'Katie,' he said, not in a murmur but quite plainly. It was more like an announcement than a declaration of desire. She found it unusually reassuring. He was recognizing her for who she was – her personality, herself, Katie Maguire, as well as her face and her figure and the way she felt and the fragrance of her.

'David,' she replied, and she found that cleansing, as if she were saying to herself, John has long gone now, and our relationship is over for ever, so why should I feel guilty making love to somebody new?

David was gentle and highly controlled, continually kissing her lips and neck and shoulders as he undressed her. He slid off the catch of her bra, and when her breasts were bared, he cupped her right breast in his left hand and rotated the ball of his thumb around her nipple, until it stiffened and knurled.

He unzipped her speckled tweed skirt and let it drop. Now she was wearing only pantyhose. She lay back on the bed so that he could take hold of the elasticated waistband and roll them off her. Once he had done that, he lay down beside her and kissed her again, and ran his fingertips all the way down her side to her hips, so that she shivered.

'Protection,' she said. 'We ought to use a condom.'

David gave her the smallest shake of his head. 'It's all right. I've been spayed. And I can promise you that I haven't been putting it about.'

He reached down between her legs and stroked her so lightly with his fingertip that she could barely feel it, and she was aching for him to stroke her harder, and quicker. The sensation that he was giving her was extraordinary. She could almost imagine that a butterfly had perched itself on her clitoris and was flapping its wings.

She grasped his shoulder and said, with a catch in her throat, 'I need you inside me, David.'

He kissed her forehead and then raised himself over her. She parted her thighs wide and took hold of his penis and positioned it between her lips. Both he and she were slippery with juice. There was a moment when they looked into each other's eyes and both of them were trying to read what the other was thinking. Then David slowly leaned his weight forward and penetrated her, as deeply as he could, until the tip of his penis touched the neck of her womb and made her jump.

He stayed deep inside her, kissing her again. The feeling of his hairless skin against her own hairless vulva was so erotic that she wanted to stay like that. It made her nerve ends tingle and the muscles of her vagina spontaneously flinch, and she thought she could almost reach orgasm without him moving.

Gradually, though, he did begin to slide himself in and out of her. She closed her eyes and listened to the soft sticky sound of them making love and it was so familiar and yet it felt so exciting and so new.

When she opened her eyes again, however, she saw that he was looking down at her with the strangest expression on his face – disinterested, rather than aroused, as if he had always known from the moment they met that she was going to give in to him.

'*David*?' she said.

'What?' he said, suddenly smiling.

'What are you thinking about?'

'Nothing. *You*. How amazing you are.'

Katie kept her eyes open as he continued to make love to her, pushing himself into her faster and harder, and gripping the quilt tightly as he approached his climax. But her own excitement had started to subside, and even as he grunted and sweated and gritted his teeth, she knew for certain that she wouldn't have an orgasm. She could almost feel it ebbing away, like an evening tide.

It's me, she thought. I've allowed myself to be manipulated into bed because I've been so frustrated and lonely and I'm having such trouble at work. I don't feel guilty about it. But I've been trained to be suspicious and I can recognize a liar when he's standing three streets away with his back turned, let alone when he's naked and right on top of me.

David made a noise that was halfway between a cough and a sob. As he climaxed, he took himself out of her and she felt the warm spatter on her stomach. He stayed on top of her for a few moments, breathing heavily. Then he rolled himself sideways so that the mattress bounced. He shuffled himself close up beside her, staring into her eyes and stroking her hair.

'I mean it,' he said. 'You're amazing. But . . . you didn't come. We'll have to do something about that.'

He reached down between her legs again but she closed her thighs and took hold of his wrist to stop him.

'I'm fine, David, I'm grand altogether. PMT, that's all.'

'Okay, so long as you're happy. There'll be other times, I'm very much hoping.'

As discreetly as she could, she wiped the semen from her stomach with a corner of the sheet. Maybe it *was* guilt that had turned her off him so abruptly. Her relationship with John may have been over, but she still loved him. *You don't stop loving people just because they're not there. You don't even stop loving them when they're dead.*

***

'Have you always shaved yourself?' she asked him, after a while. 'Like, down there?'

'Only since I was studying at UCD. I dated an Egyptian girl and she was very fussy about body hair. Hasina, her name was. She said that if a man shaves himself he presents a pure image to the gods. Also, I have to tell you, it makes sex a hundred times more pleasurable. Especially oral. That was why I kept on doing it.'

'So which gods are you presenting a pure image to?'

He stroked her forehead and traced the line of her eyebrow with his finger. 'I don't know any more. Maybe the gods who can change my life for me and make me happy again.'

***

After they had dressed they had one more drink together and then David looked at the clock on the mantelpiece and said, 'Jesus. Twenty past midnight, I'd better go.'

Katie showed him to the front door. It had stopped raining now, but the night was misty and chilly and the laurel bushes were still dripping. Over in Cobh harbour a ship let out a long, desolate cry, like a mother seal who has lost her young.

'When can I see you again?' asked David, taking hold of both of Katie's hands.

'I'm not sure. I'll have to let you know. I'm up the walls at the moment, what with this High Kings case and everything else besides.'

'But you have to sleep, surely? And I could always sleep next to you.'

145

'We'll see, David. Let's just take it one step at a time, shall we?'

David kissed her, but when he tried to kiss her again she turned her face away.

'Come on, Katie,' he grinned. 'We're lovers now, you and me.'

Eighteen

Meryl had changed the bed and was stuffing the sheets and the duvet cover into the washing machine when she heard a loud banging at the front door.

Norman was out in the back garden blowing away the leaves, and Brigid, their cleaner, wouldn't be coming today because she was taking her daughter to the dentist, so Meryl had to go to answer the door herself. Even before she got there, though, the banging was repeated, even louder this time.

'All right, all right!' she called out. 'Take it handy, would you, I'm coming!'

She opened the door and found three men standing in the porch. Two of them looked as if they could be nightclub bouncers, huge and fat and hard, almost ball-shaped, with shaven heads and pug-like faces. They were both wearing short black overcoats and open-necked white shirts. The third, who was standing further back, wore a long tan trench coat. His face was almost dead white and he had a mass of orange curls, like a bunch of Chantenay carrots. He looked as if he just stepped through a time warp from 1922, a young gunman from the Old Brigade.

'Mrs Pearse, is it?' he said, harshly. He sounded as if he was suffering from a sore throat.

'That's right. What do you want?'

'And would that be your auld feller out at the back there, blowing the leaves?'

'What if it is? Who are you?'

The breeze was ruffling the young man's curls and he pushed them back out of his eyes. 'We're friends of a friend, Mrs Pearse, and the thing of it is, he's very concerned, this friend, that you and your auld feller might have been talking to the law.'

'We haven't been talking to the law, or anybody else for that matter.'

'But you do know a feen called Derek Hagerty? Grey hair, like, pure badger, and no front teeth? Most people call him "Denny". You picked him up by the side of the road near Ballynoe, that's what my friend says. Picked him up and brought him back here.'

Meryl was beginning to feel seriously frightened. 'Derek Hagerty? No. I don't know anybody of that name.'

Norman's leaf-blower had suddenly fallen silent while he emptied the bag, and so she said, 'Why don't you talk to my husband? He'll tell you the same.'

'What, the same untruth that you're just telling us? You picked up Derek Hagerty and brought him back here and then your auld feller ran him into the city. The only trouble is, your auld feller notified the law, and believe you me that's caused a nojus heap of inconvenience all around.'

'I don't have anything more to say to you,' said Meryl. She tried to close the door but one of the bouncer-types stuck his foot in it and pushed it back open.

'Just go away,' she said. 'If you don't go away I'll ring for the guards.'

'Oh, your very good friends the guards! They were here yesterday, weren't they? So what did you tell them?'

'We told them nothing. We don't know any Derek Hagerty or any Denny and that's an end to it.'

'Oh, our friend says different. Our friend says the *law* thinks different, too, and they'll be coming back to ask you some more questions. Our friend thinks that sooner or later you'll likely be coming out with information that will place our friend in a very embarrassing situation. Right in the shite, in fact, and we can't be allowing that to happen.'

'Is this some kind of a threat?' Meryl demanded, trying to sound challenging, even though '*threat*' came out much shriller than she had intended.

'Threat?' said the carroty-curled young man, imitating Meryl's high-pitched screech. 'Not at all, Mrs Pearse. Me and my friends are not the kind to go around making threats! What's the good of a threat? A threat is only a promise, like, and everybody knows that promises always get broke.'

With that, he said, 'Call for your auld feller, would you, before he starts up that smingin again?'

One of the bouncer-types gave her a serious nod and said, 'Go on, girl.' From the tone of his voice, he didn't have to add 'if you know what's good for you'.

'Norman!' called Meryl, weakly. Then, much louder, 'Norman! Can you come here a minute?'

'What?'

'Can you come here a minute! We have visitors!'

Norman appeared through the archway in the hedge that led to the back garden. He was wearing his oldest brown tweed jacket, corduroy trousers and green rushers. He approached the porch slowly, taking off his gardening gloves and looking warily from one of the men to the other.

'What's going on, Meryl?' he asked, when none of them spoke. 'Who are these people?'

The carroty-curled young man said, 'Mr Norman Pearse, is it?'

'That's right.'

'Well, Mr Norman Pearse, I'm sorry to say that you've caused a whole rake of trouble for a friend of ours. You were specifically requested to keep your mouth shut about Derek Hagerty, you can't deny that, but you couldn't resist tipping off the law, could you?'

'Who are you?' Norman demanded.

'That's no concern of yours, Mr Pearse. You've caused enough grief already without you causing any more. All you had to do was drop off Derek Hagerty in the city and say nothing, but you just couldn't resist blabbing, you tout, could you?'

'That's because we didn't think that he was telling us the truth,' Norman snapped back. 'He was mentioned on the TV news this morning. They said he'd been kidnapped for ransom, quarter of a million euros. He told us the same story. He said he'd been kidnapped by criminals, but he'd managed to escape. The only thing is, we didn't believe him, and I think we had good reason not to.'

'Whether you believed him or not, Mr Pearse, you still had no business ringing the law.'

'And what right do you have, to tell me not to? I thought it was my civic duty. Now – I'd consider it a favour if you'd get off my property and leave me and my wife in peace.'

'Oh, I so wish we could,' said the carroty-curled young man. 'It would save an awful lot of bother and grief. But sometimes a situation arises and you can't just leave it as it is, uncorrected, like.'

'I have no idea what you mean,' said Norman, and now Meryl could hear fear in his voice.

'I mean like you'll be coming with us for a kind of a mystery tour. So if you'd care to close your front door behind you, Mrs Pearse, we have some transportation waiting in the road outside.'

'We'll be doing nothing of the sort,' Norman retorted. 'Meryl – go inside and call the guards.'

Meryl turned around, but the bouncer-type who had his foot in the doorway seized both of her arms from behind. He lifted her bodily out of the house and into the porch. She let out a breathless scream and struggled against him, but when she realized that he was far too strong for her, she let her legs give way, and sagged, so that he would have to carry her full weight. It didn't trouble him at all; he kept his grip on her arms and almost danced her down the front steps as if she were a puppet.

Norman bustled his way forward, shouting, 'Leave go of her! Leave go of her, you ape!' but the second bouncer-type grabbed the sleeve of his tweed jacket, swinging him around so that he almost lost his balance and fell over. Then he grasped Norman's right hand between both of his, crushing his knuckles so hard that the bones audibly cracked.

'Ah! Ah! *Aaaah*! Jesus!' Norman shouted. He lifted his right hand, supporting it with his left, grimacing in agony and disbelief. 'You've broken my fingers! You've broken my whole fecking hand!'

Meryl tried to twist her head around, shocked. She had never heard Norman swear before, ever. But the bouncer-type continued to frogmarch her down the garden path towards the front gate and there was nothing she could do. The other bouncer-type gave Norman a hard shove on the shoulder as if to tell him to get moving, and so he did, keeping his hand pressed flat against his chest. His face was grey and his eyes were glistening with tears.

The carroty-curled young man shut the front door and then followed them, blowing his nose on a crumpled tissue.

***

A black Volkswagen Touran people carrier with tinted windows was waiting for them by the kerb.

'I'm not going anywhere!' protested Meryl, as the bouncer-type opened up one of the rear doors and started to push her inside. 'You can't make me!'

The carroty-curled young man finished wiping his nose and then he leaned very close to her and said, 'Oh, no? And who's going to stop us? The Lord God Almighty and all of his angels can't stop us! You've heard of divine retribution, Mrs Pearse? "It is a righteous thing with God to repay with tribulation those who trouble you." Two Thessalonians, chapter one, verse six.'

'Where are you taking us?' she asked him. 'You're not going to hurt us, are you? Norman only did what he thought was right.'

'Oh, we're only going for a little trip to the seaside,' said the carroty-curled young man. Close up, Meryl thought that he even smelled of carrots. 'You like the seaside, don't you?'

'Please,' said Meryl. 'Please don't hurt us.'

The carroty-curled young man looked down and sideways. For a moment Meryl thought he was going to say something, but then he simply shrugged and turned his back on her. The bouncer-type said, 'Go on, missus. Get in. You'll be all over bruises if I have to force you, and you don't want that.'

Shivering with fright, Meryl climbed into the back seat of the Touran and the bouncer-type squashed himself in beside her. The door on the other side opened and Norman climbed in, still holding his hand against his chest. The carroty-curled young man sat in the front passenger seat, while the second bouncer-type got behind the wheel and started the engine.

As they pulled away from the kerb, the sun came out. The carroty-curled young man leaned back in his seat and said, 'How about that, Mrs Pearse? A perfect day for the seaside, wouldn't you agree?'

Meryl didn't answer him. She knew that whatever she said to him, it wouldn't make any difference, and that he would simply mock her.

They drove through Ballinlough and around Douglas village, and then they joined the main N28 and drove due southwards. The sky was pale blue with broken cloud, and apart from three or four trucks and a camper van they had the road to themselves. After a few minutes of driving the carroty-curled young man switched the radio on. There was a blurt of local news, but then he changed the station to folk music, the Bothy Band playing 'Old Hag You Have Killed Me'. Meryl reached across and gently squeezed Norman's left hand. Norman's eyes were closed from the pain of his fractured right hand, but he nodded to acknowledge her. The bouncer-type saw what she was doing and jerked his head as if to tell her to take her hand away.

Once they had passed through Snow Hill, the road narrowed, with dense hedgerows on either side. There was hardly a house in sight, only freshly ploughed fields and distant green hills, and hooded crows perched on the telegraph wires. The sun brightened and faded and brightened again, and the shadows of the clouds scurried across the fields as if they were terrified.

At last they saw the sea glittering between the hills. It was startlingly blue. They turned down a side road and into a deserted car park.

'That's it, journey's end,' said the carroty-curled young man. 'Let's take a stroll on the beach, shall we?'

'What are you going to do to us?' Norman asked him.

'Well, it's kind of a surprise, like. But considering the trouble you've been causing, and the strong possibility that you might be causing a whole lot more, you'll have to admit when you find out what it is that it's totally appropriate.'

'You're not thinking of drowning us, are you?' Meryl said.

'Wait and see,' the carroty-curled young man said, giving her a thin, lipless smile, and climbed out of the Touran. Although the day was so bright, there was a stiff breeze blowing from the sea and when Meryl climbed out, too, her hair was whipped across her face.

The five of them walked down the concrete path and on to the beach. The tide was out and jagged granite rocks were sticking out of the sand like weathered monuments. Meryl remembered this bay now, or one very much like it. Her parents had brought her here as a child and she had spent a blissful afternoon building a sandcastle for her dolls.

Seagulls screeched overhead as they walked along to a wide, flat stretch of sand. A stocky middle-aged man was sitting on one of the rocks not far away, smoking. A spade was stuck into the sand close by, and next to the spade stood a khaki jerrycan. Meryl could see that the sand had been dug up in two different places, about twenty metres apart. She had felt anxious from the moment she had answered the front door to these men, but now she felt a deep, cold sense of utter dread. She turned around, wondering if she could possibly manage to escape, but both bouncer-types were close behind her and she knew that they would grab her as soon as she started to run.

The stocky middle-aged man stood up and came across the sand to meet them. He was wearing baggy jeans and a thick cream

153

fisherman's sweater with brown stains down the front of it. His hair was grey and close-cropped and he had a broken nose and eyes that were no more than slits, so Meryl found it hard to tell if they were open or closed.

'What's the craic, boy?' he asked the carroty-curled young man, with smoke leaking out of his nostrils.

'Everything went like clockwork. No bother whatsoever. How about you? Are you all ready here?'

'Ready and waiting.'

The carroty-curled young man came over and took hold of Meryl's wrist. She let out a whimper and promptly wet herself, soaking the front of her stonewashed jeans. The carroty-curled young man shook his curls and tutted.

'First time I take you to the seaside and you do a wazz in your pants. No Mr Whippy for you, Mrs Pearse!'

Meryl's legs could barely support her as the carroty-curled young man tugged her across to one of the places where the sand had been dug up. As she approached it, she could see that the stocky middle-aged man had excavated a hole about a metre and a half deep. The sand was dark and damp and there was a small pool of water at the very bottom.

'What are you going to do? Bury me? You're not going to bury me, are you?'

'Not completely, Mrs Pearse. But if you'd care to climb in, we'll be able to estimate the depth of it much better, won't we?'

'Please, no. Don't do this. I swear on the Holy Bible that Norman and I won't say another word to the guards or anybody. I promise you! I'll pay you! Norman has money, we can pay you.'

The carroty-curled young man sniffed and wiped his nose with the back of his hand. 'It's all very well for you to be saying that, like, but you could easy change your mind once we'd let you go, and then where would we be? Sorry and all, but we can't take the risk.'

Meryl tried to twist her arm away from him, but he kept a tight hold on her sleeve and dragged her closer to the edge of the hole.

At the same time, he turned his head around and let out a piercing whistle between his teeth. One of the bouncer-types immediately crossed over and seized her with both of his hands around her waist. With a snort, he lifted her up and held her over the hole, trying to force her down into it. She kicked and struggled, but with a sudden lurch she slipped down to the bottom and found that her shoes were filling up with cold water. She jumped up three or four times, trying to pull herself out, but the hole was so deep that it came right up to her chest, and even if the sand hadn't kept sliding down when she clawed at it, she simply didn't have the strength or the leverage to lift herself up.

'Get her out of there! *Get her out of there*!' Norman shouted, his voice cracking with anger; but the second bouncer-type slapped him hard across the back of his head and said, 'Whist up, will ya, or I'll puck the fecking neck o' ya!'

In spite of that, Norman continued shouting over and over, 'Get her out of there! She's my wife! You can't hurt her! Get her out of there!' until the bouncer-type yanked him around to face him and punched him so hard in the stomach that he instantly collapsed to his knees.

'Leave him alone!' screamed Meryl, scrabbling even more frantically at the sand all around her. 'He won't tell anyone, I swear to you! *Leave him alone*!'

'You can shut your mouth, too, missus, unless you want some of the same,' snapped the carroty-curled young man. He slapped the shoulder of the stocky middle-aged man and said, 'Go on, Phelim, get to filling in, would you, boy, before this fecking weapon gives me a headache.'

Meryl stopped screaming. She could see that the bouncer-type who had punched Norman in the stomach was now bundling him bodily into the second hole. Norman was still whining for breath and for a few seconds he disappeared completely. When he eventually managed to stand up straight, chest-deep in sand, as Meryl was, his eyes were still bulging and his mouth was agape, like a stranded mullet.

Phelim went over at a leisurely pace to the rock where he had been sitting and waiting, and returned with his spade. Meryl looked up at him with what she hoped was a pleading expression, but his eyes were such slits that it was impossible for her to tell if he was moved or not. Without a word he began to shovel up some of the sand that he had excavated from the hole, and drop it back into the hole all around her.

'You can't do this,' she said, shakily. 'Do you hear what I'm saying to you? You can't do this. If you leave us like this the tide is going to come in and we won't be able to get out and we'll drown!'

Phelim said nothing, but kept on dropping sand around her until the hole was filled right up to her underarms. Not only was she panicking now, but the weight of the sand against her chest was making it hard for her to breathe.

'I'm making one last appeal to you as a Christian and a human being,' she said. Still Phelim remained stony-faced, and now he began to bang the sand flat all around her with the back of his spade. Meryl tried to snatch it, but he simply gave it a sharp, vicious twist and she had to let go, with blood welling out of a deep diagonal cut on the side of her thumb.

When he had finished he walked over to the hole where Norman was half buried, and without any hesitation he started to shovel sand into that hole, too.

O merciful God in Heaven how can this be happening? thought Meryl. It was worse than a nightmare because she knew that she wouldn't wake up and find that she had dreamed it. It went on and on, and it was so real. The tireless shushing of the sea, and the *hark-harrk-harrking* of the gulls, and the monotonous chopping sound of Phelim's shovel as he filled in the hole to make it impossible for Norman to escape.

Who could have imagined that my life would end like this? Perhaps it was God's punishment for my going out with Eoghan again, and realizing that I still had feelings for him. But I wasn't unfaithful to Norman, not even in my mind.

She looked around and she could see from the dark brown seaweed that was draped on top of the rocks how high the water would rise when the tide came in. She had never liked swimming in the sea, and she could already imagine the cold, salty brine slapping into her face, and then splashing into her mouth, and filling up her lungs.

She saw that Phelim had finished flattening the sand around Norman and it was then that she started to cry. Not loudly, because she was finding it so difficult to breathe, but a thin suppressed mew, like a kitten left out in the rain. Tears slid down her cheeks and gave her a foretaste of seawater.

She pressed her hands together and closed her eyes, and whispered all that she could remember of the prayer that Father Dolan had recited when her grandmother was on her deathbed.

O most merciful Jesus, Lover of souls, I pray thee, by the agony of Thy most Sacred Heart and by the sorrows of Thy Immaculate Mother, cleanse in Thine Own Blood this sinner who is to die this day.

Heart of Jesus, once in agony, take pity on the dying.

She knew there was more, and she wished she could recall it, but she was in too much distress, and in any case the carroty-curled young man was walking back towards her and she didn't want him to see how frightened she was.

'Well now, there's the two of you both ready,' he said. 'I told you that we didn't make threats. Only the weak and the cowardly make threats.'

'So you're just going to leave us here to drown?'

The carroty-curled young man blinked at her in mock-surprise. 'Is that what you think? Of course we're not! What kind of eejits do you think we are?'

'Then what?' she said, with her lower lip trembling.

'If we left you here, Jesus, we'd never get to see that justice was done, would we? And what if somebody was to chance along the beach and saw you here and dug you out?'

'Then – *what*?' she repeated, and now she couldn't stop herself from sobbing. 'What are you going to do to us, tell me!'

'Show her, Phelim,' said the carroty-curled young man. 'The auld feller first, so that she can have a preview.'

Phelim went back to the rocks and picked up the jerrycan. It was obviously full and heavy because it hardly swung at all as he carried it over to the place where Norman was half buried in the sand. As he levered the lid off it, Meryl realized what he was going to do, and her sobs became a low, continuous moan.

'Come on, Mrs Pearse,' said the carroty-curled young man. 'There must be worse ways of going, although for the life of me I can't think what they are, like. Not off the top of my head.'

The two bouncer-types both stepped well back while Phelim lifted the jerrycan and poured petrol all over Norman's head and shoulders. Norman held his hands up in front of his face to prevent it from stinging his eyes, but he didn't utter a sound. Meryl kept on keening with grief, as if he were already dead – and in a way he was.

She didn't want to watch what was going to happen next and she didn't want to hear it, either. Although they were only metres apart and Phelim had buried them so that they were facing each other, she could have closed her eyes and pressed her fingers into her ears, but she didn't. These were going to be Norman's last few seconds of life and she had to be a witness. Even if these men were going to kill her, too, she could take her testimony to Jesus, so that when their time came, they would be punished as they deserved to be.

'Any last words, Mr Pearse?' the carroty-curled young man called out, above the screaming of a seagull that was swooping low overhead.

Norman said nothing, but stared at Meryl with pity and sadness in his eyes. Then Phelim took a purple plastic cigarette lighter out of his pocket, flicked it alight, and calmly touched it to the back of Norman's hair.

Still Norman said nothing, and still he didn't flinch, even as flames were flickering in the wind from the top of his head and turning him into a human candle. For a few moments the flames died down, and smoke drifted towards the car park, and for a moment Meryl thought that God might have heard her and extinguished the fire with His merciful breath. Then, however, Norman's petrol-soaked jacket suddenly burst into flames and he was engulfed. He let out a single hoarse scream, but then he must have breathed in blazing petrol vapour, and all he could do was flap his arms.

Meryl could only watch him as he burned. Sometimes he was barely visible through the sheet of flames, but then the wind would blow the flames to one side, like a waving yellow banner, and she could clearly see his face blackening and his jacket turning into tatters of carbonized wool, clustered with tiny orange sparks.

Gradually his blackened face cracked, revealing the scarlet flesh underneath the skin, and then that blackened, too. He stopped flapping his arms and instead they began to stiffen. After a while the flames died down and his head and shoulders were left smouldering. Parts of his skull were exposed and he was baring his teeth in a hideous grin. Only then did Meryl lower her head and close her eyes.

The carroty-curled young man came back to her and said, 'There . . . what did I tell you? Not one word of a threat, but we won't have *him* blabbing to the law any more, will we?'

Meryl opened her eyes and looked up at him. She wanted to curse him, and call him the devil incarnate, but her stomach tightened and all she could do was bring up her breakfast, watery shreds of scrambled egg and pulpy blobs of half-digested toast.

'The state of you la,' said the carroty-curled young man. 'First you piss yourself and now you're puking your ring up. If your dear mother could see you now.'

Meryl wiped her mouth with the back of her hand. *If your dear mother could only see you, you murdering little bastard*, she thought, but she was too sick to speak, and what good would it do?

Phelim brought the jerrycan over. Meryl realized now that within the next few minutes she really was going to die, and that she was probably going to suffer greater pain than she had ever suffered in her whole life. All the same, she felt detached and calm, almost as if she weren't here on this beach at all, but somewhere far away and long ago, on a hillside overlooking Blarney Lough, and the cries that she could hear weren't seagulls at all but the sounds of children playing.

The first splash of petrol came as a shock. It was stunningly cold and it smelled so strongly that she coughed and spat and inadvertently sniffed some up her nose, which made her retch.

'For feck's sake,' said the carroty-curled young man. He tugged the jerrycan out of Phelim's grasp and emptied it over Meryl's head himself. She gasped and choked and felt that she was drowning. She even swallowed some, which made her retch yet again, but all she could do was stay where she was, imprisoned in sand, with petrol clinging to her eyelashes and dripping from the end of her nose.

When he had finished, the carroty-curled young man gave the jerrycan one last shake and then slung it aside. He held out his hand to Phelim and said, 'Lighter.'

Phelim passed him his cigarette lighter and the carroty-curled young man snapped it alight. The flame was blown out by the wind so he had to snap it alight a second time.

'Well now, like I said to your auld feller, any last words?'

She didn't answer him. Her eyes were closed now and she was sitting on the hillside overlooking Blarney Lough. He waited five more seconds, and then he leaned forward and held the lighter underneath her chin.

She jerked her chin upwards, but then her whole face burst with agony. She was blinded instantly, and the world went black. Even though she couldn't see, she could hear a crackling sound as her hair caught alight and her skin shrivelled. Then her sweater started to burn and the pain in her shoulders was so intense that she felt as if her whole being was on fire, her soul as well as her body. She tried to struggle herself free from the sand but it was hopeless. All she could think to herself was that nothing had ever hurt her like this, ever, and please God, take me now.

Soon, however, the worst of the pain began to subside, as her nerve-endings were burned away. She was still aware that she was alive, and alight, but she began to feel peaceful, as if she were a huge autumn flower with yellow petals, rather than a burning woman. Even as her skin flaked away and her tendons tightened, a strange calm filled her mind, like the tide coming in – a feeling of acceptance.

The carroty-curled young man and the two bouncer-types and Phelim all stood around until her head dropped on to her chest and it was clear that she was dead. She looked like a bald shop-window mannequin painted in patchy orange and brown and red. Her fingers had left deep furrows in the sand in front of her, but the sea would soon wash those away.

Phelim took out a packet of Carroll's and passed them around, and they all lit up with the same lighter that they had used to set fire to Norman and Meryl.

Nineteen

Katie was standing in the living room finishing her coffee when she heard a car horn tooting outside. She went to the window and drew back the net curtains. David was sitting in his silver Range Rover outside her front gate. When he saw her, he gave her a wave and blew her a kiss.

She raised her hand to acknowledge that she had seen him, but then she let the curtain fall back. The sight of him had made her feel faintly nauseous, and she went through to the kitchen and emptied the rest of her coffee down the sink.

In the light of day, she couldn't think how she had let herself give in to him. Now that she had slept, and had time to think how she was going to deal with Acting Chief Superintendent Bryan Molloy, as well as the High Kings of Erin case, she felt much less vulnerable. She still thought that in his lean, wolfish way, David was strikingly handsome, and she had to admit to herself that he was one of the most charming men that she had ever met, but she recognized him for what he was. It had been the taking of her that had aroused him; he wouldn't be interested in a long-term relationship, and she was sure that he wouldn't leave Sorcha for her. Something kept him tied to Sorcha, although she couldn't think what, if she was so violent and such a header. He had told Katie that he felt duty-bound to stay with her, but that didn't ring true.

In spite of that, she had been feeling rejected and frowzy for so many months now, ever since John had left her. She had put on over two kilos in weight and her hair never seemed to behave itself. Even if she couldn't trust him, David had reassured her that she was still attractive and sexy.

She said goodbye to Barney and drove into the city. The day was blustery but bright, which made her feel even more confident. Today I'm going to sort out Bryan Molloy, and today we're going to make some real progress with the High Kings of Erin, or whoever it was that was responsible for murdering Garda Brenda McCracken and Micky Crounan and kidnapping Derek Hagerty.

She switched on the radio and it was playing 'Banks of the Roses' by the Barra MacNeills. O Johnny, lovely Johnny, don't you leave me, they sang, but this time she remained dry-eyed.

***

Bryan Molloy was out when she arrived at the station, which she found partly frustrating and partly a relief. His secretary, Teagan, said that he had gone for a meeting at the city council offices about the Cork Foyer housing scheme for homeless young people, and that he probably wouldn't be back until very much later.

'All right, thanks, Teagan,' said Katie. She glanced around Bryan Molloy's office and noticed that his golf clubs were missing from the corner where he normally kept them propped up. She had been meaning to confront him as soon as she came in, but she could use some extra time to prepare her case more thoroughly.

There were three folders waiting for her on her desk – a report on yet another drugs ring, which had been operating out of Knocknaheeny, and an update from social services on three young Nigerian girls who had been brought into Cork last week by Michael Gerrety, allegedly to work as 'escorts'. There was also a warning from Garda headquarters in Dublin that hackers were locking people's computers, then sending them an official-looking demand, which appeared to come from An Garda Síochána, telling them that they had been logging in to unauthorized websites, or child pornography, and would have to pay a 100-euro fine to have them unlocked. This scam was called 'ransomware', which

Katie thought highly appropriate, considering the cases she was working on.

She had picked up her phone to call Detective Sergeant Ni Nuallán when Kyna herself knocked at her office door and came in.

'What's the story, Kyna? I was just about to ring you. Have we sent Derek Hagerty home yet?'

'No, he's still here. He's afraid to go home for what he thinks these High Kings of Erin are going to do him.'

'You've told him we'll give him protection? We can even arrange for him and his family to go to a safe house if he's that freaked.'

'He knows that, but he seems to think that they can get to him wherever he goes. He kept saying, "You guards can't keep me safe, you're worse than they are." I asked him what he meant by that, but he wouldn't say. I don't think I've ever come across a man as scared as he is. He's like shaking with terror. Absolutely planking it.'

'Did he give you any more clues that he might have been faking his abduction?'

Detective Sergeant Ni Nuallán said, 'I still haven't asked him outright about the bruises that Norman Pearse said were washed off. That's if our informant really *was* Norman Pearse. I haven't asked him about his mobile phone, either. Well, you did say not to.'

'I want us to interview the Pearses again before we do that. I'm sure it must have been them. How many other drivers called Norman drove past the Cineplex at that particular time, do you think? I can understand that they're probably just as scared as Derek Hagerty, but we can protect them, too, if we have to.'

'One problem,' said Detective Sergeant Ni Nuallán. 'O'Donovan and Horgan went to Ballinlough only half an hour ago to talk to them, but they're not at home. Most likely they're out shopping or something, so they probably won't be long. O'Donovan said that they'd hang around and wait for them to come back.'

Katie checked the clock on her desk and said, 'All right, we'll give them an hour or so. I've a rake of paperwork to get through, anyhow.'

At that moment, Detective Sergeant Ni Nuallán's iPhone let out a shrill, high-pitched ringtone. She took it out and said, 'Yes, Patrick?'

There was a lengthy pause while Detective O'Donovan spoke to her. She nodded a few times and said, 'Right,' and then, 'Right you are. Right. Just hold on a second, would you? I'm here with the super right now.'

'What is it?' asked Katie. 'Have the Pearses come back home?'

'Still no sign of them. But a woman just turned up at their house and when O'Donovan asked her what she wanted she said that she was a friend of Mrs Pearse from the same church, Our Lady of Lourdes. She said that Mrs Pearse had invited her for coffee this morning.'

'Any chance she might have simply forgotten?' asked Katie, and Detective Sergeant Ni Nuallán repeated the question to Detective O'Donovan.

'Very doubtful,' she repeated. 'According to this friend, they meet for coffee at the same time every week.'

'Tell O'Donovan to go all the way round the house. Tell him to look in all the windows and see if any of the doors have been left unlocked. Check for any signs of a struggle or a hurried exit, like carpets rucked up or furniture knocked over.'

Detective Sergeant ó Nuallan waited a little longer, and then Katie could hear Detective O'Donovan talking to her again.

'He says there's an electric leaf-blower in the back garden which is lying in the middle of the lawn. It's still plugged in with an extension lead that goes through the open kitchen window.'

She paused, and then she said, 'The back door's unlocked, and there's washing hanging half in and half out of the washing machine.'

Another pause, then, 'Horgan says that there are two cars still inside the garage – the green Audi A3 and a mustard-coloured Peugeot 208.'

Katie stood up. 'Jesus,' she said, 'they've been taken. I'll bet you money they've been taken.'

'O'Donovan's had a quick sconce inside the house and it doesn't appear like there's any indications of a struggle. If they have been taken, they must have gone without any kind of a fight.'

'Take Quinlan and get out there,' said Katie. 'I'll go down and see Denis MacCostagáin and see how much manpower he can muster. After that, I'm going to have that talk with Derek Hagerty, and this time it's no more Mrs Good Cop.'

'Don't you think this is jumping the gun, like?' asked Detective Sergeant Ni Nuallán. 'I mean, they're a grown-up couple and they're only late for a coffee morning. It's not like they're missing children.'

'Perhaps it is,' said Katie. 'But I'd rather risk the money and the man-hours than give Bryan Molloy another chance to say that I'm always two steps behind. Did you hear "Morning Ireland" this morning? They quoted him almost word for word. "Detective Superintendent Maguire and her team still have a fair amount of catching up to do." Thanks for nothing, Molloy.'

'You shouldn't let him get under your skin so much. He's just an old-fashioned misogynist and everybody knows what a great cop you are.'

'The trouble is, Kyna, *he's* a great cop himself, and there's no two ways about it.'

'Well, I know he made a reputation for himself in Limerick.'

'He deserved it. The way he stamped out the worst of those feuding gangs – the Ryans and the Keane-Collopys and the McCarthy-Dundons. The Duggans, too. The Duggans were pure bogmonsters. You only had to look at them the wrong way and they'd feed you to their pigs, and you'd be lucky if they'd shot you first.'

'Oh, I know all about the Duggans, for sure,' said Detective Sergeant Ni Nuallán. 'Niall Duggan, wasn't it, and those terrible twins of his, Aengus and Ruari? My friend Paul Dannehy was attached to Henry Street for a while, looking into some car-theft racket, and Ruari Duggan spat in his face and told him she'd hang his danglers on her Christmas tree.'

'That sounds like her all right,' said Katie. 'But as much as I hate to admit it, nobody was able to lay a finger on those scumbags before Bryan Molloy went in there with all guns blazing. As far as most of his fellow officers are concerned, he's still the chief boy.'

***

Superintendent Denis MacCostagáin was on the phone when she went downstairs. He was an angular, gangling man who always stooped because of his height. He had a high crest of wavy grey hair and a large, complicated nose, so that he looked like some extinct flightless bird. He was obviously harassed. The television in the corner of his office was showing a rowdy crowd scene, although the sound was turned down. The caption running underneath the picture was 'Violence Erupts At Anti-Water Demo In Cork'.

'No, no, Sergeant, for feck's sake, *no!*' he repeated. 'You absolutely *have* to keep it low-key. RTÉ are showing it live. Yes, Inspector Rooney's on his way to you now and I don't want this getting out of hand, do you deck it?'

He put down the phone and shook his head.

'What's the story?' Katie asked him.

'It's that demonstration outside County Hall against Irish Water installing smart meters on the estates. About fifteen minutes ago one of our patrol cars knocked over three protestors. Only by accident, like, and none of them was seriously hurt, but the crowd didn't see it that way.'

'So what's happened?'

'They've smashed the patrol car's windows and rolled it over on to its roof. Now the whole thing's turned ugly. They've started tearing down fencing and tossing rocks and Sergeant Mulligan's just asked me if they can use batons. Jesus! And all over water meters! You know what the protestors are saying? They don't want water meters because they think they'll make the water radioactive and they'll all die of the radiation poisoning, like Chernobyl. Every time Irish Water dig a hole and try to install a water meter the goms come along and stand in it, so that they can't.'

'I'm looking for as many feet on the ground as you can spare me,' said Katie. She told Superintendent MacCostagáin about Derek Hagerty and the Pearses, and that she urgently needed gardaí to back up Detectives O'Donovan and Horgan out at Ballinlough. 'Maybe half a dozen officers for door-to-door inquiries. I think there's a strong possibility that the Pearses have been abducted by these High Kings of Erin. If they have, they could be in serious danger.'

'You don't think these High Kings of Erin could be all a hoax? Just some eejit ripping the piss?'

'It's possible. So far we don't have any evidence one way or the other. But whoever they are, they seem to know what we're doing almost before we've thought of it ourselves, and that's what worries me more than anything. They knew that Shelagh Hagerty had told us about her husband being abducted, although God alone knows how. Because of that, they booby-trapped Mrs Hagerty's car and Garda McCracken lost her life.'

'You're not suggesting they have a stoolie here in the station?'

'No, Denis, I'm not, but I'm keeping an open mind, and I'm trying to get a step ahead of them, whoever they are, instead of being two steps behind.'

'Well, I don't honestly know how much manpower I can spare you,' Superintendent MacCostagáin told her. 'I might be able to send out a couple of cars from Togher and Carrigaline. Jim Rooney obviously has his hands full at the moment, but I'll see what I can arrange for you.'

'Thanks, Denis. Whatever you can do, I owe you.'

As she was walking along the corridor back to her own office, Katie heard her phone warbling. She hurried to pick it up, and said breathlessly, 'Yes?' It was Detective O'Donovan ringing again.

'Still no sign of the Pearses, ma'am, but Horgan's just been talking to an aul wan who lives across the road. She said she was cleaning the windows in her lounge and she saw Norman and Meryl Pearse climbing into a black van with two big fellers.'

'What time was this?' Katie asked him.

'Half ten, quarter to eleven, thereabouts, that's what she thought. She said she usually listens to the Niall Carroll show on the radio and that hadn't started yet.'

'Could she describe the van at all? Did she know what make it was? I don't suppose she managed to lamp its registration?'

'All she said, it was black with black windows along the sides. So most likely it was a people carrier of some sort.'

'All right. I'll have an alert put out for it. There can't be too many like that. There's a couple of units coming out to help you with the house-to-house and anything else you need, but they can't spare any more than that because there's some kind of a public-order problem at County Hall. Anti-water-meter demonstration. It looks like it's almost a riot.'

'Gollun, don't these eejits have anything better to do? Why don't they go and fall on their arse somewhere and make themselves some compo?'

'I'll get back to you, Patrick,' said Katie. 'I'm going to question Derek Hagerty again, see if I can't get more out of him.'

'Well, good luck to you so.'

Twenty

Derek Hagerty had just finished his lunch when Katie went down to see him – bacon and cabbage and boiled potatoes, although he had hardly touched it and it had now gone cold. He looked haggard and his eyes were rimmed with scarlet.

Katie pulled out a blue plastic chair and sat down opposite him, laying her iPhone down on the table and setting it to record. Derek Hagerty glanced up at her and then continued to stare down at the plate of food in front of him.

'You know that you're free to leave any time you want to?' Katie told him. 'You haven't been formally charged with any offence and we can't legally hold you here any longer without making a special application to the court.'

Derek Hagerty gave an almost imperceptible nod, but didn't answer.

Katie said, 'You've told us that you're in fear for your life from your abductors and that's why you're reluctant to return home. We've offered you protection, but you haven't given us any clear indication that you're prepared to accept it.'

'Everything's a mess,' said Derek Hagerty, closing his eyes and shaking his head. 'It's all such a fecking mess. I never dreamed that it would turn out like this. I never fecking dreamed it.'

'It's more of a mess than you realize, Derek,' said Katie. 'We questioned Norman and Meryl Pearse yesterday about picking you up from the roadside at Ballynoe and taking you in. They denied it. In fact, they insisted that they had never even heard of

170

you. This morning, though, I'm sorry to tell you – '

She paused, deliberately. Derek Hagerty opened his eyes and frowned at her. 'What?' he said. 'What's happened?'

'This morning it seems that the both of them were taken away from their home by at least two men. At the moment we have absolutely no idea who those men were or whether the Pearses were taken against their will. They missed a regular coffee morning with a friend of Mrs Pearse and they left their house unlocked. Both of them left their mobile phones at home, so we have no way of locating them that way.'

'Oh God,' said Derek Hagerty. 'Oh God, no.'

'Derek,' said Katie, leaning forward and staring him straight in the eyes, 'you have to tell me the truth now, the *whole* truth, before anything happens to the Pearses. This isn't a game any more. If the Pearses are hurt or murdered, then you're going to become a suspect on more than one conspiracy charge. Extortion and homicide and God knows what else. You could be locked up for the next twenty years.'

Derek Hagerty tilted his head back and took several noisy breaths through his nostrils.

Katie continued, 'I'm not going to mess with you any longer. Whoever it was who called us and said that he was dropping you off on Grand Parade, he also told us that he thought you were lying about being kidnapped. Maybe it was Norman Pearse, maybe it wasn't. He claimed that you showed him some really bad bruises, but when he allowed you take a shower he saw that those bruises had mostly washed off. He also said that you still had a mobile phone on you, and that he heard you talking to somebody while you were in the bathroom, arranging to meet them. Now, it's conceivable that what your man thought were bruises were nothing but dirt, but what I find impossible to believe is that any kidnappers would allow their victim to keep a mobile phone.'

Derek Hagerty said, 'You've known all along, then, that I haven't been straight with you?'

'Yes. I was hoping that I could coax you to tell us what really happened voluntarily. But now that somebody's taken the Pearses, there's no more time for that. Come on, Derek, I need to know if you were genuinely kidnapped, and if you were, who by. If it's all been some kind of a fraud, then I need to know that, too, and who's involved in it.'

Derek Hagerty clenched his fists tightly and lowered his head, pressing his knuckles against his temples.

'I've been such a fecking fool,' he said. 'I never knew that I could end up doing anything like this.'

'Then tell me,' said Katie. 'You'll feel so much better about it if you get it off your chest.'

'I can't. I can't tell you. They'll kill me, I know they will, but not just me. Shelagh, too, for telling you that I was kidnapped, and the kids, too, and who knows, my mother and father besides.'

'*Who*, Derek? Who are they?'

Derek Hagerty was crying now. He lowered his left fist and it squashed into what was left of his boiled potatoes. He pushed the plate aside and scraped the potato off his hand on the edge of the table, but all the time he didn't stop weeping.

'I can't tell you,' he said, at last. 'I can't tell you what they do to people who cross them. They're not scared of the law. They're not scared of nobody.'

Katie said, 'Derek – listen to me. I'm deadly serious now. When a garda gets murdered, every police officer takes that personally and we make a special effort to track down whoever was responsible and bring them to justice. When Garda McCracken was killed, *I* took it personally, and let me tell you now that I'm going to find out who did it and make them pay for what they did, even if I have to hurt people like you. You think you've been a fool? You just wait until I've finished with you.'

Derek Hagerty could do nothing but sob. He opened and closed his scab-encrusted lips like some grotesque tropical fish, but he didn't, or couldn't, say any more.

Katie sat back, waiting for him to pull himself together, but as she did so her iPhone pinged. It was a text message from Ciara on the station switchboard. JUST HAD CALL 4 U. HE SD V. IMPORTANT. I TLD HIM U BUSY BUT HE SD HED RING BACK. HE SD HES HK OF E ??

Katie stood up. 'Think on what I've said, Derek. I appreciate how frightened you are, but you have to face up to this. Otherwise, the rest of your life is going to be ruined. Your family, your business, everything.'

Derek Hagerty looked up at her miserably. 'Chalk it down,' he said. 'Don't I fecking know it.'

***

Only ten minutes after she had returned to her office, Katie's phone warbled. She picked it up and said, 'Ciara?'

'He's calling back, ma'am. The HK of E fellow. Do you want to take it?'

'Please, Ciara, put them through.'

She waited a moment and then she cleared her throat and said, 'DS Maguire. Is that who I think it is?'

'Well, that depends entirely on who you think it is.' It was the same hoarse, slurred voice that she had heard before. 'I know more about you, Detective Superintendent Maguire, than you could ever imagine possible, but even I have to admit that reading your mind is somewhat beyond me.'

'What do you want? You left a message that it was important.'

'Oh, I think you'll agree with me that it's important all right. I gather that you've been concerned about Norman and Meryl Pearse.'

'What if I have?'

'Give me some credit, Superintendent. It was Meryl Pearse who found Derek Hagerty by the side of the road, and it was Norman Pearse who shopped him.'

'That's what you say.'

'That's right, and I say that because I know for a fact that it's true, even though they wouldn't admit it to you, would they?'

Katie reached across for a ballpen and scribbled on her big yellow notepad, *HK knew that Pearses denied helping DH? How?*

'Whether they admitted it to you or not, Superintendent, they did it, but they could have saved themselves a heap of grief if they had just kept quiet about it.'

Katie was sorely tempted to ask, *Have you taken them? What have you done with them?* but she didn't want to give the caller any indication that she suspected the Pearses of having tipped off the Garda about Derek Hagerty. The High Kings of Erin might have the Pearses in captivity and they could be trying to trap her into giving them the justification for punishing them.

'Well, I know what you're thinking, Detective Superintendent,' said the hoarse voice. 'I said I couldn't read your mind, but maybe in this instance I have an inkling. You're thinking that we've abducted Norman and Meryl Pearse, and that we intend to teach them a lesson for squealing to the law. But that's where you're wrong. We *did* abduct them, and the reason for me calling you now is to put up my hand and admit it. *But* – we have absolutely no intention of teaching them a lesson. The road to hell is paved with intentions, both good and bad. No – what we set out to do to the Pearses, we've already done it.'

Katie still said nothing. She was now almost positive that the High Kings of Erin really were responsible for all the crimes for which they were claiming credit. They knew far too much about them to be hoaxers. But there was still a possibility that Norman and Meryl Pearse were still alive and unharmed, and a wrong word from her could change that instantly.

'If you want to find them, go down to Rocky Bay Beach. You know Rocky Bay Beach? It will take you only twenty minutes or so. The sea's on the turn, but it won't be high tide again till ten o'clock tonight, so you shouldn't have any trouble locating them. Good luck to ye.'

Katie said, 'Whatever you've done, or whatever you're thinking of doing, I can tell you now that you'll pay for it.'

'Oh, how many times have I heard that before? My mammy always used to threaten to smack me a clatter, but you don't frighten me, Detective Superintendent Maguire, not a bit more than my mammy ever did! Let me tell you this, the sooner you learn to rub along with us, the happier we're all going to be. You do your thing and we'll do ours, and Ireland will have its pride restored before you know it. *Éirinn go Brách.*'

With that, the caller hung up.

Twenty-One

The bell above the front door of Whelan's Music Store jangled as the carroty-curled young man stepped inside. Outside on Oliver Plunkett Street, the two bouncer-types in black suits stood on either side of the entrance, their eyes hidden by wraparound sunglasses, their hands clasped over their genitals in the classic pose of bouncers everywhere.

The carroty-curled young man walked slowly through the store, pausing for a moment to tilt his head sideways and admire the electric guitars hanging on the right-hand wall, and then the Roland and Yamaha keyboards arranged in a serried line on the left-hand side. He stopped by a drum kit and flicked his index finger against one of the crash cymbals, so that it made a soft pish!

Pat Whelan was standing with his elbows on the counter, frowning at his laptop. He looked up when the carroty-curled young man flicked the cymbal and said, 'All right there? Anything I can help you with?'

The carroty-curled young man smiled and looked around the shop as if he were roughly calculating what all of this stock was worth.

'I hear you're thinking of closing down,' he said, in his hoarse, thin voice.

'End of the month,' said Pat. 'There's twenty per cent off everything till then. What are you looking for?'

'Nothing special,' said the carroty-curled young man. 'To be truthful with you, nothing at all. Whelan's has been in business for ever, hasn't it? A real Cork institution.'

'My grandfather opened it in 1933,' Pat told him. 'Guess who bought his first guitar here?'

'Rory Gallaghcr.'

'That's right. Kim Carroll, too. His first bowed mandolin, anyhow.'

'Yes, I know. I've done a little research on you, like.'

Pat stood up straighter, although he didn't close his laptop. He was short and plumpish, with a mass of curly black hair that was beginning to turn grey, and which badly needed a cut. His face was podgy with a button of a nose and thick lips and broken veins in his cheeks. He was wearing a frayed green jacket, a crumpled-looking orange shirt, and speckled maroon bow tie. At a glance, in the back of a badly lit pub, he could have been mistaken for Dylan Thomas.

'Research?' he said. 'What was that for? Just curiosity, like?'

'You could say that,' replied the carroty-curled young man, He ran his fingernails with a soft rattle along a Korg Arranger keyboard, and then turned round to face Pat, still smiling.

'That keyboard comes with a free stand and amp, if you're interested,' said Pat.

'Well, no, Pat, I'm not really interested in buying an instrument. What I'm really interested in is keeping you in business.'

'What do you mean? I'm practically bankrupt. Why do you think I'm closing the shop down?'

'I know that you're stony broke, Pat, and I also know how much you're in for. Three hundred and forty-two thousand yoyos, and then some. You'll be sleeping with the tramps at St Vincent's House before you know it.'

'Listen, who are you?' Pat demanded. 'You've got a brass neck poking into my affairs like that.'

'No need to get yourself agitated. I'm a friend. In fact, one of a number of friends, you might say. You know about Kevin McGeever?'

'Of course I know about Kevin McGeever. He was the stupid eejit who pretended that he'd been kidnapped so that his creditors would get off his back. What an eejit.'

The carroty-curled young man raised his gingery eyebrows in agreement. 'You're right, Pat. He *was* an eejit. An eejit of the first water. But, you know, his basic idea was sound. He thought that if he disappeared for a while, and then came back looking like he'd been badly mistreated, barefoot and clatty and his fingernails grown all long, none of his creditors would press for their money, on account of they wouldn't want to be suspected of abducting him.'

'What was sound about that?' asked Pat. 'He got himself arrested for wasting Garda time, didn't he?'

'Ah! But that's because he didn't plan things right. It's no good pretending to be kidnapped if you don't have any kidnappers. All that McGeever did was to disappear off to the west of Ireland somewhere and have his girlfriend report him as missing. There was no ransom demand from any third party, no threats made on his life. That didn't ring true at all. On top of that, like, he didn't anticipate that when he was found wandering by the roadside the people who found him would take him directly to the nearest Garda station. Thick, or what? Where else did he think they were going to take him?'

'So what does any of this have to do with me?' asked Pat.

'It has *everything* to do with you, Pat,' said the carroty-curled young man. 'Right now, you are in the same unenviable position as Kevin McGeever. Granted, he was a millionaire property developer and you run a one-horse music shop, but you both owe more money than you can ever hope to pay back.'

'Go on,' said Pat, slowly closing his laptop. He had been looking through the online catalogue of the Sound Shop. Almost every price that they were offering undercut the lowest prices that he could afford to charge, and that was why his business was going under. Some days recently he had sold nothing but a harmonica or some sheet music or a single packet of guitar strings; other days, nothing at all.

'Just supposing you left your shop tomorrow evening, Pat, and a couple of fellows jumped on you? Just supposing they blindfolded you and drove you off and locked you into a room somewhere? Just supposing they contacted your wife and your sons and demanded two hundred and fifty thousand yoyos for your safe return?'

'That's ridiculous. Where would my wife and my sons get half a million euros from? My wife's not well and my sons are still at college.'

'Now that's where this little plan works so well, unlike Kevin McGeever's. Your wife goes to the Garda and informs them that you're being held hostage, although she tells them the kidnappers have warned her not to, on pain of something horrible happening to her. The Garda come up with the necessary money because they can hardly refuse if your wife has been threatened and your life is at stake.'

'Then what?' asked Pat. He had just noticed that the two bouncer-types standing outside the front door of his shop had turned away three young musicians who were regular customers. He kept on glancing at them nervously.

'We arrange a swap, like. We get the money and *you* get returned to your nearest and dearest, living and breathing and in very reasonable shape, all things considered.'

'"Very reasonable shape"? I'm not so sure I like the sound of that.'

'Come on, Pat, you have to *look* as if you've been forcibly abducted, even if you haven't. We may have to mess you up a bit and put on some make-up to look like bruises. But the deal is, we'll give you ten per cent of the ransom money, after what you might call a cooling-off period, like, so that nobody gets too suspicious. Once you get that you'll be able to afford the best dentist in Cork.'

'What about the shades? They're not just going to stand by and let you stroll off with half a million euros, are they?'

'Don't worry about the shades. They won't bother us.'

Pat thought for a moment, but then he said, 'This still won't settle my debts, though, will it? Like, what? Ten per cent of half a million is only fifty thousand.'

'Don't you worry about that, either. Kevin McGeever was right about one thing at least. Your creditors won't come after you if they think they might be suspected of kidnapping you. And we can make sure that they *are* suspected.'

Pat looked around his shop – at the tall, shiny conga drums and the music stands and the stacks of Skytec speakers and Marshall amps. Not that it was really his shop any more, and neither was any of its stock. It all belonged to the tax commissioners, and Allied Irish Bank, and his scores of impatient creditors. Three hundred and forty-two thousand euros didn't sound like much unless you didn't have it, or any chance of raising it, except by winning the lotto.

'Who are you?' he asked the carroty-curled young man.

'You don't need to know that, Pat. In fact, the less you know the healthier it will be for you and your nearest and dearest.'

Pat's first instinct was to tell the carroty-curled young man to stick his offer where the sun doesn't shine and to clear off out of his shop and never come back. Fair play, he was well up shit creek without a paddle, and his canoe may have sprung a leak, but he was still a decent man and he had never committed a single criminal act in his life, unless you counted hobbling a few Mars bars from the local sweet shop or boxing the fox when he was a kid.

But then he thought of what it would be like to sleep soundly at night, and not to wake up at two in the morning sweating and grinding his teeth and worrying about money. He thought of Mairead's constant back pain, and how he could afford to have her privately treated if he had fifty thousand euros and no outstanding debts. Not only that, he could buy her a new coat, and new shoes, and maybe even take her away to Gran Canaria for a week on a package.

He couldn't remember the last time they had eaten at a proper restaurant. He could only just remember when they had last gone out to the pictures. They had gone to see *Love, Actually* but had to leave halfway through because of Mairead's back pain. After that, he had never had enough grade to take her out again.

'So . . . supposing I said yes, I'd do it . . .'

The carroty-curled young man said nothing, but waited, smiling, for him to finish. Outside, the two bouncer-types were turning away yet another customer, a bleached-blonde violinist from the Cork Symphony Orchestra.

'. . . supposing I said yes, what would I actually have to do, like?'

'Nothing at all. We'd arrange a time and a place for you to be snatched. Then we'd drive you away and keep you hidden until your ransom was paid. Most likely you'd have to talk to your wife on the phone, pleading with her to raise the money. And we might have to pull out a couple of your teeth as proof that we really have you, but I'd hope very much that it wouldn't come to that.'

'What? Pull out my teeth? Jesus. I hate the dentist at the best of times.'

'It has to be convincing, Pat. If the shades even get a sniff of a scam they won't cough up, and after all, phone calls can easily be faked. That was the problem when they kidnapped that racehorse, Shergar. They could hardly put *him* on the phone, could they, and they couldn't prove in any other way that they had him.'

'How about my wife, Mairead . . . would *she* be in on it? I mean, would *she* be aware that it was nothing but a set-up? Like I say, she's not too well. Spinal stenosis. I wouldn't want her to suffer any stress.'

The carroty-curled young man emphatically shook his head, so that the carrots bounced. 'You'd have to keep her completely in the dark, Pat. Sounds cruel, I agree, but women are shite at telling lies.'

'But if you warn her not tell the gardaí . . . what happens if she takes you serious, like, and *doesn't* tell them? She won't be able to raise the money then, will she?'

'Oh, she'll tell them, I guarantee it, because she won't know where else to turn for help. But the gardaí mustn't have any notion at all that it's a fix.'

Pat thought for a moment, and then he said, 'Listen . . . can you give me some time to mull this over? When it comes down to it, we're talking about extortion here, aren't we?'

'Extortion? No, not really,' said the carroty-curled young man. He was drumming his fingers on the counter and it was clear that he was becoming impatient. 'It's more like the liberation of redundant public funds. The Department of Justice always budgets a certain amount of money every year for ransom demands and suchlike. It occurred to me and my friends that it would be a fierce pity if that money was never put to good use and just rolled over till next year like a lotto jackpot.'

'All the same . . .' said Pat, uncertainly.

'Just tell me you're in, Pat, and I'll set the wheels in motion.'

Pause. 'What if I say thanks, but no thanks?'

'You won't.'

'How can you be so sure?'

'Because you know as well as I do that there are far worse things that can happen to you than going bankrupt.'

'Hey, steady. You're not *threatening* me, are you?'

The carroty-curled young man raised his eyebrows again as if to say, *Holy Mary, Mother of God, you're wide at last.*

'You know O'Connell's shoe shop?' he said.

'O'Connell's, of course. That was one of the worst fires in Cork for years. Frank O'Connell ended up with third-degree burns trying to save his stock. Lost all of his shoes and half of his face, too.'

'Well, let me just say this. Frank O'Connell said thanks, but no thanks. It's a no-brainer, Pat. Me and my friends are offering you an easy way out of all of your financial worries, but now that you know how our little scheme works, we can't really take the risk of you sharing it with anybody else – like the shades, for instance.'

Pat said nothing. He should have known the moment the carroty-curled young man stepped into the shop and those two bouncer-types took up their positions outside the door that this was going to be serious trouble. In 1991, Michael Crinnion, the hardest enforcer of the O'Flynn crime family, had walked into the shop in almost exactly the same way and for years he had been forced to pay protection money and allow his shop to be used as a dropping-off point for drug-trafficking. That extortion had only come to an end when Crinnion was shot dead in a phone box by rival gang members in April of 1995.

Pat had sworn to himself then that he would never give in to criminals ever again.

'Well?' demanded the carroty-curled young man, after nearly half a minute of silence.

'Well what? I wouldn't do it for choicer, but it looks like I don't have any alternative, do I?'

'Not really, no.'

'When would you do it? Like, snatch me, I mean?'

'I'll let you know early tomorrow. But it'll be soon.'

Pat stayed behind the counter as the carroty-curled young man left the shop and he and the two bouncer-types walked off in the direction of the General Post Office. One of the bouncer-types glanced back at him through the window and gave him a gap-toothed grin. Pat was shaking and sniffing as if he had the flu.

He stepped out from behind the counter and stood in the middle of the shop, looking around him, still shaking and breathing noisily through his nostrils. Then he kicked over a drum kit, so that the bass drum boomed and the cymbals clashed. After that, he walked all the way down to the front door, kicking and pushing over keyboards and electric pianos. Finally, he took a Flying-V guitar down from the wall and smashed it against the bookcase where all the music books were stacked, again and again, until books and glass were scattered all over the floor and the guitar was shattered into pieces, its neck broken and strings dangling.

He dropped the wrecked guitar and then slowly went down on his knees, his hands covering his face, and sobbed like a child at his own helplessness.

Twenty-Two

Katie stood on the sand at Rocky Bay Beach, her hands deep in the pockets of her red duffel coat, her hair blown across her forehead by the chilly breeze that was blowing in from the sea.

The technical team had erected two bright blue vinyl tents over the incinerated bodies that they had found half buried in the sand. They had taken hundreds of photos and more than sixty plaster casts of footprints, and now they were carefully digging the bodies out. Every now and then there would be a flicker of flashlights inside the tents, and every now and then a technician would emerge from one of the tents carrying a large black bucket of sand. He would squat down and carefully sieve the sand with a fine-meshed riddle, in case the perpetrators had dropped anything incriminating. Even a cigarette end could prove damning.

The car park was packed with four patrol cars, two Technical Bureau vans, an ambulance from Cork University Hospital, Katie's own car, two Range Rovers and a Ford Transit dropside tipper in case they needed to take away a large quantity of sand for closer analysis. There were no media vehicles yet; Katie had told Tadhg McElvin not to notify them until she had visited the crime scene herself and assessed how she was going to present it to the press.

Inspector Fennessy emerged from one of the tents and walked over. He was looking gaunt, as if he hadn't been eating properly, and his circular spectacles were stuck together with a lump of yellowish Sellotape on the bridge of his hawk-like nose. The tails of his long grey herringbone overcoat flapped in the wind.

He held up a small transparent envelope. Inside it was a receipt from a credit card terminal.

'They found this in the male's back trouser pocket. It's a Visa debit card receipt for drinks at the Silver Key Bar in Ballinlough, three evenings ago. I'll have Horgan check out the card owner's identity right away.'

'Ballinlough? It's more than likely that it *is* the Pearses then, isn't it?'

Inspector Fennessy nodded. 'I'd say so. You can't tell from their faces, of course, they're almost burned down to the bone, but the rest of their bodies fit the description. A woman in her mid- to late thirties by the look of her and the way she's dressed, and a man close to sixty, I'd say.'

'What's the story with the footprints? Do they tell us anything?'

'It's hard to say for sure because there's so many of them and they're all criss-crossed and going in every direction, but we have plenty of photographs of them, as well as plaster casts, and we'll be able to sort them out once Bill Phinner can get them back to the lab. At a guess, I'd say there was at least three of them, apart from the victims, and possibly one more. All male, by the size of them, like, and the depth of their impressions, and all wearing rushers or some kind of waterproof boots, except for one.'

Katie said, 'I think they already tell us one thing at least – and it's important.'

'Oh, yeah? And what's that, like?'

'I think these High Kings of Erin are trying to show us that when it comes to the law they don't give a fiddler's. Apart from the fact that they actually rang me up and confessed that it was them who had taught the Pearses a lesson, and told me where we could find them, they plainly didn't care that they were leaving enough evidence all over the crime scene to convict them ten times over. That's if we can ever can find them.'

'Well, I have to agree with you,' said Inspector Fennessy. 'And not only that – what a fecking horrendous way to kill people, for the love of God. Why did they have to make such a holy show of it? A bullet in the back of the head in their own front lounge would have done the job just as effective. They didn't have to take them all the way to the seaside and set them alight. Like, what's all that about?'

Katie turned her face to the breeze so that her hair was blown out of her eyes. In the distance, to the east, there was a rocky grey headland, with seagulls wheeling around it. Quite unexpectedly, she felt very lonely, with the gulls crying and the sea softly seething as the tide came in, and the blue vinyl Technical Bureau tents snapping and rumbling.

She turned back to Inspector Fennessy. 'I don't think there's any doubt at all that it was deliberate, making a performance out of killing the Pearses like this. Look at the way they killed Micky Crounan, cutting off his head and baking it into that poor young couple's wedding cake. Even the Real IRA don't kill people like that. And who knows what they might do to Derek Hagerty if they can ever lay their hands on him. I've never in my life seen a man so freaked.'

'So what are they up to, then?' said Inspector Fennessy.

'Think about it, Liam. How many people have been murdered by criminal gangs in Cork in the past five years?'

'Going on forty-seven at last count – not including these two.'

'That's right, and that's quite a fair number, but almost all of them were killed by plain old ordinary shooting, weren't they? These days, if somebody gets a bullet in the back of the head on a patch of waste ground, or a double-barrelled shotgun blast in their own front hallway, they scarcely get a mention in the media. Look at Eric Cummins – shot four times while he was still holding his baby son in his arms and it barely made the front page. It seems to me that the High Kings of Erin are after publicity, as much as they can get, like they want the whole world to know about them, and that the law can't touch them. It's a kind of terror campaign.'

'And the purpose of that is – *what*, like?' asked Inspector Fennessy. 'Surely they realize that if they keep on sticking up two fingers to us, we're going to put twice as much effort into finding out who they are and hunting them down.'

'I'm not at all certain why they're doing it, Liam. Although – well – there's a couple of possibilities that I can think of. Maybe they want to give themselves such a frightening reputation that when they kidnap somebody their relatives will stump up the ransom money without any argument and without ever telling us about it. Then again, they could genuinely be political, like they claim to be – or maybe they're nothing more than attention-seekers. You remember the Brogans when they robbed all those building society branches wearing hockey masks so nobody would know it was them, and we told the media that we suspected the Quirke family – which we did, of course.'

Inspector Fennessy nodded and smiled. 'That's right, Kevin Brogan rang up the "PJ Coogan Show" raging that it was him and his brothers that had done it, but we hadn't given them the credit. What a gobdaw.'

Just then, Katie saw two more cars approaching on the narrow, hedge-lined road that led to Rocky Bay Beach – a bronze Opel Insignia with a dented driver's door and a cream Fiat Punto. There were no spaces left in the car park, so they drove halfway down the rough concrete slope that led to the beach and stopped at an angle, one close behind the other. Out of the first car climbed Dan Keane from the *Examiner*, with his photographer, and out of the second car emerged Branna MacSuibhne from the *Echo*.

Katie could see yet another car coming into view around a bend in the road, followed by a large white van with a bottle-green stripe around it and a satellite dish on the roof.

'Cross of *Christ*!' she snapped. 'Who tipped off the media?'

'Not me, ma'am,' said Inspector Fennessy, shading his eyes to watch the vehicles coming nearer. 'I can swear that to you on my estranged wife's share of my house.'

'I told Tadhg *specifically* that I didn't want them down here until the technical boys were finished and the site was cleared.'

'I'll go over and have a word,' Inspector Fennessy told her. Blue and white crime-scene tape was stretched across the path that led down to the sand, and three uniformed gardaí had already intercepted the reporters to stop them from coming any closer. Dan Keane, however, caught sight of Katie and gave her a cheery salute.

'Go on, Liam,' said Katie. 'I don't want them seeing the bodies. I don't even want them knowing how they died. It's vital that we keep this very low-key, especially if the High Kings of Erin murdered them like this for the sake of publicity. We need to deny them the oxygen.'

Inspector Fennessy walked across to talk to Dan Keane and Branna MacSuibhne, who had now been joined by Fionnuala Sweeney from RTÉ, with her cameraman and sound engineer. Fionnuala was wearing a short ginger coat to match her gingery hair, and she waved, too. Katie looked the other way and pretended that she hadn't seen her.

She was furious – so furious that her fists were clenched inside her coat pockets and she was breathing hard, as if she had just stopped running. The High Kings of Erin had now killed three people who appeared to be totally innocent, as well as a Garda officer, and at the same time they were taunting her and playing her for a fool. With this case – as Acting Chief Superintendent Bryan Molloy had so patronizingly told the media – she always seemed to be swimming against the tide.

It even occurred to her that the High Kings of Erin might have deliberately committed these murders here on the seashore as a sly reference to Bryan's remark. *Pull yourself together, girl*, she told herself, *don't let the bastards grind you down*. But in spite of that, she still couldn't work out what the High Kings' game was, or who they could possibly be. She found it hard to believe that they were really old-fashioned Irish patriots, righteously determined to punish those chancers who had ruined the country's economy. Maybe they did have some connection to the Real IRA, *Óglaigh na hÉireann*, who had frequently shot or beaten up drug-dealers in Cork for 'unrepublican behaviour', although she still thought that the killings were far too fantastical for them.

More likely, they were a professional crime gang who had concocted a far-fetched political excuse for what was nothing more than out-and-out extortion.

She was still standing there, looking out to sea, when Bill Phinner came up to her, walking so silently on the sand that she didn't hear him, and she jumped when he said, 'DS Maguire?'

'Bill! Yes, what is it?'

'We have the victims all laid out now, if you want to come and take a look.'

'What? Yes, of course, Bill. Thanks.'

She followed him back to the nearest tent. She was only halfway there when Dan Keane shouted out, 'DS Maguire! DS Maguire! Any chance of a quick word, ma'am?'

She pretended she hadn't heard him and kept on walking, but as she reached the tent and Bill Phinner was holding the flap open for her, he shouted, 'Is it true that this is Mr and Mrs Pearse, who found Derek Hagerty?'

She hesitated for a moment. She was sorely tempted to stalk over to the crime-scene tape and demand to know who the *hell* had told him that?

Bill Phinner obviously saw from her expression what she was thinking, because he said, 'You're grand, ma'am. Just come inside and see the victims. There'll be plenty of time for the media later.'

Katie glanced across at Dan Keane, who was holding out both hands appealingly, but then she nodded and ducked her head down as she entered the tent.

The lights inside were brilliant, like a television set, which made the spectacle of the two half-incinerated bodies even more unreal. They had both been dug out of the sand and laid side by side on stretchers. The tent was crowded with five technical assistants in rustling Tyvek suits and masks, and two armed gardaí. There was an eye-watering smell of vinyl and petrol and burned flesh, which reminded Katie of Paul's first and only barbecue – abandoned, thankfully, because of the rain.

She took out the large men's handkerchief that she always kept in one of her pockets, soaked in perfume.

The victims both had their arms crooked up like two toy monkey drummers, the classic posture of burns victims. Both had been burned down to chest level – the man more severely than the woman. His eyeballs were shrivelled in their sockets and where his nose had been there were only two deep triangular cavities. In fact, there was scarcely any flesh left on his head at all, although he still had some large flakes of blackened skin on the right-hand side of his skull, with hair sprouting out of them, and part of his right earlobe remained intact, resembling a thick crispy curve of bacon rind.

The man's collarbones were exposed and blackened, but below his breastbone, where he had been buried in the sand, his body was intact. He was wearing what was left of a green cable-knit sweater with some moth holes in it, a pair of worn brown corduroy trousers, and green rubber boots.

The woman had more hair than the man, but it had been charred into clumps, like the bristles of a burned sweeping brush. There was more flesh left on her face, too, pinkish-orange and glistening with intracellular fluid. Her neck and shoulders were a mass of yellow blisters, blister upon blister, although some of them were starting to wrinkle and collapse and weep.

She was wearing a pale grey cardigan with a pink cotton blouse underneath it, and a pair of black Levi jeans. Inspector Fennessy had probably been close when he guessed her age at mid- to late thirties; the jeans were tighter than an older woman would have worn, but they weren't jeggings.

On her feet she was wearing flat grey canvas deck shoes.

'The pain, I'll tell you, it must have been monstrous,' said Bill Phinner, in his dry, expressionless voice.

Katie didn't answer him. She had accompanied Bill Phinner to more crime scenes now than she could count, and the two of them had stood together and witnessed much more horrifying sights than these two burns victims – men who had been deliberately pushed into combine harvesters, a woman whose husband had pinned her against the garage wall with their car's bumper and left her for days on end to die. Yet this was the first time she had heard him utter a single word of empathy for any of the deceased.

'Did you find anything else in their pockets apart from that bar receipt?' she asked him.

'The female had a pink plastic hair slide in her cardigan pocket and a tissue in her jeans. We'll analyse them both for DNA, but that's just routine. The male had an unused cotton handkerchief and seventy-eight cents in change.'

'I'm surprised that he had a bar receipt in these trousers. They look like his gardening clothes.'

'Well, who knows?' Inspector Fennessy put in. 'Sometimes I'll be getting dressed in the morning and I'll see something that I took out of my trouser pocket the night before and pick it up. Keys, change, receipts. Maybe he meant to take it downstairs and put it in his desk, but forgot.'

'We found three cigarette ends buried in the sand around them,' said Bill Phinner. 'Something else, too, which may or may not be relevant.'

He beckoned to one of his assistants and she passed over a clear plastic evidence bag which he handed to Katie. Holding it up, Katie could see that it contained a tarnished silver medallion, oval in shape, with an embossed picture of a saint on one side and the words *Pray for Us* stamped into the reverse.

'Who's this?' she said. 'I can't quite make out the lettering.'

'Saint Nicholas. Not *only* known as Santa Claus, but the patron saint of prostitutes, among many other disreputable professions, such as thieves and pawnbrokers. Let's put it this way, he takes care of the dregs of society, so long as they promise to try and mend their ways.'

'Where was this found?' asked Katie.

191

'Underneath the right foot of the female victim. She may have been wearing it herself and the chain broke while she was trying to resist being buried, or else it belonged to one of the perpetrators. On the other hand, it's just as likely that it was lost on the beach by a swimmer or a holidaymaker weeks or months or even years ago. We'll do our best, but you can buy these things in their thousands in any religious store in Ireland, or online – www.religiousartefacts.com. We'll try the Veritas shop in Carey's Lane, see if they recognize it, but I can't say that I'm hopeful.'

'All right,' said Katie. She knelt down carefully between the two bodies and examined them both closely, keeping her scented handkerchief pressed over her nose and mouth. The woman's lips were curled up like the Joker's. It was only the effect of the searing heat, which had tightened her facial muscles, but she looked as if she were grinning in glee at the clownish tragedy of her own appearance. The man, on the other hand, could have been a thousand-year-old mummy excavated from an ancient tomb.

Little did they know when they put on these clothes this morning that they would end the day looking like this, and that it was the last time that they would ever get dressed. Katie always thought the same about traffic accident victims, sitting dead in their cars with their clean shirts on, and their teeth freshly brushed, and their stomachs still full of breakfast.

"You'll be calling Dr Reidy, then?' asked Bill Phinner, as Katie stood up straight again.

'Yes. He won't be very happy. One of his assistants has flown off to South America for some international pathology conference and the other's on paternity leave. And I think there's a golf tournament at Ballybunion he was very keen to go to.'

'Oh well, he'll have to make do with Fota. They have a couple of singles tournaments coming up next week. He can watch golf by day and post-mortify by night. I'll text you as soon as these two have been delivered to the morgue.'

Katie pushed her way out of the tent and stood outside for a moment, breathing in the salty sea air. The tide had come in a long way since she had first arrived and Bill Phinner and his team would probably have less than twenty minutes to remove the bodies. After that, the holes in the sand in which they had been buried would fill up with seawater, and all the footprints around them would be washed away, and there would no trace left of the way in which the Pearses had met their deaths.

As she was walking to the car park, Detective Horgan came towards her in a bright blue anorak. His nose was red with cold and his GAA tie was crooked.

'Visa just got back to us, ma'am.'

'Oh, yes. Good. And was it him?'

'It was him all right. Norman Anthony Pearse, Ard na Fálta, Boreenmanna Road, Ballinlough.'

'Well, unless somebody stuffed that receipt into his pocket when he wasn't looking, I think that proves it. You'd best go tell Inspector Fennessy. I'm going back to the station and then I'm calling it a day and going home.'

'Yes, ma'am.' He started to go, but then he stopped and looked at the blue vinyl tents and shook his head. 'What a way to end your life, burned alive like that. Makes you realize what all of them martyrs went through, them and that Bridget Cleary.'

Katie turned her head and looked at him quizzically, but his expression seemed perfectly serious. She never quite knew with Detective Horgan if he was taking the mickey or not. Bridget Cleary was said to have been the last-ever witch burned to death in Ireland, albeit by her husband, Michael, who set fire to her nightgown and then splashed lamp oil all over her, convinced that she was a fairy.

'Yes,' she said, and then continued walking to the car park, where the press and TV reporters were patiently waiting for her, swinging their arms and clapping their hands together to keep warm. She ducked under the crime-scene tape and went up to them.

'It *is* them, isn't it?' asked Dan Keane, taking his cigarette out of his mouth and flicking it away. 'Norman and Meryl Pearse?'

'I'll consider answering that question for you if first of all you answer one of mine. I want to know who tipped you off that we were dealing with an incident down here?'

'Ah stop, Superintendent. You know you can't ask us that.'

'If knowing the name of your informant will help me solve this crime, then I'll have you for obstruction, I promise you.'

'Well, you're more than welcome to try, but I don't think you'll get very far with it. Not after *Keena and Kennedy*.'

He didn't need to explain to Katie what he meant. In the legal action to which he was referring, *Mahon Tribunal vs Keena and Kennedy*, in 2009, the Supreme Court had upheld the right of Irish journalists to keep their sources confidential.

'So, *is* it them?' asked Branna MacSuibhne, holding out her mobile phone to record Katie's answer.

'I'm saying only this: two deceased persons were found on the beach here at Rocky Bay Beach early this afternoon and currently we're making every effort to identify them and determine how they lost their lives.'

'But you suspect that they're Norman and Meryl Pearse, the couple from Ballinlough who found Derek Hagerty by the roadside after he had escaped from the High Kings of Erin?'

'We're pursuing several different avenues of inquiry, but that's all I'm prepared to say for the time being.'

Fionnuala Sweeney said, 'Can you confirm that they were burned alive?'

Katie was beginning to grow angry again, although she tried hard not to let it show. She thought that Acting Chief Superintendent Molloy had been rash and untypically unprofessional when he told the media about the High Kings of Erin and how a married couple from Ballinlough had rescued Derek Hagerty, even if he hadn't identified them. But it was clear that these reporters knew a lot more than that. Somebody was leaking them information, and that made her job ten times more difficult. She always liked to give the media the impression that she was telling them every inconsequential detail about a crime and exactly what progress she was making in solving it, but in reality she was very selective with her press releases. She had always believed in keeping criminals in the dark about how much the Garda had found out about them, right until the very last moment when they were arrested – and even then it was important to hold back some critical details until she finally had to put together the Book of Evidence and present it to their solicitors.

She had seen too many cases in which vital evidence had gone missing or been tampered with retrospectively, and too many cases in which witnesses had been intimidated or beaten, or even killed, like Norman and Meryl Pearse.

'We'll be arranging for a post-mortem examination, of course,' said Katie. 'After that I'll be able to tell you an exact cause of death.'

'But they *were* burned?'

'I'm not saying anything more today, except to appeal for witnesses. If anybody was walking on the cliffs or the seashore around Rocky Bay this morning, would they please contact us, even if they believe they saw nothing out of the ordinary. Also, if anybody was driving on the road between Spruce Grove and Rocky Bay this morning, and passed one or more vehicles coming in the opposite direction, would they please let us know. The road is very narrow and most of the time vehicles have to slow right down and pull over on to the nearside verge to pass each other.'

Dan Keane had stuck another cigarette between his lips and lit it. He looked at Katie with one eye closed and said, 'Do you want to explain to us why you're being so unforthcoming about these murders, Superintendent? This is not like you at all. I mean usually you'll be telling us the colour of the victim's undercrackers, if he was wearing any, and what his star sign was, and what his mother-in-law cooked for her supper last night.'

'I didn't say these people were murdered, Dan. I said only that they were found deceased.'

'But they *were* murdered, weren't they?' put in Branna MacSuibhne. 'They were buried in the sand and doused with petrol and set fire to.'

'Absolutely no comment, Branna. I'll have Tadhg McElvin get in touch with you all as soon we're ready to give you more.'

'Well, I hope it's soon,' said Dan Keane, blowing out smoke. 'Otherwise tomorrow morning's banner is going to be "Why Are Garda So Secretive About Horrific Double Homicide"?'

Katie left them and walked up the slope to her car. Her feelings were more and more mixed up and she was beginning to lose confidence in her own authority. Even worse than that, she was beginning to mistrust her fellow police officers at Anglesea Street. She badly needed to know who was leaking information to the media before she had approved it, especially since the premature release of that information was making it almost impossible for her to find out what was really going on.

She climbed into her car, reversed sharply, and then started the half-hour drive back to the city.

As she drove, she found herself chanting the little jump-rope song that she had learned in high babies:

Are you a witch or are you fairy?

Or are you the wife of Michael Cleary?

Twenty-Three

Walking along the corridor, she saw that the door to Acting Chief Superintendent Molloy's office was ajar and that his lights were on. She knocked and opened the door wider. Bryan Molloy was sitting at his desk, talking on the phone. He was wearing a sandy-coloured tweed jacket and a pale green turtleneck sweater that was too tight for him around the neck. He nodded towards the chair on the opposite side of his desk, indicating that Katie should sit down, but she remained standing.

'All right, Denis,' he was saying. 'I'll see what I can do for you. No promises, mind. I may be the Acting Top Cop here at the moment, like, but I haven't been promoted to Acting God. Not yet, anyway.' 'All right.' 'Yes. Good. Good luck to you so.'

When he had finished his call, he kept the receiver held up in his hand, which gave Katie the impression that he was about to dial somebody else and that she was interrupting him. 'Yes?' he said.

'I've just come back from Rocky Bay Beach. We haven't yet formally identified the victims, but I'm certain that it's Mr and Mrs Pearse.'

'I see. Bang goes our evidence, then, that Derek Hagerty might have been faking it.'

'Not entirely. I still think there's a strong chance that we can persuade him to admit it.'

'Oh, I think you'll be fierce lucky to get him to do that. He's bricking it. And what else do you have? Norman Pearse was the only one who claimed to have seen Hagerty's bruises washed off,

197

and Norman Pearse was the only one who heard him talking on his mobile phone.'

'I realize that. But Meryl Pearse had a friend with her when she found Hagerty lying by the road. We don't know who it was yet, but we're working on it, and whoever it was might be able to help us.'

'Well, good luck with that. If Hagerty doesn't dare to speak, you don't think this friend will, do you, always supposing that you can find them? So, any road, how was the crime scene? Any good forensics?'

'Forget about the forensics for the moment – the media only showed up. Dan Keane, Fionnuala Sweeney, and that Branna girl from the *Echo*.'

'And? It was a major crime scene, on a public beach, what did you expect?'

'I expected no media at all, not until I was ready for them. I urgently need to find out who tipped them off.'

Bryan Molloy pouted out his bottom lip and shrugged. 'Could have been anybody. You know what these journos are like, they have eyes and ears everywhere.'

'No – they knew details that only somebody on the inside of this investigation could have given them. They already knew that it was Norman and Meryl Pearse and they already knew that they'd been half buried and burned.'

Bryan Molloy said nothing, but shrugged again, with his index finger still poised over his telephone keypad.

'Bryan – ' Katie demanded. 'Are you not worried in the slightest that somebody inside this station could be passing confidential information to the media? If this carries on, my investigation into these High Kings of Erin could be seriously compromised. It's causing me enough complications already.'

Bryan Molloy shook his head from side to side as if he were patiently trying to explain something to a young child. 'Katie, the security of your investigation is your responsibility, not mine. Believe it or not, I don't only have crime to take care of.

I also have national security and immigration. I have traffic management and road safety. I have community relations and antisocial behaviour. I have inter-agency cooperation to improve the quality of life for people in Cork. I have strategic planning. If we have a mole here in the station, then it's entirely down to you to sniff him out – him or *her* – and deal with them. In any case, it's most likely that it's somebody on your own team, in my opinion. Somebody with a gambling habit? Somebody who's looking for a little extra grade?'

'My team are irreproachable. All of them.'

'Oh yes? What about that detective sergeant what's-her-name? Ni Nuallán? She's an odd wan, if you ask me. Wouldn't surprise me at all if she was a carpet muncher.'

Katie said, '*Bryan* – Kyna Ni Nuallán is a very effective and highly respected member of my team, and I won't tolerate you talking about her like that.'

'So what are you going to do? Report me? Come on, Katie, don't act so grim. I was only rowling with you.'

'You think it's a joke, do you, to call one of my detectives a lesbian?'

Bryan put down his phone with a bang. 'You listen to me, Detective Superintendent Maguire, I was an inspector when you were still waving on tractors and helping snotty little kids across the road. It's not my fault that you're making a fecking bags of this investigation. I know it's complicated, but sorting out complicated, that's your fecking job. You've been wrong-footed right from the very beginning, so don't come cribbing to me about somebody leaking information. It's up to you to cover your own arse.'

Katie could think of at least three different retorts to that, but she knew that it was pointless. The only way to deal with a man like Bryan Molloy was to let him think that she had given him the last word and then wait patiently for him to become overconfident and make some foolish mistake. *If you wait by the River Lee long enough*, she thought, misquoting the Chinese warrior Sun Tzu, *you will see the body of your enemy float by.*

She took a deep breath, and then said, 'I'm putting a call in to Dr Reidy. Then I'm calling it a day. You wouldn't want to be paying me overtime for making such a pig's dinner of things, would you? I'll be talking to the media tomorrow, as soon as we've formally identified the victims.'

'Is that it, then?' said Bryan Molloy, picking up his phone again.

'Yes,' said Katie. 'That's it. I'll see you in the morning. Good luck to you so.'

Twenty-Four

It was cold and foggy when she left Anglesea Street and by the time she was driving down beside the river towards Cobh the fog was so thick that she had to slow down to 10 mph. The streetlights looked like dandelion clocks.

She turned into her driveway and was annoyed with herself for not having switched the porch light on. She still hadn't quite become accustomed to living alone – drawing the curtains in the living room if she expected to be late back, taking a Tesco ready meal out of the freezer in the morning to defrost, tidying the bed. Out of everything, that was what saddened her the most, coming back to find the bed exactly as she had left it when she woke up. Idle as he was, even Paul used to straighten the quilt and plump up the pillows.

In the darkness of the porch she had to jab her key two or three times before she found the lock. As she turned the key, a ship leaving the harbour let out a long, mournful hoot, as if to emphasize her loneliness. When she pushed open the door, however, Barney came snuffling and waffling and tail-wagging up to her. At least somebody's pleased to see me, she thought.

She went through to the nursery and locked her revolver in the chest of drawers. Looking around at the baby-blue wallpaper, she wondered if it was time to stop calling it the nursery and redecorate it, so she could use it as a home office. *Everything comes to an end*, she thought, *even though you never believe that it will. People die, lovers walk out of the door. All that remains is the rain.*

She went back into the living room, switched on the television and poured herself a large glass of Smirnoff Black Label. RTÉ's nine o'clock news would be starting in a few minutes and she wanted to see if Fionnuala Sweeney had filed a report on Rocky Bay Beach. Barney trotted over and sat close to her, resting his head on her lap. She stroked his back and tugged at his ears, which he always liked. She would have to take him for his walk later, even though it was so foggy.

The news was just beginning when her doorbell chimed. 'Out of the way, Barns,' she said, and went to answer it.

'Who is it?' she called out, standing to one side of the door. Her previous chief superintendent, Dermot O'Driscoll, had recommended that she install CCTV in her porch, but she had never got around to arranging it.

'It's me,' said a man's voice. 'David.'

She opened the door and found David Kane standing outside with a smile on his face, holding up a bottle of champagne.

'Bolly,' he said.

'David. It's late. I have a very early start tomorrow.'

'Oh, come on. It's never too late for a glass of bubbly!'

'What about Sorcha?'

'Dead to the world, as usual, with her medication. She won't wake up until eight o'clock tomorrow. Thank you, clozapine, I love you!'

'I'm sorry, David. I'm serious. I've had a very long and difficult day and I really do need to have an early night.'

'Well, we don't have to drink the bubbly now. Maybe we could have it for breakfast.'

'You can't stay the night, David,' said Katie. 'Apart from anything else, I'm not in the mood. I'm extremely tired and I haven't even eaten yet.'

'So what were you thinking of having for your dinner?'

'I don't know. Something simple and quick, like an omelette.'

'Oh, Katie, my darling, you should taste my omelettes. I'm a master chef when it comes to omelettes. I'll make one for you and you can have a glass of bubbly while you're watching me cook it. And this is the good stuff, not your Tesco Prosecco.'

'David,' said Katie, 'I need to be alone tonight. Thanks for bringing round the champagne, and thanks for the offer of an omelette, but really – no thanks.'

David frowned. 'What's the matter with you? I thought you and me were getting along famously.'

'Nothing's the matter with me, David. It's just that I need to unwind and I need to do it in peace and quiet, by myself.'

'I'll just sit there. I won't say a word.'

'David – no.'

'There is something wrong, isn't there, and it's not just the monthlies?'

'No. Nothing's wrong. Now, please – I have to take Barney for his walk and it's getting late.'

David's eyes narrowed, as if he suspected that she was lying. 'Last night you couldn't get into bed with me fast enough. Now you don't want to know. Don't tell me *you're* bipolar, too. Jesus. That would be just my luck, wouldn't it? Both my wife and my mistress, manic depressives!'

'David, I'm not your mistress, and I never will be. If you really want to know, I'm quite happy to be friends with you, but I don't want to sleep with you again.'

'What?' he said. 'You can't tell me that wasn't the best sex you ever had in your whole life?'

'I can, as a matter of fact. But that's not the issue. The simple reality is that I don't want to have an affair with you, no matter how casual it is.'

'You're serious?'

'Yes. I'm serious.'

'And that wasn't the best sex you ever had in your whole life?'

'No.'

David lowered his head and slowly stroked his chin, like a man pondering a deep mathematical problem, or a cryptic crossword clue. Then, with no warning at all, he swung the Bollinger bottle around and smashed it against the porch railing. The floor was covered in shards of shattered green glass and fizzing champagne.

David pointed his finger at Katie and said, 'You know what you are, don't you, Katie? There's a word for women like you.'

'Go away out of here,' Katie told him. 'Go home and look after your wife.'

'You're in your flowers right now, but you'll miss me. Tomorrow night when you're in bed alone you'll remember what I was like, and you'll regret it.'

'Go home, David. Either you're langered or you've been snorting something.'

'God, you're so high and mighty. Just because you're a detective, you think you have the right to treat me like I'm some kind of dirtball.'

'David, go home. If you don't go home now I'll arrest you for harassment and threatening a police officer.'

David closed his eyes for a few moments, as if he were consulting some inner advisor, and then he said, 'Okay, Katie. I'm sorry. I apologize. I lost my temper, that's all. I'm not really used to women saying no.'

He looked down at the broken glass and said, 'Do you have a dustpan and brush? I'll sweep this all up for you. I'm sorry.'

'Just go home, David. I can clear it up myself in the morning.'

'We can still be friends, though, can't we?'

Katie started to close the front door. 'I honestly don't know,' she said. 'I'll have to think about it. Now, please, go.'

David hesitated, and then he went. Katie closed the door, bolted it and slid on the security chain. Barney was standing in the hallway looking up at her expectantly, ready for his walk.

'Sorry, Barns. Not tonight. You'll have to make do with the back yard.'

After she had let him out of the kitchen door, she returned to the living room and sat down. It was only then that she realized how quickly her heart was thumping. What made her feel so stressed was not just the way in which David had lost his temper so suddenly, but the fact that she still found him sexually attractive. His violent show of frustration had alarmed her at the time, but in retrospect it had aroused her, too. She hadn't known many men who would smash a 70-euro bottle of champagne just because they wanted to go to bed with her so much.

Even though she hadn't forgotten the disinterested look on his face as he had pushed his way in and out of her, there was a lot about him that aroused her. That bald penis, almost sculptural, and the way that it had felt against her own bare skin. That self-possession and those secretive smiles, as if he knew something about her that even she didn't know. Maybe that came from years of working as a vet and learning to understand creatures that couldn't express themselves in words, only with their eyes.

She finished the dregs of her vodka and was considering pouring herself another one when Fionnuala Sweeney appeared on the TV screen, with Rocky Bay Beach behind her. The sky was growing dark, so this report must have been recorded about half past six. Katie could see that the blue Technical Bureau tents were being dismantled and the tide was already sluicing in as far as the rocks.

'The badly burned bodies of a man and a woman were found today on the beach here at Rocky Bay. Gardaí were tight-lipped about their identities and how they had died, but we understand that they were a married couple from Ballinlough, Norman and Meryl Pearse. Norman Pearse was a manager at Faraway Travel in the city centre, and his wife worked for Eason's bookstore.

'Mrs Pearse is believed to have found Derek Hagerty, the owner of Hagerty's Autos at Looney's Cross, after he had managed to escape from being abducted by the now-notorious kidnap gang calling themselves the High Kings of Erin. Mr Hagerty was in a poor condition by the roadside, but Mrs Pearse and her husband took him into their home to recover.

'Before Mr Pearse dropped off Mr Hegarty in Cork City centre, however, he informed the gardaí and Mr Hegarty was taken into protective custody, where he remains today. Reliable sources suggest that Mr and Mrs Pearse may have been punished for notifying the gardaí, and because they knew too much about Mr Hagerty's abduction, and who might be responsible.

'The same sources say that Mr and Mrs Pearse were buried up to their armpits in sand and then doused in petrol which was set alight.

'Detective Superintendent Kathleen Maguire who attended the scene today refused to confirm or deny the identities of the victims or how they had met their deaths. She also declined to comment on the suggestion that the murders may have been committed by the High Kings of Erin, who netted a quarter of a million euros in ransom money for Derek Hagerty even though he had already escaped.'

Katie could only sit and watch this report with a growing feeling of helplessness and frustration. But Bryan Molloy had been right. It was up to her to ferret out these 'reliable sources' who were leaking so much confidential information to the media. After all, he had made it clear that *he* wasn't going to do it, not the great Acting Top Cop.

She poured herself another drink and went into the kitchen. Barney was scratching at the door, so she let him in, and he brought with him the smell of damp dog hair and fog. She went to the fridge and took out three eggs, which she cracked into a Pyrex jug. The third egg crushed to pieces in her hand and all the shell dropped into the omelette mixture.

She started to fish out the fragments of broken shell with a teaspoon, but then she suddenly lost patience and threw the jug into the sink. The jug didn't break, but bounced up, so that egg was splashed all the way up the right-hand curtains and halfway across the window.

Katie didn't cry, but stood there watching the egg sliding slowly down the windowpane.

***

That night, she was woken up by the sound of shouting from next door, followed by screaming and the loud slamming of doors.

She lifted her head from the pillow and squinted at her bedside clock. It was 3.07. So much for Sorcha sleeping until morning.

The shouting and screaming went on for at least ten minutes. Katie lay there in the darkness, wondering if she should go next door and intervene, but in the end she decided it would be wiser not to. God knows what an angry David Kane would tell his wife if she tried to stick her nose in, especially after tonight's performance on the porch.

After ten minutes there was absolute silence, which in some ways was more disturbing than all the arguing. Katie remained awake for nearly an hour afterwards, but eventually she slept. She dreamed that she was back in Knocknadeenly, talking to John, trying to persuade him to come and take Barney for a walk with her, but he kept his back to her and wouldn't turn around.

'All right, then,' she said. '*Don't* come. See if I care.'

He still wouldn't turn to face her. 'I'll be gone by the time you get back,' he told her, and even in her dream she was sure that she would never see him again.

Twenty-Five

Next day, the sky was slate-grey and it was raining hard. Shoppers hurried to and fro past the windows of Pat Whelan's shop as if they were fleeing from some major disaster.

Only one customer came in all morning, at ten minutes to twelve, when Pat was almost ready to close. He was a fiftyish man with a crimson face and wet grey straggly hair. When he had closed the shop door behind him, he stood on the mat and shook his old-fashioned black rubber mackintosh with a rumble like distant thunder.

He approached the counter and said, in a slurry accent, 'The Broad Black Brimmer.'

'The Broad Black Brimmer?' asked Pat. 'What of it?'

The crimson-faced man leaned closer, and his breath was sour with last night's Guinness. 'The sheet music, if you have it, on account of me and my friends are holding a republican evening.'

'Oh yes?'

The crimson-faced man spoke with the precision of somebody who knows that he's still under the influence of drink. 'We're commemorating the amnesty that the Free State offered to the soldiers of the IRA in October 1922.'

Pat went across to the racks of sheet music and started to sort through the section devoted to the Wolfe Tones. 'And – ah – why would you be commemorating *that*, like?'

'Because the boys told them to *shtick* their amnesty, that's why.

They stayed true to the cause. And because of that, a lot more of them died. It's them we'll be honouring.'

Pat found him the sheet music of 'The Broad Black Brimmer', but as he went over to the till he couldn't stop himself from glancing apprehensively towards the street outside. Shortly after a quarter past seven that morning he had received a phone call from the carroty-curled young man, advising him in that hoarse, throaty voice to step out of his shop at noon precisely, and lock it, leaving a sign on the door saying 'Back in 5 Minutes'. That would indicate that he had intended to return, and that he hadn't been a party to his own kidnapping.

He felt tingly with nerves but at the same time felt an under-lying sense of relief. For over three years now, he hadn't been able to see any way at all to clear his debts and the future had appeared unrelentingly grim. He had already accepted that he would probably have to sell his house, and his car, and all his stock for a knock-down price. He wasn't at all sure that his marriage could survive him going bankrupt. Mairead had already talked about going to live with her sister in Waterford, and he could hardly blame her.

'You should come along,' said the crimson-faced man. 'We're holding it at Quinlan's, tomorrow night. We'll be singing all the good old favourites – "Come Out Ye Black and Tans", "The Boys of Fair Hill".'

He broke into song, waving his hands as if he were conducting a choir. 'The smell on Patrick's Bridge is wicked, how does Father Mathew stick it? Here's up them all, say the boys of Fair Hill!'

He cackled and snorted and shook his head.

Pat said, 'Thanks for the invitation, but I can't.'

'You'd have a whale of a time. At least think about it.'

'No, I can't.'

'Oh, pity. Are you going away, then?'

'Something like that.'

'Off on your holliers?'

'Something like that.'

'Oh yes? Where are you going, like?'

Pat hesitated. Then he said, 'Nowhere in particular. In fact, I just might come to Quinlan's. I could do with a night out.'

If the guards manage to trace this fellow, he was thinking, seeing as how he'll probably be the last person I talked to before I went missing, that will confirm that I had no idea at all that I was going to be kidnapped.

The crimson-faced man rolled up the sheet music and stuck it into his raincoat pocket. Pat followed him to the door to let him out.

'I'll be seeing you at Quinlan's, then, most likely,' said the crimson-faced man. He leaned out into the street and stuck out his hand, palm upwards, squinting up at the sky. 'The fecking angels are crying again. Don't know what they're so fecking sad about.' Then he teetered off down the street, stumbling over one of the high raised kerbstones and nearly falling in front of a taxi.

Pat checked his watch. Three minutes to twelve. *Oh well, deep breath, Pat, now's the time.* He went to the back of the shop to collect his khaki waterproof jacket and switch off the lights and set the alarm.

Before he left, he looked around the shop and had a strange feeling that he would never set foot in it again, although there was no logical reason why he shouldn't. Once he had received his share of the ransom money, he would at least have a chance to arrange some kind of repayment plan with his creditors, and maybe he could find a way to save the business from closure.

He locked the front door and started to walk eastwards along Oliver Plunkett Street towards Parnell Place, as he had been instructed on the phone. The rain was lashing down now and he gripped the collar of his jacket and kept his head down. A young woman in a red raincoat collided with him and almost poked out his left eye out with the spokes of her umbrella, but when she said, 'Jesus, I'm sorry!' he simply waved one hand to show her that it didn't matter, and carried on walking.

210

He reached the corner of Parnell Place and hesitated, looking south towards Parnell Bridge, blinking against the raindrops on his eyelashes. Parnell Place was one-way, with traffic coming from his right, but at that moment there was no traffic at all, only parked cars.

Now that he had locked the shop and was out on the street, he was beginning to doubt that he was doing the right thing. Perhaps by agreeing to this mock-kidnapping he was being a coward rather than a realist. All right, he was up to his ears in debt, and this ginger-haired young feen had threatened him with God knows what if he didn't play along. But he was still his own man and he had always prided himself on being afraid of nobody or nothing. Apart from that, faking his own abduction to extort money was a serious crime. If he were found out, he could face a long stretch in jail.

He looked across to the other side of the road, to the cream-painted facade of the Panda Mama Chinese Restaurant on the corner. The carroty-curled young man had told him to walk slowly over towards it. The plan was that a car would pull up in front of him, two men would climb out, and they would snatch him. Parnell Place was never too crowded, so it was unlikely that anybody would come to his assistance, but there were bound to be at least three or four witnesses.

As he stepped off the kerb, a dark blue Ford Mondeo that was parked outside Mulligan's pub started its engine and reversed out into the street. It stopped for a second as the driver changed gear, then started driving towards him with its headlights on full.

He was suddenly gripped by the thought, This is sheer fecking madness. What the feck am I doing this for? These people are criminals and I'm allowing them to take me away?

The Mondeo slithered to a halt right in front of him. Its doors were flung open and two bulky bald-headed men climbed out of it. He turned around and started running away, back along Oliver Plunkett Street, running in the road because the pavements were too crowded. He ran as fast as he could, not even looking behind him to see if the men were coming after him.

He dodged an elderly couple crossing the road in front of him and almost lost his balance, staggering like a man running too fast down a steep hill. A green An Post van blew its horn at him and a cyclist shouted something abusive that he didn't catch.

He wasn't fit. He had only recently given up smoking and he had been drinking far too much since the business had started to lose money. And just as he passed the Ovens Bar, gasping, the crimson-faced man in the black rubber raincoat stepped out in front of him, as if from nowhere at all, and seized the sleeve of his jacket. He slewed around, panting, with clear snot running from his nostrils and rain dripping from his chin. He was too breathless to speak, but he tried to wrench his arm away. The crimson-faced man clung on to him, his eyes staring and fierce, not smiling or friendly at all now, and wouldn't let him go.

'I had a feeling you might lose your bottle, boy. That's why I've been waiting here for ye.'

'Get the – get the feck off of me – '

'I will in me bollocks.'

A few seconds later, the two bouncer-types arrived and immediately seized Pat's arms. Several passers-by stopped to stare at them, but nobody made any attempt to come over and ask what was going on. It was raining too hard, and in any case they didn't look like the sort of men who would take kindly to being challenged.

'You came to a solemn agreement,' said the crimson-faced man. 'You can't go back on a solemn agreement.'

'I didn't agree to nothing,' Pat protested, as the bouncer-types tugged him back along the street, half marching and half hopping. The Mondeo had followed them, even though Oliver Plunkett Street was a pedestrian-only zone after eleven in the morning. One of the bouncer-types opened the back door and pushed Pat inside, climbing in next to him, while the other walked around the car and wedged himself in on the other side. The crimson-faced man sat himself in the front passenger seat. 'Right,' he said to the driver, 'let's get the fuck out of here.'

The driver was a young man with spiky blond hair and a red spot on the end of his nose and sunglasses, in spite of the gloom. He twisted around in his seat and reversed at speed all the way back to Parnell Place, the gearbox whining in protest.

'I want you to let me out,' said Pat, his voice quaking. 'I've been thinking about this and I've come to a decision. I don't want any part of it.'

'A bit late now, Pat,' said the crimson-faced man, without turning round.

'I won't say a word to nobody, I swear to God.'

'Too right you fecking won't. You won't get the fecking opportunity.'

'Just let me out. I can deal with my financial problems on my own.'

'You're too late, Pat. I told you. Now shut the front door, would you?'

'Listen – ' Pat began, but one of the bouncer-types took hold of his right ear and twisted it around so hard that it felt as if he were tearing it off.

'Jesus Christ!' he exclaimed, pressing his hand to the side of his head.

'It's like you were told,' said the crimson-faced man. 'Either you cooperate willingly or else we'll have to *force* you to cooperate, and we don't want to have to do that. It only makes for bad feeling.'

'Jesus Christ, that hurt.'

'I'm sure that it did, like. Now let's have some peace and quiet, shall we, unless you want more of the same.'

They were driving along Merchants Quay now, alongside the river. The crimson-faced man turned around in his seat and held out a black woollen scarf. 'Right now, Pat, we're going to put a blindfold on you. You won't mind that, will you? It's entirely for your own protection, like, so we can be sure that you can't tell anybody where we're taking you. It wouldn't be like a real kidnap, would it, if you knew where you were?'

Pat said nothing, but closed his eyes as one of the bouncer-types tied the scarf tightly around his head. It smelled strongly of cigarette smoke, and even though he kept his eyes closed it still made them water.

Twenty-Six

When Katie left for the city at seven-thirty in the morning David Kane's Range Rover was still parked in the next-door driveway, so she hadn't gone to see if Sorcha needed any help. If his tantrum on the porch last night was anything to go by, she was beginning to ask herself if he had been telling her the whole truth about his marriage, and Sorcha's violent rages. She thought that if she ever found herself married to a man who smashed champagne bottles when he was denied sex, she would probably end up doolally, too.

It was so dark in her office that she had to switch on the lights, and her desk lamp as well. The rain pattered against the windows like somebody throwing handfuls of currants at them.

She had only just started to leaf through the messages on her desk when Detective Horgan appeared at her door.

'Morning, ma'am. Miserable old day today. *Drawky*, my grannie would have called it.'

'What did you want?' Katie asked him. 'I have to go and interview Derek Hagerty again in a minute.'

Detective Horgan held up a green manila folder. 'It's Acting Chief Superintendent Molloy, ma'am. I've been checking with the Companies Registration Office in Dublin and I've discovered that he's the majority shareholder in a limited partnership called Flathead Consultants.'

'*Flathead* Consultants? And what do they do?'

'Construction consultants, apparently, whatever that means. They haven't yet lodged their accounts for last year, but in the

215

previous year they had a turnover of one and a half million euros and made a profit of six hundred and seventy thousand.'

'Construction consultants?' said Katie. 'What on earth would Bryan Molloy know about construction?'

'I suppose "construction" could cover a whole multitude of things to do with building. Getting planning permission, that kind of thing. Molloy has very close contacts with lots of politicians, doesn't he? Goes to all their fancy banquets, plays golf with them regular. They're all Masons, too.'

'Maybe you're right. So where did all of this turnover come from?'

Detective Horgan opened the file and turned over the first two pages. 'Most of it came from a company called Crossagalla Groundworks. They're a civil engineering company based in Limerick.'

'And what do we know about Crossagalla Groundworks?'

'Not much. The names of their directors and not a lot else. They have a website, but all it gives you is a list of what projects they've been involved in, like the wastewater works at Carrigrenan.'

'Okay,' said Katie. 'Why don't you get in touch with Henry Street and see what they can tell you about them? Meanwhile – look – I have to go. We're holding a media conference at eleven and apart from talking to Derek Hagerty I have to get up to speed on these Rocky Beach murders.'

Detective Horgan turned to leave the office and as he did so he almost collided with Bill Phinner, who was still wearing his lab coat, as well as his usual mournful expression. He always looked to Katie as if his dog had just died and he had lost a bundle of money on the races at Mallow, both on the same day.

'Good morning to you, Bill,' she said. 'What's the story?'

'Oh, good morning,' he said, looking over at the rain that was dribbling down the windows. 'Not that good, though. I have a leaky attic roof at home that needs fixing.'

'What about our victims? Have we identified them yet?'

'We're still waiting on the DNA. We should get the results of that in an hour or two. But the female had three fingers of her left hand curled up tight against her palm, so that the fingertips weren't burned, and we were able to take some good prints off of them.'

He laid the printouts of two sets of fingerprints on her desk, both of which had been marked with red felt-tip pen.

'We compared them with all the prints that we lifted last night from the Pearse house, and they matched all right. So the female is definitely Meryl Pearse. We'll be double-checking, of course, with the hairs we've taken from their combs and brushes, and the residue from Norman Pearse's electric razor, but I don't think there's very much doubt as to the male's identity.'

'How about the footprints?' Katie asked him.

'They were a bit of a jumble, I have to admit, but I put young Phelan on it and he has a very sharp eye for detail, that boy. Apart from the victims, there were four other people on the beach, all of them men, judging by the size of their feet and what they must have weighed. One was wearing Irish Setter RutMaster rubber boots, size ten. Another was wearing Cofra Somalia safety boots, size eleven. A third was wearing a standard pair of Dunlop wellingtons, also size eleven. The fourth was wearing an ordinary smooth-soled leather shoe, but with quite a distinctive pointed toe.'

'So if we found the people who were wearing them, you could positively identify those boots and shoes, and match them to their owners?'

'No trouble at all. Every boot and shoe impression has its own unique markings, caused by wear and tear. And every boot and shoe has perspiration inside it, and perspiration gives us DNA, just like mucus and earwax and urine and faeces and vomit – and even tears.'

'Yes, thanks a million, Bill, I know all about that, but I've not long ago had breakfast. What about the cigarette butts?'

'We've tested those for DNA, too, but like I say, we've not yet had the results back and I can't say I'm particularly hopeful that we'll be able to make a match – not until you bring in a suspect we can match them with. We're still checking the Saint Nicholas medallion, but again I don't think that can help us much until we have a suspect who might have been seen wearing it. Even then . . . you know, there are thousands of them.'

'Well, thanks, Bill,' said Katie. 'Anything else you can tell me?'

'Not at the moment. Once we're able formally to say for sure that it's Mr and Mrs Pearse, we'll be able to go through their house inch by inch for forensics and that may give us some more.'

Bill Phinner picked up his printouts and left. Katie quickly finished sorting through her messages, but there was nothing urgent that she had to attend to. An update from Detective Dooley, telling her that he had interviewed the last of the wedding guests from the Gallagher–O'Malley ceilidh, but hadn't been able to glean any more information about who might have brought the cake with Micky Crounan's head in it. An invitation to talk to the sixth-year students at Christ King Girls' Secondary School in Douglas about women's careers in law enforcement. A lengthy memo from Finola McFerren, the state solicitor, about the Michael Gerrety hearing, with a list of proposals for future prosecutions.

There was also a report from Sergeant Ni Nuallán about the continuing search for Roisin Begley. Three members of the public had reported seeing a girl who answered her description – one in Togher, on the south side of the city, and two in the city centre. This increased the possibility that she was still alive, and unharmed, but they were no nearer to discovering what had happened to her or where she might be.

She switched off her desk lamp, but before she left her office she went over to the window and stared through the raindrops at the Elysian Tower, the tallest building in Ireland, pale green and almost ghostly in the gloom. Only a few of its windows were lit up, because so many of the apartments were still unoccupied, but the lights near the top were shining. That was where Michael Gerrety lived. She could imagine him up there, talking and laughing, and she found herself breathing more deeply and narrowing her eyes, like a predatory animal. She would get him one day.

***

Katie went downstairs to Interview Room Two where Derek Hagerty was waiting for her. He was sitting at the table in the centre of the room with a polystyrene cup of tea in front of him, looking weary and unkempt, an old dog that no longer has the energy to groom itself.

In the corner of the room, a young female garda was tapping at her mobile phone, but as soon as Katie came in she dropped it in her pocket and stood up.

'That's all right,' Katie told her. 'You can take a bit of a break, if you like. I'll call you when I've finished.'

She drew out the chair opposite Derek Hagerty and sat down. He glanced up at her once, and then lowered his eyes again, staring at his cup of tea.

'Hello, Derek,' she said.

Derek Hagerty grimaced and nodded, although he didn't say anything and he didn't look up.

There was a long pause, but eventually Katie said, 'Well? Aren't you curious to know what's happened to the Pearses?'

Still he didn't look up. 'Have you found them?' he asked, with phlegm in his throat. He coughed to clear it, and then he said, 'Are they back home now?'

'Oh, we've found them all right, but they're not back home. They'll never be going back home now, except if their families decide to hold a wake there.'

Now Derek Hagerty did raise his eyes. 'They're *dead*?' he said.

'They were taken to the beach at Rocky Bay. They were half buried in the sand, and then they had petrol poured all over them, and they were set alight. We're not one hundred per cent sure if they were still alive when they were burning, but it seems unlikely that anybody would go to the trouble of burying them up to their chests if they were already dead, don't you think?'

Derek Hagerty pressed his hands to his ears as if he couldn't bear to hear any more.

'Oh God,' he said. 'Oh Jesus, dear Jesus, what have I done?'

Katie leaned forward. 'I'll tell you what you've done, Derek. You've got yourself mixed up with some very evil and heartless criminals. You can't blame yourself entirely. I don't think you had any conception of how vicious they could be. You were naive, and you were foolish, and now Norman and Meryl Pearse have both been murdered because of your naivety. But you do have a chance to redeem yourself.'

'I can't tell you anything! I can't! What if they take my Shelagh and set fire to *her*? What if they catch up with me one day, which they will, and burn me to death? Oh God, I can't stand this any more! That poor, poor woman! And her poor husband! God! All they wanted to do was help me!'

'Derek, you said that Meryl had a friend with her when she found you by the roadside.'

Derek Hagerty pulled a tissue out of the box on the table and wiped the tears from his eyes. 'She did, yes,' he sniffed.

'Do you have any idea who he was? We're worried that if we don't protect him, he could be in danger, too. It's quite clear that these people are determined to eliminate anyone who could testify against them.'

Derek Hagerty shook his head. 'I don't know for sure. I think he might have been an old boyfriend of hers. They'd been out together for a drink or something, so far as I could tell. I heard them arguing about what she was going to tell her husband. She dropped him off at Anderson's Quay before she drove me back to her house.'

'Can you describe him?'

'Not really. Not bad-looking. Brownish hair. He was wearing a dark blue coat with a light blue sweater underneath it. She called him Eoghan.'

'Eoghan? You're sure about that?'

'She said something like, "Nothing happened between us, did it, Eoghan?" Something like that.'

Katie said, 'Good. That's a start. Now tell me how you first got involved with these people who were supposed to have abducted you. Did you know any of them before this was all fixed up?'

'I'm not saying any more. I've told you about Mrs Pearse's friend, but that's only in case they try to kill him, too. If I tell you any more, and they find out about it, I won't stand an earthly.'

'You know that I could arrest you now and charge you with conspiracy? You could be facing years in jail.'

'At least I'd be safe.'

'Safe? In jail? I hope you're not serious. You don't know how many friends your co-conspirators have in jail – friends who might be only too happy to do them a favour and stick a chiv in you, or cut your throat with a razor-blade glued to a toothbrush.'

Derek Hagerty said, 'No! I'm not saying another word! You can threaten me as much as you like, but I'm not telling you anything more! Look what happened when I let it slip about the Pearses. Mother of God – they did that? They really burned them alive?'

'Yes,' said Katie. 'They really did. You'll see it on the news this evening.'

'Holy heart of Jesus. I can't bear it.'

'Derek, I'm giving you one last chance. Tell me who these people are who kidnapped you. Even if you're afraid to tell me their names, at least give me *something* to go on. It needn't come out that it was you that told me. Otherwise I won't have any alternative. I'll have to arrest you.'

'Then arrest me. And tell the media that you've arrested me. And tell them why – that I've refused to give you any information about the gang who abducted me.'

'Derek,' said Katie. 'I've no doubt at all that they're going to do the same thing to somebody else, and that more innocent people are going to be killed as collateral damage, like the Pearses, and like poor young Garda McCracken. Do you want to have *those* people on your conscience, too?'

'I'm sorry,' said Derek Hagerty. 'I can't be persuaded. Nothing that you can do to me would be as bad as what those fellows could do. They pulled out my teeth with pliers, for Christ's sake, with no anaesthetic at all except for half a bottle of Paddy's, and that almost fecking killed me. And that was when I was cooperating with them.'

'So you *were* cooperating with them?'

Derek Hagerty looked up again, startled at his own admission. 'I never said that. I never said that I cooperated. I didn't cooperate.'

Katie lifted up her iPhone. 'You did so. I have it on here.'

'Well, I didn't. I deny it. I totally deny it. I was taken by force against my will and it was only by a pure miracle that I escaped with my life. That's all. From now on, I'm keeping my mouth shut, and you can't force me to incriminate myself. If you're going to arrest me, I want to call my solicitor.'

'Have it your own way,' said Katie. 'Derek Hagerty, I am arresting you under Section Seventeen of the Criminal Justice Act 1994, for conspiracy to demand money with menaces. You are not obliged to say anything, but if you wish to do so whatever you say will be taken down in writing and may be given in evidence.'

Derek Hagerty said nothing. Katie sat staring at him for almost half a minute, giving him one more chance to change his mind. The only sounds were the rain pattering against the window and the distant echoing of somebody shouting. A door slammed. Somebody walked along the corridor outside, whistling, their rubber-soled shoes squeaking. Another door slammed.

Katie stood up. 'I don't exactly know what you've got yourself into, Derek, but I can promise you that this is not the way out of it. An officer will be with you shortly to read the charge sheet against you.'

Derek Hagerty remained silent and completely motionless. Katie had the feeling that he wanted to stay like that for ever. If time stood still, then he would never have to suffer the consequences of what he had done. But the minute hand of the clock on the wall behind him shuddered to twelve – and at that moment Pat was locking the door of his music shop on Oliver Plunkett Street and stepping out into the rain.

***

Katie found Detective Sergeant Ni Nuallán in the canteen, eating a messy corned-beef sandwich and talking to Detective Garda Nessa Goold, who had joined Katie's team only three weeks before. Detective Garda Goold was a dark-haired girl, pretty but slightly plump, with dark brown eyes and eyebrows that could have done with some plucking, and a dark brown mole on her upper lip. She stood up as Katie approached their table, but Katie waved her hand to indicate that she should sit down again.

Detective Sergeant Ni Nuallán held up her half-eaten sandwich. 'This is my last night's supper,' she explained. '*And* this morning's breakfast, *and* my lunch, too. I was wallfalling with the hunger.'

'How's it going?' asked Katie, smiling at Detective Garda Goold.

'Oh, surviving, ma'am! I think I may be getting somewhere with Roisin Begley. I have a fair description of the fellow that her school friend saw her with, or his car anyway, because they were involved in a bit of an altermacation with another driver who was coming out of the car park on Patrick's Quay. The fellow in the pay booth said it was a silvery-green Renault Mégane with a dinge in the rear offside door. All I have to do now is locate it.'

'Well, good luck with that, because Jim Begley's been ringing about every ten minutes, accusing us of gross incompetence. When I told him that we were devoting as much time as we possibly could to finding his daughter, he said we couldn't find the time in a clock shop. Well, I can hardly blame him. He and his wife must be worried sick.'

Detective Sergeant Ni Nuallán finished her mouthful of sandwich and said, 'Did you have any luck with Derek Hagerty?'

'I've formally arrested him on a charge of conspiracy to demand money with menaces. I don't think it's going to persuade him to talk, though. He's so scared of these High Kings of Erin that he'd rather face jail than tell us who they are – especially now he knows what they did to the Pearses. But . . . he did give me one little bit of information that might give us a lead. Meryl Pearse had a friend with her when she found him by the side of the road, and from what Hagerty heard them saying to each other, it sounds like he was an old boyfriend of hers. She dropped him off at Anderson's Quay before she drove Hagerty home, so that her husband wouldn't find out that she'd been out with him.

'His name was Eoghan, but that's all Hagerty heard. Brown hair, medium build. Quite good-looking. That's not a whole lot to go on, I know, but if he was a former boyfriend, it's likely that her family knows who he is. We've already warned them, haven't we, that the dead woman on Rocky Bay Beach was probably her?'

'Yes,' said Detective Sergeant Ni Nuallán. 'Her widowed mother lives in Glanmire and one of her brothers in Douglas. Sergeant Devitt went round to visit them first thing this morning and had a word with them.'

'All right,' said Katie. 'As soon as she's been formally identified, pay them a visit yourself, would you, and offer your condolences, of course, but make sure you ask them about this Eoghan. I'm not saying that he'll have anything new to tell us, even if we can find him. The odds are that he won't. But on the other hand, he might have noticed some detail when he and Meryl Pearse picked up Hagerty – something that seemed like nothing at all at the time, but that might really assist us to make a breakthrough. You never know.'

'Okay,' said Detective Sergeant Ni Nuallán. 'But what happens if I *do* find him, and he *does* have some really vital clue?'

'In that case, he's going to need us to give him some close protection. If he saw anything at all that could help us to convict the High Kings of Erin when we bring them to court, then, of course, we'll have to declare it in the Book of Evidence, and that could put him at extremely high risk. But don't let's be dancing till the music starts up.'

Twenty-Seven

They drove for about fifteen minutes, mostly uphill, which led Pat to guess that they were heading north. The acrid tobacco on the blindfold made him sneeze twice, but he had nothing to wipe his nose on except the back of his hand. The bouncer-type sitting on his right-hand side shifted uncomfortably and said, 'Don't be blowing any of your gulliers on me, boy, I just had this suit cleaned. Fecking twelve ninety-nine it cost me.'

It was still raining hard and the car's windscreen wipers squeaked monotonously. The car lurched left, and then right, and then left again; then its tyres were crunching over shingle and they came to a stop. The bouncer-type took hold of Pat's arm and helped him to climb out of the car, into the rain, and then led him across the driveway by his elbow. He tripped twice on the shingle, but each time the bouncer-type gripped his arm tighter and prevented him from falling,

'There's a step up here, boy, that's it. Then another one.'

They had entered a house now. It was warm inside, although there was a musty smell of damp wallpaper and of dust that had been heated up on rarely used radiators. The front door closed behind them and the crimson-faced man said, 'You're all right now, Pat. Let's take that blindfold off of you.'

He untied the knot at the back of Pat's head and dragged the scarf away. Pat blinked and looked around. They were standing in the gloomy hallway of a large old house. The floor was covered with rumpled Indian carpets, red and blue originally, but mostly worn down to the string. There were pale rectangular patches on the yellowish walls where pictures had once hung, and the outline of a clock, too. On the opposite side of the hallway a wide staircase led up to a half-landing, dimly illuminated by a tall stained-glass window. The window had a picture of a distant grey castle on it, with rooks flying around its turrets, and a river, with bulrushes.

A side door suddenly opened and the young carroty-curled man appeared, wringing his hands together in apparent satisfaction. 'Well, Pat, you made it, then!' he said, in that high, throaty voice. 'Good man yourself!' He was wearing a speckly grey polo-neck sweater and tight black jeans that emphasized how skinny his legs were.

Behind him, Pat could see a high-ceilinged living room, sparsely furnished with an antique ottoman and two tub-like armchairs. Through the living-room windows he could see only oak trees with their wet leaves turning rusty, so it was impossible for him to tell where they were. From the time they had been driving, he guessed they were close to Watergrasshill, but he had never seen a house of this size or age around that area, only farms and bungalows. This was more like the houses you would expect to find in Montenotte or Military Hill, but they were only minutes away from the city centre.

'He was a shade reluctant, like,' said the crimson-faced man. 'Said that he'd changed his mind and didn't want to be kidnapped after all. But we managed to persuade him otherwise.'

'I still don't want to go through with this,' Pat interrupted. 'I don't see how we have any chance at all of getting away with it, and I don't want to be ending up in jail.'

'Pat, Pat – I wouldn't have taken you for such a pessimist,' said the carroty-curled young man. 'Besides, like I told you before, you don't have a choice. Well, you *do*, like, but I wouldn't really call the graveyard much of a choice, would you?'

'So if I don't pretend to be kidnapped, you're going to kill me, is that about the size of it?'

'You have me. That is exactly the size of it.'

'Well, screw you, that's all I have to say. I'm not afraid of you, no way.'

'Listen to me, you handicap,' said the carroty-curled young man, stepping up close and prodding Pat in the chest. 'I made you a once-in-a-lifetime offer to get you out of all your financial woes and you accepted it. But now you're going back on yourself? Sorry, boy, but it doesn't work like that.'

Pat was breathing hard and his heart was thumping. Despite what he had said, he was very frightened, but at the same time he found that his fear made him bolder.

'I don't give a shite how it works. I'm not going to get myself involved in this scam and that's my very last word on it.'

At that moment a young woman came out of the living room and said, 'Did I just hear what I thought I just heard?'

Pat stared at her in disbelief. Although she was wearing a loose green cowl-neck sweater and black tights and ankle-boots, she was almost identical in appearance to the young carroty-curled man. Her carroty curls were thicker and wirier, and almost shoulder-length, but she had the same dead-white, thin-lipped face and the same pale onyx-coloured eyes. As she came closer, Pat could smell a thick, musky perfume.

'Oh, it's nothing, sis,' said the carroty-curled young man. 'Pat's having himself a mickey fit, that's all.'

'I did warn him,' said the crimson-faced man.

The young woman stared at Pat, unblinking. She had no expression on her face at all, which he found more unnerving than if she had looked irritated, or angry, or contemptuous. After a few moments she said, 'Malachi, make him change his mind, would you, boy?'

The bouncer-type who had helped Pat out of the car turned round and without any hesitation punched him so hard in the stomach that he dropped on to his knees on the threadbare carpet, unable to breathe. He heard the crimson-faced man saying '*ooff!*' in sympathy, and when he looked up everything in the hallway around him appeared to be stained dark red, with prickly stars floating in front of his eyes.

The carroty-curled girl leaned over him and spoke quietly in his ear, overwhelming him with the smell of her perfume. 'Now, Pat, are you going to go along with this or not?'

Pat couldn't draw enough breath into his lungs to say anything, but he shook his head. He had taken beatings before, behind his shop, when he had first refused to cooperate with Michael Crinnion, and although he had eventually given in when the O'Flynns had threatened to smash up his stock, he believed that he could survive any kind of punishment that these bouncer-types could dish out. When he had been bullied at school, Father Thomas used to say to him, 'Close your eyes, Patrick, and think of Saint Epipodius. He was thrown to the lions, but even as the lions chewed him up, feet first, he ignored the pain and continued to speak to God.'

Still gasping, Pat managed to climb back on to his feet. 'Well?' said the carroty-curled girl.

'No,' he declared. 'I'll not do it.'

The carroty-curled girl turned away and Malachi punched him in the stomach a second time, even harder than the first, so that he dropped down on to his knees again and his mouth filled up with bitter-tasting sick. Half-digested egg-and-bacon sandwich from Tesco.

'Let's show Pat here what happens to anyone who tries to play Molly Bán with the High Kings of Erin,' said the carroty-curled girl. 'The traditional treatment, just to make it absolutely clear who's in charge around here.'

Pat was doubled up on the floor. His stomach and ribs hurt so badly that he could have sobbed like a child. He had managed to swallow the mouthful of sick but his throat hurt now and all he could taste was bile. *Saint Epiopodius, save me*, he thought. *You're the patron saint of pain. Save me, or at least give me the strength to bear this bravely.*

The two bouncer-types grasped his arms and lifted him up on

to his feet. The carroty-curled twins led the way down the hall to another door, while the two bouncer-types half carried and half dragged Pat behind them, his feet catching on the rumpled-up carpet. As he opened the door, the carroty-curled young man turned and smiled at him and said, 'You can still change your mind, Pat. We never like to cause anybody any unnecessary distress, do we, Ruari?'

'Oh, I don't know,' said his carroty-curled twin. 'There's nothing worth watching on the box these days.'

The bouncer-type called Malachi snorted in amusement as they manhandled Pat through the door. They were now in the kitchen, which was even gloomier than the hallway, and the carroty-curled young man switched on the overhead lights, two of them, with conical green metal shades. It was almost dark outside, even though it wasn't even one o'clock yet, and the rain was beating hard against the windows.

The kitchen looked as if it was last refurbished in the 1950s, with a deep old-fashioned sink and a wooden draining board, and a dome-topped fridge. There was a large pine dresser up against the left-hand wall which bore the ghostly images of plates along its shelves. In the centre of the room stood a long pine-topped table, with thick legs and drawers underneath.

The tap in the sink had obviously been dripping for a long time, leaving a brown stain down one side, and the whole kitchen smelled of drains and mould and rat urine.

Without being told, the two bouncer-types tugged off Pat's khaki waterproof jacket, and then the salmon-pink sweater that he was wearing underneath, wrenching it over his head so hard that he almost felt that they were going to decapitate him. Next, Malachi took hold of the front of his brown and white checked shirt and tore it open, so that most of the buttons were scattered on the lino-covered floor. After that, he twisted his vest off him.

Pat stood there, stripped to the waist, his pale, crimson-bruised belly hanging over his belt, feeling cold and miserable and completely defenceless. At first he crossed his arms tightly across his chest, but he felt that made him look too much like a frightened woman covering her breasts, so he let his hands drop down by his sides.

The two bouncer-types grasped his arms again and heaved him up on to the pine table. Malachi took a choke-hold on his throat, forcing him to lie flat on his back. Then, while Malachi continued to hold him down, the other bouncer-type unbuckled his belt, jerked down his zip, and wrestled his tan-coloured corduroy trousers off him, followed by his Y-fronts.

'Fierce skid marks in those,' he said, tossing his underpants into the corner.

'What did you expect?' said Malachi. 'It's pure amazing he hasn't shit himself by now.'

Apart from his maroon Primark socks, Pat was now completely naked, the fair hairs on his legs and arms standing up from the chill, his penis shrivelled up like a dead red rose. The carroty-curled young man came and stood over him, still smiling his eerie, lipless smile, while his sister looked over his shoulder, her face still totally expressionless, as if she were wearing a white Venetian carnival mask.

'Well, Pat, we *were* hoping that you would ring your dear wife and tell her that you'd been kidnapped,' said the carroty-curled young man. 'Unfortunately, I don't think we can trust you to do that any more. It would take only one wrong word, like, and this whole carefully worked-out plan of ours could be up in a bollocks.'

Pat said nothing, but lay back on the table, his eyes darting from side to side, trying to see what Malachi and the other bouncer-type were doing. He could hear rattling, like somebody sorting through a toolbox, but at the moment they were out of his line of sight.

'Normally, you see, that phone call would be the incontrovertible proof to your wife that we really have you. But if we can't rely on you to do that, we'll have to prove it in another way. Like, the last fellow *did* make the phone call, but we weren't at all sure that his wife believed that it was really him. Just to convince her we pulled out all of his front teeth and sent them to her in a jam jar.'

'You did *what*?' said Pat. 'You pulled out *all* of his front teeth? Go away out of that! You told me you might have to pull out only the one, if that.'

'Don't be getting yourself all stooky, Pat! We weren't planning on doing that again. It was too much like hard work, yanking them all out, I can tell you. Not only that, Malachi made a right hames of it and there was blood all over the shop, and the fellow was screaming like you couldn't hear yourself think. But at the time, you know, Ruari here wanted to get her revenge.'

'Revenge for what? I don't know what the feck you're talking about.'

'You don't need to concern yourself about that. The main thing is that we do need some physical evidence that we have you, even if it isn't your teeth.'

Pat stared at him, saying nothing, but dreading what he was going to say next.

After a while, the carroty-curled young man leaned forward and said, 'Tell me, Pat, how much do you know about the High Kings of Erin?'

'The High Kings of Erin? Wait a minute, I have you. They were talking about the High Kings of Erin on the TV news. That was what the gang called themselves who kidnapped that garage owner and set off that bomb off at Merchants Quay, the one that killed that garda. Was that *you*? Is that what you're trying to tell me? Are *you* these High Kings of Erin?'

'I'm the one asking the questions here, Pat. What do you know about the High Kings of Erin, and by that I mean the original High Kings of Erin, the kings who used to rule this country before the Brits stole it from us?'

He waited. And when Pat didn't answer, he said, 'Well? You must know something about them.'

'Not much,' said Pat. 'Only what we learned in school, like. Most of them weren't real at all, though, were they? They were only told about in stories. Why?'

'Did they tell you in school that you could only be a king if there was nothing wrong with you at all? Physically, like? You had to be perfect.'

'Yes, I remember that. You couldn't have a hand missing or nothing like that.'

'That's right. If you lost an eye, or foot, or an ear, even if you lost them in a battle, then you couldn't be king any more. There was Congal Cáech, for example, who was hit in the eye by a bee, which is why they called him Cáech, which means blind in one eye, or squinty. Old Congal lost his kingdom because of that.'

Pat tried to sit up, but Malachi pushed him back down.

'Listen,' he protested, 'I don't understand a single word you're babbling on about, and I don't want to understand. The High Kings of Erin, what kind of nonsense is that? I want nothing to do with any of this. Just give me my clothes back and let me go and I'll forget that this ever happened.'

'Oh – but you really thought that *you* were the kings, didn't you?' said the carroty-curled young man. 'All you little people who borrowed so much money with not a hope in hell of ever paying it back? In the olden days, though, the real kings always had to take the blame for things going wrong, as well as the credit when things went right. If all the cows dropped dead of some cattle disease, or the crops were all beat flat because it never stopped raining, then the people would think it was the king's fault, and he would have to be sacrificed.

'Do you know what they would do? They would grab the king and drill holes through his arms, so that they could tie him down with hazel wands and he couldn't get away. Then they would beat him, and stab him, and break his arms and legs, and sometimes they would cut off his mickey and stuff it into his mouth and make him chew on it. In the end they would hammer three wooden stakes into his head, just to make sure. You should be grateful that your creditors don't do the same thing to you.'

'Why are you telling me this all this guff? I just want to get out of here.'

'I'm telling you this because we're prepared to forgive you for the harm you did to Ireland – unlike those people in the olden days. All you have to do in return is make sure that we're well rewarded for our forgiveness. We're doing a deal here. Once your ransom is paid up, you can go back to your wife and family with all of your debts forgotten, and a little bit more besides to help you to get back on to your feet. But you'll never be kings again, because we're the new High Kings of Erin now, Ruari and me and Lorcan, and apart from that you won't be perfect any more.'

'What the feck do you mean, I won't be perfect?'

'Everything has its price, Pat, as you very well know.'

'I want to go now,' said Pat. When he first said it, his voice was constricted but reasonably steady, but then he suddenly burst into tears and wept, 'I want to go now. I don't want to do this! I want to go!'

'Oh, it's far too late for that, boy. You've seen us and you know who we are. You'll just have to go through with this to the bitter end.'

'I don't want to,' he sobbed. 'I don't want to.'

'Come on, Pat,' said Ruari, the carroty-curled girl. 'Don't be such a baba.'

Pat stopped crying and wiped his eyes with the back of his hand. 'What are you going to do to me?' he said. 'You're not going to take my eye out, are you?'

'No, Pat! Take your eye out, for feck's sake! We wouldn't dream of doing such a thing! But we have to do something to make sure that you don't think that you're a king ever again. When people paid homage to the High Kings, back in the olden days, what do you think they did?'

'I don't know. How should I know?'

'They sucked their nipples, that's what they did.'

'They *what*?'

'They sucked their nipples! Don't you get it? If a man had no nipples, he couldn't be a High King, could he? That's what the High Kings did to their rivals, so that they could never depose

233

them and take their place. They cut off their nipples. It's true. You can look it up for yourself in the history books.'

As he said this, Malachi approached the side of the table. Pat noticed for the first time that he had two round warts on top of his shiny shaven head, one on either side, as if he had once had horns, but they had been filed down. He had taken off his black suit jacket and rolled up the sleeves of his billowy white shirt.

In his right hand he was holding up a pair of garden secateurs.

Pat let out a shout and again tried to roll himself off the kitchen table, but the carroty-curled young man and the other bouncer-type immediately seized him and slammed him back, so hard that he hit his head and almost bit through the tip of his tongue. He felt stunned and his mouth filled with the metallic taste of blood.

He tried once more to lift himself up, but both of his arms were being gripped tight and the girl called Ruari was holding both of his ankles, digging her sharp fingernails into his skin.

'You should be thankful we're not taking out your pearly whites, Pat,' said the carroty-curled young man. 'You should have heard your man roaring and screaming when we were doing that, even though we tanked him up with whiskey.'

Pat could do nothing but lie back, squeeze his eyes tight shut and clench his teeth. Malachi took hold of his left nipple between finger and thumb and stretched it upwards as far as he could, so that it formed a little tent of white skin. Then he opened the secateurs, positioning the curving blades just below the areola.

Saint Epipodius, let me not feel this.

His prayer, however, went unanswered. The secateurs cut through his skin and his flesh with the softest crunch, but the pain was fiercer than anything he had ever felt in his life, as if he had been branded on his chest with a red-hot iron. Malachi held up his bloody nipple in front of his face so that he could see it, but he closed his eyes tight and turned his head away. He could feel blood sliding down his side on to the table top, and the agony was unbearable.

'There,' he heard the carroty-curled young man saying. 'That wasn't so bad after all, now was it? Only one more to go!'

'*No!*' Pat begged him, shaking his head violently from side to side, his eyes still closed. 'No, please, no! I'll do anything you want! I promise you! I'll ring my wife! I'll tell her I've been kidnapped! But not again! Please!'

'What do you think, Ruari?' asked the carroty-haired young man. 'Think we can trust him, or not?'

'Not me, I wouldn't,' said Ruari. 'Besides, if you leave him with a nipple, even if it's only the one nipple, he could still pretend that he was a king now, couldn't he?'

'Well, you're probably right, sis. What do you say, Lorcan?'

The crimson-faced man was standing by the window, looking out at the rain. He turned his head and said, 'It's tradition, isn't it, and who are we to be messing with tradition?'

'Please, no,' said Pat. 'Please, in the name of Jesus.'

He tried to struggle again, but he was already numb with shock and he found that he couldn't make his arm or leg muscles do what he wanted them to do. All he could manage was to clench his fists tightly and arch his back.

Malachi pinched his right nipple and stretched that up, too. In spite of his shock, he couldn't stop himself from lifting his head and watching as Malachi opened the secateurs. This time he didn't appeal to Saint Epipodius. He knew that it was going to hurt regardless of his prayers. He thought that the best course of action would be to watch and try to persuade himself that he was observing another man having his nipple cut off, and not himself at all. Perhaps in that way he could distance himself from the pain.

But when Malachi squeezed the handles of the secateurs together, and the blades sliced through his skin, the pain was just as excruciating as it had been the first time. It seemed to take longer, too, almost as if Malachi were cutting his nipple off in slow motion. Even the soft crunching sound seemed to go on for nearly half a minute.

He saw blood spurting from his chest, but then Ruari let go of his ankles and came round unhurriedly with a grubby-looking

235

green hand towel. She pressed it against his wound, and held it there for a while, looking down at him as she did so. He didn't think he had ever seen a woman with such a white face and such finely plucked eyebrows. Her eyes were such a pale green colour that they looked more like stones than eyes, and they showed no more emotion than stones would have done.

'There now, Pat,' she said, 'that's all over. You've been put in your place now. No more playing at kings for you, boy.'

Close behind her, Malachi held up Pat's right nipple so that he could see it, then the carroty-curled young man passed him a small polythene freezer bag. He dropped the nipple into it, along with the bloodied left nipple, and passed it back.

'You see, you won't be having to make a phone call now to prove that we have you,' said the carroty-curled young man, flip-flapping the bag in front of Pat's face. 'We'll be able to send these to her, with a warning not to show them to the guards under any circumstances, but of course she will. The guards will do a DNA test to prove that they're your little titties, and then they'll pay up to have you released. See? Perfect!'

Lorcan, the crimson-faced man, came away from the window and looked down at Pat's chest, with its two circular wounds where his nipples used to be. The wound on his left side had begun to clot now, but the wound on the right was still bleeding. 'You shouldn't have changed your mind, Pat. We didn't have to do this at all. But I suppose you'll always have something to remember us by.'

Pat didn't answer him. His eyelids were fluttering and he kept losing consciousness – light, then dark, then light again – and he kept missing fragments of conversation. It was like listening to a microphone with a faulty connection.

At last he croaked, 'It doesn't – doesn't work.'

'What doesn't work, Pat?' asked Lorcan. He had tucked a cigarette between his lips and he was snapping the top of a purple plastic lighter.

'Prayer,' said Pat. 'It doesn't fecking work.'

Twenty-Eight

Katie met Michael Dempsey in the Roundy Bar on Castle Street in the city centre. It was still raining hard outside and it was dark inside, so they sat at a table under the window.

'I need you to tell me about the High Kings of Erin,' she told him, hanging her raincoat over the back of her chair.

'The High Kings of Erin?' asked Michael Dempsey. 'How long do you have?'

He was tall, at least six foot three, but round-shouldered, with thick black curly hair that was beginning to show strands of grey. He looked like the professor of history that he was, wearing a maroon corduroy jacket with elbow patches, a yellow cravat and a thick green flannel shirt. His trousers were baggy at the knees and his brown deck shoes were worn down.

'I know that there were dozens of Irish kings,' said Katie. 'But you must have seen on the news that we're trying to track down a gang of kidnappers who call themselves the High Kings of Erin.'

'You could hardly miss it. Those two people burned to death on the beach like that. And that fellow having his head cut off and baked into a wedding cake. Shocking.'

Katie said, 'The trouble is, I've received two phone calls now from these High Kings of Erin, but I still can't be sure if they're the real kidnappers or if they're hoaxing us. This always happens whenever we're dealing with a major crime and it gets well publicized – some stupid gobdaw will ring up and claim they have vital information for us, or that they committed the crime themselves. Sometimes it's

237

some header who is totally convinced in his own mind that he really *did* do it, but usually it's time-wasters – the sort of people who call the fire brigade just to see the engines come out.'

She paused while Michael Dempsey ordered coffee for them both and a raspberry pastry for himself. 'You're sure I can't tempt you?' he asked her.

Katie shook her head. 'No thanks, I'm a cake-o-holic. Once I start eating them I can't stop.'

'Well, I shouldn't either. But when you teach history you realize how short your life is, and is it worth depriving yourself? You can't eat raspberry pastries when you're lying six feet under the sod in St Joseph's Cemetery.'

'True enough,' Katie smiled. 'But what I wanted to ask you, Michael, is if you thought these murders were – I don't know, *ritualistic* in any way. Did the real High Kings of Erin kill people like that? Or even the mythical High Kings?'

'Would it make any difference?'

'Of course. If the real High Kings of Erin ever killed people like that – burning them and baking their heads into cakes – that would make me pretty sure that these new High Kings of Erin really *are* responsible for doing it. They wouldn't simply be trying to take the credit for a couple of random gang killings that were nothing to do with them.'

'I understand,' said Michael Dempsey solemnly. 'However, I can't truthfully tell you that I've ever read anything about the High Kings of Erin disposing of people in those particular ways. But, like you say, there were dozens of High Kings, more than fifty altogether, some of them mythical and some of them real, so I don't know everything that was ever written about all of them. I can tell you, though, that they were a pretty ruthless lot, on the whole. They had to be. They sacrificed innocent children and they murdered their brothers and sisters, just to stay on the throne.'

He tore open a packet of brown sugar and poured it into his coffee, then another one, and then another. 'You'll have to give me a little time to do some research.'

'I'd be very grateful, Michael,' said Katie. 'More than anything else, it might help me to understand their agenda. The two men they've abducted so far were both on the brink of bankruptcy. Why would they demand ransom money from people who patently didn't have any? Why didn't they kidnap rich people?'

She didn't tell him that she was almost certain that Derek Hagerty had aided and abetted his own kidnapping, and that the Pearses may well have been murdered because they had suspected it, too, and might have been able to give evidence in court to prove it. Neither did she say that there had been another witness who could possibly prove that Derek Hagerty had been an accomplice in his own abduction – Meryl's former fiancé, Eoghan.

Michael Dempsey said, 'You – ah – you won't be mentioning my own name in connection with this investigation, will you?'

'Of course not. My lips are sealed.'

'Well, you know that I'm more than happy to help you out. But after what happened to Gerry O'Brien . . .'

'No,' Katie assured him. 'We won't risk anything like that.' He was referring to his late colleague from the history department of Cork University, Professor Gerard O'Brien, who had assisted Katie and her team to investigate a previous series of ritual homicides. The killer had found out that Professor O'Brien was getting close to the truth about the murders and had brutally silenced him.

Michael Dempsey sipped his coffee and then he said, 'It's queer, don't you think, that this gang should be giving themselves a name like the High Kings of Erin? Quite intellectual for a Cork crime gang? About the most romantic gang name I've ever heard is the Bride Valley View Boys. Not that it's at all romantic if you know Bride Valley View.'

'That's one of the main reasons I've come to you, Michael,' said Katie. 'I need to find out if their name can give me any clues as to who they really are and what it is they're after. They may be political fanatics, or they could be using the name just for mockery, who knows? Or, like I say, it might not be them at all, and they might just be stringing me along. But they know much more about these kidnappings than they could have seen on the TV news or read in the papers, so I do have serious suspicions that they're responsible.'

'Well, Katie, the High Kings of Erin committed some terrible acts of butchery, either to survive or to get what they wanted. For instance there was Art Óenther, who was sent by his wicked stepmother Bé Chuma to fetch back to Ireland the daughter of Morgan, Delbcháem, so that he could marry her and inherit her father's throne. Before he could take her away, though, he had to kill her brother, Ailli Dubdétach, and then her mother, Coincheen, the 'dog-headed'. Coincheen had cut off the heads of all her daughter's previous suitors and impaled them on a bronze fence. So Art Óenther cut off *her* head, and Morgan's too, for good measure, and impaled *them* on the fence.'

'Mother of God, they were a bloodthirsty lot all right.'

'There are plenty of descriptions of people being burned alive, but on bonfires usually, not half buried in sand. And the only mention I can recall of people being cooked was in the reign of the High King Tigernmas, the son of Follach, which was a particularly bloody time. Tigernmas used to offer sacrifices to Crom Cruach, the fertility god. Apart from many other small children, they once included the twin babies of his own sister, Eithne. The poor little babes were boiled alive in a pottage, with herbs and grains.'

'Jesus. I'll bet Darina Allen doesn't teach you how to cook *that* recipe at Ballymaloe.'

Michael Dempsey lifted up his raspberry pastry and said, 'You're absolutely sure you wouldn't like a bite?'

'If I was tempted before, I'm certainly not tempted now. Can you imagine it? "What's for supper tonight, darling?" "Oh, just the usual, boiled twins."'

Michael Dempsey chewed and swallowed his pastry, but as he did so he was watching Katie closely. 'Something else is worrying you, isn't it?'

'What?' she said, looking up at him. 'No – nothing more than usual.'

'I don't know. You'll forgive me for saying so, but you look kind of sad.'

Katie tried to manage a smile but it turned out to be more of a pout, like a small child just about to burst into tears.

'I'm sorry,' said Michael Dempsey. 'It's none of my business. I shouldn't have stuck my snout in. Forget I ever said it.'

'No, no, you're a sensitive man, Michael. You're a sensitive man and you're right. The truth of it is that the man I thought was going to marry me – well, now he's *not* going to be marrying me.'

'He must have a screw loose, this fellow.'

'No . . . it's just that Fate with a capital F had different ideas. That can happen sometimes. He went off to America and I decided to stay here.'

'Couldn't you have gone with him?'

'Ah,' said Katie, fiddling with her coffee spoon. 'That's the sixty-four thousand yoyo question. But no, not really. I have a city of over half a million people to look after. I couldn't just walk away and leave them, could I?'

Michael Dempsey continued to watch her for a while and then he said, 'Do you know what I've learned, more than anything else, from all of my years of studying history? I've learned that life is filled with overwhelming sadness.'

'Oh, come on now, Michael, don't be so depressing. The day's dark enough.'

'No, it's true, Katie. No matter how wonderful life is, no matter how exhilarating, no matter how filled it is with joy and love, in the end it's always over.'

Katie looked up at him again and this time she saw that there were tears in his eyes. She reached across the table and laid her hand on top of his.

'Michael . . . what's wrong?'

He shook his head and took out his crumpled handkerchief and blew his nose. 'Sorry . . . sorry. I shouldn't have intruded. It's just that my mother passed away last week and now I can recognize sadness wherever I see it. I never realized before how much of it there was about.'

This time Katie managed a genuine smile, although it was more a smile of understanding than of good humour. 'You and me both, Michael. You and me both.'

***

On her way back to the station she received a text message from Detective Sergeant Ni Nuállan, asking where she was, and by the time she walked into the office, shaking her umbrella and taking off her raincoat, Kyna was already there waiting for her. Her blonde hair had been cut even shorter than usual, shaved up the back of her neck, which emphasized her sharp cheekbones and her strong, almost masculine jawline.

'I talked to Mrs Collins, Meryl's mother,' she told Katie. 'She's in bits about Meryl, but she still wanted to help as much as she could. She lost her husband to throat cancer and her only son in a motorcycle accident, both within three months of each other, so she doesn't think that fate has been very fair to her this year, to say the least.'

'Strange you should say that,' said Katie. She sat down at her desk and quickly leafed through the messages on it. 'I was talking about fate not half an hour ago with Michael Dempsey from the university history department, how unkind it can be. Anyway, did you have any luck with Eoghan?'

Detective Sergeant Ni Nuallán took out her notebook. 'Eoghan met Meryl when they were kids at school. Carroll his surname is, Eoghan Carroll. Mrs Collins said that she and her late husband both liked Eoghan. He was always polite, she said, and he always held his knife and fork properly, and he came from a very respectable family. His father worked for the county council. Everybody assumed that Eoghan and Meryl would be married when they were old enough.'

'So, what happened?' asked Katie, standing up. 'How did Meryl end up marrying a travel agent more than twenty years older than she was?'

'Usual story,' said Detective Sergeant Ni Nuallán. 'Eoghan went off to find a job in England and met somebody else. Well, met somebody else and made her pregnant.'

Katie was standing by the window now. She pressed her fingertip to the glass where a raindrop was dribbling down but, of course, she couldn't stop it. She couldn't help thinking of John. He must have found some other woman by now. He was too attractive a man not to. Some other woman he would marry, and cherish, and make pregnant.

'Mrs Collins told me that Meryl rang her three days ago to say that she had bumped into Eoghan,' said Detective Sergeant Ni Nuallán.

'So Eoghan settled back to Ireland?'

'No, no. He only came over from England for a couple of weeks to visit his parents, but his wife didn't join him because of their kids having to go to school. His meeting with Meryl was pure accidental. He'd walked into Eason's looking to buy some pens or something, that's all – didn't even realize Meryl was working there. He asked her to go out with him for a bit of a catch-up, like, but she told her mother that she wasn't sure if she ought to go. Norman was very possessive, mostly on account of their age difference.'

'But if Eoghan was over here for a couple of weeks, he may *still* be here?'

'Oh, for sure, I'm almost certain that he is. Mrs Collins gave me his parents' address in Carrigaline and a couple of the local garda went round there for me and took a sconce. There was nobody at home at the time but there was an Avis car parked in the driveway, so they noted the number. Eoghan Carroll rented it from the airport ten days ago and he's not due to return it until Saturday. This afternoon he's probably out somewhere with his parents, but I think he's still here in the country all right. Crannagh, The Grove, Carrigaline, just off Church Road.'

'Is somebody from Carrigaline keeping an eye on the place for you?'

'Sergeant Barry said that he's pushed for manpower at the moment but he promised to send a car past the house every hour or so, just to check. He'll call me as soon as they see that the Carrolls are back home.'

'Okay, Kyna, that's grand. Like I said before, I still shouldn't think that Eoghan can tell us anything useful, but you never know.'

Just as Detective Sergeant Ni Nuallán was leaving Katie's office, Inspector Fennessy came in. 'Ma'am?' he said. 'You'll be delighted to know that I found Fergal ó Floinn.'

'Well done! But of course he denied everything. I'll bet he denied even knowing that a bomb had gone off.'

'No, he didn't, he knew about it all right. But I very much doubt that he made it or planted it himself. He's in Blair's Hill Nursing Home and the staff are surprisingly intolerant when it comes to the residents bringing in Semtex and timing devices and putting bombs together, even in the quiet room.'

'Well, I suppose that lets *him* off the hook.'

'Amazingly, he tried to be helpful,' said Inspector Fennessy. 'I don't know if he's mellowed as he's grown older, or if he's turned to religion since he's been at Blair's Hill. Maybe he's seeking absolution for all the innocent people in Belfast he's blown to bits over the years, now that he's so close to meeting his maker.'

'He tried to be *helpful*?' asked Katie. 'I wouldn't mention Fergal ó Floinn and a helpful man on the same day.'

'You say that, but he gave me a hint about the Merchants Quay bomb. He said that one of his visitors had seen Clearie O'Hely in the centre of Cork the day before.'

'Clearie O'Hely? There's a rave from the grave.'

'That's no proof in itself, Clearie just being here in Cork. But of course Fergal ó Floinn trained him in bomb-making back in the seventies. He was always a prime suspect for that Palace Barracks bombing in Holywood, wasn't he, although the peelers could never prove it?'

Katie frowned and said, 'I don't think we've ever had the slightest sniff of Clearie O'Hely operating in Cork. If you'd asked me, I would have guessed he was dead by now.'

'I was surprised myself when Fergal told me he'd been seen around here. Apart from that time he spent in Belfast, O'Hely's a Limerick boy through and through. He used to work for the Duggans more than anybody, didn't he? They had him blowing up ATMs and building society safes and the doors off security vans. Well, that's until the sainted Niall Duggan got what he so richly deserved.'

'Oh yes,' said Katie. 'Shot dead wearing his mistress's white satin dressing gown, if I remember – much to his wife's annoyance. I seem to remember that she was only angry because somebody else had shot him before she had the chance to do it herself.'

'I doubt if his mistress was best pleased, either,' said Inspector Fennessy. 'But I'd say we have to accept that times have changed. There's much more cross-pollination between the gangs in Cork and the gangs in Limerick than there ever used to be.'

'"Cross-contamination", I'd call it,' Katie put in.

'I blame all those improvements to the N20 myself. You have to admit that since they've made the road better, we've seen more scobes from Limerick in town than we ever used to. In fact, we've seen a general increase in scobes from all over.'

'Go and tell Bill Phinner, in any case,' said Katie. 'It could very well help the technical boys to identify the bomb-maker if they know that Clearie O'Hely might have had a hand in it. It always surprises me how bomb-makers can't help themselves leaving their own telltale trademarks on their handiwork, like the way they twist the wires, or the type of tape they use.'

She turned away from the window. 'As for me . . . I'll go and have a word with Bryan Molloy, reluctant as I am. If anybody knows about Limerick gangs, then he does.'

'Rather you than me, that's all I can say.'

Twenty-Nine

When she knocked at the door of Bryan Molloy's office, he surprised her by looking up from his desk and waving her inside with a smile on his face.

'Katie!' he said. 'What's the craic? Fancy a cup of coffee? I'm just about send Teagan to fetch me one, and some of them Kimberley biscuits, too. I think I'm addicted.'

'No, thanks, I'm grand altogether,' said Katie, sitting down opposite him. 'I had coffee only an hour ago. I was meeting with Professor Michael Dempsey from the university history department.'

'Oh yes?' said Bryan Molloy. 'And what was all that about?'

Katie had never seen him so breezy before. She almost preferred him when he was being openly unpleasant, but here he was, smiling at her and cheerfully rubbing his hands together as if he couldn't wait for her to give him the latest update.

'He specializes in Irish mediaeval history and so he knows as much about the High Kings of Erin as anybody. I've asked him to see if the real High Kings ever killed any of their enemies in the way that the Pearses and Micky Crounan were killed. I'm trying to establish if the fellow who's been ringing me up is the genuine article or if he's bluffing.'

'That's good thinking, Katie. Yes, that's very astute, I'd say. I'll be interested to see what your professor comes up with. So, what other lines of inquiry do you have going? Did you manage to wring any more out of Derek Hagerty yet? He's still with us, isn't he? We're going to have to decide what to do with him. He can't stay here at Anglesea Street for ever – not unless we start charging him rent!'

Bryan Molloy let out a sharp bark of laughter and sat back in his chair, his fingers laced across his stomach, clearly pleased with himself.

Katie said, 'I don't know if it's going to lead us anywhere, but he gave me enough information for us to track down the friend that Meryl Pearse had with her when she found him by the roadside.'

'Oh, well, that's something, I suppose,' said Bryan Molloy, although he didn't look very impressed. 'Hasn't he come out and named any of these High Kings of Erin, or given us some idea of what they look like?'

'He's too scared. It was as much as I could do to get the name of Meryl's friend out of him. He may have been party to his own kidnap to begin with, but now he's totally terrified and he won't say a word.'

'So who *was* her friend?'

'An old flame of hers, her childhood sweetheart as a matter of fact. Apparently they were out for a drink together for old times' sake. Eoghan Carroll his name is. He lives in England now but just at the moment he's visiting his parents in Carrigaline. He was out today, but as soon as he gets home DS Ni Nuallán will go round and see if he can help us with any new information.'

'Eoghan Carroll? His da's not *Brendan* Carroll is he, by any chance? I play golf with a fellow from Carrigaline called Brendan Carroll. Lives just off the Ballea Road.'

'No,' said Katie. 'Eoghan's father is called Paul and his mother is called Mary and they live in The Grove.'

'Oh. Can't be him, then!' Bryan Molloy gave another bark of laughter. Katie had the feeling that she was trying to have a conversation with an exuberant dog.

'I'm not giving up on Derek Hagerty yet, not by any means,' she told him. 'I'm hoping that his sense of guilt will win through in the end. He's quite aware that if he colluded in his own kidnapping then he's just as responsible for Garda McCracken's murder as the rest of the gang. I can't keep him under arrest for very much longer, though, not without moving things forward. I have to get him into the District Court by noon tomorrow.'

Bryan Molloy leaned forward again, and for a moment Katie thought he was going to say something sarcastic. But he kept on smiling and said, 'Listen, Katie, I'm sure you'll crack this one. You're a great detective and you have a grand team working for you. I know we haven't always got along together as well as we should have done, and mostly that's been my fault, like. I can only plead stress. It hasn't been easy, taking over from Dermot at such short notice, and Cork is not the same kettle of fish at all as Limerick – like, I don't know half the councillors here, or the clergy. I don't know half the fecking criminals, for that matter.'

'You're a stonecutter, though,' said Katie, nodding towards the triangular Masonic clock on his desk. 'That must help.'

'Of course,' said Bryan Molloy. He didn't seem offended in the least by Katie saying that – or if he was, he wasn't showing it. 'Nothing like the old secret handshake to open doors for you. Not that we really *do* have a secret handshake. We don't sacrifice virgins, either.'

He pushed his chair back and stood up. 'What I'm trying to say to you, Katie, is that maybe you and me can call a truce, like. I'll support you one hundred and ten per cent, and maybe you can stop your detectives poking around in my private accounts. They won't find anything untoward, because there's nothing untoward to find, which makes the whole exercise a provocation and nothing more.'

'It's not really in my remit, Bryan,' Katie told him. 'The Public Accounts Committee asked us to look into the financial affairs of several officers in the division, and that's mostly been done with their full cooperation. You know what it was all about. There were so many allegations of favours being done, especially after that penalty points affair, and the Kieran Boylan drugs business.'

Bryan Molloy didn't answer immediately, but slowly licked his lips, as if he could taste something vaguely disagreeable. She could almost hear him thinking what Commissioner Martin Callinan had said about Garda whistleblowers before he had decided to resign: '*disgusting*'.

Instead, he nodded and said, 'Very well. But if you have any questions, you could come directly to me, you know. I'd be only too happy to help out. I'll let your people have my bank statements if you want them, but they'll only see that I've been spending too much money on golf club subscriptions.'

'All right, Bryan,' said Katie. 'I might even take you up on that.'

He picked up his phone and started to prod out a number, but just as she turned to leave, Katie said, 'By the way, Clearie O'Hely's been seen around the city.'

Bryan Molloy stopped dialling, although he didn't look up.

'Just thought I'd mention it,' Katie added. 'You know, considering his reputation with bombs and all. Unusual to see him here in Cork.'

'It's a free country,' said Bryan Molloy. 'A man can go wherever he pleases, even if he does have a reputation.'

'I just wondered if you'd heard anything, that's all. You know, the old Delmege Park telegraph.'

Now Bryan Molloy raised his eyes. He was still smiling, but his smile looked tight now, and forced, as if he were trying hard to stop it from turning into a scowl. 'No,' he said. 'Not a *whisper*.' He whispered the word '*whisper*', which for some reason made it sound threatening.

'Right you are, then,' said Katie, and left his office. She almost collided with his secretary, Teagan, as she came in carrying a mug of coffee and a plate of Kimberley biscuits.

Purely out of mischief, Katie took one of his biscuits and bit into it as she walked along the corridor back to her office. As she did so, though, an inexplicable feeling of unease began to come over her. It was the same unease she felt when she wasn't sure whether she had double-locked the front door before she left home, or had left a candle burning in the living room. She stopped and turned round, frowning. Something unsettling had happened in that encounter with Bryan Molloy, but she wasn't sure exactly what it was.

When she reached her office, she dropped the half-eaten biscuit into her waste bin. Outside it was still dark, and the rain was lashing against her windows harder than ever, like mad people flailing their arms against the glass, trying to break in.

Thirty

When Detective Sergeant Ni Nuallán and Detective Garda Goold turned into The Grove, they saw that there were three vehicles parked outside the house named Crannagh – the Avis rental car that Eoghan was using while he was visiting his parents, a tan-coloured Volvo estate, and a black Volkswagen people carrier with tinted windows.

The rain had eased off now. The sky was still grey but as bright as a migraine, and the pavements were starting to dry.

'Looks like they have visitors,' said Detective Garda Goold.

'Yes,' said Detective Sergeant Ni Nuallán, narrowing her eyes. She was trying to focus on the two bulky men in black suits and white shirts who were standing in the porch of the Carroll house, talking to somebody in the open doorway. The men's heads were both white, as if they were bandaged like the Invisible Man. She wished that she had worn her glasses – her eyesight had been getting worse lately. She unbuckled her seat belt and opened the door of their silver Toyota before Detective Garda Goold had even brought it to a halt.

The Grove was a quiet cul-de-sac of two-storey, four-bedroom properties, painted white, with low hedges in between them. As Detective Sergeant Ni Nuallán reached the concrete drive in front of the Carroll property she could hear a woman inside the house screaming shrilly and a man shouting, 'Get off me! Leave go of me! Get the hell out of here!'

The man was mid-thirtyish, with brown hair and a bottle-green sweater, and he was wrestling with the two bulky men in black in the hallway. Now that she was nearer, Detective Sergeant Ni Nuallán could see that both of the bulky men had plastic shopping bags tied around their heads, with holes torn open for their eyes and mouths. They were like a thuggish and frightening version of the Rubberbandits, the hip-hop duo from Limerick who wore the same kind of plastic-bag masks. She guessed that the man who was shouting was Eoghan Carroll. One of the bulky men had clamped one hand around the back of his neck and seized his right wrist with the other hand, and was trying to tug him off balance and out of the hallway.

'*Garda*!' shouted Detective Sergeant Ni Nuallán, hurrying forward. 'Garda – let him go!'

The bulky man ignored her, heaving Eoghan into the porch and swinging him around so that he collided with the front of the Volvo estate. Eoghan fell sideways to the ground, in between the Volvo and his rented Opel Insignia, but the bulky man reached down and dragged him up on to his feet again.

Detective Sergeant Ni Nuallán shouted, '*Garda*! Let him go or I'll arrest you!'

She tried to seize the collar of the bulky man's jacket, but his companion stepped over, gripped the sleeve of her coat and wrenched her away. As she stumbled, he pushed her so hard in the chest that she toppled into the hawthorn hedge behind her, hitting her head against the wall of the house.

She tried to struggle to her feet, but the bulky man kicked her in the shin, and then the hip, and spat at her and snapped, 'Next time, mind yer own fecking business, ya bitch!'

Again she tried to get up, but he kicked her shin yet again, even harder this time, and her blue woollen coat was hopelessly snagged by the hawthorn spikes. Her head felt as if it had been cracked in half. She looked up at him, but all she could see was his eyes staring at her out of the holes in the plastic shopping bag, and his thick red lips. There was a pale red C across the side of his face, but that was only C for Centra supermarket.

The two of them started to drag Eoghan away from the house. He was still struggling and shouting, 'Leave go of me! Leave go of me, you bastard!' and now his father had emerged from the house, brandishing an aluminium walking stick, while his mother continued screaming in breathless panic.

Now, however, Detective Garda Goold came forward and stood between the two bulky men and the Volkswagen people carrier. She held up her right hand almost as if she were directing traffic in the middle of Patrick Street and she cried out, 'Stop! Garda! Stop right there! I said *stop*!'

Even Detective Sergeant Ni Nuallán wouldn't have taken her for a police officer. She was so young, and what with her brown wavy hair and the mole on her upper lip and her duffel coat she looked more like a sociology student.

One of the bulky men went straight up to her and pushed her out of the way. He opened the rear door of the people carrier and his associate started to force Eoghan inside. By now Detective Sergeant Ni Nuallán had managed to tug herself free from the hawthorn hedge and pull her phone out of her coat pocket to call for backup. Eoghan's father had caught up with the bulky man who was manhandling his son and started to hit him across the back with his walking stick. The other bulky man punched him on the cheek and he spun wildly away, as if he were dancing a jig, and tumbled heavily on to the pavement.

Detective Garda Goold caught hold of the open door of the people carrier and wouldn't allow the bulky man to close it. He wrestled with her and hit her on the shoulder with his fist and swung the door violently from side to side, but still she clung on.

'*Nessa*!' shouted Detective Sergeant Ni Nuallán, limping down the driveway to help her. '*Nessa, let them go*!'

But Detective Garda Goold held on to the door handle and wouldn't loosen her grip. Inside the back of the people carrier Eoghan was struggling, too.

Detective Sergeant Ni Nuallán shouted, 'Nessa! Leave it! We have backup coming! They won't get away!'

But then the bulky man stopped trying to force Detective Garda Goold to release her hold on the door, and instead he turned round and drew out a large grey automatic pistol from underneath his jacket.

He pointed it first at Detective Sergeant Ni Nuallán, directly at her face. 'Hold it dere, girl,' he warned her, in a thick Limerick accent. 'Don't ye be movin' a muscle.'

Detective Sergeant Ni Nuallán stopped beside the Volvo estate and lifted both hands. 'Nessa,' she said.

'Yeah, come on, Nessa, let go of the feckin' door,' said the bulky man with the pistol, without looking round at her.

'Let this fellow out and then I will,' said Detective Garda Goold.

'Nessa,' the bulky man repeated. 'Would you ever let go of that feckin' door?'

'Nessa, let it go,' said Detective Sergeant Ni Nuallán.

'We're Garda detectives,' said Detective Garda Goold. 'You're under arrest, both of you, for public order offences and assault.'

Detective Sergeant Ni Nuallán's head was banging so loudly she thought that everybody around her must be able to hear it. What made it bang even harder was the dread of what was certainly going to happen next, unless Detective Garda Goold immediately backed away.

She was about to say, 'Nessa,' one more time, but the bulky man turned round and without any hesitation at all shot Detective Garda Goold point-blank in the mouth. The noise of the shot was deafening and the lower part of Detective Garda Goold's face exploded like a huge scarlet chrysanthemum. She pitched backwards on to the pavement and lay there with her arms and her legs spreadeagled, her eyes staring up at the grey clouds, twitching and jerking.

The bulky man kept his pistol pointing at Detective Sergeant Ni Nuallán as he opened the front passenger door of the people carrier and heaved himself in. His companion slammed the rear door, walked round, and climbed in behind the wheel.

Without any hurry at all, they drove off, turning left at the end of The Grove to head north, towards Douglas and Cork.

Detective Sergeant Ni Nuallán rushed over and knelt down beside Detective Garda Goold. Her jaw had been completely blown away and her tongue was hanging down like a tattered scarlet scarf, but she was still breathing bubbles of blood.

'Oh, Nessa,' said Detective Sergeant Ni Nuallán. 'Oh, Nessa you poor, poor darling!'

Eoghan's father had managed to get back on to his feet now. 'I'll call for an ambulance right away,' he said.

'And can you bring me some warm blankets, please,' said Detective Sergeant Ni Nuallán. 'Warm blankets and some gauze if you have any, to try and stop the bleeding. Or a face cloth, or a towel, anything.'

By now, neighbours had started to emerge from their houses to see what was happening. They stood a little way away, as if they were figures in a religious tableau, while Detective Sergeant Ni Nuallán knelt beside Detective Garda Goold and held her hand tightly, and prayed for her.

***

Katie was still halfway through her paperwork when her phone rang.

'It's Kyna here, ma'am. Nessa Goold's been shot.'

'What? When?'

'Only a few minutes ago. She was shot in the face, but she's still conscious and we've called for an ambulance.'

'Who shot her?'

'There were two big fellows already at the Carroll house when we arrived there to talk to Eoghan. They were taking Eoghan away with them, forcibly like, but Nessa tried to stop them. That was when one of them pulled out a gun and shot her point-blank.'

'Mother of God. I'll come out there now. What kind of vehicle did they have, these fellows? I don't suppose you got their number, did you?'

'So far as I could see, they didn't have one. But they were driving a black VW Touran and the windows were all black, so it sounds very much like the black people carrier that Horgan's witness saw outside the Pearses' house when *they* were abducted. They took a left at the end of the road, heading towards the city, although of course they could have turned off in any direction.'

'What did they look like, these two fellows?'

'Well, like I say, *big*. But they both had plastic shopping bags over their heads, like the Rubberbandits, so I couldn't see their faces. They were both wearing the same – white shirts, short black coats. They looked like the kind of fellows you'd see on the door of a pub or a nightclub on a Saturday night.'

'I'll have a bulletin put out for them right now. How's Nessa doing?'

'Still about the same, but the ambulance has just turned the corner, thank God.'

'Listen, Kyna,' said Katie. 'Wait till the first patrol cars arrive to cordon off the place where she was shot, then go to the hospital and stay with her. I'll have Patrick contact her next of kin for me.'

She put down the receiver and punched out Superintendent Denis MacCostagáin's number. Oh dear Jesus, she thought, Detective Garda Goold is so young. Please don't let us lose another one, not like Brenda McCracken.

And as she waited for Superintendent MacCostagáin to answer, she couldn't help but wonder what Eoghan Carroll had in store for him. *Not another live cremation*, she prayed. *Not another beheading. Not another self-congratulatory act of pure sadism by the High Kings of Erin.*

***

Two Garda patrol cars were already at The Grove when Katie arrived, although the ambulance had just left. Detective Sergeant Ni Nuallán was standing beside her own car with the door open, ready to follow it, but she was still talking to one of the gardaí.

As Katie came up to her, she could see how shocked she was. Her face was pale and she was trembling, and her mouth was puckered like a child who is just about to burst into tears.

'I'll be going to the hospital now,' she said. 'The paramedics said it was touch-and-go, like. They couldn't be sure, but they thought that the bullet might have severed her spinal cord. Even if she survives, there's a strong possibility that she's going to be totally paralysed.'

Katie gave Kyna's arm a reassuring squeeze. Her instinct was to hold her close and allow her to let out all of her distress by sobbing, but she was a superintendent and Kyna was a sergeant, and this was a crime scene, and other officers were watching.

One of the gardaí came up and said, 'I've located the spent cartridge case, ma'am. Just over there, by the fence. I've put a marker next to it so. Looks like 9mm Parabellum.'

'Well, that narrows it down to sixty per cent of every handgun in the world,' said Katie. 'Have you found any other forensics?'

'There's a white shirt button which looks like it's been torn off, but that's all. I've marked that, too.'

'Okay. Good man yourself,' said Katie. 'The technical boys will be here soon, but keep looking around.'

Detective Sergeant Ni Nuallán said, 'I'll call you as soon as I know any more about Nessa.' She climbed into her car and drove off, just as Detectives O'Donovan and Horgan arrived and pulled into the kerb on the opposite side of the road.

The bloodstained pavement where Detective Garda Goold had been shot was cordoned off now, and two officers were stretching a groundsheet over it in case it starting raining again, but the bloodstains wouldn't tell them anything they didn't already know. Even if she didn't die, thought Katie, Detective Garda Goold's life had effectively been brought to an end.

She was still standing there, feeling helpless and bitter, when Detectives O'Donovan and Horgan came across the road.

'So, what's the story with Nessa?' Detective O'Donovan asked her. 'Is she going to be okay?'

Katie shook her head. 'She'll be lucky to survive. Or then again, maybe she won't.'

'Jesus. That poor, poor girl. I really liked her. She had so much enthusiasm, you know? What about this ex-boyfriend fellow?'

'Eoghan Carroll? God knows. According to DS Ni Nuallán he was hauled off by two men who looked like bouncers, in a similar type of vehicle to that the Pearses were taken off in. They were both wearing shopping bags like masks.'

'Sounds like them High Kings of Erin again, then, doesn't it? What the hell kind of a game are they playing at, that's what I'd like to know. Did you ever know *any* criminal go to this sort of length to nobble every potential witness?'

'Much more to the point, Patrick, how did they know that Eoghan *was* a potential witness?' asked Katie. 'How did they know we were on our way here to talk to him? How did they know that he was staying with his parents, and where they live?'

'Don't ask me,' said Detective O'Donovan. 'I wouldn't have the first idea.'

'Well, neither have I, or else I wouldn't be asking you. But I don't have any doubt at all now that someone inside Anglesea Street is tipping off the High Kings of Erin about every step we're taking to gather evidence against them.'

'But come on. Why in God's name would anybody at the station want to do that?'

'Blackmail, bribery, who knows? Bryan Molloy said it could be somebody with a gambling problem. Anyway, listen, let's go and talk to Eoghan's parents and see what they have to say about what happened.'

Katie and the two detectives went into the house, where Mrs Carroll was sitting in the corner being comforted by a female garda, while Mr Carroll stood by the window, with his hands in his pockets, morosely smoking. The house smelled of cats and cigarette smoke and was decorated in beiges and browns, with chocolate-brown armchairs and a patterned beige carpet, and a reproduction over the fireplace of an autumn scene in the Wicklow

Mountains. Even the cat in Mrs Carroll's lap was brown. She was stroking it so quickly and furiously that it looked as if she were trying to get it to catch fire.

'Mr and Mrs Carroll?' said Katie. 'Hello there. I'm Detective Superintendent Maguire.'

'Detective *Superintendent*?' said Mr Carroll, with smoke leaking out of his nostrils. 'The top brass, hey?'

'One of my detectives has been shot and critically injured, Mr Carroll. Apart from that, there's every likelihood that your son's abduction may be connected with a number of other very serious crimes, including murder.'

'Those men won't hurt him, will they?' asked Mrs Carroll. 'They said they wanted to have a word with him, that's all.'

'To be honest with you, Mrs Carroll, I simply don't know what their intentions are,' Katie admitted. 'But I've put out a wide-scale alert with a description of Eoghan and the two men and their vehicle, so I doubt if they'll be able to get very far.'

Mr Carroll coughed and then he said, 'Who are those scumbags? What would they have wanted to talk to Eoghan about? You said it was connected with some other crimes, like. Eoghan hasn't done anything wrong, has he?'

'He was a possible witness to a fraud,' said Katie. 'That's all I can tell you at the moment.'

But Mrs Carroll said, 'Pauly – you saw on the news that couple that was burned to death on the beach at Rocky Bay.'

'So? Yes, that was terrible, like. Terrible. But what did that have to do with our Eoghan?'

'The woman that was burned, Pauly, that was Meryl.'

'*Meryl*? Not Meryl Collins that Eoghan was engaged to? You're codding me!'

'No, it was her all right. Eoghan told me because he was worried about why she was killed.'

'What did *he* have to worry about?'

'They were out together, him and Meryl, a couple of days back, and they found this fellow lying by the side of the road. The fellow told them he'd been kidnapped but managed to get away, but Eoghan thought that maybe Meryl and her husband were killed because of that.'

'He was out with Meryl? What in the name of Jesus was he doing out with her? She's a married woman – well, she *was*, God rest her soul – and Eoghan's a married man!'

'They were only having a drink together for old times' sake, Pauly, nothing more.'

Mr Carroll's cigarette had burned right down to the filter so he crushed it out in a brown glass ashtray, shook out another one and lit it. 'Well, thank you very much, Mary, for sharing your secrets with me! What else has been going on in this house that I don't know about?'

'Eoghan didn't want to worry you, that's all. And he was afraid you might report it to the police or do something rash, and apart from that he didn't want his Patsy finding out.'

'Jesus, woman, don't you ever learn that secrets bring nothing but trouble? If I'd have thought that Eoghan was in any kind of danger I would have got him out of here. But now what? He's been taken away to God alone knows where and a guard's been shot.'

He turned to Katie and blew out smoke and said, 'Women! Jesus! What can you do with them?'

Katie said, 'If you could just tell me exactly what happened when these men came to take Eoghan.'

'They took him, that's all. They came to the door with those bags tied around their heads, the two of them, and they bust their way in and they took him. There was nothing I could do.'

'Did they knock on the door?'

'No, they rang the doorbell. I thought it was the coal delivery, from Blackpool. They should have delivered our coal today.'

'Horgan, stick some evidence tape over the doorbell, would you?' said Katie. 'We don't want anybody else touching it until the technical team have taken a print.' Then she turned back to Mr and Mrs Carroll. 'What did they say, these men? Did they say anything at all?'

'Only to Eoghan,' said Mrs Carroll. 'They said, "Come on, you, there's some people want a word with you!" That's all.'

'So what did Eoghan do? Do you think he knew who they were, or that he might have been expecting them?'

'I don't think so. Not at all. Well, you couldn't tell *who* they were, could you, with those bags on their heads? They were enough to scare you half to death. Eoghan was sitting at the kitchen table, working with his laptop. When they busted in, he asked them who they were and what the hell they thought they were doing, but they just grabbed hold of him and dragged him right out of the house, even though he was kicking and fighting, like. They spilled hot tea all over the floor. Well, look at it.'

'Don't mop that up yet, Mrs Carroll,' said Katie. 'There may be footprints in it.'

Mrs Carroll nodded, but then she suddenly started weeping, bending forwards and clutching her cat so tightly that it wrestled its way out of her arms and jumped on to the floor.

'Oh, dear Mother of God, what are they going to do to him? What are they going to do to my Eoghan? Oh God, what in Heaven's name tempted him to go out with that girl again? Now she's dead and Eoghan's been taken and the whole world feels like it's coming to the end!'

Mr Carroll went over and stood behind her, patting her on the back and saying, 'There, there, girl, don't you worry. They won't hurt our Eoghan. What's he done to upset those fellows? Nothing at all. The worst they'll do is give him a few clatters and Eoghan can take care of himself, like. You know that.'

He took another drag on his cigarette and looked across at Katie and shook his head as if to say, *Women*! *Jesus, Joseph and Mary*! *What can you do?*

Thirty-One

Katie stayed at The Grove until twenty past three in the morning, although there was no real need for her to do so. Shortly after two o'clock it started to rain again, that very fine prickly rain that can soak through a woollen sweater in minutes, and when the technical team arrived they erected one of their blue vinyl tents over the pavement. They set up floodlights, too, and three of them got down on their hands and knees in their white Tyvek suits and combed the Carrolls' front driveway and their scrubby little front garden. Another two went inside to lift any prints that the kidnappers might have left on the doorbell button and to take photographs of the tea-spattered kitchen floor.

Donald Mullen from RTÉ turned up just before 1 a.m., with his ENG cameraman and a sound technician. He was wearing a short black rain cape with a pointed hood, like a weary middle-aged leprechaun, and there were creases under his eyes as if he had just got out of bed. He was followed shortly after by Francis Byrne, a portly freelance reporter from the *Examiner* in a trench coat as tight as a sausage skin. He had flaking red cheeks and a comb-over, and he looked and smelled as if he had been drinking for most of the previous evening. Katie recognized him from the press bench at the District Court.

'So – the High Kings of Erin have been at it again, Detective Superintendent?' was the very first question he asked her.

'Who told you that?' Katie retorted.

262

Francis Byrne tapped the side of his nose with his biro. 'Sorry, ma'am! Can't possibly reveal my sources.'

Donald Mullen's cameraman switched on his light and for a few seconds Katie was blinded.

'Do you want to tell us what happened here, ma'am?' asked Donald Mullen, holding out his microphone.

Katie brushed the rain from her hair and turned to the camera. 'I'm sorry to say that there was a shooting here in Carrigaline yesterday afternoon and that a detective garda was seriously injured. She was unsuccessfully trying to prevent the abduction by two unidentified assailants of a man who had come back here from England to visit his parents.'

'Can you give us the name of the detective garda who was shot?'

'Not yet,' she said. 'The officer was taken to the University Hospital for emergency treatment and I'm still awaiting an update. We'll be able to release the name as soon as the next of kin have been informed.'

'But what about the fellow who was abducted?' asked Francis Byrne. 'Who was he?'

'His name is Eoghan Carroll. He lives in England permanently these days but his parents still reside here in Carrigaline. He's an audio engineer.'

'An audio engineer? So why was he abducted?'

'At this moment in time, we're not at all sure.'

'But what exactly was the Garda's interest in him?'

'What do you mean?'

'Well, if your detectives arrived to find Mr Carroll in mid-abduction, they must have been coming here to talk to him for some reason – maybe arrest him even. Don't tell me they were just passing and saw him being abducted by chance? Apart from the coincidental timing, The Grove is a dead end, like.'

Katie said, 'I'm sorry, I can't give you any further details yet.'

'But didn't you believe that Mr Carroll might have information that could help you in your investigation into the High Kings of Erin? That's true, isn't it? And that being the case, it looks like the

High Kings of Erin have stolen another march on you, wouldn't you say?'

'Francis, you can come up with as many suppositions you like, but I'm not going to make any further comment, not right now. At the moment, my main concern is Mr Carroll's safety and most of all the condition of the officer who was shot here.'

Francis Byrne stuck out his lower lip like a disappointed baby and shrugged. 'Oh well. I know you have to take care of your own. But there's no doubt, is there, that this was the work of the High Kings of Erin and that they're running rings around you? That's two local businessmen kidnapped, with one of them decapitated, a man and his wife burned to death on a beach, one garda blown to smithereens and another shot. The High Kings have even been on the phone to you, boasting what they've done, but how much nearer have you got to feeling their collars?'

'How do you know they've been on the phone to me?' Katie demanded.

The rain fell softly and silently between them, illuminated by the TV camera so that Katie would appear on the screen as if she were veiled.

Again Francis Byrne tapped his well-chewed biro on the side of his nose. 'Can't say, ma'am. But you're not denying it, are you?'

'Not denying it, not confirming it. Now, unless you have some information that might assist me in my inquiries, I suggest you go and breathe your secondhand Murphy's fumes over somebody else.'

'Oh, you're a hard woman, Detective Superintendent. Everybody says so.'

'I hope for your sake that you didn't drive here,' Katie told him. 'If you so much as open a car door, I'll have you breathalysed.'

Francis Byrne gave her a leering smile. 'I'm happy to say that my auld doll drove me here, and the most intoxicating drink *she* ever takes is Barry's Tea with a cough drop in it.'

***

Katie had been asleep for less than half an hour when her front doorbell chimed. She opened her eyes and tried to focus on the clock beside her bed. Seven thirty-seven a.m. Who on earth could it be at this time of the morning? It couldn't be connected with work because they would have phoned her first. It was gloomy outside and it was raining hard, so it wouldn't be the window cleaner, either.

She had made up her mind to ignore it when the doorbell chimed again, and then again. She hesitated for a few seconds and then she threw back the quilt and sat up. Mother of God, what did this person want so urgently? She was wearing only a Cork GAA T-shirt, so she stood up and went across to the door where her thick pink flannelette dressing gown was hanging.

'All right!' she called out, her voice still hoarse from sleep. 'I'm coming!'

She walked along the hallway, scratching her scalp and trying to tidy her hair. She turned off the alarm, but before she opened the door she said, 'Who is it?'

'Sorcha. Sorcha Kane, from next door.'

Katie immediately slid back the bolts and the safety chain and opened the door. Sorcha was standing in the porch, drenched, wearing nothing but a long white nightdress that was spattered all the way down the front with blood. She had long brown hair, thick and tangled and knotted, which half covered her face. In spite of that, Katie could immediately see that her right eye was crimson and completely closed up, and that a small triangular flap of skin had been torn open on the bridge of her nose, as if she had been hit with a signet ring.

'My God, Sorcha, come in!' said Katie. She reached out and took hold of Sorcha's arm and helped her into the hallway. Her shoulders were hunched like a little old lady's and she was shaking uncontrollably all over. Katie guided her into the living room and said, 'There, sit down there. I'll bring you a towel. You can dry yourself and then you can put this on.' She took off her dressing gown and laid it over the back of the couch.

Sorcha perched herself on the edge of the couch, but then almost immediately she stood up again.

'I'm so sorry,' she said. 'I should never have bothered you. It's not for you to worry about. I'll just go back home. He'll be even more angry if he finds out I've called on you.'

'Sorcha, sit down. It's not a bother at all.'

'But he'll be so *angry*!' said Sorcha, and she was almost squeaking.

'I don't give a knacker's bang how angry he is, darling. He'd better not try doing to *me* what he's clearly been doing to you. Now sit down, *please*. I won't be a second.'

She went to the airing cupboard and came back with a thick white bath towel. 'Here,' she said. 'Get yourself dry and I'll put on the kettle. What would you like? Tea or coffee? Or chocolate, if you like.'

Sorcha looked down at the towel that Katie had laid across her knees. She lowered her head for a moment and then she started to sob – deep, wrenching sobs that sounded as if the alveoli in her lungs were being ripped apart.

'I can't,' she wept. 'I can't. I can't do anything any more.'

Katie came back over and knelt down in front of her. She took hold of her hands and held them tight. As she did so, she noticed that Sorcha's wrists were both bruised and that two of the fingers on her left hand were crooked, which indicated that they must have been broken at one time but failed to set properly.

'Sorcha,' she said gently, but Sorcha didn't look up. All Katie could see was that dark tangle of wet brown hair. 'David said that all of your arguments, all of that shouting and screaming, that was all your fault. He said you were bipolar – manic depressive – and that you have terrible rages and smash things.'

'It *is* my fault,' said Sorcha. 'I shouldn't make him angry. He only punishes me when I make him angry.'

'*Are* you bipolar?'

Sorcha shook her head. 'I don't know what that means.'

'Do you suffer from mood swings? You know, happy one minute but really depressed the next?'

Again Sorcha shook her head. 'I do try to please him. I'm always trying to think of ways to please him. I cook his favourite meals, but most of the time he throws them at me. I made him a summer shirt once but all he did was rip it to pieces.'

'But what makes him so angry?'

Sorcha started to sob again. 'I don't know,' she said. 'I try and I try but I just don't know. It must be my fault, but I don't understand what I keep doing wrong.'

Katie laid the towel to one side and took hold of Sorcha's shoulders. 'Come on,' she said, 'let's get you dry and warm and then you'll begin to feel better.'

She helped Sorcha to stand up, then pulled the soaking-wet nightgown over her head. She didn't say anything when she saw Sorcha naked, but she was horrified. She was so thin that her breasts were nothing but two semicircular flaps against her ribcage, and her pelvis protruded like the rim of a washbasin. Her legs were barely thicker than broom handles.

But it wasn't her emaciation that disturbed Katie so much as the obvious beatings and other mistreatment that she had been suffering. Her body was tattooed all over with bruises, some yellow and faded, some still purplish. Others were crimson, so they had obviously been inflicted only hours ago. She had teeth marks and scabs all around her nipples, as if they had been bitten, and bitten hard enough to break the skin, and there were runnels of dried blood down the insides of her thighs, so Katie could only guess what had been done to her there.

'I never wanted anybody to see me like this,' said Sorcha. 'I'm so ashamed.'

'Sorcha, there's only one person in your relationship who needs to be ashamed,' Katie told her. 'Look, you're shivering with cold. Come and have a warm shower and wash your hair, too, and then you'll feel much better.'

She led Sorcha through to the bathroom and ran the shower for her. She took off her T-shirt and climbed in with her and while Sorcha simply stood there with her eyes closed and her head bowed, Katie shampooed her hair for her and washed her all over with tea-tree shower gel.

After she had rinsed her hair, with the warm water still cascading over them, she held Sorcha closely in her arms and tried to make her feel her strength and her sympathy, as well as her determination that she was never going to be beaten or abused ever again.

Almost a minute passed and then Sorcha looked up, her right eye still closed, but her left eye dark and glittering. 'You're not an angel, are you?' she said. 'It feels like you're an angel.'

***

Katie gave Sorcha a pair of her knickers and some warm blue woollen tights, as well as a navy-blue tweed skirt and a pale blue roll-neck sweater. Then she made them both some coffee and brought out some oat biscuits, although Sorcha only nibbled at the edge of one of them.

Barney came trotting into the living room and sat close beside Sorcha with his head on the couch, looking up at her soulfully, as if he understood how much she was suffering.

Katie had looked out of the kitchen window and seen that the next-door driveway was still empty, with no sign of David's Range Rover.

'Do you know when David's going to be back?' she asked.

'He's gone to Kinsale for the day. There's some kind of veterinary conference at the Trident Hotel. He doesn't usually get in till late from one of those things, if he gets in at all. Especially if he finds a woman that he likes.'

'He tells you about his affairs with other women?'

Sorcha nodded. 'This woman I was with last night, she was a dream compared with you. Beautiful eyes, beautiful figure, and she really appreciated me for who I am. Unlike you, you stupid waste of space, with your missing teeth and your face like chewed toffee.'

For a moment, Katie was concerned that David might have told Sorcha that he had taken *her* to bed, too, but Sorcha didn't seem to know about that – or if she did, she was simply too anaesthetized by David's brutality to care.

'Let's go back next door and collect your clothes and your toothbrush and anything else you need,' said Katie. 'Then I can take you to the Cuanlee Refuge. They're really welcoming there. They'll probably arrange for you to see a doctor, too. I think you ought to have a check-up.'

'Can't I stay here with you?'

'That's impossible, Sorcha, I'm sorry. I'm out on duty for most of the time and I wouldn't want to leave you alone in the house with David right next door. But once I have you settled at Cuanlee, I'll immediately get in touch with Gallchnó Crann, which is a project I'm involved in to take care of battered and intimidated women. They'll give you all the help and support you need to sort your life out. I'll be having a word with David myself, believe me.'

'You're not going to arrest him?' asked Sorcha, fearfully.

'It depends if you want to make a formal complaint of domestic violence, and even if you don't I still might consider it, after what he's done to you. Otherwise, you can go to the District Court and ask for a barring order so that David has to leave the house and never come anywhere near you. As soon as you apply, the judge will grant you a protection order, or an interim barring order, pending your hearing. Whatever you decide, Sorcha, you need to get away from that man. Look at you. Listen to yourself. He's beaten you physically, but worse than that, he's beaten you mentally. You've just become David's punchbag, somebody he can use whenever he feels like it to take out his frustrations on.'

'I can't collect my clothes,' said Sorcha. 'I don't have a door key. David's never given me a door key.'

'That's no problem,' said Katie. 'One of the skills they teach us in the Garda is lock-picking. And if I can't open the door like that, they also teach us housebreaking.'

'You won't cause any damage? David will go mental if you cause any damage.'

'Sorcha, it doesn't matter how angry he gets. He's not going to hurt you again. You don't even have to *see* him again, ever, if you don't want to. You did the right thing coming here to me this morning. It's all over. All of the shouting, all of the pain. It's finished.'

Sorcha sat on the couch in Katie's pale blue sweater, which was much too big for her, looking nervy and miserable. Barney licked her hand and made a noise deep in the back of his throat as if he was trying to say, *There, see, you're safe now.*

Thirty-Two

While Katie waited in the hallway of the Kanes' house, Detective Sergeant Ni Nuallán called her.

'I'm still here at the hospital,' she said. 'Nessa's parents are here, too, and two of her sisters.'

'How is she?'

'It's not good news, I'm afraid. They operated on her for nearly five hours last night, but the bullet damaged her spinal cord and even if she survives she won't be able to breathe unaided, apart from having no feeling at all below the neck.'

'Oh God. All right, Kyna. Thanks. I'll have Patrick relieve you if you want to go home for a rest.'

'No, I'd rather stay, ma'am. There's a bed here that I can use if I need to sleep. The surgeon didn't say so in as many words, but I don't think she has very long and I want to be here.'

'Okay, if that's what you want. I have a couple of things to take care of first and then I'll come right over.'

Sorcha came out of the bedroom, pulling a purple wheeled suitcase behind her. She stopped in the hallway and looked into the living room, and then at the kitchen. Katie could see pieces of broken blue and white china on the kitchen floor, and a brown splash mark up the wall which looked like gravy.

'Have you got everything you need?' she asked Sorcha.

'Not really,' said Sorcha. 'But I'm ready to go.'

They left the house and Katie lifted Sorcha's suitcase into the back of her Ford Focus. It had stopped raining at last and a pale

271

lemon sun was visible behind the clouds. As Katie drove into the city, Sorcha talked almost ceaselessly, as if she were trying to persuade herself that she was doing the right thing by leaving David and that she wasn't to blame for making him lose his temper and hitting her.

'I asked myself so many times why I didn't leave him. But what would have happened to him if I had? The trouble is, I loved him. I *still* love him, even if I have a thousand reasons not to. And I'm sure that he loves me. He wouldn't hit me if he didn't love me, would he? He wouldn't even *talk* to me, would he, if he didn't love me, let alone punish me?'

Katie drove along by the river until she reached the Cuanlee building on Kyrls Quay. When she had parked, Sorcha sat for a moment with her hand pressed over her mouth as if she were trying to remember something important.

'Come on, Sorcha,' Katie told her. 'You know you have to do this. You can't go back now.'

'No, you're right,' said Sorcha. 'I need to get back into the real world again. I've totally forgotten what it's like.'

***

Katie drove back to Anglesea Street and went up to her office. Detective O'Donovan came in to see her almost at once. His shiny brown tie was crooked and he was eating a snack-size pork pie.

'No trace of that people carrier,' he said, with his mouth full. 'It's probably tucked away in some garage or workshop by now, or somebody's barn.'

'Well, all we can do is keep looking. How many vehicles of that description are there in Cork?'

'City-wide, only twelve black people carriers, of all makes. County-wide, thirty-eight. Nationwide, one hundred and eleven. We've tracked down the owners of all the black people carriers in the city. Three of them are abroad at the moment, two of the vehicles are off the road, and the remaining seven are either being used as taxis or for private hire, or their owners have credible alibis. Either that, or they're too old and feeble to kidnap anybody.'

Katie said, 'These two thugs who kidnapped Eoghan Carroll, surely somebody must reck them? They may have had bags on their heads, but the way that Detective Sergeant Ni Nuallán described them, they sounded like Tweedledum and Tweedledee. You can't mistake a pair like that.'

'They didn't ring any bells with me and nobody else has spoken up and said that they know them. They could have been the Flynn brothers, Joey and Dermot, except that Joey's dead and Dermot's in the nuthouse at Carraig Mor.'

Katie checked her wristwatch. 'Look, keep me in touch, I'm going to the hospital to see Nessa Goold and then I have to attend the District Court with Derek Hagerty. We need to widen the search for this people carrier. I'll be making a statement to the media when I get back, so with any luck somebody who knows these two scumbags will come forward. I'm seriously concerned for Eoghan, though, I have to admit. If he's really been taken by the High Kings of Erin, God alone knows what they could do to him.'

She went over to the coat stand to take down her raincoat, but as she did so, her phone rang.

'Oh, get it for me, Patrick, would you? Whoever it is, tell them I'm not here.'

Detective O'Donovan picked it up and said, 'Patrick O'Donovan here. The DS has left for the hospital. You can probably get her on her mobile.'

He listened for a moment, but then he put his hand over the receiver and said, 'I think you'd better un-leave for the hospital, ma'am. It's Inspector Fennessy. There's a woman who's just come in to report that her husband's been kidnapped.'

Katie hung up her raincoat again and went across to take the phone out of Detective O'Donovan's hand. 'Liam?' she said. 'Where is she? Okay, grand. Thanks. I'll be right down.'

**

The woman who was sitting in the interview room with Inspector Fennessy was tall and angular, with choppy grey hair that looked as if she had cut it herself. She wore no make-up and her eyebrows were unplucked and she reminded Katie of her history teacher from school. She was wearing a light green trench coat with the belt tightly twisted around a very thin waist, and green lace-up shoes.

'This is Mrs Mairead Whelan, ma'am,' said Liam Fennessy, standing up. 'Mrs Whelan, this is Detective Superintendent Maguire, and this is Detective O'Donovan.'

'They *warned* me not to come to you,' said Mairead Whelan, in a voice that was almost a whine. She stood up, too, clutching a large brown leather handbag with curled-up straps. 'They said that they couldn't be held responsible for what would happen to Pat if I did tell the guards. But I didn't know where else to turn. They said they'd do all sorts of horrible things to him if I didn't pay up, but how can I pay up? Pat's way over his overdraft limit and I only have sixty-seven euros left in my Permanent Bank account.'

'Please, Mairead, sit down and try to be calm,' said Katie. 'If your husband's missing and there are people demanding a ransom from you, you did the right thing coming here.'

'But what if they *hurt* him? What if they murder him? I can't pay them two hundred thousand euros! Where in the name of Jesus would I get two hundred and fifty thousand euros?'

She sat down, still clutching her bag tightly, and Katie sat down, too, with Detective O'Donovan sitting on her left. Liam Fennessy remained where he was, standing, with his arms folded. Katie glanced up at him and she thought he had that haunted look again. She badly needed his support at this moment, and she didn't want him cracking up. Ever since Bryan Molloy had taken over as Acting Chief Superintendent she had felt that fault lines had been opening up in the structure of Anglesea Street and that all of the officers in the station were acting more cautiously, watching their backs, working less as a team.

'What's your husband's name, Mairead?' Katie asked her.

'Pat – Patrick Whelan, the owner of Whelan's Music Store on Oliver Plunkett Street.'

'Well, I know it, of course. In fact I know him. He helped to organize that music festival last year, didn't he, in aid of the Good Shepherd Services? When did he go missing?'

'He closes the shop at six sharp and he's always in for his tea by half past. Once or twice he used to come in later because some old musician friend of his might have come into the shop, you know, and asked him out for a drink. But he always called me if he was going to do that, and of course these days he hasn't been able to afford to go to the pub.'

'So he didn't come in last night?'

'No, and I was fierce worried I can tell you. I kept ringing his mobile but there was no answer at all. When he didn't come in by midnight I was going to ring you anyway. But then about a quarter to twelve I got this phone call.'

Mairead Whelan's lower lip was trembling and she was very close to tears. Katie reached across the table and said, 'Go on, Mairead. You're doing really well.'

'I thought it was Pat, but of course it wasn't Pat. It was this fellow who said that Pat had been kidnapped and that I had three days to come up with two hundred and fifty thousand euros or else I would never see Pat again, or at least I would never see him again the way that I was used to seeing him.'

'Did he say what he meant by that?' asked Detective O'Donovan.

Tears had been filling Mairead's eyes but now they suddenly dropped down her checks. 'He said that I would either see him in a coffin, dead, or else he'd be alive but not kicking, because he'd have no legs, and no arms either, and he wouldn't be able to tell me what had happened because they would have cut out his tongue with a straightrazor.'

'Come on, don't get too upset. Your man was only trying to scare you. Did he tell you where to deliver the money?'

'No. He said he'd ring me this afternoon sometime and see

how my fund-raising was coming along. Then, when I had the whole two hundred and fifty thousand, he'd give me instructions on when and where to hand it over.'

One of her tears dripped on to the back of Katie's hand, and then another, but Katie didn't take it away. 'Did the man tell you who he was? Or who he represented?'

'I'm sorry?'

'What I mean is, did he say that Pat had been kidnapped by any particular gang?'

'No, he didn't give me any names.'

Katie said, 'Patrick, would you fetch that latest recording for me? The one about the Pearses. It's on my desk, next to the clock.'

Detective O'Donovan left the interview room. Liam Fennessy sat down now and said to Mairead Whelan, 'So Pat's overdrawn at the bank? Has business been going badly?'

'Terrible bad. Disastrous. He's having to close the shop at the end of the month. Everybody buys on the interweb these days. I don't know how we're going to manage.'

Liam glanced at Katie as if to say *there's definitely a pattern here*. Micky Crounan with his bakery and Derek Hagerty with his auto workshop. Now Pat Whelan and his music store. All of them bankrupt or near-bankrupt, but all of them kidnapped for ransom.

Detective O'Donovan came back with the DVD recording of Katie's last conversation with the man who claimed he was speaking for the High Kings of Erin. He slotted it into the interview recorder and switched it on. Katie used the remote control to fast-forward it until she came to a part that was appropriate for Mairead Whelan to hear.

'Let me tell you this,' said the husky-voiced caller, 'the sooner you learn to rub along with us, the happier we're all going to be. You do your thing and we'll do ours, and Ireland will have its pride restored before you know it. *Éirinn go Brách.*'

'That's him!' said Mairead, firmly. She took out a tissue and smartly wiped her eyes, and sniffed. 'That's the cancery bastard who called me!'

Katie was taken aback by her vehemence. 'You're sure about that? You don't want to listen to any more?'

'No, I don't have to. That was him all right. God rot him.'

Katie said, 'All right, Mairead. What I have to do now is talk to my superior officers to see what we can do about the ransom money. But, please – you must *not* breathe a single word of this to anybody, not even your closest relatives or your closest friends. If Pat's been kidnapped by the people I think he's been kidnapped by, they're likely to go after anybody who can identify them, or give even the smallest scrap of evidence against them. I'm not going to beat around the bush, Mairead, they'll kill them, and not pleasantly. I'm afraid it's as simple as that.'

'Mother of God,' said Mairead Whelan. 'I shouldn't have come here, should I?'

'What choice did you have?' Katie asked her. 'How else could you have hoped to find enough money to pay them off? Besides, I'm going to make sure that you have close protection from now on. It'll be discreet, plain-clothes protection, so that the kidnappers won't realize that you've contacted us. Where do you live?'

'The Lodge, Ard na Laoi, just off the Middle Glanmire Road.'

'All right, then. Detective O'Donovan here will make a note of your phone numbers and all your particulars. When the kidnappers ring you again, we'll be recording your conversation and with any luck we may be able to trace where they're calling from, too. Meanwhile, when you *do* talk to them, Mairead, try your very best not to sound angry and resentful, no matter how you really feel. You'll have a detective with you the whole time to help you through it. Just tell them that you're doing everything you can to get hold of the money, and you're hopeful that you'll be able to pay them off well within the three days.'

'Are you sure I've done the right thing? What if they find out that I've come here and they kill Pat? How am I ever going to forgive myself?'

Katie stood up. 'You'll get him back, Mairead. I promise you that. Patrick – if you can make a note of all of Mairead's details and run through any of her husband's business background that she knows about. You know – aggressive creditors, outstanding court orders, things like that. I have to go and brief Chief Superintendent Molloy.' She paused, then she added, '*Acting* Chief Superintendent Molloy.'

***

Halfway along the corridor to Bryan Molloy's office, Katie's mobile phone rang. She saw that it was Detective Sergeant Ni Nuallán calling. She was probably wondering why she hadn't arrived at the hospital yet.

'Kyna? I won't be too much longer. Something's come up. Another broke businessman's been kidnapped, would you believe? Pat Whelan, the owner of Whelan's Music Store. His wife's here now. I just have to talk to Molloy and then I'll be with you.'

'You don't have to hurry,' said Detective Sergeant Ni Nuallán. She was silent for a very long time, and then she said, 'Nessa passed away five minutes ago. Father Buckley from the hospital chaplaincy came up to give her the last rites.'

'Oh no,' said Katie. 'Dear God in heaven.' She couldn't think of anything else to say. She remembered a consultant psychiatrist at Templemore telling her group of trainee gardaí, 'Much more often than most people, you will find yourselves being hit unexpectedly and devastatingly hard by emotions such as fear, and disgust, and pity, and grief. I am not suggesting for a moment that you could or should make yourself immune to such emotions. You wouldn't be human if you did. But while you are on duty, you must keep calm and rational and level-headed. Learn to suppress any reactive outbursts until later. Shout or weep or break things by all means, but wait until you get home.'

'I'll come over as soon as I can,' she told Detective Sergeant Ni Nuallán, and then she continued along the corridor to Bryan Molloy's office. Before she knocked on his door, though, she took a deep breath to steady herself, and held it. *Wait until you get home.*

Acting Chief Superintendent Molloy was standing behind his desk in his shirtsleeves, going over his diary appointments with his secretary, Teagan.

'Now, look here, girl,' he was saying, 'how can I show up for that meeting of the Southern Law Association if at one and the same time I'm supposed to be giving an after-dinner speech to the Cork Business Association? Mind you, if only these people would stop associating with each other, we'd all have a quieter life!'

He looked up when Katie came in. 'Katie! How's that young detective of yours? Any news?'

'I just heard from DS Ni Nuallán at the hospital. She died a short time ago. It may have been a blessing, considering that she would have been paralysed for the rest of her life.'

'Ah well, I'm sorry to hear it. Very sorry. I'll be writing a letter of condolence to her family.'

He was about to go back to his diary, but then he realized that Katie hadn't just come to tell him that.

'You haven't found that witness fellow, have you? The fellow from Carrigaline?'

'Not yet, no. But a woman has just come in to tell us that her husband's been kidnapped. Mairead Whelan – her husband Pat owns Whelan's, which is one of the oldest music stories in Cork.'

'Has she heard from the kidnappers at all? He hasn't just walked out on her?'

'Oh no. They've called her. They want two hundred and fifty thousand euros, they said, or else they'll kill him or amputate his arms and legs and cut out his tongue.'

'Holy Mary! Did they say who they were?'

'No, but I played Mrs Whelan the recording of the last call I received from the fellow who said that he was speaking on behalf of the High Kings of Erin. She swore blind that it was one and the same as the fellow who rang her.'

Bryan Molloy turned to his secretary and said, 'Teagan, would you give us a moment, please?'

Teagan gave Katie a quick, sympathetic smile, as if she could guess what she was in for, picked up the diary and left the office, closing the door very quietly behind her.

'Sit down,' said Bryan Molloy.

Katie sat down opposite his desk and crossed her legs, but said nothing.

'What am I going to tell the media?' Bryan Molloy asked her. 'More important than that, what am I going to tell Jimmy O'Reilly?'

'For the time being, you should tell the media nothing at all,' said Katie. 'The kidnappers warned Mairead Whelan that if she reported her husband's abduction to the Garda they'd kill him at once. As for Assistant Commissioner O'Reilly, you can tell him the truth, that the so-called High Kings of Erin have taken another bankrupt businessman and want nearly a quarter of a million euros for his safe return.'

'No, no, Katie, I don't think you have me. What am I going to tell him about our hopeless inability to stop these High Kings of Erin? How am I going to explain that we are making absolutely no progress at all in identifying who they are and why they're doing what they're doing?'

'Bryan, we *are* making progress,' Katie insisted. 'We have witness descriptions of at least two of the offenders, and their vehicle, and I don't think it's going to be long before we get a breakthrough. It certainly doesn't help that they seem to be receiving inside information from somebody here in the station.'

'Oh, that again! You're sure about that, are you? I'm beginning to think that's nothing more than an excuse for your incompetence. You don't seem to be able to get a handle on this at all, Katie. You say you've made progress, but at what price? We have two young gardaí dead now, as well as three known homicides – Micky Crounan and the Pearses. We've lost a whole heap of public money paying for the freedom of a man who already happened to be free. Now it looks like we're going to pay almost as much again to get this Whelan fellow released – even if he manages to escape, too, which he may very well do – although I doubt if you'll get know about it before it's too late. And where is our last surviving witness to Derek Hagerty's abduction, I ask? Bundled away by the High Kings of Erin before we could ask him even a single question.'

'Bryan, you're being unfair,' Katie retorted. 'My team have been working all the hours that God sends them to break this case, but you know yourself that the evidence is less than minimal. We have the saw marks left on Micky Crounan's vertebrae, we have the footprints left on Rocky Bay Beach, we have a fingerprint lifted from the Carrolls' doorbell in Carrigaline, and two sightings of two bald gorillas in black suits, who nobody has yet come forward to identify. Plus some bits and pieces of bomb that may or may not have been put together by Clearie O'Hely.

'I'm hopeful, though, that Derek Hagerty will break, sooner or later, especially now that he's been charged.' She checked her watch. 'Talking of that, I have to be at the District Court in fifteen minutes.'

'What for?' asked Bryan Molloy. 'How can you possibly pursue your case against Derek Hagerty when you have no witnesses left alive and no material evidence?'

'Bryan, no messing,' Katie snapped at him, 'I'm beginning to wonder whose side you're on.'

Bryan Molloy's eyes bulged and he repeatedly jabbed his finger at her 'I'll tell you whose side I'm on! I'm on the side of efficiency and effectiveness in clearing up serious crime in this city! You know how I dealt with the gangs in Limerick? They thought they were hard, but I was harder than they were. I didn't give them an inch, not a fecking inch, and I'm not going to give an inch to any of the gangs here in Cork, whatever they call themselves. But it takes good team management to be efficient and it takes good intelligence and first-class detective work to be effective, and you, girl, are seriously falling short.'

Katie said, 'This is your idea of a truce, is it? This is your idea of us "rubbing along together"?'

'Katie, you don't have to call a truce with somebody who doesn't have anything to offer you. And up until now, what have you come up with?'

'You don't know me at all, Bryan,' said Katie. 'You don't know the way I work or what connections I have, and I can promise you that one day soon you're going to regret talking to me like this.'

'I'm shaking in my boots,' grinned Bryan Molloy. 'Meanwhile, if you or one of your team will be so kind, I'll need some detailed background information on this Whelan kidnap so that I can talk to Jimmy O'Reilly again and see if he can authorize another two hundred and fifty thousand euros ransom money. I don't know if he'll be able to let us have that much, but if he can, we'd better not lose it this time.'

Katie was about to lash back at him that no crime ever got solved by sarcasm, but she bit her lip. *Wait until you get home.*

Instead, she said, 'Detective O'Donovan's taking down Mairead Whelan's particulars right now. I'll ask him to send them up to you.'

'And what are you going to do about Derek Hagerty?'

'I'll drop the charge against him, for the time being anyway, although I still think I could make it stick. Believe me, there's enough holes in his story to strain the poppies.'

'Drop it,' said Bryan Molloy. 'We don't want to look even more cack-handed than we do already. And you'll have to turf him out, whether he wants to go or not. This is the Garda station, not the fecking Simon Shelter.'

'We have a safe house in Macroom that should be free in a day or two. In the meantime, he could go back to his own home. It would give him the chance to sort out his affairs, cancel his newspapers or whatever and pack what he needs. But we'd have to give him round-the-clock protection.'

'As long as it's only a couple of days and no more than that. For the love of God, Katie, we can't afford many more officers out on protection duty. We simply don't have the manpower, and if you saw the overtime costs you'd pass out on the spot.'

282

'I'll see what I can arrange with Denis,' Katie told him.

As she opened the office door to leave, Bryan Molloy said, 'There doesn't have to be this enmity between us, Katie. But you have to prove to me that you're on top of these kidnappings. I can't go on making excuses for you for very much longer.'

Katie pretended that she hadn't heard that, and walked out into the corridor without closing the door behind her.

Thirty-Three

The door opened and Eoghan heard floorboards creaking, and people breathing, and the sound of their clothes rustling. He could smell perfume, too, heavy and musky, similar to the Jovan perfume that his wife, Patsy, sprayed on herself far too liberally whenever she went out in the evening.

He was blindfolded with what felt like a woollen scarf, knotted so tightly at the back of his head that it was bringing on one of his headaches. His wrists were bound behind his back with gaffer tape and his shoes had been taken away. He was lying on his right side, very awkwardly, on what felt like carpet that was worn down to the backing.

Wherever he was, it was chilly and smelled strongly of damp, like most old houses in Cork. He was trembling with the cold and also with the shock of being dragged away from his parents' house and seeing that young detective shot, right in the face. On top of that, his bladder was so full that it was painful.

He heard shuffles and murmurs and then somebody came up and squatted down close to him, and sniffed. Then a thin, abrasive voice said, 'So! You're the fellow who found Derek Hagerty lying by the roadside, along with that Pearse woman.'

'Do you think you could untie me here? I'm absolutely bursting for a slash.'

'Oh, just piss in your kecks, I don't mind. What I want to know is, what did you think when you picked up Derek Hagerty?'

'Is that his name?' said Eoghan. 'To me and Meryl, he called himself Denny.'

'Denny, Derek. Whatever he called himself, what did you think?'

'What do you mean, what did I think? I thought we ought to call an ambulance or take him to the nearest Garda station, that's what I thought. But he begged us not to, said he was scared for his life. He was totally shitting it, so Meryl said she'd take him back to her house, God rest her soul.'

'You know that she's dead?' the thin voice asked him.

'Of course. It's been all over the news. It was horrible, her getting all burned up like that. She and I were going to be married once upon a time.'

'Yes, I know about that. You have my sympathy, believe me.'

'Was she killed because of this Denny fellow? This Hagerty, or whatever his name is? Am *I* here because of him? I was going to go to the cops about it, but my father told me that it would be safer for me to forget about it altogether and go back to England a couple of days early, just in case. I wish I had now.'

'Do you know the names of the people who killed her?'

Eoghan had to squeeze his eyes tight shut and clench his thighs together for a moment to stop himself from urinating. Then he said, 'No, of course I don't. Even the cops don't know. How could I?'

'Did Derek Hagerty tell you who had kidnapped him? Did *he* mention any names?'

'No, the people who took him, he said he'd never seen them before.'

'Did you believe him?'

'I didn't have any reason not to.'

'Ah, no. I have a strong suspicion, Eoghan, that you did *not* believe him.'

'For Christ's sake!' Eoghan retorted. 'Why should I have not believed him? I didn't care one way or the other! He was all bloody and bruised and the smell off of him was rank. All I wanted to do was for us to get rid of him as soon as we could. To be honest with you, I didn't even want to pick him up in the first place.'

'But you had an inkling that he wasn't telling you the truth, didn't you?'

'Like I say, it didn't matter to me one way or the other. Not a hat of shite, believe me.'

'All the same, you *did* think that he could have been lying about what happened to him, or exaggerating at the very least?'

'No. Yes. I don't know.'

'If you didn't suspect that he wasn't telling you the truth, why did the Pearses call the guards?'

'How should I know? Listen, I really need to go to the jacks and I don't want to wet my pants, thank you very much.'

'Okay, okay. I'll do a deal with you. I'll let you go and relieve yourself and then we'll come to an arrangement, you and me.'

'Arrangement?'

'Go and water the horses first. I can't stand talking to someone so twitchy. Malachi?'

Eoghan heard somebody else approaching and then his left arm was grasped tightly and he was hauled up on to his feet as easily as if he had been a young child. Because he was still completely blindfolded he had to stagger to correct his balance, but then his left arm was grasped again and he felt the tape around his wrists being sliced apart with a very sharp knife.

A hard hand gripped his right shoulder and, with stumbling steps, he was pushed straight along a corridor for about thirty or forty feet, then tugged to the left, and then stopped. He heard a door open and a growly voice said, 'There you are. You can sit down to piss. Don't want it spraying all over the shop.'

He unbuttoned his trousers and sat down. The toilet seat was wooden and rickety and the varnish was peeling, but he didn't care about that. As he emptied his bladder, he thought, *My hands are free now, and there's only this one fellow close enough to stop me. If I can surprise him, maybe there's a good chance that I can get out of here.* He could hear the thin-voiced man talking and a young woman replying to him, but he couldn't make out what they were saying, so they were obviously some distance away.

He knew it would be dangerous. If they had been prepared to shoot a detective garda who had tried to stop them, they would have no compunction at all about shooting him. In fact, he was almost one hundred per cent sure that was what they were going to do anyway. For some reason, the thin-voiced man seemed to be sure that he knew something incriminating about Derek Hagerty's escape, even though he didn't – or if he did, he wasn't aware that he knew it. Whatever it was, though, it had been motive enough for them to murder Meryl and her husband, and horribly.

Behind his woollen blindfold, his eyes prickled with tears. Meryl. Oh God, Meryl. I loved you so much. Why did I take you on that stupid drive up to Fermoy? Did I really believe that you would go to bed with me? And Patsy. How is Patsy going to cope, if they kill me?

'Aren't you fecking finished yet?' the growly voice demanded. 'You're putting the Shannon to shame in there.'

Eoghan stood up, pulled up his trousers and zipped up his fly. He groped around for a few seconds as if he were fruitlessly searching for something, and then backed out of the toilet and said, 'Can't find the handle to flush it.'

'Jesus, out the way, would you,' said the growly voice. Eoghan was roughly pushed aside, but as soon as that happened he reached up with both hands and wrenched the scarf down from his eyes. It had been knotted so tightly that it hurt his nose when he tugged it down, and he couldn't get it over his chin.

He blinked in the sudden light. One of the bald-headed bouncer-types who had kidnapped him was stretching up to reach the cistern arm because the toilet chain was missing. Eoghan hunched his head down and shoulder-tackled him, as hard as he could, just like in rugby at school, and the bouncer-type hit the wall and dropped down between the wall and the lavatory bowl, so that for a few moments he was wedged in the corner.

'What the *feck* do ye think ye're playin' at, ye feckin' gowl!' the bouncer-type screamed at him. He grabbed hold of the toilet seat to pull himself up, but its fastenings gave way and he fell back again, with the toilet seat landing in his lap.

Eoghan limped along the short distance to the end of the corridor until he reached the high-ceilinged hallway. He hesitated for a split second, looking for the best way to escape. All of the doors around the hallway were closed, and might be locked, and he didn't want to risk running upstairs and trying to hide. He crossed over to the front door and hurriedly jiggled off the security chain. The two cast-iron bolts were both stiff, but he managed to force them back, the bottom one by kicking it with his stockinged foot, and then he pulled down the door handle and tugged. He tugged it again and again, but the door was double-locked and wouldn't open.

'So – thinking of taking a walk, were you, Eoghan?' said that thin, scraping voice. 'I thought you and me agreed that we had business to talk over.'

Eoghan turned around. The two bouncer-types with their black suits and shiny bald heads had positioned themselves on either side of the hallway, blocking the way to the stairs and the kitchen. Between them stood the carroty-curled brother and sister, Aengus and Ruari, both dressed in grey chalk-striped jackets, as well as Lorcan, the crimson-faced man, whose grey hair was even wilder and more straggly than ever, and who had a strange, distracted smile on his face, almost beatific, as if he were high.

Eoghan looked tensely from one to the other, slightly crouched down. He felt like a cornered animal.

'Now why don't you come back to the lounge, Eoghan?' said Aengus. 'You never gave me the chance to explain what I had in mind. Jesus! I can't believe you rushing off like that without even saying "see ye".'

'What in God's name can you and me possibly have to agree about?' said Eoghan. His words sounded flat and expressionless, as if they were being repeated by a translator standing beside him.

'Well, come here, sham, and I'll tell you,' said Aengus. Without saying anything else, he turned and walked back along the corridor, accompanied by Ruari and Lorcan, although the two bouncer-types waited in the hallway for Eoghan to follow them. He hesitated for a moment, but then he did. He knew that he had no alternative.

They went through to the large gloomy drawing room. Aengus and Ruari sat together on the ottoman while Lorcan went over and perched himself on one of the window seats. The two bouncer-types stood in the background, hands clasped together, silent and unmoving. Eoghan sat in one of the tub-like armchairs. Either the seat cushion was too flat or the sides were too high, but it made him feel diminished and small.

Aengus started to twist one of his carroty curls around his left index finger, around and around. 'You know something, sham, I was almost coming around to believing you. That's why I let you have a comfort break. I was coming around to trusting you, ninety-nine per cent at least.'

'What do you mean?'

'Well, you seemed sincere enough, like. Maybe you *did* take Derek Hagerty's story at face value. Which, of course, you were supposed to.'

'Am I a prisoner here?' asked Eoghan, and again his voice sounded flat and unfamiliar.

'Of course not. But I'd prefer it if you stayed here until we got things sorted. You realize that you've complimicated the situation *enaaarmously* by taking off your blindfold. Not only for us, but mostly for yourself, like. Before, we could have dropped you off somewhere inconvenient and let you find your way home and that would have been an end to it.'

'Why can't you do that now?'

'Oh, come on, Eoghan, use your brains. You've seen us now. You know who we are. You can identify us in a court of law.'

'I don't have the first idea who you are, and if the price of getting out of here is to forget I ever saw you or witnessed one of these two feens shooting a garda, then that's a price I'm more than willing to pay. As for Denny, or Derek Hagerty, or whatever you want to call him, I didn't see anything at all when we found him by the roadside that made me suspicious, and neither did he say anything that made me doubt that he wasn't telling us the truth. Not while I was with him, anyway. I can't vouch for what Meryl thought, or her husband.'

Staring out of the window with a freshly lit cigarette, Lorcan said, 'I think you're missing the point, Mr Carroll. It's all very well your promising us now that you won't rat us out to the law, but we don't have any guarantee that you won't change your mind as soon as you're safely back in England. It would only take an e-mail to Anglesea Street, now wouldn't it, or an anonymous phone call?'

'What more can I give you than my word?' said Eoghan.

Lorcan breathed smoke out of his nostrils. It had started to rain again and silver droplets were spotting the window. 'You can give us your cooperation, that's what you can give us.'

'Cooperation to do what, exactly?'

'Get yourself released, of course. You could call your bowl feen and tell him that you've been abducted but treated fair so far, but you'd need him to cough up a bit of money to get you free.'

'That's ridiculous. My father doesn't have any money. He's retired from the council on a pension.'

'Oh, he can find the money all right. You won't be asking for much, only fifty thousand euros, say. He can find that.'

'Fifty thousand euros? How? The only way he could raise that kind of money would be to sell his house. The stress of it would kill him. He has a weak heart as it is.'

'Oh, don't you worry,' said Lorcan. 'The Garda will help him. Especially if you tell your father that Derek Hagerty admitted to you that he helped to arrange his own kidnap, so that he wouldn't have to pay his creditors.'

'But he didn't. He said nothing to me at all except that he'd been beaten and all his front teeth were pulled out with pliers.'

'Again, Mr Carroll, you're missing the point. Derek Hagerty won't talk, but the shades are convinced that he was a willing party to his own abduction. They believe that he knows full well who was supposed to have taken him. But – since *he* won't talk – they're desperate for witnesses. It's highly likely that the Pearses found out the truth somehow, or they wouldn't have notified the guards when they gave Derek Hagerty a lift into the city, so that they could pick him up and take him in for questioning. But, sadly, the Pearses are no longer in any fit state to testify.'

Eoghan was still shivering and he found it hard to make sense of anything that Lorcan was saying.

'I'm supposed to ring my father and tell him that I know for sure that Derek Hagerty was faking it?'

'That's it, you have it. But you also have to tell him that you managed to persuade *us* that he told you nothing. That's the reason we haven't silenced you for good and all, like the Pearses. All we're asking for is a small amount of recompense for the trouble you've caused us, and then we'll let you go.'

Eoghan glanced towards Aengus and Ruari. They were sitting side by side in their matching jackets, both expressionless. With their flour-white faces and their carroty curls they looked more like two life-size marionettes than real people, and Eoghan found them more frightening than anybody he had ever encountered in his life.

'Why should I do anything you want me to do?' he challenged them. 'You murdered my Meryl. Burned her alive! Christ, you sound like you're proud of yourselves for killing her!'

Lorcan shrugged. 'She should have listened to you, Mr Carroll. She should have left Hagerty where he was, or minded her own, at the very least.'

'Are you those High Kings of Erin they've been talking about on the news?' Eoghan demanded. 'Is that who you are?'

'Well, well, the light has shone through at last!' said Aengus, with a sudden smile. 'The very same. The great notorious High Kings of Erin! Not *all* of them, of course. There are more of us, like, all over the country. But all of us are sworn to do the same thing, and that's to restore Ireland's pride in herself and to punish those scobes who brought her so low.'

Eoghan didn't know what to say to that. He couldn't really understand what Aengus or Lorcan were talking about, or follow their logic, if there was any logic to it.

'So . . . will you do it?' asked Aengus. 'You'll agree to make the phone call and ask your father for the money?'

'And what if I will not?' said Eoghan.

Aengus looked at Ruari and then across at Lorcan.

Lorcan was about to light another cigarette. 'Oh, you will, I think,' he said, with the cigarette waggling between his lips.

Thirty-Four

Katie was due to meet with Derek Hagerty and his solicitor at two o'clock that afternoon to discuss the provisional withdrawal of the charge against him and how the Garda were planning to protect him and his family after he had left Anglesea Street.

However, she postponed the meeting for an hour because she had something more important to do. She drove to the hospital in Wilton to pay her respects to Detective Garda Goold and to give her condolences to her family.

The mortuary was silent and dimly lit. Rain was starting to patter against the clerestory windows and the mortuary attendant's shoes made a scrunching sound on the highly polished vinyl floor. After the attendant had folded back the pale green sheet that covered Nessa Goold's body, Katie stood for a long time staring in sadness at her lumpy, ruined face. The surgeons had attempted to suture back the flaps of flesh around her mouth, but Katie could see that even if she had survived she would have had to suffer months, or years, of reconstructive surgery.

She crossed herself and spoke the same words that her father had spoken over her mother's open casket all those years ago, and over the casket of his second wife-to-be, Ailish, after she had died in a car crash less than six months ago.

'*Solas geal na bhFlaithis ar a hanam.*'

'May the joyful light of heaven shine on her soul,' translated Detective Sergeant Ni Nuallán, coming up behind her. 'Poor creature. She deserves a Scott Medal for what she did.'

293

'Stupid, stupid girl,' said Katie. 'What in the name of Jesus possessed her to try and stop some scumbag with a gun when she wasn't armed herself? I'm so cross with her. But, no, you're right. She does deserve a medal. How old was she?'

'She'd be twenty-four next Friday. We were going to take her to the Long Island for cocktails and get her hammered.'

Katie stood beside the trolley for a long time without saying anything. This wasn't Nessa Goold any longer, after all. This was just the body that had carried her through her short and tragic life. Nessa Goold herself was elsewhere, in the hands of God.

She and Kyna left the mortuary and went to the relatives' room. There she found Nessa's father and mother, as well as her grandmother and two of her brothers. They were all red-eyed and looking miserable, but the men stood up when Katie came into the room.

'Do sit down,' she said, and she sat down herself, beside the softly bubbling fish tank. 'I just want to tell you that every officer at Anglesea Street has been shocked and saddened by Nessa's passing. She had such a great future ahead of her in the Garda and I can't imagine why fate was so cruel as to snatch her away from us so young.'

Nessa's mother began to sob, with her handkerchief pressed against her mouth, and her father put his arm around her and held her close.

Katie said, 'Detective Sergeant Ni Nuallán said to me that Nessa's courage deserved a Scott Medal. That's the medal for bravery that is awarded once a year to gardaí who have knowingly risked their lives to protect others.

'I want you to know that I'll be writing to the interim commissioner to recommend that Nessa is chosen for the highest award, the gold medal. It's the least I can do to honour her. She was a very courageous and selfless young woman, and even though we're all feeling such pain at losing her, we should also be feeling tremendous pride.'

She shook hands with all of the family and embraced Nessa's mother, and then she and Kyna left. Standing on the steps outside the hospital, buttoning up her raincoat, Katie said, 'I swear to God that Nessa Goold is going to be the last of our officers murdered by the High Kings of Erin. I swear it.'

'So, what's the plan?'

Katie started to answer but her words were drowned out by a deafening burst of thunder right over the hospital roof. She waited for a moment, until its last echoes had crumbled away, and then she said, 'I hate to admit it, Kyna, but Bryan Molloy is absolutely right. The High Kings of Erin have been making me play catch-up, right from the very beginning. I'm always two steps behind them. What I have to do is find a way to get ahead of them somehow – to try and anticipate what they're thinking of doing next, so I can catch them at it.'

They started to hurry together towards Katie's car. The rain wasn't heavy, but it was cold and spiky, as if somebody were casually and vindictively throwing lengths of wire at them.

Once they had settled into their seats and slammed the doors, Kyna said, 'What about Pat Whelan? Do you think he's faked his kidnapping, too?'

'We still don't have definitive proof that Derek Hagerty faked *his*. But my instinct is, yes, this is the pattern. The High Kings of Erin approach a businessman who's right on the edge of going bust and suggest he colludes in his own abduction. It's very much like what Kevin McGeever tried to do – pretend that he'd been kidnapped to get his creditors off his back – only much more carefully worked out.'

They were driving along the South Ring now and there was another rumble of thunder right overhead. The rain began to drum on the roof of the car so loudly that they could hardly hear each other.

'But what about Micky Crounan?' shouted Kyna. 'If he was colluding in his own abduction, how did he end up getting his head cut off? And even Derek Hagerty had all those teeth pulled out.

You wouldn't collude with that, would you? I know I wouldn't. I go to jelly if the dentist tells me that I have to have a filling.'

'I don't know the answer to that yet,' Katie told her. 'But I'm beginning to wonder if these High Kings of Erin ever have any intention of letting their victims go free, whether the ransom's been paid or not. Even if they were kidnapped willingly, their victims can still identify them, so the High Kings are always going to regard them as a liability. And look what extremes they're prepared to go to, to silence any witnesses.'

'They didn't kill Derek Hagerty, though, did they?' said Kyna.

'Because Derek Hagerty escaped. Or *claims* he escaped.'

'I know. But why did he need to escape at all if he was colluding in his own kidnap – unless, of course, he began to suspect that they weren't going to let him go when the ransom was paid?'

'I'm sure that his escape was a fake,' said Katie. 'His whole kidnap was a fake. The High Kings wanted Derek Hagerty discovered by some innocent passing motorist, so that his story sounded genuine. The trouble is, it didn't go according to plan. I don't think they bargained on somebody like Norman Pearse suspecting that it was all a put-up job.'

Katie slowed down for the Magic Roundabout, where the heavy rain had slowed the traffic even more than usual.

Kyna said, 'But think about it. Why did they have to pretend that he'd escaped? They knew they were going to collect the ransom money anyway. What did they actually think they were going to gain by it?'

'I don't know,' said Katie. 'The only thing they did gain out of it was to make a show of us. We handed over a quarter of a million euros of public money when we didn't have to – if only we'd been aware that Derek Hagerty was already free. On top of that, of course, there was the bomb and Garda McCracken losing her life, and that made us look a thousand times more incompetent, and almost criminally negligent.'

Kyna nodded. 'Exactly. They made us look like bungling eejits. But maybe that was all they were trying to do – nothing more than that. Maybe that was the whole point of it, neither more nor less. And you have to admit they succeeded.'

'Well, it could be you're right,' said Katie. 'We've been getting a very bad press lately. God knows what they're going to say when they find out that Pat Whelan's been kidnapped. Not that they're going to know about it – not just yet, anyway.'

'Actually, ma'am, I hate to say this, but the media haven't been giving us such a hard time, not the force in general. It's been you, personally. Didn't you see the *Examiner* this morning?'

'No. It was on my desk but I didn't have time to read it.'

'Didn't Tadhg McElvin tell you about it?'

'No. I haven't seen Tadhg since yesterday.'

'Jesus, he should have done. There's an editorial that says something like 'Is A Woman Cop Tough Enough To Fight Cork's New Crime Wave?' Fergal Byrne wrote it. It's all about you, and the High Kings of Erin running rings around you.'

'Oh, come on. The press have been sniping at me with monotonous regularity ever since I was appointed,' said Katie. 'They don't like me because I never give them all the juicy scandalous details they're panting for and I don't go out drinking with them.'

'Well, yes. But they also had a comment from Bryan Molloy, saying how he'd sorted out the gangs in the Limerick by cracking down on them so hard, and if you didn't arrest the High Kings of Erin pretty soon he was going to bring in the same zero-tolerance policies in Cork. He didn't say so in so many words, but the implication was that he doesn't think you're up to the job, being a woman, and the public shouldn't have any faith in you.'

Katie was driving into the city on the South Link Road now, under the Old Blackrock Road overpass. Up ahead of her, even through the rain, she could see the green glass tower of the Elysian, where Michael Gerrety lived. Right now, however, her mind was much more troubled by the High Kings of Erin than Michael Gerrety.

'I'm going to be talking to Derek Hagerty now, and his solicitor,' she said. 'I'm going to give him one last chance to tell me the truth.'

'And if he still won't?'

'Then I'm going to show Bryan Molloy what zero-tolerance is really all about. You just watch me.'

***

Derek Hagerty was sitting with his solicitor in the interview room. He was looking even more gaunt and exhausted than yesterday, but he had showered and shaved that morning and he was wearing an ill-fitting tan-coloured suit with a shiny orange tie – all in preparation for the District Court appearance that Katie had called off.

His solicitor, Margaret Rooney, was a tiresome young woman who handled legal-aid cases for a South Mall solicitor's firm called Sharkey's. She had upswept glasses and a French pleat and very thick ankles. When Katie came into the room she made a point of glaring at her watch.

'I'm sorry if I've kept you,' said Katie. 'As you've probably heard, a young detective garda has died from a gunshot wound and I needed to give my condolences to her family.'

'Yes, well, we were very disturbed by that, too,' said Margaret Rooney. 'It seems like this city's becoming more and more like the Wild West every day.'

Katie ignored that remark. Instead, she opened the folder that she had brought into the interview room with her and said, 'We've withdrawn the charge against Mr Hagerty of conspiracy to commit fraud, but that's for one reason only, and that is insufficient evidence. However, I want to make it clear to him that we will continue to investigate the circumstances of his supposed abduction and his supposed escape from that abduction.'

'I'm not sure that I'm too happy with the word "supposed",' said Margaret Rooney, interrupting her. 'My client has been through a deeply traumatic experience at the hands of a vicious kidnap gang and I would have thought that he deserved support and sympathy rather than suspicion.'

Katie turned to Derek Hagerty. 'Derek,' she said, 'you've come so close to admitting what you did. I don't think you went into it thinking for a moment that anybody was going to get hurt, let alone killed. But I can tell you this in strictest confidence – the detective garda who was shot was trying to prevent two men from abducting the young fellow who found you along with Meryl Pearse.'

'*What?*' said Derek Hagerty.

'His name is Eoghan Carroll. It's our guess that they took him because – rightly or wrongly – they thought he might have information to prove that you weren't really kidnapped at all.'

'Now hold on a minute!' Margaret Rooney chipped in. 'My client completely refutes your suggestion that he colluded in his own abduction.'

'If that's the case, what possible motive did those men have for taking somebody they thought might be a witness?'

'I don't know, Detective Superintendent, and my client has no more to say on the matter.'

'Whatever their motive, Ms Rooney, clearly it was strong enough for them to think that it was worth them shooting and killing a police officer.'

'Are you going to protect me? Me and my family?' Derek Hagerty put in. 'You did promise that you were going to give me protection.'

'Yes, we're going to give you protection,' said Katie. 'You'll be going back to your own home today and we'll post officers on watch around the clock. We have a property just outside Macroom that will be ready for occupancy by the weekend, and you and Shelagh will be able to move there until we feel that it's safe for you to come back.'

'And how long do you think *that* will be?' asked Margaret Rooney sharply. 'It doesn't sound as if you're making very much headway in this investigation.'

'Don't believe everything you read in the papers, Ms Rooney,' said Katie. 'But I'm going to tell you one more thing in confidence.

Another bankrupt businessman has gone missing and the same people are claiming that they've abducted him.'

'These High Kings of Erin?' asked Margaret Rooney.

'We don't know for sure who they are. But it's possible that he's made a similar arrangement to the one that *you* made with them, Derek – I know, I know, you're completely denying it. But we're gravely concerned for his safety whatever he's agreed to do. And, of course, we're equally worried about Eoghan Carroll.'

She paused for a moment, watching Derek as his eyes darted from one side of the room to the other and he fiddled with his tie. *Come on, Derek*, she thought. *Things can only get worse before they get better. Just have the courage to come out with it and tell me what really happened.*

But Derek Hagerty gave her a guilty, wounded look, and said nothing. Margaret Rooney stood up and crammed all her papers into her briefcase.

'We'll be going now, then,' she said. 'I was told that there's a car waiting for Mr Hagerty in the car park.'

Katie stood up, too. 'Derek?' she said, but he still wouldn't speak.

'All right,' she said. 'Have it your way. But you know very well what the consequences are going to be if you stay silent.'

Margaret Rooney said, 'Please, Detective Superintendent, don't try to make my client feel responsible for something that hasn't happened yet. He has a perfect right to safeguard his own life, and those of his family, before he starts worrying about the hypothetical deaths of other people.'

'Oh, that's all right, then,' said Katie. 'I shall think about that when I'm attending the hypothetical funeral of Detective Garda Goold.'

***

Katie went downstairs with Derek Hagerty and Margaret Rooney to the car park doorway, where a short, stocky protection officer was waiting for him. The officer was wearing a dark blue anorak with rain spots on it and smelled of cigarettes.

'Mr Hagerty?' said the protection officer. 'Your code name for now is Matthew McGinty. That's just for the sake of security, like. You know, in case of phone hacking, or being overheard.'

Katie said nothing as Derek Hagerty was led across the car park to a black Mondeo. It was drizzling and so she stayed in the doorway, with Margaret Rooney standing too close beside her. On the building overlooking the car park, at least twenty hooded crows were perched, looking bedraggled in the rain. They hopped and fluttered a little when the Mondeo's doors slammed, but they didn't fly away.

'That's that for now, then,' said Margaret Rooney.

Katie gave her a chilly smile. 'For now, yes. Ms Rooney, I'm sure you can find your own way out, can't you?'

***

Derek Hagerty sat in the back of the Mondeo next to the protection officer.

The driver's eyes were hovering surrealistically in the rear-view mirror. 'Tivoli Estate, isn't it?'

'That's right,' said Derek, clearing his throat. 'Head directly along the Lower Glanmire Road until you get to Trafalgar Hill and I'll direct you from there.'

'I *do* know where the Tivoli Estate is,' the driver told him, as he drove out of the Garda station car park. He turned left on to Old Station Road, past the Elysian and then up Albert Street towards the river.

There was hardly any traffic, but halfway up Albert Street there was a pedestrian crossing, with two men in khaki raincoats standing beside it, waiting to cross. They must have already pushed the button before the Mondeo appeared around the corner, because the lights turned to red just before it reached them.

'For feck's sake,' complained the driver, slowing down. 'There's nothing coming at all. Idle feckers could have strolled across with no trouble whatsoever.'

As soon as the Mondeo had stopped, however, one of the men stepped out in front of it and stayed there, while the other man approached the passenger side where Derek Hagerty was sitting. Both men were wearing wraparound dark glasses.

The protection officer said, '*Shite*!' and thrust his hand into the front of his coat, but he was seconds too late. There was a muffled sneezing sound and the window next to Derek Hagerty shattered as if a bucketful of ice had been emptied into his lap.

The driver immediately tugged the Mondeo's gearstick into reverse and slammed his foot down on the accelerator pedal. The car lurched backwards with a squitter of tyres and collided with a loud bang with a Butlers minibus that was just pulling up behind them.

By now the two men in raincoats were already hurrying away down the pedestrian alley beside the ACC Bank. The Mondeo driver changed gear and shot forward, speeding the last fifty metres to Albert Quay.

'Hospital!' shouted the protection officer. 'There's blood all over!'

'I'll have to take the Western Road,' said the driver. He was trying to stay calm but he was panting. 'There's some kind of a hold-up on the South Ring, I heard. Big lorry broken down or something like that.'

They sped through the city centre, weaving in and out of the traffic and running one red light after another. The Mondeo had no siren but the driver had his headlights on full and repeatedly blasted his horn. Derek Hagerty was slumped forward in his seat, swaying from side to side as they swerved around corners and overtook buses. While they were driving so fast it was impossible for the protection officer to see exactly how serious his injuries were, but the legs of his tan-coloured trousers were soaked maroon with blood and he could see pinkish lumps on his shoes that could have been brain tissue.

As they turned into Washington Street, the protection officer called in to the station.

'Doyle here. McGinty's been hit. Shot. That's right. I think it's bad. We're taking him to the Wilton Hilton right now.'

He paused, listening, and then he said, 'Just passing the city courthouse now. Okay. That'll be grand. Okay. Two fellers stopped us at the pedestrian crossing on Albert Street, the one right next to Albert Road. Browny sort of raincoats, the both of them, and sunglasses. Heavy build I'd say. One stood in front of the car to block us while the other one shot McGinty right through the window. Sounded like he was using a silencer. Then they ran off towards Eglington Street.'

As they reached Victoria Cross and turned south down Wilton Road towards the hospital they heard a siren and a patrol car, with its blue lights flashing, came out of a side road on their left and drove ahead of them, clearing the way.

They turned sharply into the hospital car park which made Derek Hagerty flop sideways across the protection officer's thigh. It was then that he could see that there had been no point in them rushing him to A&E so fast. Derek Hagerty must have turned his head away as the man in the raincoat approached the car, because there was a bullet hole immediately behind his left ear and a triangular piece of his left temple had been blown away and lay on the floor, like a large fragment of a broken teacup. Glistening beige blobs of his left frontal lobe were still clinging to the back of the passenger seat in front of him.

The driver pulled up in front of the hospital entrance and two orderlies came hurrying out, wheeling a trolley, as well as two male nurses, one tall and white and the other short and Indonesian. One of the orderlies opened the car door and the Indonesian nurse leaned over to take a look inside.

After only a few seconds he stood up straight, shaking his head. 'I'm afraid it's directly to the mortuary with this poor fellow,' he said. 'Do you know who he is? You are police, yes, correct? Do you know his next of kin?'

The protection officer took out a cigarette and tucked it between his lips. 'Yes,' he said, with the cigarette waggling, 'we know who he is, and we also know his next of kin.'

'I'm sorry, no smoking on the hospital grounds,' the Indonesian nurse told him, as he flicked his lighter. 'We have to consider our patients' health.'

The protection officer looked at Derek Hagerty in the back of the car, soaked in blood and glittering with broken glass.

'Oh sure,' he said. 'Wouldn't want him getting lung cancer on top of having his head blown off, would we?'

Thirty-Five

Katie had only just returned to her desk with a cup of coffee when her phone rang. More thunder was grumbling somewhere in the near-distance, southwards, over the airport.

'It's Liam Fennessy, ma'am. Gerry Doyle's just called in to say that Derek Hagerty's been shot.'

'What? He's been shot? I can't believe it. I saw him leave here with Gerry not five minutes ago. What happened? Where is he?'

'It seems like they were ambushed at the pedestrian crossing on Albert Street, you know, right beside the junction with Albert Road. Two fellows in raincoats. They shot him through the car window. They're taking him to CUH now.'

'Do we know how badly he's been hurt?'

'Not yet, but I'll get back to you as soon as I hear.'

Katie sat down. She felt deeply shaken, as if the floor were going to open up beneath her and she was going to drop three floors to the basement, still sitting in her chair, with her desk and everything else crashing down, too.

Apart from Inspector Fennessy, Detective Sergeant Ni Nuallán and Detective O'Donovan, no other members of her team had been advised as to when Derek Hagerty was going to be driven home, and as far as she knew Superintendent Denis MacCostagáin had briefed only four of his gardaí about it – the officers who would be on twenty-four hour protection duty. So how in the name of God had the killer known which car he would be travelling in, and exactly when it was going to be leaving the Garda station, and what route it was going to be taking?

If there had been any doubt at all in her mind that somebody in the station was passing information to the High Kings of Erin, this had dispelled it completely. But it only made her feel more helpless and frustrated. How could she possibly hope to catch them if they knew everything that she was planning to do before she did it?

In her mind she had already started to work out a scheme that could lead to their entrapment, and she had been thinking of discussing it with all of her detectives, and with Denis MacCostagáin, too. Now, however, she felt she ought to keep it to herself, at least until she had some idea of who the station's informer might be.

She prised the lid off her coffee, but she didn't really feel like it now. What she really felt like was a drink. She picked up the stack of manila folders that had been left on her desk and started to go through them, although she was so shocked and angry that she found it difficult to concentrate. Detective Horgan had given her a progress report on a Lithuanian gang suspected of smuggling heroin into the country through the ferry port at Ringaskiddy in two white vans. The vans were now parked in a yard in Gurranbraher and were being kept under observation until somebody from the gang came to collect them.

Katie was still reading through this when Detective Dooley knocked at her door. He was a chatty, dapper young man with a heart-shaped face and intensely blue eyes. His brushed-up black hair and slim-fit suit made him look about twenty-two, but he was actually ten years older. Katie had found that his looks made him particularly useful for infiltrating the bars and pubs and nightclubs in Cork where bangers and bóg were being hawked around.

'What's the story, Robert?' she asked him.

Detective Dooley gave her a cherubic smile and without a word dropped a computer printout on top of the file in front of her. It was a picture of a pouty blonde girl lounging on a heap of cushions, wearing only a red lace bra and panties, with the caption 'Samantha

New Girl In Town Will Give You The Massage Of Your Life With A Happy Ending'.

'Recognize her?' asked Detective Dooley.

'Holy Mother of God,' said Katie, peering at the picture more closely. 'She's wearing a wig, isn't she, but I'd swear that's Roisin Begley.'

'Chalk it down. That's our Roisin all right.'

'But legally she's still a child? She's not seventeen yet, is she?'

'No, not yet, although she will be in only three weeks' time. Her birthday's on November the nineteenth. But apart from her age – look whose website she's advertising on.'

Underneath the picture, the text read, 'I am a stunning sexy blonde model lovely slim dress size 8 natural 34D pert breasts. I have an art of awakening and heightening second to none €150 per session.' Beneath that there was a line which said 'Brought To You By Cork Fantasy Girls'.

'Would you believe it?' said Katie. 'Michael Gerrety's website. But if she's not seventeen yet – ? Michael Gerrety goes to any lengths not to advertise underage girls. I know that doesn't stop him farming them out to other pimps. But he's quite aware that we'll be down on him like a ton of bricks if he does.'

'Well, I've been hanging around Roisin's school and chatting to some of her friends,' said Detective Dooley. 'They all say that she was ever the wild one, always messing around with boys, even though her parents thought she was Saint Roisin the Spotless. She never wore knickers to school and even gave one boy a gobble during geography. Strangely enough, he took up the priesthood after he left. But judging by what her friends said, I don't believe that she was abducted at all, I think she went willingly with one of Gerrety's talent scouts she met at some club.

'One of her pals told me she was always making out she was older than she really was – like she pretended to be seventeen when she was only fifteen and a bit. Now, it wouldn't surprise me at all if she's told Michael Gerrety that she's reached her seventeenth birthday already. You know – just to impress him, and to get herself on to his website, so she can make herself some decent money. A hundred and fifty for a massage, that's a lot. Most of them girls are charging no more than fifty.'

'That's grand work, Robert,' said Katie. 'I'm really impressed you got those girls to talk to you like that.'

'Oh, it's my natural charm,' grinned Detective Dooley. 'My mam's mam always said that I was a sexy biscuit.'

'Modest, too. That's what I like. Well, whatever, we have to set this up with the utmost care. We probably won't get another chance to nail Gerrety for a long, long time – if ever – and we don't want to blow it on a legal technicality.'

'Gerrety's always doggy wide,' said Detective Dooley. 'Cork Fantasy Girls never openly advertises sex services or sexual intercourse, and the site specifically warns the girls not to do it.'

'I know that,' Katie told him. 'But what we have to do is to prove that Roisin is offering sex to her clients as well as a massage, and to establish that she's using the money she makes to pay Gerrety for running her advertisement on his website – as well as anything else that he's providing her with, like accommodation. She's a schoolgirl, she can't afford to be renting a flat of her own. More than likely, she's staying at one of his places . . . and if it's a brothel, we'll have even more to charge him with. Reckless endangerment – "causing or permitting a child to be placed in a situation which creates a substantial risk to the child of being a victim of sexual abuse". That means a fine with no upper limit if he's found guilty, or ten years' detention.'

'First of all, I need to find out where she's located,' said Detective Dooley. 'If she's in a known brothel, then we shouldn't have a problem. If she's somewhere else, like a B & B or some-body's private house, well, it could be more tricky. But if she goes out clubbing at all, I have a couple of girlfriends who might be able to meet up with her and wheedle something incriminating out of her. Like you say, though – softly, softly, catchee slapper.'

He was about to leave when Katie's phone warbled.

'Liam Fennessy here again, ma'am. Gerry Doyle just called in from the hospital. Derek Hagerty was dead on arrival. He was shot point-blank in the head. Blew half his brains out. Gerry said that he never stood a chance.'

'Oh, no,' said Katie. 'That's just tragic.'

She covered the receiver with her hand and said to Detective Dooley, 'Derek Hagerty. We were driving him home and somebody's shot him. He's dead.'

'Mother of God.'

Katie returned to her conversation with Inspector Fennessy. 'It's unbelievable. There he was, totally refusing to give us any information about the High Kings of Erin, and they go and murder him anyway. It really makes me worried for Eoghan Carroll. And Pat Whelan, too, for that matter. Any word on Whelan yet? They haven't rung Mrs Whelan back yet, have they?'

'No, but the sound boys have wired up her phone and Detective Garda Callum's in with her, as well as a female garda.'

'All right,' said Katie. 'I suppose I'd better go and talk to Molloy about the ransom money.'

'Well, you're in luck, I'd say. You can talk direct to Jimmy O'Reilly, too. He came back from Dublin about an hour ago.'

'Oh, Jesus.'

Detective Dooley frowned at her, but Katie waved her hand at him to tell him not to worry and that he could go.

'I'll get back to you as soon as I find where Roisin's at,' he told her.

'Thanks, Robert. I could do with some good news, believe me.'

***

'So tell me, Katie, is this *ever* going to end?' demanded Assistant Commissioner O'Reilly. 'How many *more* times are you going to be coming to me, begging me for ransom money?'

Katie glanced across at Acting Chief Superintendent Molloy for some sign of support, but he was prodding at his iPhone and pretending not to listen.

'With luck, sir, this will be the last time,' she said. 'These High Kings of Erin are very ruthless and they're making sure that everybody knows how brutal they are. I think that's an integral part of their strategy, like. Nobody's going to dare to give evidence against them if they think they're going to be horribly murdered. But I have a number of ideas which I believe will help to entrap them.'

'Oh! Well, that's something!' said Assistant Commissioner O'Reilly. 'Can we *hear* these ideas?'

'They're not really complete yet, sir, but I'll be holding a full briefing within a day or two. At the moment, though, I think our most urgent priority is arranging the release of Pat Whelan and Eoghan Carroll, preferably without their heads cut off or their teeth pulled out.'

Assistant Commissioner O'Reilly sucked in his cheeks so hard that he looked cadaverous. He always reminded Katie of Peter Cushing in *Star Wars*. Even when he wasn't throwing a togo about somebody's supposed inefficiency, he always looked sour, with his grey hair slicked back from his bony forehead and his dead grey eyes and pinched-together lips. Every discussion that Katie had ever had with him had not only been short and unpleasant, but inconclusive, too. He seemed to think that every officer under his command ought to be able to read his mind, without him having to go to the bother of spelling out what it was that he required them to do. Then, of course, he would be furious if they hadn't done it.

'If I put in a requisition for this new ransom payment, Katie, that's going to amount altogether to four hundred and fifty thousand euros of public money.'

'I understand that, sir,' said Katie. *I can count.*

'That's a further two hundred thousand we're at risk of losing, and that's more than Kieran Fitzpatrick was given for his golden handshake – although not too much more.'

'I'm very conscious of that, sir,' Katie told him. She knew that he had been badly rankled by the lump sum paid to his predecessor as assistant commissioner for the Southern Region. He never failed to mention it every time they discussed anything at all, even drug-trafficking. ('That package of smack might have been worth one hundred and eighty thousand euros, but that was less than Kieran Fitzpatrick was given for his golden handshake. Can you believe that?')

'Provided I can convince Dublin to approve it, I'll sign off the ransom payment this time,' said Assistant Commissioner O'Reilly. 'I'm doing it with the deepest reluctance, though, I have to tell you. And before you make any arrangements for a handover, make absolutely certain that they really *do* have this Whelan fellow and that he's still alive.'

'I'll insist that they give us some proof, of course, even if his wife can just hear him talking to her on the telephone.'

'Very well. But I will also need to know how you're going to make sure that these High Kings of Erin *do* release him, once the ransom's paid, and how you intend to use the handover to catch them, if that's what you're planning to do. You do understand what the repercussions will be, don't you, if they make a fool of you again?'

Bryan Molloy glanced up from jabbing at his iPhone, and smiled.

Thirty-Six

By 8.15 that evening there had been no calls from the High Kings of Erin to Mairead Whelan or to Eoghan Carroll's parents, so Katie decided to call it a night and go home. She was so tired that she felt as if all her joints had stiffened so that she barely had the strength to get up from her desk and walk down to the car park. Her back ached. She was hungry, too, although she thought that she was probably too exhausted to cook anything sensible. All she had eaten since breakfast was a pulled ham ciabatta from O'Brien's and some ginger biscuits.

At least it wasn't raining as she drove home. She knew that Barney would want his evening walk up to the tennis club, but he would have to be satisfied with being let out into the back yard. Ever since John had left her, she had been wondering if it was fair to keep him, since he had to spend most of his day cooped up in the house. But John had given him to her after her black Labrador, Sergeant, had been killed, and she was too sentimentally attached to give him away. It would be like admitting that all of the happy times she had spent with John had gone for ever.

She let herself into the house and Barney came bustling up to her, with his tail thrashing.

'It's all right, Barns,' she said, tugging at his ears. 'Mam's just a little tired and hormonal, that's all. You can thank Jimmy O'Reilly for that.'

She unlocked the kitchen door to let Barney out into the yard and then went back into the hallway to hang up her raincoat.

John's raincoat was still hanging there and she leaned against it and smelled it, but it didn't smell of him, only of raincoat. She could have cried, but her tears all seemed to have dried up. She went into the living room and poured herself a vodka and switched on the news on the television.

As she sat down on the couch, the reports from the Middle East ended and Acting Chief Superintendent Molloy appeared, with the caption 'Kidnap Victim Shot Dead In Cork'.

'Oh, I don't believe this,' said Katie, out loud, and turned up the sound.

Bryan Molloy was saying, ' – ambushed by two gunmen on Albert Street on his way, ironically, into witness protection. The kidnap gang calling itself the High Kings of Erin seem to be stopping at nothing to prevent themselves from being identified, and we openly admit that our detectives have been unable to determine exactly who they are. All I can say is that we're now doing everything we can to put a stop to their abductions, although their silencing of witnesses has been so brutal that we can understand why anybody would be reluctant to come forward with evidence that might help us catch and convict them.

'However, if you do have any information about the kidnapping of Derek Hagerty or if you witnessed the shooting on Albert Street this afternoon, we urge you to call your local Garda station or Crimestoppers on 1800 250 025. I can assure you that anything you say will be treated in strictest confidence. Even if you think that what you have to say is not particularly relevant, it may help to put our detectives on to the scent. Right at this moment, believe me, they urgently need your help.'

He's doing it again, thought Katie. He's undermining me. He's the only person I know who can turn a public appeal for help into a hatchet job. Or maybe I'm just being too sensitive. After all, everything that he said was true.

She finished her drink, but she didn't pour herself another one. What was the point of getting drunk on her own? What she needed was somebody to talk to. Barney was scratching at the kitchen door, but there was no point in talking to him, and in any case he hadn't been outside long enough.

She was still trying to decide if she wanted to make herself something to eat when her doorbell chimed. She stood up and went to the living-room door, but then she hesitated. She wasn't expecting anybody from the station, or any of her friends, so there was only one person it could be.

The doorbell chimed again. She went up to the door and called out, 'Who is it?'

'Who do you think?'

'What do you want? It's late.'

'I need to talk to you.'

'Well, you can talk to me tomorrow. It's late and I have nothing to say to you right now.'

'I need to know what's happened to Sorcha. I came home this evening and she's not there. She's gone. She's even taken a suitcase and some of her clothes.'

Katie waited for a moment, and then she said, 'She's safe, David. That's all I'm going to say to you tonight. She's safe and she's being well taken care of.'

'So you know where she is?'

'Yes, and I'll tell you tomorrow.'

'If you can tell me tomorrow, why can't you tell me now?'

'Because tomorrow she'll have a protection order against you and you won't be able to go near her, that's why.'

'What? What are you talking about, protection order?'

'That's all I'm going to say to you, David. Now, go back home and I'll discuss it with you in the morning.'

There was a long silence from outside, but Katie hadn't heard David leave and she was sure that he was still standing in the porch.

'David – ' she began.

'Can't we just talk about it?' he begged her. 'I know I've done wrong, Katie. I know I've treated Sorcha badly. But whatever she's said to you, it's not all my fault. Far from it.'

'David, go home.'

'I desperately need some help here, Katie. I don't know how to deal with this situation at all. I don't have anybody to discuss it with, because it always seems like I'm in the wrong. But if you had any idea what it's like, living with Sorcha.'

Katie waited, but it was obvious that David was going to stay outside until she agreed to talk to him.

'All right,' she said, sliding back the safety chain and unlocking the door. 'I'll talk to you. But for five minutes only, and I'm still not telling you where Sorcha is.'

David was standing in the porch looking dishevelled. His dark curly hair was messed up and although he was wearing a brown tweed jacket, his crumpled shirt tails were hanging out. His eyes were puffy and as soon as he stepped into the hallway Katie could smell that he had been drinking. He lurched against the raincoats and then steadied himself by placing the flat of his hand against the opposite wall.

'David, you're langered,' said Katie. 'I hope you weren't driving like that.'

'Oh! I'm sorry! I forgot you were a detective superintendent and not the interfering slutbag who lives next door!'

'I can't talk to you when you're like this,' Katie told him. 'Go home and get yourself sober and I'll come round and see you in the morning.'

David stared at her. 'Did I *ask* you to stick your nose into my marriage?' he said. 'You were all sympathetic to me when you were gagging for a shag, weren't you? But now look at you? All high and mighty and judgemental! How dare you to think that you can come between me and my wife? What gives you the right, you supercilious bitch?'

Katie said, 'Go home, David. I'm not telling you again.'

'And if I don't? Then what? You'll arrest me? What for? Defending a husband's right to tell his psychotic wife to behave herself?'

Katie grasped the sleeve of David's jacket and tried to turn him towards the front door, which was still wide open. Immediately,

David reached behind him and slammed it shut. His face was flushed and contorted, barely recognizable, as if he had suddenly been possessed by some demon. He pushed Katie back along the hallway with both hands, so that she staggered and lost her balance and her shoulder hit the frame of the living-room door.

'You *think* – !' David shouted at her. 'You *think* that you can tell me how to treat my own wife! What gives you the right? What gives *you* the fecking right? You may be a detective, Detective Superintendent, but you're still a slutbag, and I won't be given lessons in how to behave by some slutbag! Do you hear me?'

Katie backed into the living room, glancing behind her to make sure that she didn't stumble over the coffee table. Her heart was beating hard, but she had faced up to drunken and violent men plenty of times before. As a young garda, she had patrolled outside Waxy's and Rearden's and Buckley's on a Saturday night, and David didn't make her feel afraid.

'So what happened?' said David. 'Sorcha came around to you whining, did she? She always does that, wherever we are. "Oh, he's been beating me! Oh, he gave me such a slap!" Don't you realize that's the only way that any human man could possibly deal with her?'

'David, get out of here, now, and go home,' Katie warned him. 'I don't want to arrest you, but unless you leave I swear that I will.'

David advanced on her and shoved her again, and then again. She fell backwards on to the couch and he toppled heavily on top of her. He seized her right wrist and forced her arm straight upwards, while at the same time grabbing the hem of her skirt and twisting it right up almost to her waist.

'So you think you can play dirty with me, do you?' he hissed at her, right in her face, so that she could feel his spit prickling all over her cheeks and she was overwhelmed by the smell of whiskey. 'You think you can flirt with me and jeopardize my professional reputation and mess up my marriage? You just wait until I report you to your superiors. Then we'll see who can play dirty!'

His hand fumbled underneath her bottom until he found the elastic of her thong.

'First of all, though,' he panted, 'how about some compensation for that bottle of Bolly you made me break? Yes? How about that? Only fair, don't you think? And you know you like it, don't you, even though you make out you don't!'

Katie didn't answer him. Instead, she tensed every muscle in her body and then heaved herself sideways so that David fell off her and on to the carpet.

'Jesus!' he said, reaching out for the edge of the coffee table to pull himself up. 'What the hell did you do that for? I thought you wanted it!'

Katie sat up and then climbed over him. He snatched at her ankle, but she trod on his stomach so that he gasped and said, '*Shit*!' and let her go.

'Now, get out of here,' she told him. 'Get out of my house and don't ever come back.'

David levered himself up between the couch and the coffee table and eventually managed to stand. He stood there, swaying, one eye closed because he couldn't focus with both eyes. 'You know what you are?' he blurted. 'You're a fecking witch. I should have known that the day I first saw you. I'll tell you something, witch, if anybody deserves a fecking belt, it's you.'

He lurched towards her, raising his arm as if he intended to slap her. Instead of backing away, though, Katie took a step forward, lifted herself up on the balls of her feet and swung her right leg in a side roundhouse kick, so that her shin struck him hard in the ribs.

David doubled up and staggered to his left. As he did so, Katie punched him directly on the cheekbone with her elbow. He fell sideways on to the floor, staring at the carpet.

Almost a minute went past, with David still staring at the carpet and Katie standing over him. At last he managed to sit up, wincing. There was a crimson bruise on his right cheek and his right eye was already beginning to close.

'*You've hurt me,*' he whispered. His voice was tiny, like a miniature man shut up inside a matchbox. '*You've really, really hurt me. I think you've broken my ribs.*'

'Do you want me to call for an ambulance?' asked Katie.

David took a deep breath and shook his head. 'There's nothing they can do for broken ribs. Don't worry. I'm a doctor. I have plenty of painkillers.'

'Do you want a hand up?'

'No, thank you. I don't want anything more from you, ever. I wish I'd never set eyes on you.'

'Well, the feeling is mutual, David, I can assure you. Now I'd very much appreciate it if you'd get up and leave. I'll ask the people who are looking after Sorcha to ring you in the morning, but you'll be hearing from the court, too.'

David managed to climb to his feet. He shuffled out of the living room into the hallway and Katie opened the front door for him. He paused for a few moments before he stepped outside, as if he wanted to say something to her, but either he was in too much pain or else he couldn't think of anything venomous enough, or both.

Katie watched him as he crept back next door. She felt sick with contempt at his arroagance and his stupidity, and disgusted at her own weakness, too. How on earth could she have found him so attractive? Even in his drunken anger, hadn't it occurred to him that since she was a Garda officer she would be highly trained in self-defence? Every Saturday morning she still went to Muay Thai kickboxing sessions.

She closed the front door and locked it. She went back into the living room and tidied the cushions on the couch. She looked around and felt very empty and lonely . *How did my life come to this?* she thought. But then she heard Barney whuffling and scratching at the kitchen door again, and she went through to let him in.

Thirty-Seven

Pat Whelan heard voices and opened his eyes. Above him was the sharply sloping ceiling of an attic room and when he turned his head to one side he saw that he was lying on a single bed with a thin horsehair mattress covered by a scratchy pink wool blanket. The room was gloomy: the only light came from a dormer window, grimy-glassed and speckled with raindrops, through which he could see only dull, charcoal-grey clouds.

He heard footsteps mounting uncarpeted stairs, and voices growing louder. 'Oh, but they will, I'm sure of it,' a young woman was saying, right outside the door. 'They know what will happen if they don't. What they *don't* know is that the very same thing will happen if they do.'

He made an effort to sit up, but when he did so his chest was gripped with such agonizing pain that he let out a child-like whimper and dropped back on to the blanket. He felt as if his ribcage had been mercilessly beaten with a metal bar and then his nipples branded with a red-hot iron. When he looked down he saw that a white gauze bandage had been wrapped several times around his chest, and that there were dark brown spots of dried blood where his nipples had been. Apart from the bandage, he was wearing only a pair of grubby grey tracksuit bottoms which he had never seen before in his life.

The door opened and the carroty-haired twins, Aengus and Ruari, came in, followed by Lorcan. Aengus was wearing a lime-green roll-neck sweater, while Ruari was dressed in a dark brown

sweater and an orange tartan skirt. Lorcan was all dressed in black
– black jacket, black shirt – but still crimson-faced, as if he had
just returned from a wake where there had been plenty to drink.

'Did I hear you bawling there, Patrick?' asked Aengus, leaning
over him. 'I think we might have some ibuprofen downstairs if
you're still feeling any pain.'

'What the hell did you do that to me for?' Pat croaked at him.
'That was just sadistic.'

'Oh, come on,' said Aengus. 'If you'd been a shade more
cooperative we wouldn't have had to touch you at all. But we had
to show you who was in charge here, like, and that's the way the
great High Kings always did it. There's nobody going to be sucking
your tits in future, and that's for sure.'

'You're a total header. You're all total headers.'

'There's no call to be offensive, Pat. The fact of it is we needed
some proof that we have you and snipping your tits off was much
less drastic than pulling out your teeth or cutting your mickey off.
Anyway, you'll be glad to hear that they were sent to your wife by
express post which means that she'll receive them this morning.
Here – I've brought you this phone so that you can give her a ring
and see if the guards have managed to drum up the ransom for her.'

'I swear to God I wish I'd never got myself involved in this.'

'You didn't have a choice, Pat,' put in Lorcan, lighting a cigarette. 'Well, you *did*, when you started to borrow more money from
the bank than you could afford to pay back. You need to tell your
wife that, on the phone. Tell her that you're surviving, just about.
But tell her why we took you.'

'I don't see what difference a doonchie overdraft like mine could
have made to the whole Irish economy,' Pat protested.

'On its own, you're right, Pat, it was a drop in the ocean. But
there were tens of thousands of other small businessmen who
did the same as you, and even if tens of thousands of drops don't
quite make an ocean, they're enough to sink the fecking ship. Did
you ever hear somebody say "there'll be the devil to pay"? Well,
the devil is the sailor's name for the gap between two planks in

a ship's hull, and to pay the devil meant to seal that gap with hot pitch. Except that when it came to the Irish economy, we had no hot pitch ready to seal it up with, because of people like you who never gave a thought for tomorrow.'

'Here,' said Aengus, and handed Pat an iPhone. 'Give your missus a call. Tell her what your situation is and who has you and why you're here, and most of all ask her if she's managing to raise the money.'

'I hate to do this to her. She's sick enough as it is and I've let her down so many times lately this will break her melt.'

'Pat, call her. Otherwise we might have to send her another piece of you, just to doubly prove that we have you, and you wouldn't like us to do that, would you?'

Grimacing, Pat lifted himself up so that he was supporting himself on his left elbow. 'If Mairead's told the guards that I've been kidnapped they might trace this call, mightn't they?'

Aengus shook his head. 'Not with that phone they won't. Now, get on with it.'

Pat dialled his home number and waited for Mairead to answer. The phone's speaker was switched on so that Aengus and Ruari and Lorcan could hear it, too.

'Hello?' said Mairead. 'Who is this?' She sounded out of breath and very close to tears.

'It's Pat, May. It's me.'

'Oh, Pat! Oh, God! Are you all right? I had these terrible things in the post this morning! There was a letter with them saying they'd been cut off of you! Tell me they haven't really done that!'

'They did, May. They took me yesterday when I was leaving the shop and now they have me locked up. They said they had to cut something off of me to prove that they really had me,'

'Oh, God, I can't believe it. Are you all right?'

'Well, I'm hurting still, of course, but I'm okay otherwise. You haven't told the Garda, have you, or anyone else?'

There was a moment's pause. Pat could hear his Mairead trying to suppress her sobs, and he looked up at Aengus and

Ruari with undisguised hatred. Aengus smiled, but Ruari remained expressionless. The strong smell of her perfume was already filling the room.

'May – ' Pat repeated, 'you haven't told the Garda, have you?'

'No,' said Mairead. He had never heard her sound so deeply miserable, even when her back pain was at its worst. 'This fellow rang me yesterday and said that if I told the guards that you'd been kidnapped he couldn't guarantee what might happen to you. He said I had to find two hundred and fifty thousand euros by Saturday midnight or else I might never see you alive again, or they'd do something terrible to you like amputate your arms and legs. And after what I got in the post this morning, I believe them, Pat. I believe they'll do it if I can't find the money for them. I do.'

'But how are you going to find so much money?'

'I don't know, Pat. My sister Maureen has a bit put aside and the father has a pension I can lend a borrow from, although I'd have to pay him back.'

'Of course, pet. We'll find a way, tell him. And don't give up hope. These people who took me, they call themselves the High Kings of Erin like the old kings of Ireland. They say that they're punishing all the small businessmen like me because we ruined the country by spending money that we didn't have. Well, no, it doesn't make a whole lot of sense to me, either, but that's what they say. They're not criminals, they say, they're patriots.'

'Pat – ' Mairead began, and for one moment Pat thought that she was going to admit that she had contacted the Garda after all. He prayed that she had, because he was completely convinced now that when the High Kings of Erin had said that they would mutilate or murder him if they didn't get their ransom money, it had been no empty threat.

'May,' he said. 'The leprechauns.'

'What?' she said, but then she obviously understood what he was telling her. When their children had been small, they had cautioned each other when they were having an adult conversation and they thought that the children might be able to overhear them by saying 'sshh . . . the leprechauns'.

Aengus took the phone out of his hand and switched it off. 'Leprechauns? What's all that about?'

'Nothing at all. Just a pet name. Nothing.'

'What did I say to you?' grinned Aengus. 'Women are shite when it comes to telling lies. You could tell that she's contacted the shades already.'

'She swore that she hadn't. You heard her for yourself.'

'Of course she did. She was trying to keep you alive, as any good wife would. But she will, if she hasn't already, and you can thank your lucky stars for that, Pat.'

Wincing with pain, Pat eased himself back on the mattress. 'How can you know that?'

'Because we're the High Kings of Erin and there's nothing in our kingdom that we don't know about, that's how.'

Ruari came up close to the side of his bed and looked down at him coldly. 'You did well, Pat,' she said. 'Not long now and this should all be over.'

Pat looked back up at her, breathing in that musky perfume with every agonizing breath, so that he could actually taste it. He didn't find her words reassuring at all. All he felt was utter hopelessness, like the time when he was five years old and he had lost his mother in the English Market and thought that he would never see her again.

Thirty-Eight

By the time Katie left the house to take Barney for his morning walk, David's Range Rover had already gone from the driveway next door. The clouds were low and grey, but there was a fresh, salty south-west breeze blowing in from the harbour and that helped to wake her up. She hadn't managed to fall asleep until well past three o'clock in the morning, thinking about David and how he had attacked her.

She had a hectic day ahead of her and she had to be at her most alert. It was likely that the High Kings of Erin would contact Mairead Whelan sometime later and give her their final instructions for handing over the ransom money. Assistant Commissioner O'Reilly would only authorize the payment, however, if Katie could convince him that she had an effective plan for making an arrest and recovering the cash before it was shared out and laundered. The serial number of every single note would have been recorded, even though the High Kings of Erin had insisted that they be non-sequential, but once a note had been through pubs and grocery stores and betting shops it was almost impossible to trace who had handled it.

She had the beginnings of an idea of how she might trap them, although ultimately it would depend on where and when and how they wanted the drop to take place. What worried her was that their informer inside Anglesea Street could well tip them off about what she planned to do before she could put it into action. She didn't know who she could trust and who to keep in the dark.

On a more positive note, she had already worked out how to set up Roisin Begley. She needed Roisin to admit that she was offering sexual intercourse as well as massage, and that at least some of the money she was making she was paying to Michael Gerrety. It was vital that they didn't make the same mistake as the gardaí in County Louth last year, who had entered a brothel without identifying themselves as police officers and subsequently had their case thrown out of court. She wanted to see Michael Gerrety convicted so much that it was almost like a constant headache, but he had the best lawyers in Cork and it would take only one procedural error to see him go free again.

She went into the Day Today store on the corner of Grove Garden to buy herself a cheese and tomato sandwich and a newspaper. As she untied Barney on her way out, her iPhone rang. Barney looked up at her and made that disappointed noise in the back of his throat, as if he knew that she would have to hurry him back home and go rushing off to Anglesea Street.

It was Inspector Fennessy calling her. 'Good morning, ma'am. Sorry to ring you so early.'

'What is it, Liam? I'll be leaving the house in fifteen minutes tops. Can't it wait?'

'I just thought you should know that Mairead Whelan received a package in the post first thing this morning.'

'Oh God. What? Not teeth.'

'A bit grislier than that. Nipples.'

'You're codding me. *Nipples*?'

An elderly man who was walking past her turned his head and gave her a look of alarm.

Inspector Fennessy said, 'There's a note with them claiming that they were cut off her husband, to prove that they have him, and that he'll be contacting her later this morning. She has no way of telling for sure if they're his, but she reckons they are.'

'All right, Liam. I'm out with the dog right now, but I'll come in directly. Where are these nipples now?'

'Bill Phinner's sending one of his technicians around to collect them, and the note, too. He can take blood and DNA samples and send them off to the deputy state pathologist for further tests if he has to.'

'Jesus. This gets worse by the minute. No news about Eoghan Carroll, I suppose?'

'Not yet, no. All we can do is keep our fingers crossed that they haven't barbecued him like the Pearses.'

'Okay. I'll see you in a half-hour so.'

***

When she walked into the station from the car park, she found Detective O'Donovan waiting for her by the front desk, blowing his nose.

'Pat Whelan's rung his missus,' he said, stuffing his handkerchief back into his pocket. 'We haven't been able to pinpoint where the call came from exactly, but it was close to the city, northside. We have it recorded, though.'

'How does he sound?'

'Not too good, I'd say. Sick as a box of frogs, in fact. From what he said, I think we can be sure those nipples they sent to his missus are actually his.'

They went upstairs in the lift to the second floor. 'She hasn't heard from the High Kings of Erin again?'

'Not yet, no. But I don't doubt that she will. Pat was insistent, though, that she shouldn't tell us or anyone else that he'd been kidnapped. She swore blind that she hadn't, but I don't know whether he believed her or not. Or if *they* did, whoever they are.'

They walked together along the corridor to Katie's office. Detective O'Donovan said, 'I have to say I'm totally puggalized by them warning the victims' relatives not to contact the Garda. They pick on people to kidnap who are practically bankrupt. How do they think their relatives are going to raise so much money unless they come to us for help? Nobody else is going to hand them two hundred and fifty thousand yoyos with not a hope in hell of ever getting it back.'

Katie stopped at her office door. She looked up at Detective O'Donovan, with his rusty-coloured hair and his sea-green eyes and his tie all crooked, and from the expression on his face and the question he had just asked her she felt that she could trust him.

'I'll tell you what I think,' she said. 'I think the High Kings of Erin are fully aware that their victims' relatives will get in touch with us. In fact, I believe they want them to. They're vicious, but they're also very cute, and I think the only mistake they've made so far is to bungle Derek Hagerty's so-called escape. They killed him to keep him quiet, but I think they would have killed him anyway, eventually, just like they killed the Pearses, and Micky Crounan, too, and unless we can find a way to stop them I think they're going to kill Pat Whelan and Eoghan Carroll.'

'So you don't think that they're going to let Pat go free, even after they've collected their ransom?'

'No, I don't. And I think the only reason they warn their victims' relatives not to contact us is to hamper our investigation. Think about it: it deters us from making an immediate appeal for witnesses after somebody like Pat Whelan has been snatched. It restricts our surveillance on the victims' homes and it makes it much more difficult to set up an ambush when the money gets handed over.

'Not only that, but if anybody gets hurt or killed, then we get the blame for being incompetent because we knew that the relatives had been warned not to get in touch with us. Whatever happens, we can't win.'

Detective O'Donovan followed her into her office. 'We could refuse to pay the ransom, couldn't we? Then what would they do?'

'I think you know that as well as I do. They'd kill their victims anyway and we'd still get the blame. They'd call us heartless as well as incompetent.'

Detective O'Donovan took out an Olympus voice recorder and laid it down on her desk. 'This is Pat's call to Mairead, any road.

There's one or two voices in the background and the sound boys are trying to enhance them, like.'

He switched the recorder on and Katie heard Mairead Whelan saying, 'Hello? *Who is this?*' and then Pat saying, '*It's Pat, May. It's me.*'

Before she could listen to the rest of the conversation, however, her phone rang. It was Acting Chief Superintendent Molloy's secretary, Teagan.

'DS Maguire? The Chief Superintendent says could you come to his office, please?'

'Yes, okay. Tell him five minutes, would you? I've only just got in.'

'I think he wants you to come now, ma'am.'

'Well, whatever he wants, he's going to have to wait. I'm busy at the moment.'

She put down the phone, but after less than ten seconds it rang again. This time it was Acting Chief Superintendent Molloy himself.

'Katie? I need to talk to you right now.'

'Bryan – I've just told your secretary that I'm busy. I'm listening to evidence. I'll be with you as soon as I can.'

'No, you won't, Katie. There's been a complaint made against you and I need to discuss it with you immediately.'

'A complaint? From whom? What kind of complaint?'

'I'll tell you when you come to my office, and I'd very much appreciate it if you'd do that now.'

Katie said to Detective O'Donovan, 'I'm sorry, Patrick, I'm going to have to leave this for now. Molloy wants to see me. I'll come and find you and listen to the rest of it when I'm finished with him.'

She could see that Detective O'Donovan badly wanted to ask her what was wrong, but she simply gave him a quick, tight smile and left her office.

Acting Chief Superintendent Molloy's door was open, which was unusual for him. He was sitting at his desk with his fingers steepled and his forehead furrowed, as if he were a judge at a tribunal.

Assistant Commissioner O'Reilly was there, too, standing by the window, so that all Katie could see of him was his lean silhouette, with his slicked-back hair and his aquiline nose.

'So what's this complaint?' Katie demanded. 'You do realize how much I have on my plate today, Bryan?'

Bryan Molloy picked up a sheet of notepaper and leaned back in his chair. 'At ten forty-seven this morning a thirty-six-year-old male came into the station to lodge a formal complaint against you, namely of assault with intent to cause bodily harm.'

'You're not serious.'

'Oh, I'm serious all right. The complainant's name is David ó Catháin, a veterinary surgeon of Lee Vista, Carrig View, Great Island. As I understand it, he's your next-door neighbour.'

'And he's complained that I've assaulted him?'

'He claims that he called on you yesterday evening because he came home to discover that his wife was missing. He was extremely worried about her whereabouts because she suffers from mental instability, but since you are a senior police officer he assumed that you might be able to offer him some advice and assistance.'

'The man is a chronic wife-beater,' said Katie. 'His wife had come to me earlier and she was so badly battered that I took her to the Cuanlee Refuge. He turned up at my door late in the evening, langered and very angry. When I let him in, he attempted to assault me. I retaliated with a single kick and a blow with my elbow. After that he left.'

'That's not the way he tells it,' put in Assistant Commissioner O'Reilly, turning away from the window. 'The way he tells it, you were the worse for drink yourself and you told him that you had managed to get rid of his wife so that you and he could continue a sexual relationship which you had already initiated with him, without her interference.'

'He said *what*? You should see the state of the poor woman. She's bruises and bites all over. You can get in touch with Brigid

McNulty at Cuanlee yourself and ask her.'

'I'm asking *you*, Katie,' said Jimmy O'Reilly. 'Is it true that you had intimate relations with this David ó Catháin?'

'I refuse to answer that,' Katie retorted. 'If a formal complaint has been made against me, then I'll need to consult with a lawyer.'

Bryan Molloy held up the sheet of notepaper. 'David ó Catháin states categorically that after his wife suffered an acute mental episode one evening he came to you to ask for moral support. Instead, you invited him into your bedroom and enticed him into sexual relations. He admits that he allowed you to take advantage of his extreme emotional distress, but that he regretted it immediately and that after that evening he had no wish for the incident to be repeated. Subsequently, you asked him around to your house on several occasions, but each time he politely declined, explaining to you that he was deeply attached to his wife and his priority was to take care of her.'

'I'm not answering any of those accusations,' said Katie.

'You understand that a thorough investigation will have to be conducted,' said Jimmy O'Reilly. 'Questions will have to be asked about your suitability to remain in the position of detective super-intendent, especially in the light of your recent poor performance in regard to the kidnappings by the High Kings of Erin.'

'David ó Catháin's accusations are not related in any way to my investigations of the High Kings of Erin.'

'Yes, Katie, you can say that. But any police psychologist will tell you that the stresses that occur in an officer's working life almost always take a toll on their personal life. And this is clearly what has happened here.'

'I resent that,' Katie snapped back at him. 'We are making slow but positive progress in the High Kings of Erin case, and David ó Catháin's version of events is completely distorted and mostly untrue.'

'But you *did* have sexual relations with him?' asked Bryan Molloy, smiling one of his smug, golf-club smiles.

'Bryan – I am not answering any more questions without

legal representation,' said Katie, trying to keep her voice steady, although inside she was trembling with suppressed anger. She felt like stalking over to him and tipping his desk over on top of him.

'You're entitled to that, of course,' said Jimmy O'Reilly. 'But considering your rank and the seriousness of the allegation against you, I am going to forward this matter to the Garda Ombudsman Commission. In the meantime, you will have to consider yourself suspended from duty. Make sure you hand in your ID badge and your weapon.'

'That is ridiculous, sir. I am right in the middle of dealing with two life-threatening situations with regard to Pat Whelan being kidnapped, and Eoghan Carroll having been taken. It's quite possible that Eoghan may already have been murdered.'

'I'm aware of that, of course. Bryan has been keeping me up to date.'

'That's not the half of it,' Katie protested. She held up her hand and counted off the points she was making with her fingers. 'I am also supervising the investigations into the murders of Garda McCracken and Detective Garda Goold, as well as the killing of Norman and Meryl Pearse, and the shooting of Derek Hagerty – not to mention Micky Crounan being beheaded. Plus, I am close to indicting Michael Gerrety on a charge of reckless endangerment. Plus, I have two major drugs operations running. Plus countless other cases, including the prosecution of twenty-three people under the Public Order Act after that water-meter riot at County Hall.'

'I'm conscious of your considerable workload, Katie. Maybe that's part of your problem. But Inspector Fennessy is perfectly capable of taking over the supervision of your ongoing cases for the time being, and Bryan has suggested that we draft in a very experienced inspector from Limerick to assist him.'

'With all due respect, sir, do you really understand what you're proposing here?' Katie demanded. 'One of the most cold-blooded gangs of kidnappers and extortionists and murderers that we have ever known in Cork is still unidentified and at liberty, and the lives of two of their victims are hanging in the balance even as we speak. And you want to suspend me because my abusive next-door neighbour is cribbing that I gave him a kick?'

Jimmy O'Reilly came up uncomfortably close to her, although he didn't look her in the eye. He looked instead at the lapels of her maroon tweed jacket, as if he had seen a stray bit of fluff on one of them and was debating with himself whether he ought to pick it off.

'I was never keen on your appointment, Katie, but the instructions came from Dublin Castle that they wanted a woman in a senior position for public-relations purposes. As it turns out, I was right and they were wrong. You can't promote officers beyond their level of competence just because they happen to have a bosom.'

Katie stared at him. She could hardly believe what he had said to her. She looked across at Bryan Molloy, but he still had that all-boys-together smirk on his face.

Without saying another word, she turned and walked out.

'*Katie*!' she heard Bryan Molloy calling out when she was halfway along the corridor. Then, '*Detective Superintendent*!'

She didn't answer. She went into her own office and stood behind her desk, breathing hard, wondering what to do next. She had an urgent duty to try and save Pat Whelan and Eoghan Carroll, if they were still alive, and she also had the responsibility of catching and prosecuting the High Kings of Erin. How could they possibly suspend her?

She was still standing there when Detective Sergeant Ni Nuallán knocked at her door.

'Yes?' she said distractedly.

'Mr and Mrs Carroll have received a phone call from the High Kings of Erin.'

'When?'

'Only about ten minutes ago.'

'What did they say? They haven't harmed Eoghan, have they?'

'No, but they said they had him captive and they want fifty thousand euros for his release.'

'Otherwise they'll do what?'

'They didn't say what would happen to him if the Carrolls didn't pay up, but I don't think they needed to.'

'Well, you'd better tell Inspector Fennessy,' said Katie.

'I will, of course.'

Detective Sergeant Ni Nuallán hesitated, as if she were waiting for Katie to say something else.

'Is that all?' she asked her.

'What do you mean, "is that all"?'

'I mean, don't you want to hear the recording? It definitely sounds like the same scobe who called you. That high, raspy voice, like.'

Katie said, 'I'll be down in a minute to talk to Inspector Fennessy myself. The thing of it is, I've had an official complaint made against me. Jimmy O'Reilly has relieved me of duty until it's cleared up.'

She found it hard to blink back the tears, although she didn't feel sorry for herself. They were tears of frustration, because she really believed that now she had thought of a way to outwit the High Kings of Erin – and they were tears of anger at Jimmy O'Reilly's coarse misogyny. She had been so close to saying to him, 'Oh, and I suppose *you* were promoted because you happen to have a prick, is that it?'

Detective Sergeant Ni Nuallán came towards her and raised her arms as if she were about to hug her in sympathy. As much as it would have comforted her, however, Katie waved her away. 'No, Kyna. I'll deal with it. I have enough trouble as it is. It's that next-door neighbour of mine, the one I was telling you about. He went for me – tried to push me around. I think he might even have raped me if I'd given him the chance. I slapped him a kick, that's all.'

'But if you were just protecting yourself, and he deserved it, that's so unfair. Like, what's O'Reilly thinking of?'

'I wish I knew, Kyna. Maybe I'd understand then what in the name of Jesus is going on in this place. I'll tell you, I'm beginning to smell something seriously rotten in this station. I only wish I knew what it was.'

Thirty-Nine

From somewhere downstairs, Pat Whelan heard voices and laughter and doors slamming. Almost immediately afterwards, he heard car engines starting up outside, one after the other, at least three of them, and the crunching of tyres on shingle. Another door slammed, and then there was silence.

He waited for a short while and then he eased himself up into a sitting position, sucking in his breath, and swung his legs off the side of the bed. His chest was still tender and his ribs were so bruised that he could have groaned out loud, but he bit his lower lip, and sniffed deeply, and stayed where he was, not moving, until the pain subsided.

The silence downstairs was broken for a few seconds by somebody tunelessly whistling, but then even that stopped. Another door closed, but much more quietly than before.

He managed to stand up and shuffle slowly across the attic. He tried the doorknob, expecting the door to be locked, but it opened easily. Outside, there was a long landing with two skylights and another door at the very far end. He could smell bacon, which reminded him that he hadn't eaten anything since the High Kings of Erin had brought him here. They had left a two-litre bottle of Ishka spring water beside his bed, but even if they had given him biscuits or sandwiches he probably would have found swallowing too painful.

He stood in the open doorway, wondering what he ought to do. If three cars had left the house, there couldn't be more than two people left here to guard him, Before they had beaten and mutilated him like this, he might have taken his chances and tried to escape. In the state he was in, though, he knew that he was no match for anybody. Even that girl, Ruari, could stop him, anaemic and thin as she was.

He was still standing there when the door at the far end of the landing suddenly opened. He was about to step back and quickly close his door when he saw a young man emerge, rubbing his wrists and looking cautiously around him.

The young man caught sight of him and stopped still, but with the bloodstained bandages around his chest and his baggy grey tracksuit bottoms it must have been plain that he wasn't one of the High Kings of Erin.

'Hey,' called the young man, although not too loudly. 'You're not one of them, are you?'

Pat shook his head. 'Look at the state of me la. What do you think?'

The young man came out of his room and walked along the landing. 'Shit,' he said, as he came nearer. 'What the hell did they do to you?'

'Cut my fecking nipples off. Part of their great historical tradition, they said, so that I could never be a king.'

He held out his hand and said, 'Pat's the name, Pat Whelan. Maybe you know my music store on Oliver Plunkett Street. Whelan's.'

'Of course, yes. I bought a kazoo in there once when I was about nine. Eoghan Carroll. Cut your nipples off, Jesus. What did you do to deserve that?'

'Well, it's a long story,' said Pat. He didn't think it was wise to tell this young man too much about his faked kidnap and how he had changed his mind about it – not until he knew more about him. 'I was giving them ire, for some reason. I'm not too sure myself. They're not what you'd call forgiving. How about you?'

Eoghan glanced down the staircase. The smell of frying bacon was stronger than ever. 'They seem to think that I was a witness to something shady that they'd been up to, even though I wasn't. They came around to my parents' house and dragged me out of the door and shot and killed a garda while they were doing it. Now they won't let me go unless my parents come up with fifty thousand euros. It's pure insanity.'

He held up his wrists and showed Pat the deep scarlet dents in them. 'They had me tied to the bed with washing line but the bed frame was sharp metal and I kept on rubbing and rubbing and in the end I managed to fray it right through.'

Pat said, 'We need to get ourselves out of here. I think they're going to top us for sure, whether anybody pays off our ransom money or not. They don't want nobody knowing who they are.'

'They don't have to worry about me. I don't have the faintest notion who they are.'

'No, well, neither do I. But what I mean is we know what they look like, don't we, and if they got themselves arrested we could pick them out in one of them what-do-you-call-thems – identity parades.'

'So what do you suggest?' asked Eoghan. 'They can't think there's too much chance of us getting out of here or they would have locked our doors, wouldn't they? I tried to get out before but it was hopeless.'

Pat said, 'I just heard three cars leave and as far as I know there's only five of them, so at the most there's only two of them still here.'

'Yes, but it could be the two who took me away from my parents' house. They were built like red-brick shithouses, the both of them.'

'So what are we going to do? Sit in our rooms and wait for them to come back and cut our throats or blow our heads off or beat us to death?'

'No way,' said Eoghan. 'They don't know yet that I've got myself untied, do they? If you start moaning and complaining real loud like you're in terrible agony then they're bound to come up to see what's wrong with you, aren't they?'

'Oh, yes, and then what?'

'There's a stool in my room. When the first one of them gets to the top of the stairs I'll jump out and smack him with it.'

Pat looked dubious. 'And you think that's going to put him out of action?'

'There's a chance. Those stairs are fierce steep, aren't they?'

'And what about the other fellow?'

'Well, we don't know who's down there, do we? It could be those foxy-haired twins, the girl and her brother. I reckon I could take them on.'

'But supposing it's not the twins? Supposing it's the red-brick shithouses?'

'Listen,' said Eoghan, 'do you want to get out of here or not?'

'Of course I do. Like I said, I'm not going to sit here like some turkey waiting for Christmas.'

'Then let's just go for it. What have we got to lose?'

'Well, nothing at all. So long as you realize I'll be no use at all if it comes to a fight. I can hardly take a breath, let alone give anyone a beating.'

'We'll just have to take our chances,' said Eoghan. 'You go back to your room and when I give you the signal, start moaning. I'll be hiding back here at the top of the stairs. When you hear me whack whoever it is comes up, come out quick and we'll make a break for it.'

Pat hesitated for a moment, listening. Again, he could hear a door opening and closing downstairs, and more of that tuneless whistling. Actually, he recognized that it wasn't completely tuneless: it was 'The Fields of Athenry', but whistled flat. He could hear the words inside his head. 'It's so lonely round the fields of Athenry . . .'

He looked at Eoghan. He didn't know him from Adam and yet here he was agreeing to join him in a totally reckless attempt at escape. What if he were nothing but a header? What if the High

Kings of Erin had kept him tied up because he was some kind of a psycho?

'Are we going for it then?' asked Eoghan impatiently. 'We'd better do it quick because the others could be coming back at any moment and then we'd be fucked.'

'All right, let's go for it,' Pat agreed. Whatever happens it couldn't be worse than having my nipples cut off. And if we do manage to escape, I can make sure these High Kings of Erin are locked up for good, which is less than they deserve. Eoghan gave him the thumbs up and he shuffled back to his room, feeling frightened but strangely excited, too. He had never been involved in a fight in his life, not even in the school playground.

Pat left the door a few inches ajar and then went over and sat on the bed. He waited for what seemed like well over a minute, although it was probably less than half that. Eventually he heard Eoghan call out, '*Okay, Pat*! *Let's hear you*! *Give it all you've got*!'

He took a deep, painful breath and then let out a long, warbling howl, like a dog crushed under a car wheel.

'*Louder*!' Eoghan urged him.

He howled again and then he sobbed for breath, although the sobbing was genuine because his ribs hurt so much.

'More!' said Eoghan, in a stage whisper. 'They're talking to themselves downstairs, I can hear them.'

Pat breathed in yet again and this time screamed as high as he could, and went on and on screaming until he ran completely out of air. He leaned forward, his eyes shut tight in agony, trying to summon up the strength to scream again, but he couldn't.

It didn't matter, though. Eoghan hissed, '*They're coming*!' and Pat could hear footsteps stamping up the stairs. He stood up and went over to the door, ready to come out when Eoghan hit the first of the gang to reach the landing.

Malachi appeared at the top of the stairs, his face flushed and his white shirtsleeves rolled up. He saw Pat peering out of his half-open door and he started to say, 'What in the name o' – '

Eoghan stepped out from behind him, holding a heavy oak stool high up over his right shoulder. He leaned back a little and then swung the stool around hard, so that the edge of its seat struck Malachi on the side of his head, about an inch above his ear. The noise was extraordinary, *clokk*! – as if Malachi's skull were hollow. He pitched backwards, his feet doing a scrabbling, complicated dance, his left hand trying to snatch the banister rail to stop himself from falling, but he lost his footing and went thumping and banging down the narrow staircase. He slithered down the last few stairs, head first, and then hit the first-floor landing with a crack.

He lay there, both arms spread wide, his shiny black loafers still resting on the stairs, looking up at Eoghan with an expression of disbelief. He blinked, so it was clear he wasn't dead, but he didn't appear able to move. He looked as if he had been crucified upside down.

Pat came out on to the landing and stared down at him. Still Malachi didn't move, although he blinked again, and opened and closed his mouth.

'Malachi?' came a shout from the hallway below. 'Malachi, what the feck was all that fecking racket about? You didn't push that fecking spastic down the stairs, did ye?'

'For Christ's sake,' said Pat. 'Look – he has a gun on him!'

The grey steel butt of an automatic pistol was just visible sticking out of the waistband of Malachi's trousers. He wasn't making any attempt to pull it out – he was still lying on his back with his arms outstretched. Eoghan dropped the stool with a clatter and swung himself down the staircase, grasping the banister rails on both sides like a gymnast on the parallel bars. He climbed awkwardly over Malachi and when Malachi made no move to prevent him, he tugged out the pistol with two or three jerks and then stepped away from him.

'It's all right, I have it,' he said, holding the pistol up for Pat to see. 'I think his neck must be broke.'

'Malachi!' came another shout from downstairs. 'Are you

making us this fecking breakfast or not? The fecking beans have just pinged! Malachi!'

Pat came down the stairs and Eoghan helped him to step over Malachi's outstretched body. Malachi opened and closed his mouth again, but the only sound that came out of him was '*urrrrrr . . .*'

'Jesus,' said Pat.

'What? You're not feeling sorry for him, are you?' said Eoghan. 'This is one of the two who shot a woman garda right in the face. Come on, let's get out of here!'

'*Urrrrrr . . .*' said Malachi, rolling his eyes.

'And *urrrrr* to you, too, you murdering scumbag,' said Eoghan. 'It might be human to *urrrrrr*, but I'm not going to be divine and forgive you!'

They headed for the wider flight of stairs that would take them down to the hallway. Before they had reached them, however, the head of the second bouncer-type appeared over the top of the banisters as he came trudging up to see why Malachi hadn't answered him.

As soon as he saw Pat and Eoghan walking towards him, and Malachi lying prone on the landing behind them, his mouth dropped open. 'What the *feck* – !'

Eoghan lifted Malachi's pistol, pointed it at him and pulled the trigger, but the safety catch was still on and it didn't fire. Immediately the bouncer-type turned around and began to jump back down the stairs, two and three at a time.

Eoghan ran to the top of the staircase, pointed the pistol with both hands and fired at him again. This time the pistol went off, and the shot was so loud that Pat was deafened. It missed, though, and the bouncer-type leaped to the bottom of the stairs, staggered for a second, and then turned towards the kitchen.

Eoghan hurried halfway down the staircase, leaned over the banisters and fired again, almost directly downwards. The bouncer-type had almost made it to the kitchen door but he clapped his left hand to his shoulder and dropped heavily on to his knees.

Eoghan quickly went down the remainder of the stairs to the

hallway. The bouncer-type was trying to shuffle his way towards the kitchen on his knees, rucking up the threadbare carpet as he did so. Eoghan walked around so that he was facing him and pointed the pistol at his face.

'Go on, then, shoot me,' croaked the bouncer-type. Blood was glistening between his fingers and staining the front of his shirt. 'I'll bet you don't have the fecking neck.'

'I'm not going to shoot you,' said Eoghan. 'I'm not a murderer like you High Kings of Erin.'

'Oh yeah? Then what have you done to Malachi?'

'Malachi tripped and fell down the stairs, that's all. Nothing that a lifetime in a wheelchair won't put right. No – I'm not going to shoot you. All me and my friend want to do is get out of here, so that you won't be able to extort ransom money to have us set free. The only thing we want apart from that is to forget that we ever knew you.'

The bouncer-type slowly shook his head from side to side. 'You won't ever be able to forget us, I can promise you that, sham. You can hide yourselves anywhere you like, we'll find you and we'll do for you.'

'Well, dream on,' said Eoghan.

Pat had come down the stairs to join him now. The bouncer-type looked up at him and then spat blood and saliva on to the floor.

'Let's go,' said Eoghan. 'But you can't go out with those bandages showing. There, look, in the kitchen, there's a jacket hanging over the back of that chair. Take that.'

'That's Malachi's jacket,' the bouncer-type protested.

'So what?' said Eoghan. 'He won't be needing it any more. All he'll be needing is a hospital gown.'

Pat went into the kitchen and lifted the jacket off the chair. There was still a strong smell of bacon everywhere, and the frying pan was crowded with curled-up rashers. When he put on the jacket it hung on him like a large black tent, but it would help to keep him warm and it would hide his bloodstained bandages. In the inside pocket he found a black pigskin wallet which contained a driving licence in the name of Malachi Brawley, a colour photograph of a round-faced woman with a double chin and frizzy blonde hair, and three twenty-euro notes.

'Keep the money,' said Eoghan. 'Compensation for your injuries. We're going to need some grade, anyhow.'

The bouncer-type coughed and blood and saliva ran down his chin. His eyes were nearly closed and he was swaying on his knees.

'What are we going to do about him?' asked Pat. 'The other one, too, Malachi. He's going to need medical attention.'

'Let's get away from here first,' said Eoghan. 'Then we can call 112, anonymous, like.'

They left by the kitchen door. It had been bolted and locked, but they found the key lying close to it on the kitchen counter. Outside, they found themselves in a tangled, overgrown garden with brick walls all around it and beds filled with slimy brown and yellow weeds. At the end of the garden path there was a gate with peeling pale blue paint. It, too, was locked, but the wood was so damp and rotten that Eoghan only had to kick it twice and the lock came away from the crossbar.

On the other side of the gate there was a deserted country road and fields.

'You realize, don't you, that we can't go home yet?' said Eoghan. 'If we do, those murdering bastards will come after us, no messing. And our families, too.'

'I know that,' said Pat. 'I'm going to call my Mairead and make sure that she goes to stay with one of her cousins where they won't be able to find her. But we also need to call the Garda and tell them that we've got away and that they don't need to pay the ransom money, and we can also tell them what those High Kings of Erin look like. I reckon you and me will see those scumbags locked up, Eoghan. Revenge is sweet.'

They walked along the road for a while in silence, both of them thinking about how they had managed to escape and what they were faced with now.

'Do you know what you look like in that jacket?' asked Eoghan Carroll, as they came to a road junction.

'No,' said Pat. He was looking around, trying to decide which would be the best way for them to go. There were no direction signs and he had no clear idea where they were except that they could be somewhere between Upper Bridestown and Keame, but that was only a guess.

'You look like a kid who's dressed up in his old fellow's clothes.'

'Well, do you know something?' Pat replied. 'Right at this moment, I feel exactly like I did when I was a kid, coming home from school. Tired, hungry, bruised all over and totally fecking bewildered.'

Forty

Katie was fastening her large brown leather satchel, all ready to leave her office, when Inspector Fennessy came in. He was wearing new thick-rimmed spectacles, which made him look like a college lecturer.

'I'm fierce sorry about them suspending you, ma'am. I don't know what to say.'

'Well, I appreciate it, Liam, but I don't think there's a whole lot that anybody *can* say, except that Jimmy O'Reilly has been waiting for an opportunity like this ever since I was first promoted, and Bryan Molloy isn't exactly the picture of disappointment either.'

Her phone rang. She looked at it, wondering if she ought to answer it. After the tenth or eleventh ring, Inspector Fennessy picked it up.

'Hello. DS Maguire has just left the station. Who's calling her?'

He listened for a moment and then reached across Katie's desk for a sheet of paper and a pen. He jotted down a few notes and then said, 'All right. Grand. Yes. This is Inspector Fennessy you're talking to. We'll send a couple of detectives and a technical team directly. Yes. Good. I will, of course.'

'What was that about?' asked Katie. 'Not that it's any of my concern. Not for the time being, anyway.'

'Oh, I'd say that it *is* your concern, ma'am. Very much so. That was Sergeant Mahoney from Ballincollig. He says that they've discovered a man's body and they suspect that it's the rest of Micky Crounan.'

'Serious? Where did they find it?'

'It was only by chance, he said. It's underneath some freshly laid asphalt on the road that runs south from the Lisheens round-about on the N27. They've only uncovered one arm so far but it looks like he's been flattened, he said, like somebody had driven a roadroller over him. But whoever laid the asphalt on top of him, they left three of his fingertips sticking out by the side of the road.'

'It sounds like a miracle that anybody found him.'

'It was a roller-blind sales rep. He was on his way to Munster Blinds in Killumney but as soon as he got off the main road he stopped to take a leak. He was right in the middle of relieving himself when he saw these fingers. I'll bet that stopped him in mid-flow.'

Katie said, 'What makes Sergeant Mahoney think that it's Micky Crounan?'

'He can't be totally sure, but one of Crounan's identifying features was the silver ring he always wore on his left-hand pinkie. His wife gave it to him when they first met twenty-seven years ago and he never took it off. The ring's gone, but there's an indentation on one of the fingers and black stains on the skin which would suggest that the deceased was wearing a silver ring before he was squashticated.'

'That's surely going to help us, though, isn't it, the way they disposed of his body? You couldn't do that single-handed, could you – flatten a man's body with a roadroller and then cover it over with asphalt? You'd need a whole resurfacing crew. So there must have been more than a few accessories, as well as witnesses. Pity there's no law of misprision any more.'

'Well, I'll go out there myself with Bill Phinner,' said Inspector Fennessy. 'I don't know how they're going to separate his remains from the asphalt, but I shouldn't think it's going to be easy.'

'I'll come with you,' said Katie, picking up her satchel.

'Oh, I'm not sure about that. I thought that if you were suspended – '

'I don't give a fiddler's, Liam. This is still my case even if I'm not officially working on it. I won't comment. I won't interfere. I just need to see the evidence for myself.'

'I'll let you see the photographs and all the forensics.'

'It's not enough, Liam. I have to get the feel of this first-hand. I think I'm beginning to understand what's going on here, with these High Kings of Erin. Only piece by piece, like one of those thousand-piece jigsaws, you know, but every extra piece helps.'

'I'm sorry, but I won't be able to take you along with me in my car,' said Inspector Fennessy. 'Not without getting a bollocking from Molloy.'

'All right. I have you. But I'm going out there anyway, even if I'll be nothing more than a civilian nosy parker.'

'I can't stop you from doing that. I will say this, though – be very careful of these people. You could end up losing a whole lot more than just your job.'

Katie stared at him narrowly, holding her satchel close to her chest as if to protect herself. 'What are you talking about, Liam? What are you not telling me?'

'Nothing at all, ma'am, except you need to be double wide. You don't play games with the kind of sham-feens who can burn people alive and cut off a fellow's head and flatten the rest of him with a roadroller. And you don't play games with the kind of sham-feens who can end your career as easy as look at you.'

Inspector Fennessy took off his glasses and cleaned the lenses on his pale lilac tie. Katie kept on staring at him while he did so. She felt strongly that he was trying to say something important to her, but that he was afraid to put it into simple English.

'Look – I'll have to be heading off,' he said, putting his glasses back on again. 'I may see you there, out at Lisheens. If I do, though, I think it's best for both of us if we make out that we don't.'

He paused, and then he said, 'You've seen me through some difficult times, ma'am, and I don't want you to think that I'm not grateful. When I was going through all of that trouble with Caitlin you weren't soft on me, but you did appreciate why I was acting towards her the way I was. You were the only person who understood me, and that meant a lot, and still does.'

'All right, Liam,' said Katie. 'I'll see you after. Or not, rather.'

* * *

Before she drove out to Lisheens, Katie phoned her solicitor, Douglas Rooney. He was in court until lunchtime, defending a man charged with taking out his pit-bull terrier without a muzzle. She explained to his secretary why she needed to see him and made an appointment for later in the day.

A pale silvery sun began to shine as she drove westwards on the Cork Ring and the wet road in front of her was so dazzling that she had to put on her sunglasses. She turned off the N27 at Lisheens, but when she reached the small roundabout at the top of the slip road she found that there were cones across the road that led to Killumney, and a Road Closed sign.

She stopped and climbed out of her car so that she could move two of the cones to one side. Then she drove around the Road Closed sign and headed south. On either side there were only flat fields and hedges and stunted trees, without even a cow in sight. About a half-mile up ahead of her, though, she could see Garda patrol cars and several other cars and vans, including a green and white outside broadcast van from RTÉ, and a yellow JCB digger.

She parked her Focus as close behind the RTÉ van as she could, so that it was half-hidden from the gardaí and the TV crew and all the other people milling around in the centre of the road. Inspector Fennessy hadn't yet arrived but she could see Detective Sergeant Ni Nuallán talking to Sergeant Mahoney from the Ballincollig Garda station, as well as Detectives O'Donovan and Horgan. She turned up the collar of her raincoat and kept herself close beside the RTÉ sound technician, and nobody challenged her. She guessed that any gardaí who recognized her would not yet have heard that she had been suspended, and those who didn't know who she was probably assumed she was with the TV crew. In any case, everybody's attention was directed to the side of the road where the roller-blind rep had discovered the fingertips.

Katie couldn't go up as close to the victim's remains as she would have liked, so that she could examine them in detail, but she could see them reasonably well from where she was standing. The victim's hand was palm upwards, with the fingertips slightly lifted, and she could clearly make out the silver-stained indentation on his pinkie. The Ballincollig gardaí had chipped and levered away the solidified asphalt from his knuckles down to his left collarbone. His fingertips had remained unscathed, but the skin of his arm had been charred black and crisp by the eighty-degree heat and most of it had flaked off. His muscles had been roasted to the colour of overdone beef and his bones were cracked and stained brown by the asphalt.

The left side of his ribcage was just visible. He had been so comprehensively crushed that his body was less than five centimetres thick. Katie could only think that Sergeant Mahoney's assumption had been right and that he had been flattened by a roadroller. There were no humps or bumps on the finished road surface to indicate that a man was buried underneath it.

She looked around. This was an isolated spot, with no houses in sight, and although it connected the N27 with the trading estate at Killumney it was probably deserted in the evenings and for most of the day on Sundays. Three or four crows were perched on the telephone wires, their feathers fluttering, but there was no other sign of life.

She was turning to leave when Detective O'Donovan caught sight of her and quickly walked over.

'Ma'am?' he said. 'You're not going away, are you? I didn't even see you arrive.'

'That's because I'm not really here,' Katie told him. 'If you think you've seen me, you haven't.'

Detective O'Donovan said, 'What? I'm sorry. I don't follow you.'

'It hasn't been officially announced yet, Patrick, so don't go spreading it about. O'Reilly has suspended me.'

'*Suspended* you? Serious? What for, in the name of Jesus?'

'All I can tell you at the moment is that there's been a formal complaint lodged against me. I'm disputing it, of course, but in the meantime I'm at home on dog-walking duty. Or supposed to be.'

'I can't believe it. What about these kidnaps? Who's going to be in charge?'

'Talk to Inspector Fennessy. He should be here soon. He's taking over for the time being, along with some inspector from Limerick.'

'I can't believe it,' Detective O'Donovan repeated, shaking his head.

'Don't worry,' said Katie. 'I'll have it all sorted before you know it. I'll see you later so.'

She walked back to her car. Before she reached it, though, she saw an elderly man pedalling slowly and unsteadily towards her on a bicycle. He was wearing a tweed cap and a tweed jacket with frayed elbows and corduroy trousers. As he drew alongside her, he came to an abrupt stop and took off his cap and brushed back his straggly white hair. He had a bulbous nose and lips that were deepy furrowed from wearing false teeth, and his chin was covered with white prickly stubble. His breath reeked of stale alcohol and cigarettes.

'Haven't they dug that poor fellow out yet?' he asked.

'Not yet, no.'

'They could use an ordinary pick and shovel. It's only been a few days, so that tarmac will still be softish.'

'You know what happened here?'

'I do, of course. I only saw it with my own eyes. Well, I didn't realize then that it was a fellow they was laying the road over. I thought they was fixing it, that's all. But I thought it was queer that they was doing it so late, you know, when it was almost totally dark, like.'

'When was this?'

'Friday evening last week. I do a bit of gardening for a woman in The Brambles, up by Tanner Park. I was coming back late because she cooked packet and tripe for me special as a thank you, and we had a few scoops with it, too.'

'So where do you live?'

'Lisheen Fields. It's only ten minutes on the bike.'

'So you actually saw them laying the road here?'

'That's right.'

'How many of them were there?'

'Five, I'd say. Maybe six. I had to wheel my bike through the fecking field just to get past them and my boots got all muddy. I would have stopped to ask what they was doing but they was making so much of a racket with the paver that I couldn't hear myself think and, besides, I have to confess to you that I was more than partially langered.'

Katie glanced back towards the gardaí and the TV crew still gathered around the side of the road.

'You've told the guards what you saw?' she asked.

The elderly man stared at her as if she had said something deeply offensive. 'Now, why would I have done that?'

'It could help them to find out who did this, that's why.'

'Guards? I wouldn't piss on them if they was on fire. All the trouble I've had with the guards in my life. You're not a guard, are you?'

'Oh, come on, do I look like one?'

'Of course not. Fine beoir like you. But any road, I recognized one of the lads who was laying down the black stuff and I wasn't going to rat on him, was I? His dad's an old chum of mine.'

'You *know* one of them?'

'For sure. Kenny Boyle, that's Billy Boyle's youngest. Kilshane Tarmac he works for. "We're Streets Ahead!" That's their motto. Grand, isn't it? "We're Streets Ahead!"'

He shook his head in amusement and kept on shaking it. Then he suddenly said, 'You wouldn't be having the time on you, would you? I promised the auld wan I'd be home by two. She'll kill me stone dead if I'm not.'

'Don't worry, you won't be late,' Katie told him. 'It was good to talk to you. Maybe we'll bump into each other again. My name's Katie. What's yours?'

'Fergal. Fergal O'Donnell. If you need your garden trimming any time, Katie, you just let me know. I'm in the phone book. Fergal O'Donnell, Hollyglen Cottage, Lisheen Fields. Weeding, lawn mowing, hedge trimming, you just say the word!'

'Thanks a million, Fergal,' said Katie. 'I might take you up on that.'

Fergal O'Donnell climbed on to his bicycle and pedalled slowly past the crime scene and away down the road. Katie watched him weave erratically from side to side, wondering if she ought to walk back and tell Detective Sergeant Ni Nuallán what he had just said to her.

However, she stayed where she was, almost feeling as if her feet were stuck to the road. She knew that it was her moral obligation to pass on the names of Kenny Boyle and Kilshane Tarmac. But for one thing, she was suspended and she was not supposed to be here at all.

More importantly, though, Fergal O'Donnell's information might have given her a lead that she could follow all the way back to the High Kings of Erin – to identify them and to arrest them.

Under the law, Fergal O'Donnell had no duty to report to the Garda what he had witnessed; and since Katie was under suspension, she questioned whether she was duty-bound to report it, either. If she kept the information to herself, it could possibly give her a way to show that she wasn't the dithering, hormonal woman that Acting Chief Inspector Molloy had been repeatedly trying to suggest she was.

She hadn't felt so torn in her whole career, even when a vengeful Nigerian woman had threatened to shoot one of Michael Gerrety's pimps and she had failed to pull the trigger of her own gun to stop her.

One by one, lazily, the crows lifted themselves off the telegraph wires and flapped away. For some reason that she couldn't articulate, Katie took that as a sign. She unlocked her car, climbed in, and started the engine.

On the way back to the N27 she looked in her rear-view mirror and saw that the JCB had started to lift up the road surface. Then, as she reached the roundabout, she saw Inspector Fennessy driving up the slip road. She could still turn back and tell him what Fergal O'Donnell had said.

She drove all the way around the roundabout, in a complete 360-degree circle, but in the end she took the slip road down to join the main dual carriageway back to Cork.

Forty-One

As soon as she had returned home and taken off her raincoat Katie went through to the living room, sat down in front of the coffee table and opened up her laptop. While she waited for it to load, she tugged her gun out of its holster and laid it on the table beside the computer. She would go to Anglesea Street and hand it in when she went to meet her solicitor.

Barney stood in the hallway, wagging his tail very slowly and looking puzzled, because she usually took him out for a walk whenever she came back.

'It's all right, Barns,' she said. 'As soon as I've done this, I'll take you to see grandpa.'

She had nine e-mails waiting for her, but she ignored them and typed in *Kilshane Tarmac.*

The company's website featured a photograph of a red Dynapac asphalt paver with two workmen in overalls standing beside it with their thumbs up. Underneath was the motto that Fergus O'Donnell had found so amusing, 'We're Streets Ahead'.

What caught Katie's attention was that Kilshane Tarmac was based on Dublin Road, Mitchelstown, but their registered address was given as Crossagalla, in Limerick. At the very foot of the home page there was a line of tiny type that said, 'A Division of Crossagalla Groundworks'.

She scribbled a note of that and then sat back, frowning at the screen. As Detective Horgan had discovered, Crossagalla Groundworks was the principal source of income for Flathead Consultants, and the majority shareholder in Flathead Consultants was Acting Chief Superintendent Bryan Molloy. So what in the name of all that was holy did this mean? A subsidiary of the company that had paid Bryan Molloy over a million and a half euros in the previous financial year had deliberately attempted to conceal the remains of a homicide victim. If the asphalt laying hadn't been undertaken under cover of darkness, which was probably why the workmen hadn't noticed that they had left the man's fingertips protruding from the side of the road, nobody would ever have discovered what had happened to him.

The real question was, what kind of relationship did Bryan Molloy have with Crossagalla Groundworks, if any, and had he known that Kilshane Tarmac had sent out a team to obliterate any evidence of what had happened to Micky Crounan – assuming, of course, that it *was* Micky Crounan? Whoever the body belonged to, the workmen who had buried him in asphalt were all guilty of aiding and abetting a homicide, and it was highly likely that the directors of Kilshane Tarmac were equally culpable.

Katie could see that she needed to investigate the disposal of this body with extreme caution. There was a long chain of command to be followed, link by link, and she didn't want to rattle that chain until she had found out who was at the end of it, and how dangerous they might be. She had to find Kenny Boyle first and see what she could get out of him, and then confront the owners of Kilshane Tarmac and the directors of Crossagalla Groundworks. She needed to do it quickly, too, before any public announcement was made that she had been suspended.

She sorely wished that she had a contact at Anglesea Street whom she could trust implicitly. She was reasonably confident that Liam Fennessy and Kyna Ni Nuallán and Patrick O'Donovan were all reliable, and that none of them had been tipping off the High Kings of Erin about their ongoing investigation – but at the same time, she couldn't be entirely sure. In the past, she had known several senior Garda officers who had accepted pay-offs from crime gangs. Most of their service records had been exemplary, but they had run into money problems for one reason or another – gambling usually, or buying shares in companies that had collapsed in 2008 – and taking bribes had seemed like an easy way to get out of debt. If they turned a blind eye to a traffic violation, or a minor assault, or the selling of Es in nightclubs, who did it hurt?

She looked up the directors of Kilshane Tarmac. One of them – Lorcan Devitt – was also a director of Crossagalla Groundworks. She logged on to PULSE, the police computer, and was relieved to find that Assistant Commissioner O'Reilly hadn't yet thought of ordering her access to it to be blocked. Lorcan Devitt's name appeared on PULSE three times. Each time he had been charged with threatening behaviour or assault, but all three charges had subsequently been dropped because of insufficient evidence. No witnesses could be found who were prepared to give evidence against him in open court.

The second of the three charges related to an incident in August 2011 outside Mickey Martin's pub on Thomas Street in Limerick, when a young man had been slashed diagonally across the lips with a razor. The charge had been dropped, but it gave Katie the lead she was looking for. The twenty-year-old victim had been a member of the Dundon crime family, and Lorcan Devitt had not been charged alone: one of the three men arrested with him had been the late Niall Duggan. That was proof enough for Katie that Lorcan Devitt was closely connected to one of Limerick's most notorious gangs. Of course, Niall Duggan was dead now, but it was common knowledge that his twin children, Aengus and Ruari, were still running the family business – drug-dealing and extortion and car-theft. Katie had seen reports that out of 805 cars stolen in Limerick in the past year, at least half were suspected to have been taken by the Duggans.

There was something else that Katie knew about the Duggans. In 2009 they had pretended to kidnap two members of the Ryan family and demanded sixty thousand euros for their release. What nobody had known at the time was that the Ryans and the Duggans, once sworn enemies, had agreed to make up and share the city's drugs' trade between them, as well as protection rackets and ATM robberies. A stool pigeon had later exposed the 'abduction' as a fake, but by then the ransom money had been paid over and, presumably, split between the kidnappers and the kidnapped.

Katie went over to the drinks table and poured herself a glass of vodka. It was too early to drink and she knew that she needed to keep a clear head, but the ramifications of what she was discovering were overwhelming. She had never relied on hunches. Even if they proved to be correct, they invariably led to corners being cut and bad police work, and it was no good standing in the witness box in the Criminal Court and telling the judge that a defendant was guilty of manslaughter 'because I feel it in my water'.

All the same, from that one casual remark that Fergal O'Donnell had made that afternoon, she now believed it highly probable that the Duggans were the High Kings of Erin, or at least some of them. And it also seemed highly probable that Acting Chief Superintendent Molloy was connected to them somehow, even if it was only financially. He might not be directly involved in the kidnappings and killings, but it was conceivable that he was being generously remunerated to look the other way.

If he was, that would explain his bullying and his persistent attempts to undermine her authority. If she were to find out that he was being bribed by the High Kings of Erin, then he would have to go the way of Garda Commissioner Martin Callinan and justice minister Alan Shatter, and at the very least resign.

'Oh, Barns,' she said, stroking Barney's ears. 'What in the name of Jesus am I going to do now?'

She had started to search for more information about Flathead Consultants when her doorbell chimed. Barney ran to the front door and barked, while Katie picked up her gun from the coffee table and tucked it behind one of the cushions. Then she went into the hallway and called out, 'Who is it?'

'It's me,' said a familiar voice. 'It's David. I need to talk to you.'

***

Katie opened the door. David was standing in the porch in a navy-blue suit, complete with waistcoat, and a pink silk tie. His hair was neatly combed and she could smell a strong musky aftershave. As smart as he was, though, his right eye was plum-coloured and so swollen that he could hardly see out of it.

'Well?' she said. 'What do you need to talk about?'

'I'd find it a whole lot easier if I could come inside.'

'That's all right,' said Katie. 'I can hear you perfectly well where you are.'

'I went to the Garda station this morning and filed a complaint against you, for assaulting me.'

'I know that, of course.'

David took two or three deep breaths, and then he said, 'I want you to understand that I didn't do it with malice.'

'Oh, is that right? You tried to attack me, David, and I defended myself as anybody would, man or woman.'

'Well, that's your interpretation. I wasn't attacking you, Katie. Far from it.'

'What else would you call pushing me over and attempting to rape me?'

David lifted up both of his hands in exasperation. 'Why do women always say that?'

'Why do women always say what?'

'Why do women always call it rape just because they're not exactly in the mood for it? You know how I feel about you, Katie. That time we first made love, that was amazing. You can hardly blame me for assuming that was the beginning of something special. I know you've had your period and everything, and you're stressed about work, this High Kings of Erin thing. But you did lead me on.'

Katie didn't know what to say. She couldn't work out if he was deluded or manipulative or simply stupid.

David hesitated for a few moments and then he leaned towards her with his left arm raised and his hand resting against the door frame, as if he wanted to say something affectionate and confidential.

'The thing of it is, Katie, I'm more than ready to withdraw my complaint.'

'Oh, I see. You're prepared to admit that you did try to rape me, after all?'

'Of course not,' said David. 'But I am willing to say that it was nothing more than a lovers' quarrel.'

'*What*? Are you cracked?'

'Not at all. If you and I are lovers, then that'll be the truth, won't it?'

Katie said, 'Let me get this straight. What you're actually saying is that you'll withdraw your complaint against me if I agree to have sex with you?'

'"Have sex" doesn't make it sound very romantic, does it? But okay, if you put it like that. I really like you, Katie. You're a very attractive woman. You and I could be fantastic together.'

'And what about Sorcha?'

'What about Sorcha? She's a mentaller. She doesn't need me. She needs a psychiatrist.'

Katie looked at him for a while, leaning against her door frame, confident and casual as if he were chatting her up in a bar. He gave her a small 'how about it?' kind of a smile and then grinned at her, baring his teeth.

'Do you know something?' she said. 'What you have just suggested to me comes close to being an arrestable offence. I wish to God it was. Now, get off my porch and never come anywhere near me again. I wish I had never set eyes on you.'

David took his hand away from the door frame and stood up straight. 'You're serious, aren't you?' he said.

Katie looked back at him with contempt. Then, without saying another word, she closed the door in his face.

'Well,' he said loudly. 'That's pretty unequivocal, I'd say. At least I know my position now and it's certainly not on top of you, is it, Detective Superintendent?'

Forty-Two

Katie leaned back against the coats that were hanging in the hallway. Although she wasn't physically afraid of David, she still found that she was trembling.

After a moment she went back into the living room and switched off her laptop. She could continue her research into Flathead Consultants later. As soon as Barney saw her do that, his tail started wagging briskly and he jumped up at her.

'Come on, Barns,' she said. 'Let's go out and get ourselves a breath of fresh air.'

When she opened the front door she saw that David's Range Rover had already gone from the next-door driveway. She let Barney jump up into the back of her Focus and then climbed into the driver's seat herself. She held on to the steering wheel tightly for a while, willing herself not to think about David any more and not to be angry. He was worse than scum. He didn't deserve to be spat on. Yet she still felt that she had been in a fight with him, even if it was only a verbal fight, and lost. He had a way about him of making her feel worthless.

She drove up to the Passage West ferry terminal and joined the queue of cars to board the *Glenbrook*. It took only four minutes to cross over to Monkstown but she climbed out of her car and stood by the rail, feeling a sense of relief that she was leaving an unpleasant experience well behind her. The sky was cloudy but bright, lending a dull shine to the River Lee, like tarnished silver. A smug, damp breeze was blowing from the south-west, as if it were telling her that this dry weather wasn't going to last very much longer and that it was soon going to rain, and heavily, and persistently.

Her father had been planning to move from his tall Victorian house in Monkstown but that was when he and Ailish were going to be married. The house would have been far too large, even for the two of them. and it was damp and run-down and badly needed new slates on the roof.

After Ailish had died, however, her father had chosen to stay. The house had already been crowded with memories of Katie's mother and now the ghost of Ailish was there, too, and he couldn't bear to sell it. 'They left me, the both of them,' he had told Katie. 'But I'm not going to leave them, not ever.'

Katie parked in the driveway and went up the steps to the front door. The ivy that clung to the front of the green-painted house was beginning to turn crimson and yellow and it rustled in the breeze. Katie shivered, thinking of David.

Her father opened the door and stood looking at her as if he didn't know who she was. He had lost weight, so that his face was drawn and sallow and his nose looked even more prominent, and he was unshaven. He was wearing a drooping beige shawl-collar cardigan that needed a wash and baggy brown corduroy trousers and slippers that were frayed as if a cat had been clawing at them.

'Kathleen!' he whispered.

'Well, I'm glad you recognized me,' said Katie. 'How are you, Dad? Can me and Barney come in?'

'Of course you can. How have you been? I'm sorry, but the house is a bit of a tip at the moment. I keep meaning to advertise for a new cleaner, you know, but the days go by. How long is it now since I last saw you?'

Katie followed him into the living room. The house was chilly and smelled damp. There was dust on the window sills and a vase of dead roses hanging their heads on a side table. The kitchen door was open and Katie could see plates stacked in the sink and at least half a dozen dirty teacups. A loaf of Brennans bread was standing on the table but had fallen sideways so that several slices were hanging out of the bright yellow packet.

'I'm sorry, Dad. I meant to come and see you last week,' said Katie. 'The trouble is, I've been up the walls with these kidnapping cases.'

Her father eased himself painfully down in his high-backed armchair, as if his joints were seizing up. She noticed that the seat cushions were thick with biscuit crumbs and the carpet all around was spotted with stains. She sat down on the sofa close to him and Barney sat down beside her, with a whine in the back of his throat.

'Would you like me to make you a cup of tea?' Katie asked her father.

'No, I'm grand, thanks. I just had one. At least I think I did. Anyway, I've run out of tea bags.'

'I thought Moirin was doing the messages for you.'

'Yes, well, she does. But I forgot to put tea bags on my list.'

'She could have checked.'

'Oh, well, yes. But fair play to her, she has her hands full looking after Siobhán, and that husband of hers is like a lighthouse in the Bog of Allen.'

'Listen, I'll go to the shop and buy you some tea bags before I go back home. Is there anything else you need, apart from a new housekeeper?'

Her father shook his head. She didn't want to say anything to him but he smelled. For him to lose Ailish was the most disastrous thing that could have happened because, apart from making him happy, she always took good care of him. There was almost no possibility that he would find another woman who would love him as much as Ailish had, especially the state of him now.

'So, how's things at Anglesea Street?' he asked her. 'Have you heard from Dermot O'Driscoll at all?'

Chief Superintendent Dermot O'Driscoll had been a sergeant when Katie's father was an inspector. He had championed Katie's promotion to detective superintendent, against fierce hostility from other officers, simply because he had believed in her professional abilities and female intuition. Earlier this year, however, he had been diagnosed with prostate cancer and was presently on extended sick leave.

'He called into the station two weeks ago,' said Katie. 'They're still giving him radiotherapy and hormone treatment at Bon Secours, but he was cheerful enough. I have no idea if he'll ever be able to come back to work.'

'Dermot's a good man. He was always a good man. When you see him again, tell him I wish him the best, won't you?'

Katie's father sucked at his teeth for a while, his eyes focused on the past. Then he looked across at Katie and said, 'What's this kidnapping then? You did say kidnapping?'

'Haven't you seen it on the news? It's been the top story almost every day.'

'I haven't watched the telly since Ailish passed. She always had the telly on, morning till night, whether she was watching it or not. It reminds me too much of her, just the sound of it.'

As briefly as she could, Katie told him about the abductions of Micky Crounan and Derek Hagerty and Pat Whelan and Eoghan Carroll. She told him about the bomb at Merchants Quay that had killed Garda Brenda McCracken and the shooting in Carrigaline of Detective Garda Nessa Goold. She also told him how the Pearses had been incinerated on the beach at at Rocky Bay.

'Mother of God,' said her father. 'Do you know who's behind it?'

'They call themselves the High Kings of Erin. One of them has rung me to claim responsibility for everything they've done. They're proud of it, would you believe? They say that they're patriots. They want to restore Ireland's pride after the collapse of the economy and they're doing it by punishing all of those small businessmen who borrowed more money than they could ever afford to pay back.'

'The High Kings of Erin? That's who they say they are? Really?'

'Why? Does that mean something?'

Katie's father reached into the pocket of his cardigan and took out a scrumpled-up tissue to wipe his nose. 'I should say it means something. It was the High Kings of Erin who forced me to retire early.'

'What? You never told me. I always thought you retired early because of your heart.'

'No, there was never anything wrong with my heart. That was just the story that they made me agree to. Maybe it's just a coincidence, these kidnappers of yours using the same name, like. After all, there's that folk band, too, isn't there, the High Kings? But the High Kings of Erin as I knew them – they were all gardaí.'

'What, like a secret society? Like the Knights of Saint Columbanus or the Fenians or the Freemasons?'

'That's right.'

'But why did they force you to retire early? What were they up to?'

'They always claimed that they were being charitable, and I suppose they were, in a way. But they were running a scam that wasn't so different in its way from the penalty points racket that Martin Callinan and Alan Shatter had to resign for.'

'So they were wiping points off driving licences for people who could do them favours?'

'They were, yes, but a whole lot more than that,' said Katie's father. 'They weren't just erasing penalty points. They were dropping all kinds of charges – fraud, rape, drug-dealing, you name it – so long as the offenders paid them enough. Sometimes they were paid thousands. You remember Kieran Beasley?'

'Kieran Beasley? Yes, that rings a bell. He was charged with running some kind of Ponzi scheme in computer software, wasn't he? Whatever happened to him?'

'Absolutely nothing happened to him, Katie. He was charged with fraud but before he was due to appear in court he paid the High Kings of Erin nearly quarter of a million punts and all the evidence against him mysteriously vanished. I think your friend Michael Gerrety paid to have some sex charges dropped, too. The same thing happened again and again, quite regular, like, for years.'

'So what was charitable about that?' asked Katie.

'The High Kings of Erin donated at least two thirds of the money to various needy causes, like the ISPCC and the L'Arche Community. The rest they kept for themselves, as "expenses".'

'That's unbelievable.'

'Well – they justified what they were doing by saying that it was better for the money to go to the poor and the needy rather than the state, in fines, and if any of the offenders had been jailed it would only have cost the country more money to keep them in prison – nearly eighty thousand euros a year, at the last estimate. Well, you know that.'

Katie shook her head. 'I suppose there's some kind of twisted logic to it. But what happened? Why did they make you retire?'

'Because me and another inspector, Tom Keaveney, we found out what was going on. We were investigating a drug-running gang that was based in Limerick but were smuggling cocaine through Ringaskiddy. We arrested three mules from Eastern Europe and confiscated nearly one and a half million pounds' worth of drugs that they had hidden in their shoes. But two days later we were approached by this fellow from Limerick who said that he'd happily pay us if we forgot all about the charges and let the mules go.

'Of course, we told him there was no chance at all, and that we could arrest *him* for attempting to bribe two police officers. But he just laughed at us and said that he'd paid to get members of his gang off charges a rake of times. If we didn't accept his offer, he'd go public and tell the newspapers and TV the names of the gardaí who had taken his money before.'

'So what did you do?' asked Katie.

'Me and Tom told him that we didn't believe him. We were worried, of course, that this was some kind of a set-up by the Garda Ombudsman and that we were being secretly filmed or recorded, and that if we took money off him we'd be charged ourselves with corruption. But he said that he'd paid money at least five times to a group of gardaí who called themselves the High Kings of Erin, and that these High Kings of Erin had assured him that it would all go to charity. He had taken it for granted that every Garda officer was involved in this same racket, which was why he had offered to pay us.

'Again, we told him that we didn't believe him, but he said that we should go and ask the officers he had done business with.'

'So he told you who they were?'

Her father wiped his nose again, and nodded.

'Well – who were they? Aren't you going to tell me?'

'I swore that I would never mention this to anybody, ever again. The High Kings of Erin said that they would burn down my house if I did, with me in it, and that they would hurt my family, too – especially you, Katie, because you were a garda yourself. Has it never occurred to you why you faced such fierce opposition when Dermot wanted to have you promoted? It wasn't just prejudice because you were a woman. They were afraid that I might have told you who the High Kings of Erin were. And that was one of the reasons I never told you why I retired before my time. I was protecting you, pet, as well as myself.'

For a few moments Katie said nothing. Her father's words gradually sank into her consciousness like a leaky rowing boat. As chilly and damp as it already was, his house now felt even chillier, and gloomier, and more oppressive. It was so hard for her to accept that he had been living in fear ever since he had retired from the force. She had worshipped him ever since she was small, and boasted about him at school, and the stories he used to tell her about arresting notorious Cork criminals had been one of the reasons why she had decided to make a career herself in An Garda Síochána.

Now he was telling her that he had discovered that some of his fellow officers were corrupt – but because they had threatened his life if he exposed them, he had never had the nerve to face up to them. She had always believed that he was afraid of nobody and nothing.

'Dad,' she said, reaching across and taking hold of his hand. His fingers were icy-cold and gnarled and he had semicircles of black dirt under his nails. He was still wearing the wedding ring that he had first put on when he married Katie's mother and had never taken off. Ailish had told him that he could keep it on after he was married to her. 'You don't stop loving people just because they're dead.'

'Dad, you have to tell me who they were, the High Kings of Erin.'

'No, Katie, I can't. I don't care about myself any more, but I'm not having you or any of your sisters put at risk.'

'Dad, I've been suspended. I've been making hardly any progress at all with these kidnapping cases and now somebody's made a complaint against me and Jimmy O'Reilly has used it an excuse to pack me off on gardening leave.'

'What? Jimmy O'Reilly? He can't do that, surely.'

'Dad, he's the assistant commissioner now, not a superintendent like he was when you knew him. He can pretty much do what he likes. The complaint came from my next-door neighbour, who's been acting the maggot, to put it mildly. I'm going to see my solicitor when I leave here and I'm sure I can get it all sorted out. But if I can find out who these High Kings of Erin are, it will really help me to get back my credibility. Even the media have been suggesting that I'm not up to my job.'

She paused and squeezed his hand, trying to transfer a little warmth. 'It just seems to me like too much of a coincidence that your High Kings of Erin were extorting money and that my High Kings of Erin are doing the same, even though they're doing it by kidnapping people rather than dropping charges against them.'

Her father looked at her with eyes as grey and watery as the River Lee outside. 'Thomas Keaveney and I went to the Garda confidential recipient and reported what was going on. He said that he'd set up an investigation, but after only two weeks he came back and said that he'd found no evidence of any wrongdoing.

'We could have taken what we knew to the Garda Ombudsman, but by then we were both getting so much stick for turning Turk. Nobody would sit next to us in the canteen. My car was scratched almost every day and the tyres let down. One night in the middle of the night the doorbell rang and when I went to answer it I found a dead rat tied to the door handle.'

'Dad, I need every scrap of evidence that I can get,' Katie persisted. 'I've already discovered that Bryan Molloy may have some financial links to the tarmac company that tried to bury Micky Crounan's body under the road. He may be totally innocent. Paul and I had shares in Lee Waterside Developments when they were doing a babs and never had a clue what they were up to. But this needs to be looked into, Dad. It's urgent. Two young gardaí have already lost their lives, as well as four civilians at least.'

There was a long, long silence. Barney heard cats mating in the back garden and immediately trotted to the French doors at the other end of the living room and stood there wuffing in disapproval, misting up the window with his breath.

Katie let her father take his time. He may have been vilified by his fellow officers and eventually forced to retire, and it must have been almost unbearable for him to become a whistleblower, but he still retained his old loyalties.

At last, he turned his head away, as if he were addressing some imaginary board of inquiry sitting in front of the fireplace.

'I'm only repeating what I was told, and the fellow who told me wasn't what you might describe as reputable, so I can't vouch for it one hundred per cent.'

'I understand that and of course I'll take it into account,' said Katie, equally formally.

Her father hesitated even longer, still staring at the black and empty grate. Katie was about to prompt him again when he said, 'Superintendent Stephen Fitzgerald. Do you remember him? The High Kings of Erin was his idea, according to this fellow from Limerick, and he was like the ringleader.'

'I remember Stephen Fitzgerald,' said Katie. 'We always called him Superintendent Shouty.'

'He did have a very short fuse,' agreed her father . 'Of course, he's dead now. Aortic aneurysm on the golf course. In his time, though, he was one of the best officers we had. Very good with protests and demonstrations, always had everything planned out right to the very last detail, although woe betide you if you made a bags of it. He'd shout the head off your shoulders.'

'I wonder what made him start the High Kings of Erin,' said Katie.

'He started to have serious money trouble, as far as I know. His wife was very ill, cervical cancer I think, and her treatment was very expensive. Apart from that, he lost a packet with bad investments on the stock exchange. I suppose he thought that if he gave most of the money to charity then it wouldn't be so immoral.'

'So what other names did this Limerick fellow give you?'

'I can't remember all of them.'

'Then tell me the ones you do remember. Come on, Dad. You've already told me Stephen Fitzgerald.'

'Yes, but he's in the cemetery. The rest are still with us.'

'Dad, listen to me! I get threatened every day of the week. You know as well as I do that it goes with the job.'

'Yes,' said her father, twisting himself around to face her. 'But you don't have children!'

She could tell by the expression on his face that he realized instantly what he had said, and that he could have bitten off his tongue. She had never recovered from little Seamus being taken from her. How cold he had been in his pale blue Babygro when she had lifted him out of his cot, his reddish hair still sticking up from sleeping.

'I'm truly sorry, Katie – ' said her father. 'I didn't mean – '

'It's all right, Dad. I know what you meant. Now, please, just tell me the names. As many as you can.'

'There were eight of them altogether, so the fellow said. Jimmy O'Reilly you know already. Then there was Seamus Grant, he was only an inspector in those days, and Bryan Molloy, both of them from Limerick. And Superintendent Jack McGovern from Tip, and Sergeant Harris from Ballincollig and another sergeant from Togher although I don't recall his name. McConnell or McConnaigh, something like that. Oh, and another inspector

. . . Padraig Duffy, from Fermoy, I believe.'

'Jimmy O'Reilly and Bryan Molloy – they were *both* High Kings of Erin?'

'You're not going to tell them that you know, are you? I'm warning you, Katie, you'll be in danger of your life. I don't want anybody coming to my door to tell me that they've found you floating in Tivoli Harbour.'

'Don't you worry, Dad. I'm not naive enough to go marching into their offices and accuse them to their faces of taking bribes and perverting the course of justice. I'm going to be a little more subtle than that. Besides, I still don't know how they're connected to the High Kings of Erin who claim to have carried out these kidnaps. Or even if they *are* connected.'

She took hold of his hand again. 'I may not have any children to protect, but I do have a father to look after.'

'I'm so sorry, pet. I never should have said such a thing.'

'Forget it, Dad. Life has to go on, no matter what. But there's one more name you can give me, if you know it. Who was your man from Limerick? The fellow who told you all about the High Kings of Erin?'

'Now, he's somebody you really don't want to be messing with, Katie. I mean it.'

'Dad – you seem to be forgetting that I'm a detective super-intendent. Messing with dangerous and undesirable people, that's my job. I'm not your little Katie-waytie any more, playing with her plastic ponies on the back step.'

Her father gave her a small, resigned smile. 'Yes, you're right. But where do they go to, Katie, the happy times? Why are they always over?'

'You'll have to ask God that. I don't know.'

'You've probably heard of him, this fellow. He was Niall Duggan's right-hand man before Niall Duggan was shot. He's suspected of murder, arson, drug-dealing, robbery, threatening behaviour and possession of illegal firearms, although he's never been convicted for any of them.'

'You're talking about Lorcan Devitt,' said Katie.

'The very man. Face as red as a beetroot, long, wild hair, boozy breath like a knacker on dole day. But he's not at all what he seems, that man. He's a cute hoor, and he's very dangerous.'

Katie said, 'I'll be careful, Dad, I promise you. And nobody will know that you told me those names. Now let me go to McKenzie's for you and buy you whatever you need, and while I'm there I'll stick a card in the window advertising for a housekeeper for you.'

'Oh, I'm all right, pet. You don't have to fuss. I can manage.'

'No, Dad, you *can't*. You're still grieving, and nobody expects you to take care of yourself. I''ll come back again tomorrow afternoon and see how you're getting on. I'll call Moirin, too.'

Her father followed her to the front door. He gave her a kiss with his prickly cheek and grasped her shoulder tightly. 'You're a grand girl, Katie. You never let me down. If your mother could only see us now.' He paused, and then he said, 'If only we could see your mother.'

***

She was still in McKenzie's Express Convenience Store buying tea bags and biscuits and cheese for her father when her mobile phone rang.

It was her solicitor, Douglas Rooney. He had been held up in court and would have to postpone their meeting until tomorrow at 3.30. She didn't really mind. It was growing dark now and it had already started to rain and Barney was eager for a walk. She was feeling unusually tired, too, and the thought of driving back into the city in the rush-hour traffic was very much less than appealing.

She still hadn't handed in her revolver to the Anglesea Street armoury, but nobody had contacted her about it and she could do it tomorrow before she went to South Mall to see the solicitor.

She drove back to her father's house and gave him the messages, as well as a bunch of fresh yellow roses. Once she had arranged the flowers in a vase for him, she said, 'Make sure you have something to eat tonight, Dad, even if it's only a takeaway. And you can have a bath, too. I've turned on the hot water for you.'

Again, he accompanied her to the front door. It was raining hard now and ghostly swathes of spray were drifting across the river.

'And think about getting the roof fixed,' Katie told him.

'Oh, yes. The roof,' he said, vaguely. But then he took hold of her hands and said. 'I should never have told you those names, you know. Maybe you'd best forget them.'

'Dad – '

'I know, I know. You can look after yourself. In the name of Jesus, though, watch out for those High Kings of Erin, whoever they are, and don't cross that Lorcan Devitt. He'll have your tripes out before you can blink.'

Forty-Three

Pat Whelan and Eoghan Carroll arrived in Cork City centre shortly after dark. They had walked for over two hours along narrow country roads, hiding themselves behind hedges or dropping down into ditches whenever they heard a vehicle approaching in case it was the High Kings of Erin coming after them. Eventually, however, they had reached the R639 which led directly south to Glanmire, which was only seven kilometres to the east of the city, and had managed to hitch a lift from a chain-smoking, chain-swearing van driver who was delivering second-hand gearboxes to a car repair shop in Glasheen.

'You'd never fecking believe some of the fecking customers we get, they fecking ring you and say to us, okay, if I bring my car in this afternoon do you think you could service it and fit new brake pads by five o'clock? I mean forget about the other fecking five cars we've already got booked in for that same fecking day, just fecking drop everything for them.'

'Terrible,' said Eoghan. 'Some people don't think, do they?'

'No, they fecking don't. They have shite for brains.'

Pat was so tired that he couldn't even speak, leaning his head against the passenger-side window. The wounds on his chest were throbbing so painfully that he was sure they had become infected.

The van driver dropped them off by the statue of Father Matthew at the top of Patrick Street and they cut through Winthrop Street to Oliver Plunkett Street. Pat wasn't thinking of going back to his shop. The High Kings of Erin could well come looking for them there, even if they weren't watching it already, and in any case he no longer had the keys to get in. However the Café Zing two doors away had closed down only a month ago and he was sure that they could break into it through the small courtyard at the back and use it as a refuge for the night.

Before they tried that, though, they went to one of the two Eircom phone booths on the corner of Caroline Street. They looked up and down the street to see if there was anybody who was obviously keeping a lookout for them, but it had started to rain now, suddenly and heavily, and almost everybody was hurrying for shelter.

Pat had only the three twenty-euro notes he had taken from Malachi's wallet, but Eoghan had enough small change in his pocket for them to use the payphone.

Pat called Mairead first. When she answered, he said, 'This is me. Is that you?'

'*Pat*! Mother of God! Where are you, Pat? Are you all right?'

'Listen, love, I have to be very quick. The gang who call themselves the High Kings of Erin were holding me and this fellow Eoghan Carroll hostage, but we've managed to escape. I'm safe now, for the moment, and so is he, but we're almost certain that they're going to come looking for us. You need to leave the house right now, love, and I mean like *immediately*. Go to your cousin Clodagh's, or maybe your brother's. Don't tell anybody where you've gone, not even the guards, and don't tell anybody that you've heard from me. I'm serious, Mairead. These people are very, very dangerous, these High Kings of Erin. They're killers.'

'But they rang me this afternoon, Pat,' said Mairead. 'They gave me instructions where they wanted me to hand over the ransom money, and that inspector told me that the Garda have the money all ready for them. If you've escaped, like, they won't have to pay it, will they? But they'll have to know you've escaped.'

'Mairead, the money doesn't matter, it's only paper. We're hoping that the guards can catch the High Kings of Erin when they hand over the ransom, especially if we tell them that we're safe. But if they give the guards the slip and they don't get their money, they'll be sure to be wanting to take out their revenge on us. If it comes to it, let them have their ransom, for the love of God.'

'Pat – '

'No, Mairead, if they get their money, maybe they'll leave us alone and we can live in peace. I know that I'll probably have to declare myself bankrupt, but I'd rather be bankrupt than dead, any day. Now, grab whatever you need to take with you, love. I mean it. Grab whatever you need, and go. I love you. I'll be in touch with you again as soon as I can.'

He handed the warm receiver to Eoghan, who punched out the number for his parents. After a long wait his father answered. 'Dad?' he said. 'It's Eoghan. Yes, it really is. I know. But I'm alive and kicking.'

He gave them the same warning that Pat had given to his wife. The Carrolls, too, had already been told by the High Kings of Erin when and where to hand over the ransom money.

'Don't say a word to anyone, Dad. You saw what happened to that young detective woman. You and Mum don't want to spend the rest of your lives looking over your shoulders in case somebody's coming for you.'

'I'm not afraid of scumbags like that,' his father retorted. 'Besides, they don't deserve the money.'

'Dad, this is no time to be playing the hero. If they don't get arrested and they don't get their money, then the chances are that they'll find me and they'll kill me, and if they can't find me, then they'll kill you instead. Or maybe they'll kill all of us. When Pat and I were escaping, we hurt those two big fellows who snatched me out of your house, and badly. One of them, I think I broke his neck. They're not going to forgive us for that in a hurry.'

'Well . . .' said his father, grudgingly.

'*Go*, Dad! You and Mum get out of the house as quick as you can. If you go to Petra's, I'll call you there. If you go somewhere else, let Petra know where you are, so that I can contact you. Now, *go*!'

Pat and Eoghan left the phone booth, looking up and down the street again, their hands cupped over their foreheads to shield their eyes from the rain. Then Pat said, 'Come on. We can get through to the back of the cafe from Pembroke Street.'

'Let's hope they left some coffee there when they closed down,' said Eoghan.

'Oh yes. And a fridgeful of food, and two comfortable beds. You'll be lucky, boy.'

Forty-Four

Katie took Barney for a short walk along the river front, with the rain drumming on her umbrella. When she got back home, she undressed and took a shower, and then wrapped herself up in her pink towelling bathrobe, with her hair in a turban. She couldn't think why she felt so exhausted. Of course, she had been under even more stress than usual, both at work and at home, but she kept herself fit and she had always prided herself on her stamina.

'You wear me out,' John had said to her, early one morning. 'You chase criminals all day but you can still keep going all night!'

She poured herself a large glass of Smirnoff Black Label, but when she lifted it to her lips and smelled it she realized that she didn't feel like vodka after all. She poured it carefully back into the bottle and switched on the kettle for a mug of tea instead. Then she went back into the living room and opened her laptop.

Flathead Consultants had no website and no Facebook or Twitter pages. They didn't appear on LinkedIn or any other business network. There was a company in California called Flathead Enterprises, but they were website developers and they certainly didn't look as if they would have links to a company that buried headless bodies in asphalt.

The milk smelled off, or maybe it was just the smell of Barney drying off in his basket beside the radiator, but in any case Katie took her tea black. When she sat down at her laptop again she typed in 'High Kings of Erin Flathead'.

Instantly, up came the legend of Eógan, King of Munster. His wife was Moncha, who was the only daughter of the blind druid Dil Maccu Crecga.

One day, Dil Maccu Crecga came to Eógan and urged him to make love to Moncha that night. He had sensed that the king would die the next day in battle against the Alban armies of Lugaid Mac Con, and he would need an heir if his dynasty was to continue. Sure enough, Eógan and Moncha conceived a son that night – and sure enough, during the battle at Maige Mucrama the following afternoon, Eógan was put to the sword.

Nine months later Moncha went into labour, but her father had foretold that if her son was born on that particular day he would become nothing more than the chief jester of Ireland. If he were to be born the day after, however, he would be crowned King of Munster and found the dynasty of the Eóganacht.

Determined that her son would be king, Moncha sat on a rock for the whole day and night, preventing him from leaving her womb. He was born the next day, but the top of his head was pressed flat, so he was given the name Fiachu Muillethan, Fiachu the Flathead.

Flat-headed or not, he became King of Munster, one of the High Kings of Erin, although Moncha died giving birth to him and he was left an orphan.

Katie closed her laptop and sat back. This was another link between Bryan Molloy and the High Kings of Erin, but only a very tenuous one and it was far from being proof that he was actively involved with them. What she needed to do now was to find if there was a connection between the old High Kings of Erin, the corrupt Garda officers that her father had told her about, and the new High Kings of Erin, who were organizing the kidnapping of Cork's small businessmen.

Her phone rang. It was her sister, Moirin, who hadn't called her for weeks.

'I just rang Dad,' she said. 'He said you criticized me for not buying him tea bags. I don't know how you have the *neck*! You see him yourself only once in a blue moon and who do you have to take care of? You want to try looking after Siobhán for a day, with a mental age of nine but almost a nymphomaniac, and then you can criticize me all you like.'

'Moirin, I didn't criticize you. I never would. I think you're a saint.'

'You wish I *was* a saint, you mean, so that you could inherit all of Dad's house when he passes over.'

Katie leaned back on the couch, closing her eyes and letting the phone drop on to the seat cushion beside her. She could still hear Moirin's tinny little voice, but she couldn't make out what she was saying. After a while, though, she could hear her snapping out, '*Hello? Hello? Are you there, Katie? Katie?*'

There was a moment's silence, then a sharp click as Moirin put down the phone, and then there was nothing but the dialling tone.

Katie thought of her grandmother, who always used to say, 'Some people love to hear ill of themselves. There's nothing they enjoy more than feeling aggrieved.'

***

The next morning she woke up much later than usual and lay staring at the digital clock beside her bed as it changed from 8.12 to 8.13. She closed her eyes and when she opened them again it was 8.36. She threw back the duvet and sat up, furiously scratching her scalp. She had used a new shampoo last night and it had made her itch.

She had just fastened her bra and reached for the dark green roll-neck sweater that she was going to wear today when her mobile phone rang. She picked it up from the bedside table but didn't recognize the caller's number. It started with 061, the code for Limerick.

'Hello?' she said, cautiously. 'Who is this?'

'Is that Detective Superintendent Kathleen Maguire?' asked a wheezy male voice.

'Who wants to know?'

'Gary Cannon. Formerly *Sergeant* Gary Cannon, formerly based at Henry Street, in Limerick.'

'Oh, yes. And who gave you my number?'

'The daughter of an old Garda friend of mine who knows that I mean you no harm and that I'm only trying to do you some good. Kyna Ni Nuallán. Her father is Terry ó Nuallán. He was a sergeant, too, at Roxboro Road.'

Katie said, 'All right, then. You've got through to DS Maguire. Why are you ringing me?'

'I heard that you've been suspended from duty. Well – Terry told me.'

'It hasn't been announced officially yet,' said Katie. 'But, yes. I'm seeing my lawyer about it this afternoon.'

'It was Bryan Molloy who suspended you, wasn't it?'

Katie was extremely reluctant to discuss her suspension on the phone with a wheezy-voiced stranger, but he gave her the feeling that he had something to tell her that might help her. He already knew that she had been suspended, so there was no point in trying to hide *that* from him, and she didn't have to tell him anything more.

'I was given the sack myself by Bryan Molloy,' said Gary Cannon. 'That was less than three weeks before I'd put in twenty-five years of reckonable service, so you can imagine what damage that did to my pension.'

'What exactly do you want, Mr Cannon?'

'Oh, you can call me Gary, if you like. I can't really tell you what I want over the blower, for reasons that you're probably aware of. But there's somebody I think you might care to meet. Can you get yourself to Limerick by noon, say, or shortly after?'

'You want me to come to Limerick?' asked Katie.

'I wouldn't suggest it if I didn't think it would be worth your while, believe me.'

'Well . . . all right. Supposing I do?'

'Are you fairly well acquainted with Limerick? Do you know Saint Mary's Cathedral?'

'Yes, of course I do.'

'Behind Saint Mary's Cathedral is Nicholas Street and about a third of the way down Nicholas Street is a small bar with a red front called the Cauldron.'

'I've heard of the Cauldron, yes.'

'Okay, then. Me and this somebody I think you might care to meet, we'll be in the Cauldron at twelve o'clock sharp. You'll recognize me because I'll be wearing a green jacket and a green cap, and I'll be sitting at a table on the left-hand side of the bar as you come in.'

Katie was about to ask Gary Cannon if he could give her at least a notion of what this 'somebody' wanted to tell her, but he hung up. She sat on the side of the bed wondering what she ought to do. If Gary Cannon really was a friend of Kyna's father, then she was fairly sure that she could trust him, but she only had his word for it. And what could this 'somebody' have to say that would make it worth her while driving all the way up to Limerick in the rain?

She stood up and finished dressing, pulling on her bottle-green tights and black wool skirt. As she was putting on her make-up in the bathroom, she looked at her reflection and knew by the look in her eyes that she had decided to go. It was strictly against regulations, but she decided to take her revolver with her, too. She could hand it in to the armoury when she came back to Cork. But as her father had always said, 'The only person you can trust is the person you see in the mirror, and even they can let you down when you're least expecting it.'

Forty-Five

Katie drove up to Limerick through Mitchelstown so that she could stop and take a look at the Kilshane Tarmac depot on the Dublin Road. Behind grey steel palisade railings she could see a grey concrete office building and a high corrugated-iron shelter, like a barn with no sides, under which two large pavers were parked, as well as a trench roller and two compactors. There was a pungent smell of asphalt in the air.

She could make out several people in shirtsleeves inside the offices, and a group of four or five workmen in orange high-visibility jackets were standing in the yard outside, smoking. She was tempted to go inside and ask questions about the road they had laid near Ballincollig, but she wanted to find out much more about the High Kings of Erin before she showed her hand. Apart from Fergal O'Donnell, and the team of labourers who had done it, she assumed that she was the only person who knew that Kilshane Tarmac was responsible for spreading asphalt over that body, and she wanted them to continue to believe that they had got away with it. Not only that, she didn't have the legal authority at the moment and she didn't want to have her fight for reinstatement compromised by any further complaints.

She continued her drive northwards to Limerick. An hour later, a few minutes before twelve, she turned into Nicholas Street – a long, narrow street of small, flat-fronted houses, which on a wet day like this looked particularly dismal. It had two pubs in it, the Cauldron and the Mucky Duck, and a derelict demolition

381

site overgrown with weeds and supported by rusty scaffolding. Further down, even St Mary's Cathedral had turned its back on Nicholas Street, presenting it with nothing but a rough grey stone wall.

She parked outside the Cauldron's red-painted facade and went inside. The small bar was crowded with noisy drinkers and the large flat-screen TV was showing a hurling match between Limerick and Kilkenny, where the clouds were so dark that the stadium lights had been switched on. She had no trouble finding Gary Cannon. As he had told her, he was sitting at a table on the left-hand side, next to a mirror advertisement for Smithwick's ale, wearing a green cap and a green jacket with leather patches on the elbows.

Beside him sat a woman of about forty-five years old, with wiry dyed-black hair, false eyelashes that looked as if she had used them to sweep a chimney, and sticky, crimson lipstick. She was wearing a tight black wool dress which clung to her enormous breasts and wide, double-barrelled hips, and her wrists jangled with gold and silver bracelets. In spite of her blowsy appearance, however, Katie could see that she was actually quite handsome, with strong cheekbones and cat-like amethyst eyes.

Gary Cannon stood up and offered Katie his hand. 'I'm Gary, Katie, and this is Jilleen. What would you care to drink?'

'Nothing, thank you, for the moment, Gary,' said Katie, but at the same time Limerick scored a goal and the noise in the bar was so overwhelming that she had to shout.

'I'll have another Power's and ginger if you're getting one,' said Jilleen.

While Gary went to the bar, Katie sat down and took out her mobile phone. Jilleen gave her a ghost of a smile but said nothing.

'Is this your regular bar?' Katie asked her.

Jilleen shook her head. 'I usually drink at Ma Reilly's. Gary wanted us to meet here because nobody will reck us.'

'I see. Does he not want anybody to know that we've met?'

'Let's just say that it would be better if nobody did.'

'All right. His actual words were that you might have something interesting to tell me.'

'Oh, not just *tell* you,' said Jilleen. 'I have something interesting to give you, too.'

'Really?'

Gary came back from the bar with a pint of Guinness for himself and a whiskey and ginger for Jilleen. 'You're sure I can't tempt you?' he asked Katie.

'No, thanks,' she said. 'I'm driving.' All the same, she was surprised that she didn't even feel like one.

Gary swallowed some Guinness and wiped the foam from his upper lip with the back of his hand. 'Has Jilleen told you anything yet?'

'No, nothing, except that you wanted us to meet in a place where we wouldn't be recognized.'

'Well, that's right. I mean, it's not so bad if I'm recognized, which one or two of them might, because I've felt a few of their collars over the years, especially that fat fellow at the end of the bar with the wild white Ronnie, but he's so langered already I don't suppose he'd know his own mother if she walked in – not that she would, because she's dead, but you know what I mean. If her ghost walked in, like.'

'I don't think anybody in Limerick would recognize *me*,' said Katie.

'No, but it's Jilleen, see. If we'd met in Ma Reilly's, they'd be asking her all kinds of questions after about what she was doing talking to me, like, and who the divil were you, and she didn't want to go to the trouble of making stuff up. The guards are about as popular here as a dose of the scutters.'

'My brother was Donie Quaid,' said Jilleen, as if that explained everything. She was wearing a strong, oily perfume and it was beginning to make Katie feel short of breath, almost as if she were asthmatic.

'The Quaids were one of the Moyross estate families who were always feuding with each other, like the Ryans and the Keane-

Collopys,' Gary Cannon explained.

'Yes, I've heard about them,' said Katie. 'The Quaids were always fighting with the Duggans, weren't they?'

'That's right,' said Gary Cannon. 'It was all hell let loose between those two families. Shootings, stabbings, beatings, setting fire to each other's houses and blowing up each other's cars. I think the death toll was nineteen altogether, in the space of just three years.'

'I thought that was one of the feuds that Bryan Molloy put a stop to.'

'He did. There was a big article about it in the *Leader*, how Molloy had persuaded the Quaids and the Duggans to bury the hatchet, and this time not in each other's heads.'

'So? Whatever we think about him, surely that was something he was rightly commended for.'

'Ah, but it was *how* he did it,' said Gary Cannon. He turned to Jilleen and said, 'Go on, Jilleen, you tell her.'

Jilleen quickly looked around and then said, 'He paid my brother Donie to murder Niall Duggan.'

'Am I hearing this right?' said Katie. 'Bryan Molloy gave your brother money to shoot Niall Duggan?'

'Two thousand euros. He bought a motorbike with it.'

'I'm surprised that Niall Duggan allowed a Quaid get anywhere near him. Didn't he have security?'

'He did, yes. But the thing of it was, Donie was always kind of a mediator, if you know what I mean. He never carried a knife himself and he never got himself involved in any kind of trouble. When things got really bad between the Quaids and the Duggans, he would try to calm down the both of them. He was the only Quaid that Neil Duggan would ever give the time of day. That's why Molloy chose him.'

'Without Niall, the Duggans were Ebenezer Screwed,' Gary Cannon put in. 'The twins were too young to run a gang like that and in those days they were both caked out of their heads on coke most of the time. Lorcan Devitt could have maybe taken over but

Molloy deliberately put it about that it was Devitt who had paid to have Niall Duggan murdered in order to take over the gang himself, so none of the Duggan family trusted him for two or three years after that. It was only because Devitt stuck with them and found some backers to set up the Shenanigans nightclub for them that they started to believe that it wasn't him who did it.'

'But nobody ever knew that your brother had done it?'

Jilleen shook her wiry black hair and her bracelets jingled. 'Even *I* didn't know until he was dead and we were the closest that brother and sister could ever get. Talk about your poetic justice, he fell off of the same fecking motorbike that he had bought with the money that Molloy had given him to shoot Niall Duggan. He left me a letter saying that he'd done it and if he ever died sudden and didn't get the time to ask for forgiveness could I please light a candle for him in Saint Munchin's and tell God that he was mortally sorry.'

'Do you still have that letter?' asked Katie. 'Is that what you were going to give me?'

'Yes, I still have it, and yes, I've brought it for you. But I've brought something else besides.'

Underneath the table she had a large hessian bag and out of it she pulled out a plastic Aldi shopping bag with a brown padded envelope inside it. Again she looked around to make sure nobody was watching and then she passed the shopping bag over to Katie. 'The letter's in there, too, girl.'

From the weight of the brown padded envelope, Katie immediately guessed what was in it. It wasn't stuck down, so she opened it a little and took a quick look inside.

'Molloy told him to throw it off the Thomond Bridge into the river, that's what he says in his letter. But he didn't, because he was afraid that Lorcan Devitt would be coming for him and he would need to keep it to defend himself.'

'Does he say in the letter where he got it?' asked Katie.

'Molloy gave it to him. Like I say, Donie himself never even carried a penknife, let alone a gun.'

Gary Cannon leaned forward across the table and spoke in a low voice so that nobody in the Cauldron bar could overhear him. 'I found out that Molloy had paid Donie to kill Duggan the very next day after he shot him,' said Gary Cannon. 'It wasn't the most difficult piece of police work I ever did. One of my snouts said that he'd met Donie in Lorcan Bourke's bar and he was mouldy drunk and crying like a babby. He told my snout what he'd done and that Molloy had given him the money and the gun to do it.'

'So what did you do?'

'Like an eejit, I went to Molloy and asked him about it. Well, he was a good cop and he'd sorted this city out like no cop had ever managed to do before him. But I shouldn't have done, should I? I should have taken it straight to the top. Molloy really lost it. He told me that I was talking shite. When I said that my snout was always reliable and that maybe I ought to bring Donie Quaid in for questioning, he told me right out of the blue that he was going to dismiss me for taking bribes from drug-dealers. When I asked him what bribes I was supposed to have taken, and who from, he said that he could produce multiple witnesses, no bother. He also said that if I made any kind of a protest to Chief Superintendent Meehan, or anyone else, I'd regret it for the rest of my days. In fact, if I ever said anything to anybody *ever* to suggest that he'd been responsible for Niall Duggan being shot, I'd better phone a priest and ask him to give me the last rites urgent-like.'

'So what's changed your mind?' asked Katie.

'Hearing from Terry ó Nuallán that Molloy had suspended you, that's what did it. Kyna told him that you were always a brilliant cop and she thought that there was something fierce fishy going on. The way Kyna tells it, Molloy has been working ever since he was sent down to Cork to pull the rug out from under you, and it's not just because you're a woman. He's up to something, and he doesn't want you finding out what it is.

'I thought to myself, if I had a senior cop like you on my side, there would be a chance now of getting my revenge on Molloy.

That's not the only reason, though. I'll confess to you now that I've lost my job with the council and I'm serious skint. If I could get my full Garda pension retrospective like I should have got it, plus maybe some compo for wrongful dismissal, that would just about save my life.

'That's why I went looking for Jilleen, to see if she could help me at all. And lo and behold, she still had the letter and the very shooter that Molloy gave Donie to do away with Niall Duggan.'

Katie said, 'What you've given me, this is very important evidence – especially ths gun. It looks like a SIG Sauer P226, which is one of the pistols issued to the Garda Emergency Response Unit. We can check the serial number to find out where it came from, and if it *is* a Garda-issue weapon, we can check who it was signed out to, or when and how it went missing.

'More than that, we can check the striations on the bullet that was used to kill Niall Duggan against the rifling of the pistol barrel. That's always presuming we still have the bullet, which I would guess that we do.'

'You can do *what*?' frowned Jilleen. 'I'm sorry, what you said then, that was all Greek to me.'

'All gun barrels have unique imperfections,' Katie explained. 'When you fire a bullet through them the imperfections scratch the bullet and our forensic technicians can match them together. It's a bit like a barcode on your shopping.'

'What will you do now?' Gary Cannon asked her.

'Nothing hasty, Gary,' Katie told him. 'I'm not going to make the same mistake as you and ask Bryan Molloy about this to his face. As you and I have both found out to our cost, he's not to be messed with. He has a lot of friends and allies in the force, and in County Hall, too. Now, if you and Jilleen will excuse me, I have to get back to Cork to see my lawyer.'

She stood up and shook Gary Cannon's hand. As she did so, though, Jilleen looked up and said, 'There's one more thing.'

'Go on,' Katie coaxed her.

'Not in here, though. Let's go outside.'

Gary Cannon went to fetch Jilleen's purple raincoat for her and shrugged on his own cheap waterproof windcheater. They left the Cauldron and went outside on to Nicholas Street. Jilleen immediately reached into her bag for a packet of cigarettes, took one out and lit it.

'Sorry, but I've been dying for a fag.'

They walked together down towards St Mary's Cathedral, with Gary Cannon walking in the road because the pavement was so narrow. Jilleen blew out smoke and said, 'I think the Duggans have found out that Donie shot Niall. That's the reason I told Gary here about it, in case they gave me any trouble.'

'How did the Duggans find out?'

'I'm not *totally* sure that they know, but I told Donie's son Sean about it, about a month ago. Sean's just thirteen now.'

'What made you do that?' asked Katie. The rain had eased off now and a strong, fresh wind was blowing up the street from the river. Katie was thankful for it because it blew away the smell of Jilleen's perfume and her cigarette smoke.

'I never meant to tell him, ever,' said Jilleen. 'But the poor kid was getting bullied something terrible at school. I told him if his da was still alive he would have gone around to the playground and knocked those bullies' heads together. Sean said his da never would have done, because what he had heard about his da, he was a softie and never got into any fights or nothing.

'So I told him that his da had been a stronger man than all of those bullies put together, not to mention any other Moyross scummer. I told him that his da had single-handed finished the fighting between the Quaids and the Duggans and made this city a better place for everybody to live in altogether.'

'And you told him how Donie had done that?'

'That's right.'

'Did you tell him about Bryan Molloy giving him the gun?'

'I might have done, yes.'

'So you did?'

'Yes. No. Well, yes. I think I probably did.'

'So you think that Sean might have boasted about to it to the Duggans? Any boy would, especially if he was being bullied.'

'He doesn't know any of the Duggans. The Quaid and the Duggan boys might not be throwing petrol bombs at each other any more, but that doesn't mean that they're bum-chums. But there's a lad in Sean's class who's the son of Lorcan Devitt's younger brother, Phelim. This boy was one of the worst of the bullies and I think Sean might have told him.'

They had reached St Mary's now and turned right so that they were walking beside the cathedral wall. High above them, the cathedral's tower had all the grey ruggedness of a castle in a fantasy novel. Jilleen finished her cigarette right down to the filter and then flicked it across the street.

Katie could feel the heavy weight of the SIG Sauer automatic in the Aldi bag she was carrying. Gary Cannon was saying something about the cathedral being the oldest building in Limerick, if not the entire world, and that Oliver Cromwell's men had used it to stable their horses, but her mind was racing and she was only half listening to him.

They stopped at the corner of St Augustine's Place. Katie said, 'I really must get back now. But thank you for what you've told me, Jilleen, and thank you, Gary. Do you have an e-mail address or a mobile number so I can keep in touch with you?'

'Not exactly at the moment,' said Gary Cannon. 'I can tell you my home number, though.'

Katie entered that into her iPhone, as well as Jilleen's mobile phone number.

'Good luck to you so,' said Gary Cannon. 'Let's hope that justice is done at last.'

Katie gave them both a wry smile. 'That's my job,' she said. 'Justice.'

At least it was before I was suspended, she thought, as she walked back up Nicholas Street. Now my job is getting my own back.

Forty-Six

Detective Sergeant Ni Nuallán knocked on the half-open door of Inspector Fennessy's office, but there was no answer. She pushed it open wider and saw that he wasn't there, although his computer was still logged on and there was a cup of coffee beside it, with the lid still on.

She walked over and dropped on to his desk the folder that she had been preparing for him on drug-arrest statistics. As she was turning to leave, his phone rang. She reached over and picked it up and said, 'Inspector Fennessy's office.'

Ciara on the switchboard said, 'Is that DS Ni Nuallán? The caller wants to talk to whoever's in charge of the High Kings of Erin case. He says he's in a phone booth with not much change and it's desperate.'

'Okay, put him through,' said Detective Sergeant Ni Nuallán.

Almost at once, a panicky voice said, 'Is it you who's investigating the High Kings of Erin?'

'The senior officer is Inspector Liam Fennessy, but he's not in his office just now. My name's Detective Sergeant Kyna Ni Nuallán. I can help you.'

'Listen, I'm calling you from a phone booth. I have to be quick because I don't have much money and I think they might be watching us. This is Pat Whelan of Whelan's Music Store who was supposed to have been kidnapped by the High Kings of Erin, and I have Eoghan Carroll with me. He was taken in Carrigaline when that garda was shot.'

'I can send a patrol car round to you directly,' said Detective Sergeant Ni Nuallán. 'Which phone booth are you calling from?'

'Don't do that, just listen. Eoghan and I escaped yesterday from the house where they were holding us. It's somewhere up near Bridestown. We've both been beaten a bit, but nothing too serious. I've told my wife to find somewhere safe to hide herself and Eoghan's done the same for his parents.'

'Pat, please, tell me where you are. We can come and pick you up and give you protection.'

'I'm sorry. I'm not telling you where we are until I hear that the High Kings of Erin have either been arrested or else they've been paid their money and got away with it. It's not that I don't trust you personally – it's just that Eoghan thinks that somebody tipped them off that he was there when that fellow Hagerty was found and that you wanted to question him about it. He's sure that's why they came for him. Serious, who could have known about that? You have to admit that it could only have been a guard, or somebody who works at the Garda station.'

'You're safe, though, and reasonably well?' Detective Sergeant Ni Nuallán asked him. 'Is there any way I can contact you?'

'Not until we hear that the High Kings of Erin are safely locked up, or that they've taken their money and run. If you don't manage to catch them, of course, we're going to have to talk about protection. Those headers don't like anybody staying alive to give evidence against them, as you very well know.'

'Pat, can you just describe them to me?' said Detective Sergeant Ni Nuallán. 'Give me some idea what they look like, or how they talk, or anything else that might help me to identify them. Do they have an accent? How do they dress? Do they have an unusual smell about them? Please, Pat. *Anything.*'

But then the phone went dead and all she could hear was an endless beeping. Either Pat had run out of change or else he had deliberately hung up. What disturbed Detective Sergeant Ni Nuallán most of all was that neither he nor Eoghan Carroll felt that they could trust the Garda to take care of them. Katie had strongly suspected that somebody at Anglesea Street was passing information to the High Kings of Erin and now Detective Sergeant Ni Nuallán was sure of it.

She had just replaced the receiver when Inspector Fennessy walked in, closely followed by Superintendent Denis MacCostagáin.

'Ah! Kyna! Anything I can help you with?'

'I've just taken a phone call for you,' said Detective Sergeant Ni Nuallán. 'You won't ever believe who it was.'

'Oh. It wasn't the lotto, was it, telling me that I'm a multi-millionaire?'

'Almost as good. It was Pat Whelan.'

Inspector Fennessy flinched, almost as if a wasp had suddenly flown close to his face. 'Come here to me? Pat Whelan? You mean Pat Whelan who's been kidnapped?'

'The very same,' said Detective Sergeant Ni Nuallán. 'He was ringing from a payphone. He says that he and Eoghan Carroll have both escaped from the High Kings of Erin. They've gone into hiding and they've sent their families off, too, in case the High Kings of Erin come looking for them at home.'

'Well, there's a turn-up for the books,' said Superintendent MacCostagáin, with what almost amounted to a smile. 'If they've managed to escape, that's going to save us a quarter of a million euros of public money. I should think that Jimmy O'Reilly's going to be opening a bottle or two tonight!'

'Ah, no, it can't be true,' said Inspector Fennessy. 'It's one of your hoax phone calls, that's what it is. What did the fellow sound like?'

'Very scared. I'd say he was shaking.'

'Well, of course he was. He was scared that you were going to catch on that he was taking the piss. Shaking? Shaking with laughter, more like.'

'Did he tell you where he was calling from?' asked Superintendent MacCostagáin.

'No, he didn't. There was some traffic noise, like you'd expect, but nothing special. We'll have it recorded and we can probably trace it back, but if it was a phone booth that's not going to help us much.'

'I'd say we ought to be fair cautious about this,' said Superintendent McCostagain. 'Maybe we should hold off paying this ransom until the High Kings of Erin can give us further proof that they're still holding Whelan and Carroll as hostages.'

'It's a hoax,' said Inspector Fennessy. 'They tried to pull the same kind of a stunt with Derek Hagerty. There he was, making out that he'd escaped, while all the time he'd colluded in his own kidnapping right from the start. They only shot him because he messed the whole thing up and was going to give evidence against them.

'This sounds to me like the same trick backwards. Somebody calls pretending to be Pat Whelan and says that he and Eoghan Carroll have escaped, but we can't be sure that he's telling the truth because they're in hiding, so what do we do? If we don't pay the ransom money according to the arrangements they've given us, the two of them will probably end up dead, if they're not dead already, and then we'll be blamed for causing their deaths from incompetence.'

He imitated a high woman's voice. '"Oh, but Pat Whelan rung us up and told me the two of them were still alive." "Oh – how did I know it was really Pat Whelan who was calling?" "Because he said he was."

'Listen – if we *do* hand over the money and Whelan and Carroll are set free unharmed, then at least we'll be given *some* credit, for being humanitarian, if nothing else.'

'Wait a minute,' said Detective Sergeant Ni Nuallán. 'Suppose we hand over the money but it turns out that they're dead already?' She was trying not to show how angry she was at Inspector Fennessy mimicking the way she spoke and trying to suggest that she was naive and gullible. 'Suppose we hand over the money and the High Kings of Erin set them free but then they kill them later, like Derek Hagerty, so that they can't give evidence against them?'

'What if the moon drops into Cobh harbour and the whole of Cork is drowned by a tsunami?' Inspector Fennessy retorted. 'We

393

can't deal in fanciful theories, Kyna. We have two men here whose lives are in jeopardy and we can't afford to take any unnecessary chances. We already have the cash wrapped up, according to the High Kings of Erin's instructions. Superintendent MacCostagáin and I are meeting here now to go over the best way to maximize our chances of arresting them and at the same time minimizing the risk to the hostages.'

'So that call I just answered, you're going to ignore it completely?'

'Like I say, the overwhelming likelihood is that it's a hoax. Either that, or the High Kings of Erin are trying to make us look like fools when it comes to the media coverage. They did it with Derek Hagerty. They did it with the Pearses. I don't want to give them the opportunity to do it again.'

Inspector Fennessy laid his hand on her shoulder and said, as reassuringly as he could, 'After Superintendent MacCostagáin and I have finished our discussion, Kyna, I promise you that I'll listen to the conversation you had with this fellow. If it sounds even remotely like your man might be authentic, I'll ask the sound technicians to see if they can match it to the voice of the real Pat Whelan. But I have to tell you that I'm very, very sceptical. Once bitten, like. Especially with these High Kings of Erin. They're laughing at us, all the way to the bank.'

Detective Sergeant Ni Nuallán nodded towards the green folder she had left on his desk. 'Those drug-arrest statistics you asked for.'

'Great. Thank you. I won't be able to look over them today, though. The ransom money for both hostages is supposed to be handed over at eleven this evening. We have a hell of a lot of preparation to do in a very short space of time. We'll be holding a general tactical meeting at thirteen hundred hours, so I'll talk to you again then.'

He paused and smiled at her, and said, 'Sorry if I'm stressed, Kyna. Thank you for fielding that call. Don't worry. If we plan everything carefully, tonight may see the end of the High Kings of Erin.'

***

Detective Sergeant Ni Nuallán was walking back along the corridor when the lift doors opened ahead of her and Katie stepped out.

'Kyna,' said Katie. 'I was hoping to see you. I wanted to thank you for telling your dad about my suspension. His friend Gary Cannon called me and gave me some sound information. I can't tell you all about it now, but I think it might make all the difference.'

'You haven't been in to see Molloy, have you, ma'am?'

'No, not yet. I've just come back from a meeting with my solicitor and he's advised me to say nothing at all to Molloy – or to Jimmy O'Reilly, either.'

'What are you going to do?'

'Well, my solicitor is going to be getting in touch with the Ombudsman for me, requesting an urgent review. Other than that, all I can do is go home and watch TV. I just came in to the station to hand in my gun. Is Liam Fennessy in? I thought I'd try and get a quick update on the High Kings of Erin.'

Detective Sergeant Ni Nuallán glanced up and down the corridor to make sure that nobody else was there and then she said, 'There was a phone call for Inspector Fennessy, only about ten minutes ago. He wasn't in his office so I took it. The fellow on the other end said he was Pat Whelan and that he and Eoghan Carroll had managed to escape from the High Kings of Erin.'

'*Serious*? Do you think it was genuine, this call?'

'It sounded like it to me. He said that he and Eoghan had got away and they were hiding somewhere, although he wouldn't say where. He said he'd told his wife to leave home until the High Kings of Erin were caught. Eoghan had told his parents to do the same.'

'And of course you told Inspector Fennessy?'

Detective Sergeant Ni Nuallán nodded. 'He came back almost as soon as I'd put down the phone. I don't know why, but he seemed to be sure that it was only somebody wheeling me. Either that, he said, or else the High Kings of Erin were trying to make fools out of us again, like they did with Derek Hagerty.'

'So what's he going to do about it, this call?' asked Katie.

'Nothing at all, as far as I can make out. He's having a meeting with Superintendent MacCostagáin right now about how they're going to set up the handover of the ransom money this evening. He said he'd have a listen to the phone call after, but he didn't seem to set much store by it.'

'You mean he's still planning to hand over the money even though there's a chance that Pat and Eoghan could both have escaped?'

'It looks like it. Unless he listens to the phone call and decides that it's not mockeyah after all.'

'I need to have a word,' said Katie. 'I don't care if I'm suspended or not.'

'Ma'am – ' began Detective Sergeant Ni Nuallán, but she could see that Katie was determined. She lifted both hands as if to say, *Go ahead, then, good luck to you so*, and watched as Katie walked briskly along to Inspector Fennessy's office.

Katie knocked once, opened the door and walked straight in. Inspector Fennessy and Superintendent MacCostagáin were standing over a side table which had a large-scale map of Cork City spread out on top of it. They both looked at Katie in surprise and then they looked at each other, plainly at a loss as to how they should react.

'As I understand it, Katie,' said Superintendent MacCostagáin, 'you shouldn't officially be here. Not while you're under suspension.'

He said it kindly, not as an admonition, shrugging his shoulders at the same time to make it clear that her suspension hadn't been any of his doing and that he didn't agree with it.

Inspector Fennessy said, 'He's right, I'm afraid, ma'am. This makes things kind of awkward, like, to say the least.'

Katie approached the table and looked down at the map. She could see that there were red circles and arrows and rectangles drawn around the English Market.

'Is that where you're going to hand over the ransom money?' she asked.

'I'm sorry, ma'am,' said Inspector Fennessy. 'I can't tell you what the arrangements are.'

'I've just been talking to Detective Sergeant Ni Nuallán,' Katie told him. 'She told me about the phone call she took from Pat Whelan.'

'*Allegedly* from Pat Whelan, but I doubt very much if it was really him.'

'Why do you doubt it? What makes you so sure that the call wasn't genuine?'

'With respect, ma'am, the High Kings of Erin have form when it comes to "escaped kidnap victims" – in inverted commas.'

'Have you told Jimmy O'Reilly about the phone call? He's ultimately responsible for all of that money, after all.'

'Assistant Commissioner O'Reilly and Chief Superintendent Molloy are both insistent that we get the hostages released unharmed. The surest way to do that is to pay the ransom. We can worry afterwards about how we're going to get the money back.'

'Yes, but have you told them about the phone call?'

'I will be, of course. At the moment the superintendent and I are working on how to keep tracks on the High Kings of Erin once they've been paid.'

Before Katie could answer, Detective O'Donovan appeared at the door. When he saw Katie his eyes darted from side to side as if he was uncertain whether he should say anything or not.

'What is it, Patrick?' asked Inspector Fennessy. 'We're right in the middle of things here.'

'Bill Phinner's just called me,' said Detective O'Donovan. 'They extricated the remains that were found under the road surface at Lisheens and brought them back to the lab. Well, he said that there was more asphalt than body, but they've managed to identify him. It's a he, and he's headless, and the saw marks on the neck match the saw marks on Micky Crounan's head. So it was Micky Crounan all right.'

'Do we know who laid the asphalt?' asked Inspector Fennessy. 'That wasn't a small job, like, and it was professional. Somebody must know who did it.'

'We're working on it,' said Detective O'Donovan. 'Bill Phinner said they would have needed a roadroller as well as an asphalt paver. The body was pressed about as thin as a paperback book, that's what he said. Even without its head it was over two metres tall and one point eight metres wide.'

Katie said nothing. Although she knew that Kilshane Tarmac had laid the asphalt, she still didn't know who the informant inside the station was. She had a very small edge over everybody else involved in this investigation and she didn't want to give it away just yet – at least until she was officially reinstated. It was significant, though, that the body under the road surface had been positively identified as Micky Crounan. That meant that the High Kings of Erin had arranged the body's interment, and that increased the likelihood that Acting Chief Superintendent Bryan Molloy was somehow connected to them.

'Okay, Patrick, thanks,' said Inspector Fennessy. 'I'll see you at thirteen hundred so, at the tactical meeting.'

When Detective O'Donovan had gone, Katie said, 'Liam, is it okay if I have a quick personal word with you in private before I go? You don't mind, do you, Denis?'

'Not at all,' said Superintendent MacCostagáin. 'I need to go to the jakes in any case. Too many cups of green tea this morning.'

He left and closed the door behind him. Inspector Fennessy went over to his desk and pulled out a chair so that Katie could sit down, but she stayed standing.

'Is this about Caitlin?' he asked her. 'She hasn't been bothering you again, has she? I can have a word with her if you like, although I'd rather not, to be honest with you.'

'No, Liam,' said Katie. 'It's not about Caitlin.'

'You're all right, are you, ma'am? You're sorting out this suspension business? I know that O'Reilly had to do it, as a formality, but what a time to lose you.'

'Don't worry about my suspension, Liam. This is more import-ant. I'm pretty sure now that I've worked out what's happening here, with these High Kings of Erin, and who they are.'

'Really?' he said, frowning at her. He sat down at his desk and the pale grey light from the window reflected in his glasses so that she could no longer see his eyes.

'I haven't tied up all the loose ends yet and I'm not quite ready to take it to the GSOC, but you need to be aware of this – although how you're going to handle it, I'm not entirely sure.'

'Why would you want to take it the GSOC?'

'Because I'm one hundred per cent certain now that the High Kings of Erin are the Duggan gang from Limerick. And I'm ninety-nine per cent certain that they've been able to get away with so much because Bryan Molloy is obstructing everything we're doing to catch them.'

Inspector Fennessy said, 'Molloy! Come on, ma'am. I know you're allergic to Molloy. You have every reason in the world not to like him. I can't stand the scobe myself. But why would he undermine his own investigation? It doesn't make any sense.'

'He's undermining it because the Duggans are blackmailing him.'

'What?'

'You know that the Duggans and the Quaid family were at total war with each other for years before Molloy took over as superintendent?'

'Of course. But Molloy stopped that war overnight. You don't have to *like* the man to recognize that he's one of the best cops that Limerick ever had. But what are they blackmailing him for?'

'It was the way he stopped the war between the Quaids and the Duggans. He secretly paid one of the Quaids to kill Niall Duggan. It was a Garda-financed hit.'

'You're codding me. How did you find that out?'

'It was Donie Quaid who did it. He's been dead a few years now, but before he died he left a letter admitting that he was the killer. To cut a long story short, the Duggans found out about it only a few weeks ago – just before the High Kings of Erin arrived here in Cork, coincidentally, and "kidnapped" Micky Crounan – in inverted commas.'

'That's still no proof that Molloy is being blackmailed.'

'You're right, and that's why I'm not quite ready to take it to the Ombudsman. But I have other evidence that Molloy set up a racket some time ago that was also called the High Kings of Erin. No gangs involved – it was all senior gardaí soliciting bribes in return for dropping criminal charges and for wiping penalty points off driving licences.

'The Duggans must have known about this racket, which is why they've called themselves the High Kings of Erin, too. It's deliberate mockery. They're challenging the Garda to take action against them, but they know we won't because too many high-ranking officers were involved in it.'

'But stall there for a minute,' said Inspector Fennessy. 'If what you're saying is true, why didn't the Duggans come out with all this before?'

'Only one reason I can think of,' said Katie. '*They* had probably been paying some of those bribes themselves, to escape whatever they'd been charged with, and if they blew the whistle on the High Kings of Erin they would have been rearrested.'

Inspector Fennessy stood up and walked to the window. It was raining again. He took off his glasses and chewed at the end of them.

'What you've just told me, ma'am, Jesus. You've placed me in a savage awkward situation here. You're suspended, like, but now you've come in and accused the officer who suspended you of turning a blind eye to kidnap and extortion and murder – including two gardaí getting killed.'

Katie stood watching him for a while.

'It's your decision, Liam. And I'm not just talking about Molloy. I believe this goes further up the ladder. I've been given information that Jimmy O'Reilly was one of the original High Kings of Erin, too.'

'Holy Mary, Mother of God,' said Inspector Fennessy. 'This doesn't get any better, does it?'

'No, it doesn't. And it could get worse. Judging by their past records, it's conceivable that O'Reilly and Molloy are not only aiding and abetting these kidnaps, but taking a cut of the proceeds. Molloy's so-called consultancy has a very healthy annual income. Some of it comes from Crossagalla Groundworks, as we know, but it would be very interesting to discover where the rest of it originates.'

Katie didn't mention Kilshane Tarmac or the company's connection with Crossagalla Groundworks, but she did say, 'One more thing. Molloy's consultancy calls itself Flathead Consultants and "Flathead" was one of the High Kings of Erin.'

Inspector Fennessy was about to say something when there was a rap at the door and Superintendent MacCostagáin came back in. 'That fecking hand-dryer!' he complained. 'It's worse than a fecking force ten gale! Good thing I don't wear a wig or it would have blown clear across the toilet and out the fecking window! Then somebody could have taken a potshot at it, thinking it was a crow!"

He waited for Katie and Inspector Fennessy to laugh, but they both remained serious. Katie said to Inspector Fennessy, 'I'm not in a position to tell you what to do next, Liam. But if I were you, I'd listen to Kyna's phone call before I decided what action I was going to take.'

With that, she nodded to Superintendent MacCostagáin and left the office. She met only two gardaí on the way out of the station and both of them muttered, '*Ma'am*,' but averted their eyes, as if they had passed a ghost in the corridor.

Forty-Seven

Katie drove home. There was nothing else she could do. She could only hope that Liam Fennessy had taken her seriously enough to listen to the phone call that was supposed to have come from Pat Whelan, and that he would either cancel the handover of the ransom money or spring a trap that would catch whoever came to collect it.

She had never felt so frustrated in the whole of her career. The more she found out about the High Kings of Erin, both past and present, the more confident she was that she could be very close to making some spectacular arrests. She was aware how devastating it would be for An Garda Síochána if Acting Chief Superintendent Molloy really was embroiled with the Duggans, and she was also aware that she would probably be the least popular officer in the entire force if she were to expose him.

But she saw this investigation as a crusade – a crusade to find justice for Garda Brenda McCracken and Detective Garda Nessa Goold, as well as the Pearses, Norman and Meryl, and Micky Crounan, and Derek Hagerty.

If she became a pariah, then so be it. At least she would have upheld the oath she had sworn when she became a garda – and she would have avenged her father's dismissal, too, even if it was fifteen years too late.

The rain stopped and the sun came out as she arrived home. David's Range Rover was parked in the driveway next door and there was smoke coming out of his chimney. She had thought of going to talk to him and trying to persuade him to withdraw his complaint against her, but she knew that he would simply take that as sexual surrender. She knew that the price she would have to pay for having her suspension lifted would be unwilling intercourse.

After she had hung up her raincoat she took two pairs of latex evidence gloves out of the inside pocket. She went into the living-room and laid the brown padded envelope that Jilleen had given her down on the coffee table. Then she went through to the kitchen to open the back door so that Barney could go outside. She filled the kettle and switched it on, although she didn't really feel like a cup of tea. These past two or three days, she hadn't known what she fancied to eat and drink, although she couldn't stop thinking about pepperoni pizza which she usually hated.

She sat down on the couch in the living room and pulled on both pairs of evidence gloves before she tipped up the envelope and let the pistol slide out. A double thickness of latex would prevent any of her own DNA contaminating whatever DNA might still be found on it, if any.

She had correctly identified the pistol when she first glimpsed it in the Cauldron bar. It was a SIG Sauer 226, a heavy, full-sized semi-automatic that was issued to the armed response units of An Garda Síochána. Turning it over, she saw that the identification numbers had been filed off. That was no problem; it was almost always possible to restore the original numbers by chemical etching with Fry's reagent or by sprinkling with Magnaflux magnetized filings. The numbers would show if the pistol had been taken from a Garda armoury or if it was a stray weapon that had come off the street. If it had been taken from a Garda armoury, it would be easy to find out which one and who had last signed for it.

Katie had to assume that Limerick's crime-scene examiners would have kept the bullets that were taken from Niall Duggan's body, and any ejected cartridge cases that had been lying around, so long as Donie Quaid hadn't stopped to pick them up. If they had, this gun could be positively matched to Niall Duggan's murder.

She slid out the magazine and was surprised to see that it was still loaded. It was designed to take ten 9mm rounds and there were seven left.

She put the gun back into the envelope and sat back on the couch. Everything that had happened to her in the past few days was churning round and round in her head like multicoloured clothes in a washing machine. She kept hearing Jimmy O'Reilly saying to her, '*You can't promote officers beyond their level of competence just because they happen to have a bosom,*' and she kept seeing Bryan Molloy behind him, smirking. She saw Jilleen walking down Nicholas Street blowing out smoke and she thought she could still smell her overpowering perfume. She saw Kyna looking pretty with her short blonde hair, but anxious-eyed, and Liam standing by the window, indecisively chewing on his glasses.

She closed her eyes. Within minutes she was fast asleep.

***

Her doorbell chimed. She opened her eyes and looked around her. The living room was gloomy now because the sun had disappeared behind the clouds again. She checked her watch and saw that it was 3.27. She had been sleeping for almost an hour.

The doorbell chimed again and this time Barney barked twice. He was still in the back yard and she would have to let him in. First, though, she got up from the couch and went into the hallway and called out, 'Yes? Who is it?'

'Delivery,' said a young man's throaty voice.

'Delivery from whom? I'm not expecting anything.'

'It's from the Garda station. They said it was urgent.'

'Okay. Hold on a minute.'

She thought, I know what it is. All the official documents relating to my suspension. Probably a caution, too, that I am not permitted to enter the premises at Anglesea Street or to engage in any discussions with other officers regarding ongoing investigations. Thank you, Jimmy O'Reilly. Thank you, Bryan Molloy. And most of all, thank you, David Kane.

She opened the front door. It was raining very softly, which made a prickling sound in the bushes. A young man was standing on the steps that led up to the porch – a young man with carroty-coloured curls and a face as pale as candle wax. He was wearing a brown trilby hat and a long trench coat with a tight belt around the waist.

Not far behind him, standing next to Katie's car, was a young woman who must have been the man's twin. She, too, had carroty-coloured hair, but much thicker and longer, whole bunches of carrots; but she, too, had a waxy-pale face, although her false eyelashes were black with mascara, so that her eyes looked like two spiders. She was wearing a yellow raincoat with a hood.

By the front gate an older man in an old-fashioned black rubber raincoat was standing, smoking a cigarette. His face was rough and reddish, and he looked like the sort of fellow you might see sleeping drunk in a doorway on Maylor Street.

'Detective Superintendent Maguire, how are you?' said the young man, smiling.

'Aengus and Ruari Duggan,' said Katie.

'Oh, you recognize us?'

'I've seen enough mugshots of you. Why wouldn't I? What do you want?'

Aengus Duggan turned around to smile at Ruari and then turned back again. 'I think it would be preferable for all concerned if we say what we have to say to you indoors. Won't you invite us in?'

Katie had already noticed that Aengus had his hand in his right-hand raincoat pocket and that there was a lumpy shape inside it which was almost certainly a pistol. He had noticed that she had noticed, too, and that was possibly one of the reasons why he was smiling.

'Who's that?' she said, pointing towards the man smoking by the gate. 'That's never Lorcan Devitt, is it?'

'Oh, you're good,' said Aengus. 'That's Lorcan all right.'

'Time hasn't been very kind to him, has it?' said Katie, narrowing her eyes so that she could see him better. 'We need to update his mugshot and no mistake.'

'Lorcan!' called out Aengus. 'Detective Superintendent Maguire says you look like a cream cracker!'

Lorcan didn't answer, only laughed and coughed.

'Well, let's be going in, shall we?' said Aengus. 'Wouldn't want to disturb the neighbours, nice posh street like this.'

'I don't think so,' said Katie. She could feel her heart beating hard and a crawling sensation up her back. She was trying to work out if she could step back and slam the front door shut before Aengus could pull out his pistol and shoot at her. The door wasn't bulletproof, but if she threw herself backwards on to the floor she might be able to escape being hit.

'Come on, now,' said Aengus, climbing the first step up to the porch. 'There's no point at all in your being difficult about this, like. It would only make things more unpleasant for all of us.'

Katie said, 'Don't you come any closer,' although she had no idea at all how she could stop him.

Aengus was about to reply when they heard a door slam and David Kane appeared from next door, zipping up a long khaki waterproof jacket. He looked at Katie and then he looked at Aengus and Ruari Duggan, and then at Lorcan Devitt.

He stopped and said, 'Oh. You have visitors. I'll come back later.'

Katie said nothing, but mutely shook her head and stared wide-eyed at David as if to warn him, these aren't visitors, these are three highly dangerous criminals.

David had been half turning away, but then he caught Katie's look and looked again at the Duggans, and said, 'What? What is it? These people aren't giving you any bother, are they?'

'Just hop off, will you, boy?' said Aengus, in his harsh, high-pitched voice.

David walked towards Aengus and said, 'Excuse me. What did you just say to me?'

'I told you to fecking hop off, so hop off, unless you want another shiner to match the one you've got already.'

Katie took advantage of the momentary face-off between them to step back into her doorway and make a grab for the door, but her heel caught on the mat and she stumbled. Without any hesitation Aengus yanked out his pistol from his raincoat pocket.

What happened next seemed like an action replay, in slow motion. Aengus pointed his pistol at her and cocked it, but as he did so David bounded on to the porch and threw himself in front of her, with both his arms flung up like a goalie trying to save a penalty.

Katie tumbled backwards on to the floor, with David on top of her. She heard a sharp crack, and then another, and another, and the side of her face was splashed with warm blood and brains and splinters of bone. She kicked herself backwards, once, and then again, and managed to force herself out from underneath David's body.

She had a blurry split-second glimpse of Aengus's carroty-curled hair and his waxy-white face as he stalked towards the front door, but she twisted herself around and scrambled on all fours into the living room. She picked up the SIG Sauer from the coffee table, thumbed off the safety catch and rolled on to her back, holding it with both hands and aiming it at the living-room doorway.

Aengus appeared in the doorway almost at once, holding his pistol so that it was pointing upwards. Katie fired once, and the bang was so loud that she felt as if somebody had boxed her ears. Aengus fell sideways into the hallway, his head towards the front door, but now she could only see his legs. Outside, Ruari shrilled out, 'Aengus! *Aengus!*'

Katie climbed to her feet and stepped cautiously sideways, crouching down with her gun held stiffly out in front of her. She knew that she had hit Aengus, but she had no way of telling how seriously he was hurt. He still had his pistol, and if she went out into the hallway he might fire back at her. Not only that, Ruari could well be armed, too, and so could Lorcan Devitt.

She was still approaching the doorway when she heard Ruari coming into the house. '*Aengus!*' she shrieked. '*Oh, Aengus! Mother of God, Aengus! Look at the state of you!*'

It sounded as if Aengus was badly wounded, so Katie took a deep breath and stepped out of the living room. David's body was lying diagonally across the hallway and Aengus was lying halfway on top of him. He had dropped his pistol on to the carpet. His face was even whiter than before and there was blood sliding out of the side of his open mouth, but his eyes were open, even though his eyelids were flickering, and he was breathing. Ruari was kneeling on the doormat and leaning over him, stroking and tugging at his carroty curls.

Lorcan Devitt was standing outside in the porch. The afternoon was so gloomy and his rubber raincoat was so dark that all Katie could see him of was a black silhouette, except for the dull shine of the pistol that he was holding.

'Drop the weapon, Devitt,' she told him.

'I will in my balls.'

'I'll call for an ambulance,' she said, keeping her gun aimed directly at Lorcan Devitt's midriff. She knew that her voice sounded shaky but she was confident that now she had the upper hand.

'Don't fecking bother yourself,' snapped Ruari. 'We're taking my brother out of here and we'll find our own doctor, thanks, you fecking witch.'

'You don't have a hope of getting away with this,' said Katie. 'You've murdered a man right in front of me.'

'Oh yes? You just try and get yourself a conviction, Missus Detective Superintendent As-Was,' Lorcan Devitt retorted. Then, 'Come on, girl, I'll lend you a hand there. Let's get him into the car and make tracks.'

'You need to stay where you are,' Katie warned them. 'I'm going to call for an ambulance now, and backup, too. You're both under arrest.'

'Let's call this a Mexican stand-off,' said Lorcan Devitt. 'We're taking Aengus away with us now and you're not going to prevent us, because if you try to drop either one of us, the other one of us will drop *you*. Ruari, pick up that shooter.'

Ruari picked up Aengus's pistol and pushed it into her pocket. Lorcan Devitt shifted his pistol to his left hand so that he could keep it pointed at Katie while he bent over and helped Ruari to drag Aengus over David's body and on to the porch.

Katie glanced quickly down at David to make sure that he was really dead. His head was at angle so that he appeared to be looking up at the cut-glass light fixture on the ceiling. A bullet had gone directly into his right eye and blown the back of his skull off. Apart from the blood and glutinous brain matter that had sprayed over Katie, there was more of it splashed up the floral wallpaper and on to Katie's raincoat.

Between them, Lorcan Devitt and Ruari managed to heave Aengus on to his feet. Each of them hooked one of his arms around their shoulders and between them they helped him to shuffle up the driveway. He was groaning and spluttering, but he was obviously semi-conscious at least. From the dark red patch on his trench coat Katie could see that she had hit him in the right side of his chest and had probably punctured his lung. She went out on to the porch as the three of them reached the front gate, but Lorcan Devitt had been keeping an eye on her and he turned himself around and pointed his pistol at her and called out, 'Don't even think about it, Detective Fecking Superintendent Fecking Maguire!'

They disappeared from sight, off to the right, but almost at once Katie heard car doors slamming and an engine starting up, so they must have parked close to her house. She hurried back inside, stepping over David's body, and picked up her car keys from the kitchen. She knew that she should be calling for an ambulance and backup, but she was determined not to let the Duggans get away with this – the Duggans and everybody else who had allowed them to kidnap and extort money and murder two of the most promising young officers at Anglesea Street.

She ran out to her car, climbed into the driver's seat and started the engine. She backed out of her driveway into the road, right in front of a van that blared its horn at her. She ignored it and pressed down hard on the accelerator pedal, heading north.

The Duggans came to kill me, she thought, as she drove faster and faster, looking up ahead for any sign of them. They came to kill me, but why? And who told them where I live?

She sped past the Passage West ferry terminal at more than 80 mph, then up ahead of her she saw tail lights. She stamped her foot down even harder and caught up with them, and then she could see that they belonged to a black Touran people carrier, the same kind of vehicle that had been used to abduct the Pearses and Eoghan Carroll.

She flashed her lights and blew her horn and swerved to the right to try and overtake it, but the Touran swerved, too, preventing her from driving past. She dropped back a little, but then she put her foot down again, right to the floor this time, and rammed the Touran as hard as she could.

There was a *bosh*! and a jolt, and the Touran slewed from side to side. Katie's seat belt cut deeply into her shoulder, but she put her foot down yet again and collided with the Touran even harder.

This time, with its tyres screaming an operatic chorus, the Touran careered to the left and hit the end of a low concrete wall. Katie heard the shearing thump of its collision as she sped past it, and immediately pressed her foot down hard on the brake, her car sliding sideways until she stopped. She spun the steering wheel and turned around. As she drove back she groped her hand across to the passenger seat to make sure that the SIG Sauer automatic was still there.

When she reached the wreck of the Touran, however, she saw that its entire front end had been crumpled by its collision with the wall and orange flames were already licking out from underneath it. She parked on the opposite side of the road and climbed out, pushing the gun into the waistband of her skirt. There were no other cars in sight and she had left her mobile phone at home.

She crossed the road. The Touran's windscreen had been shattered, so that it was frosted and opaque. When she looked in through the driver's-side window, however, she could see Lorcan Devitt leaning forward over the steering wheel, which was draped with the now-deflated airbag. His eyes were closed and his grey hair was wildly awry, as if he had been given an electric shock.

She tugged the handle and the door creaked open. She gripped the sleeve of Lorcan's black rubber raincoat and pulled it. At first she couldn't budge him, but when she took hold of the back of his collar as well as his sleeve and pulled at him even harder, he tipped sideways out of his seat and she was able to drag him out on to the road.

The flames were now leaping even higher out of the back of the wreck and hissing and spitting in the rain. Katie tried to see in through the dark-tinted rear windows of the Touran, but all she could make out was a pale oval shape which was jerking fitfully from side to side, like somebody waving a lamp. She tried the door handle but the door was either locked or jammed, so she knocked with her knuckles on the window and shouted, 'Ruari! Can you hear me? The door's stuck! Can you open it from inside?'

There was no answer, so she knocked again. '*Ruari! Can you hear me?*'

Almost at once, Ruari let out a high-pitched shriek, and then another. 'My feet are trapped! My feet are trapped under the seat! I can't get out! My feet are trapped!'

'Can you reach the door handle? Can you open the door?'

'My feet are trapped! It's so hot in here! Get us out of here! Please God get us out of here!'

Katie yanked the gun out of her waistband, gripped the barrel and hit the window with the butt. The first time she did it, she made only a star-shaped crack in the glass. She hit it again, and again, and then it shattered and dropped out, and she could see inside.

Ruari was sitting on the opposite side of the people carrier and it was her pale face that Katie had seen moving from side to side. Aengus was leaning against her shoulder. His eyes were open but it was clear that his bullet wound had left him too weak to move.

'Get us out of here, for the love of God!' screamed Ruari. 'Get us out of here!'

Flames were now jumping up against the Touran's rear window as if a pack of fiery wolves were trying to get in. The rear tyre was ablaze and Katie had to hold up her hand to shield her face from the heat. She pushed the gun back into her waistband and reached inside the broken window to find the door handle. She levered it outwards, but the door still refused to open.

'*Get us out of here*!' Ruari shrieked at her, and her face was like *The Scream*.

Aengus lifted his head and turned to stare at Katie as if he couldn't understand what was happening. He opened and closed his mouth, and then he, too, let out a high, hoarse, meaningless cry. It was more like an animal, or a baby, than a man.

Katie pulled at the door handle again and again, but the door must have been shunted back into its frame by the impact of the crash. She was thinking of trying to climb over the wall and reach the door on the other side when she heard an ominous buckling sound. Burning petrol suddenly poured out over the road and the Touran's rear window burst with the heat.

She took two or three quick steps backwards and then she turned around and ran back across the road, throwing herself down on to the high, wet, grassy embankment, among thistles and teasels.

As she did so, the Touran blew up. The blast was so powerful that the people carrier was lifted two or three feet clear of the road surface and then dropped down again with a rending crash. Katie was hit by the shock wave first, as if somebody in the street had rudely pushed her, and then she felt an oven-like wave of heat against her face.

The vehicle was now a fiercely blazing skeleton. Katie walked cautiously back across the road, but the heat was still too intense for her to go more than halfway. She saw that Lorcan Devitt had recovered consciousness, because he had crawled further away from the wreck and was now sitting up with his back against the wall, holding his head in his hands.

Inside the back of the Touran she could see both Aengus and Ruari Duggan. The explosion had probably killed both of them outright, but they were still both sitting up, their carroty curls blackened, their faces stretched with heat so that they appeared to be grinning, their raincoats on fire. They looked like two religious effigies burning on a bonfire.

Katie took out her gun again and went over to Lorcan Devitt.

'Lorcan,' she said, 'give me your weapon.'

Without looking up at her, Lorcan Devitt reached inside his raincoat and handed it to her, butt first.

'Do you have a mobile phone on you, Lorcan?'

Lorcan Devitt fumbled in another pocket and then passed her an iPhone. If anybody living around here had heard the Touran exploding, and seen the flames, she guessed they would have called the emergency services already, but all the same she pressed out 112.

'They're dead, then, the terrible twins?' said Lorcan Devitt, still without raising his eyes.

'I'm afraid so.'

'Oh well. Always had it coming to them, I suppose. They thought they were magic, but nobody's magic, are they, Detective Superintendent Maguire?'

'No, Lorcan, nobody's magic.'

Forty-Eight

Katie called the fire brigade and the ambulance service, and then she rang Inspector Fennessy.

'Liam?' she said. 'DS Maguire.'

'DS Maguire?' he said, as if he couldn't quite believe it.

'Liam, the Duggans have just come after me.'

'What?'

She stood in the road beside Lorcan Devitt while the soft rain fizzled on the burned-out wreck of the Touran. Trying to keep her voice steady, she told Inspector Fennessy everything that had happened and told him to send out at least two patrol cars and a technical team. 'The Duggans are dead, Liam. Even if that call that Kyna took was nothing but a hoax, you still don't have to hand over the ransom money. I very much doubt if anybody will turn up to collect it, not now.'

'Jesus,' said Inspector Fennessy. 'I'd better call Molloy.'

'No, don't,' said Katie. 'I'll come into the station later and tell him all about it myself, if he's still there.'

'He's not here at the station at the moment, but he's bound to hear about it. I'll have to call MacCostagáin and even if McCostagain doesn't tell him, the media will be swarming all over you like flies before you know it.'

'I'm sure he *will* hear about it, Liam, before I get the chance to tell him. But I still want to tell him to his face. You don't get many chances in life to get your own back, but this is one of them.'

The skin on the right side of her face was beginning to feel tight, so when she had made all the calls she needed to she switched on the iPhone's camera and looked at herself. Below her right cheekbone there was an S-shaped swirl of dried blood, David's blood, with several tiny fragments of bone stuck to it, ike some kind of primitive face decoration.

Her stomach knotted with nausea, but she swallowed hard and the feeling of sickness subsided. She pushed the iPhone into her pocket and pointed her gun stiff-armed at Lorcan Devitt.

'Stay there,' she told him. 'Don't even think about moving.'

'Oh, I will, yeah.'

She crossed the road to her car, took a pack of wet-wipes out of the glovebox and sat in the driving seat, still pointing the gun at Lorcan Devitt with her right hand but rubbing her cheek over and over again with a tissue, so hard that it hurt.

**

It was past midnight before the fire brigade had finished making sure that the burned-out wreck was no longer a fire hazard and an ambulance had arrived to check that Lorcan Devitt had suffered no serious injuries and would not need hospital treatment. The two paramedics peered with morbid curiosity at the incinerated bodies in the back seat of the Touran, but they didn't touch them. Aengus and Ruari were so badly charred that it would take a pathology specialist to remove them without damaging them too severely.

Four Garda patrol cars turned up, too. Two officers handcuffed Lorcan Devitt and drove him off to Anglesea Street, to be charged and detained. Four others cordoned off the crash site, set up reflective signs in the road and directed what little traffic there was. They also called a tow-truck from Glanmire to winch up the Touran off the road and take it to the Technical Bureau garage at the back of Anglesea Street.

A plump middle-aged female garda drove Katie home, while her partner followed them in Katie's Focus. Katie said nothing to her all the way back. The shock of what had happened was beginning to make her feel shivery and weak, and when they arrived outside her house she barely had the strength to walk inside. The female garda held on to her elbow to help her.

A second ambulance was already outside her house, as well as two patrol cars and a van from the Technical Bureau. David Kane's body was still lying in the hallway, staring one-eyed at the ceiling. Two technicians were hunched over him, taking flash photographs, and with every flash his body appeared to twitch, as if he had a nervous tic.

Bill Phinner was there, too. He climbed out of his car when he saw Katie and said, 'Are you okay, ma'am? You're looking more than a little shook there, if you don't mind my saying so.'

'I'll be all right, Bill. How long are you going to be?'

'Oh, three or four more hours yet. It's probably better if you go to a hotel or something for the rest of the night. We can lock up when we're done.'

'No, I'd rather stay. I want my own bed tonight, thanks, and I have my dog to look after.'

'You're sure about that, ma'am?' asked the female garda, sympathetically.

'I'm sure. This man gave his life for me. I don't know why. I thought he hated me, but perhaps he loved me. I don't know. I don't think I'll ever know.'

***

Katie stayed in the living room until Bill Phinner came in and said, 'We're all finished now, ma'am. You can get somebody in to do the cleaning for you now. I have a number if you want it. They're very good with human remains.'

'Thanks, Bill.'

He stood there for a while, as if he wanted to say something meaningful, but then he simply flapped his hand and said, 'Goodnight to you, then. Or good morning.'

'Goodnight, Bill.'

***

The next morning, Katie went in to see Assistant Commissioner O'Reilly as soon as he arrived at the station. He was still hanging up his raincoat when she knocked at his office door.

'Ah, Katie,' he said. 'I guessed that I'd be seeing you bright and early.' He inclined his head towards the folded copy of the *Examiner* on his desk. Katie couldn't read the headline from where she was standing but she could see the front-page pictures of Aengus and Ruari Duggan, and the burned-out Touran.

'You'll know about David ó Catháin, then,' said Katie.

'Of course. Denis MacCostagáin gave me a full briefing late last night.'

'Under the circumstances, I'm asking you to revoke my suspension. David ó Catháin is no longer alive to pursue his complaint, which in any case I refuted absolutely, and there are no other witnesses.'

'Well . . . I hope you realize that I'll have to make a report,' said Assistant Commissioner O'Reilly. 'But, yes, I regret that you're right. Under the circumstances, I have very little option but to reinstate you. I'm not saying that it pleases me, but now and then we all have to swallow a bitter pill or two.'

'I'm sorry that you feel that way about it,' said Katie. 'But at least I'll be able to go down now and start to question Lorcan Devitt.'

'Hmph,' said Assistant Commissioner O'Reilly. 'I don't suppose he'll have very much to say to you. That Duggan gang were always a tight-lipped lot.'

'Yes, sir. But that was when the twins were still alive and everybody in the gang was in fear of getting them riled up. All Devitt has to worry about now is getting the best deal out of us that he can. I'm sure he'll have a whole heap of things to tell me, especially about the High Kings of Erin.'

Assistant Commissioner O'Reilly cocked his head to one side. 'Are you trying to say something, Katie?'

'About the High Kings of Erin, sir? Which particular High Kings of Erin would you be referring to?'

Assistant Commissioner O'Reilly's expression darkened like rain clouds coming in from the west, and his eyebrows furrowed. He took a breath and Katie could tell that he was about to say something, but then he bit his lip and said nothing at all. She looked back at him, not smiling, but trying to show him with her eyes that she knew all about the High Kings of Erin racket that he and Bryan Molly had been involved in, even if she couldn't prove it. Even more satisfying than that, she could tell that he had realized that she knew.

'I'll be sure to report back to you after, sir,' she said.

'Yes, Katie. You do that.'

***

She entered the interview room to find that Detective O'Donovan was already there, talking to Lorcan Devitt about last night's game between Cork and Kilkenny.

A burly uniformed garda was sitting in the opposite corner of the room with his arms folded, as impassive as an art installation in the Crawford Gallery.

Katie pulled out a chair and sat down. She reached into her pocket and took out a pack of Carroll's cigarettes and a red plastic lighter, which she laid on the table. Lorcan eyed them and said, 'I thought Garda stations were no-smoking zones. Health and safety, EU regulations and all that shite.'

'They are, Lorcan, but I thought you would probably be gasping, and one good turn deserves another.'

Lorcan still didn't reach for the cigarettes, although he didn't take his eyes off them. 'Who said that I would be doing you a good turn, Detective Superintendent?'

'Oh, I know you will, Lorcan. You have nothing to lose and so much to gain. If you tell me everything you know about the High Kings of Erin, I can testify to the judge that you were deeply remorseful about your life of crime, and most cooperative, and that he should take that into consideration when he sentences you.'

Lorcan Devitt shrugged and nodded. He opened the pack of cigarettes, took one out and gripped it between teeth so brown that they looked as if they had been varnished. He lit it and took a deep, deep drag, which he didn't blow out directly, but let it leak out in dribs and drabs as he talked.

Detective O'Donovan switched on the recorder and Katie said, 'Go ahead, then, Lorcan. Tell me in your own words.'

She asked him no questions to begin with, but simply let him ramble on, smoking and gesturing and pulling faces as he did so. The burly garda in the corner gave a single cough, but otherwise he said nothing and didn't move a muscle.

Lorcan Devitt didn't tell the story chronologically and he constantly changed the subject and digressed and gave irrelevant explanations, but gradually he confirmed almost everything that Katie had come to suspect about the High Kings of Erin, who they were, and how they had been trying to scam public funds.

'It was Molloy who said we should go for the small businessmen who were very nearly bankrupt. He said that would give us some kind of moral justification, like. The High Kings of Erin restoring Ireland's pride! More important than that, your small businessman would be likely to agree to go along with it. Because of that, we wouldn't have to set up any kind of ambush or deal with any security guards like we would have had to do with rich people.

'Rich people would have given us a rake of trouble, no question about it. If you kidnap Paddy Poorboy, who gives a shite? But if you kidnap Pearse Lyons or Dermot Desmond or Martin Naughton . . . then you're catching a Celtic Tiger by the tail and no fecking mistake.

'We still had problems with them, though. We told Micky Crounan we needed some of his teeth to prove we had him, but after we'd tugged out a few he changed his mind and said that he didn't want to have anything more to do with it. He got so bothersome that one of the twins topped him in the end, I don't know which one of them. We were going to dump him in the river, but Molloy said we needed to do something spectacular so that the media would take notice.

'As you know, like, we were holding a gun to Molloy's head all the time on account of we'd found out about him ordering a hit on Niall. I had the feeling right from the start, though, that Molloy really relished it.. He enjoyed playing the righteous cop to the media, whiter than white, when all the time he was blatantly scamming the system. He liked the money, too. Oh, he definitely liked the money.

'All in all, I think the only thing that worried Molloy was you, Detective Superintendent Maguire. That was why he dreamed up that plan of Derek Hagerty getting away. We made a right hames of that, though. Didn't count on that Pearse fellow sussing it out. And then he tried to fix things by paying Clearie O'Hely to make us a bomb, which was supposed to make you look even more of an amateur. The bomb was a shade more powerful than he'd counted on, though. He didn't reckon on that young garda getting killed.

'Molloy always said we couldn't have any witnesses who could identify us, because in the end that would lead back to him. That's why we did for the Pearses, and that's why we took that Carroll fellow . . . and in the end, that's why we took out Derek Hagerty, although Derek Hagerty never saw our faces.'

He lit another cigarette and breathed smoke out of his nostrils, closing his eyes for a moment in pleasure.

When he opened them again, he said, 'That's why he sent us to take you out, Detective Superintendent Maguire. Very urgent, he said. Top fecking priority. Somehow you'd found out about the way he'd done for Niall, although he couldn't think how. "If you don't take out that fecking woman," that's exactly what he said, "we'll all of us be stuck in the slammer for the rest of our lives, with no fecking remission."'

'So all the time, Bryan Molloy was telling you in advance what we were doing to catch you?'

'Well, not *him* directly.'

'If not him directly, then who?'

'Inspector Fennessy, he was like the go-between. He'd ring me up and say, "Molloy says that two detectives are on their way to Carrigaline to question the Carroll fellow, make sure you lift him before they get there."'

Katie felt herself growing cold. Liam Fennessy had been passing information to the High Kings of Erin? Liam Fennessy? Of all the officers in the station, she thought she could trust him the most. She and Liam had always worked so closely together, and she had helped him as much as she could when his marriage to Caitlin had broken up. She knew that he was always affected by the stress of his job, but she had never imagined that he could betray her like this.

Detective O'Donovan turned and looked at her, and she could see that he was as shocked as she was.

'What about Pat Whelan and Eoghan Carroll?' she asked Lorcan Devitt.

'What about them? Pair of shites. If we could have found them we would have cut *their* fecking heads off, too.'

'So they did escape?'

'Of course they fecking escaped! Not only did they fecking escape, they fecking put both of my cousins in the hospital. They pushed Malachi downstairs and broke his fecking neck, so that he's going to be a quadraplongic for the rest of his life, and then they took his gun and shot Ezra in the shoulder and it looks like he's never going to have the proper use of his arm again. He used to be a snooker champion, too. Well, pub snooker champion, at Dolan's.'

'And you have no idea where they are, Pat Whelan and Eoghan Carroll?'

'Like I said, if I knew where the scumbags were and I wasn't stuck in here I'd cut their fecking heads off and have them baked into some hundred-year-old lady's birthday cake. It'd be big enough.'

'But you were still going to collect the ransom for them?' asked Katie.

'Why not? So long as you lot didn't know that they had escaped, we could take the money and run. That was the idea, anyway, and we could settle the score with Whelan and Carroll later, when they showed themselves.'

'But Inspector Fennessy knew that they'd got away?'

'Of course he fecking knew. I told him myself.'

'How much were you paying him?'

'Ten per cent. And Molloy was getting twenty.'

Katie sat watching him smoke for a while, then she said, 'I think we can take a break right now. I'll have somebody bring you some coffee or some tea, if you'd like some. We can talk again later.'

'Oh, you're off to have a quiet word with Inspector Fennessy, I imagine?' said Lorcan Devitt, slyly.

'Tea or coffee?' snapped Katie.

Forty-Nine

Katie and Detective O'Donovan went as quickly as they could to Inspector Fennessy's office, but they could hear his phone ringing unanswered as they walked along the corridor, and when they reached his office there was no sign of him. His computer was switched off and the folders on his desk were unopened.

Next, they went to Acting Chief Superintendent Molloy's office. He wasn't there, either. His computer screen was blank, too, and his golf clubs were gone.

Katie knocked at the door of his secretary's office.

'Teagan, do you know where ACS Molloy has got himself to?'

'Oh . . . he went out about an hour ago. He said he had a racial integration meeting at County Hall.'

'Did he give you any idea when he was coming back?"

'He wasn't sure. He said he might be playing golf this afternoon.'

'Did he say where?'

Teagan shook her head. 'It's usually Fota. Do you want me to try calling him for you?'

'Don't bother,' Katie told her. 'I don't think he'll be picking up.'

***

Now Katie and Detectiove O'Donovan went to Assistant Commissioner O'Reilly's office. He was sitting at his desk reading the latest BAILII report on Supreme Court decisions, and when Katie and Detective O'Donovan walked straight in without knocking he looked up in annoyance.

'I've been questioning Lorcan Devitt,' said Katie.

'And that somehow entitles you to walk in here without an appointment and without even knocking?'

Katie ignored that retort. 'Lorcan Devitt has confirmed something I already knew . . . that Bryan Molloy was being blackmailed by the Duggans to assist them in their kidnap operation. Apparently Liam Fennessy was involved in it, too, although I don't yet know what leverage they might have against him.'

Assistant Commissioner O'Reilly opened and closed his mouth like a large bottom-feeding fish. Then he said, 'And . . . you believe him? Devitt's a leading member of one of the worst crime gangs in Limerick, for the love of God. He'd tell you anything at all to reduce his sentence.'

'I know, sir, but I have another witness, apart from him. A very credible witness.'

Assistant Commisioner O'Reilly reached across his desk for his phone. 'Let's have Bryan up here and see what *he* has to say about it. Have you any idea what damage this could do? I can't believe this! You're only two hours back from being suspended and already you've turned my whole day into a fecking catastrophe!'

'He's not there, sir,' Katie said, quietly, as Assistant Commissioner O'Reilly started to punch out Molloy's extension number. 'He's not there and neither is Inspector Fennessy.'

Assistant Commissioner O'Reilly slammed the receiver down. 'Then where are they?' he demanded.

'Your guess is as good as mine, sir.'

'Jesus, this *is* a fecking catastrophe! Find them! Find the both of them! You're detectives, for Christ's sake! Find them! And not a word of this to anybody! If this gets out the whole fecking roof is going to fall in!'

Katie called both of their mobile phones again and again, but there was no reply from either of them. Eventually she went downstairs with Detective O'Donovan to the CCTV control room and asked the Crime Prevention Officer to check when Acting Chief Superintendent Bryan Molloy and Inspector Fennessy might have driven out of the station car park, and where they went.

Acting Chief Superintendent Molloy had driven into the station car park in his black Mercedes S-Class at 8.07 a.m., but left only twelve minutes later. He had driven along Merchants Quay and then crossed the River Lee by the Christy Ring Bridge to take the N20 due northwards.

'I'd say he's on his way back to Limerick,' said Detective O'Donovan. He checked the clock and said, 'Well, he'll have got there by now, easy, especially in that motor.'

Inspector Fennessy had left the station car park in his metallic green Mondeo only a few minutes later. He had driven northwards, too, but on the N9 towards Fermoy.

'Are you going to put out a bulletin on them?' asked Detective O'Donovan.

Katie shook her head. 'If we do that, Jimmy O'Reilly's right, the roof will fall in. We need to be really, really careful. They're not dangerous to the public, either of them, and we have to think about the reputation of the force as a whole. I'll contact DS Brown at Henry Street. He'll know who Molloy's friends are, and where he's likely to go if he thinks he's in any kind of trouble. As for Liam Fennessy . . . I don't know. It might be worth waiting to see if and when and where he turns up. He must have been under an awful lot of pressure of some kind to get involved in this.'

Katie went back to her office and switched on her desktop computer. There was a message on her phone from the press office, asking her to call back as soon as she could about the Duggans, and the shooting at her house of David Kane.

She went into her small private toilet and stared at herself in the mirror over the washbasin. She looked almost as waxy-white as one of the Duggan twins, and there were dark circles under her eyes. She had showered this morning and washed her hair but it still looked like a crow's nest, and although she had put on her maroon suit which usually made her feel quite smart, it seemed too tight across the bust today, and her breasts felt sensitive.

All the same, Katie, she said to herself, you've done it. You've beaten the High Kings of Erin. They're finished, both the original High Kings of Erin and the new High Kings of Erin, the Duggan gang and Bryan Molloy.

There was so much to clear up. She had to find Bryan Molloy and Liam Fennessy, wherever they were. She also had to track down Pat Whelan and Eoghan Carroll, and find out how they had managed to escape, and if they would have to face charges of assault for the injuries they had inflicted on Lorcan Devitt's two cousins. Under EU law, even criminals had rights.

She fixed her make-up and then she went back to her desk to call James Brown in Limerick and the press office downstairs. She hadn't even had the chance to pick up her phone, though, when Detective Dooley knocked at her door.

'Robert,' she said. 'Come on in. How's it going with Roisin Begley?'

'Well, see for yourself,' grinned Detective Dooley. He opened the door wider and led a pretty young girl into the office. Her dark brown hair was long and straight and shiny, and she was wearing a very short pink dress, with Detective Dooley's tan leather jacket hung over her shoulders. Her emerald green eye make-up and her bright pink lipstick gave her the appearance of a little plastic doll.

'Roisin herself,' said Detective Dooley, proudly, and smiled at the girl and squeezed her hand. 'I answered her advertisement and went around to see her and she told me the whole story. She thought that working for Michael Gerrety was going to be sexy and glamorous and exciting – didn't you, Roisin, that's what Gerrety promised you? She thought she was going to meet all these hunky rich fellers and make loads of money so that she could drive down Pana in her own sports car and stick up two fingers to all of her old schoolfriends, and her dad and mum, too!'

Katie stood up and held out her hands to her. 'So what happened, Roisin? It didn't turn out at all like that, did it?'

Roisin Begley suddenly pressed her fists up to her face and burst into tears. She tottered on her high red heels into Katie's arms and Katie held her tight while she sobbed and shook and let out a howl that sounded like all of the pain and disappointment and degradation she had suffered turned into a single long plainsong.

'Come on, sit down, Roisin, and tell me all about it,' said Katie. She led her over to the grey leather couch beside the window and put her arm around her.

'It was terrible,' Roisin wept. 'It made me sick to my stomach. First of all I met these two fellows in Starr's and I thought they were funny and smart and they always had so much money. They took me to parties and discos and we had such a great time.'

She started howling again, so that she could hardly breathe. Katie turned to Detective Dooley and said, 'Bring her a glass of water, would you, Robert? There's a glass in the toilet there.'

'After three or four times they said I would make a fabulous masseuse, you know. All I had to do was give these guys a massage and I would make so much money. They took me to see Michael Gerrety right at the top of the Elysian and Michael Gerrety said I was gorgeous. He gave me champagne and we went to bed together and it was just like a dream.'

'Wait a minute. Michael Gerrety took you to bed, and he had sex with you?'

Roisin sniffed and wiped her eyes with her fingers, until her green eye make-up was all smeary. 'He was such a great lover. I thought that every man I gave a massage to was going to be the same.'

'Did he know how old you were?' asked Katie.

'I told him seventeen because the boys I met at Starr's said you had to be seventeen to be a masseuse.'

'But you weren't seventeen?'

'No. Sixteen. I'm not seventeen till November the nineteenth/'

Katie handed her a glass of water, and then she asked her,

'What did Michael Gerrety do after that?'

'He took me to this house in Knocka and showed me this room and said he was going to set up a website for me and all these men would come around and all I had to do was give them a massage.'

'That was all? Just a massage?'

'Well, all I had to do was rub their mickeys. I don't know how to do that proper Thai massage. But Michael Gerrety said that if they asked for anything more I could give it to them, you know, and I could ask for lots more money.'

More tears ran down her cheeks, although this time she didn't howl, and she gradually managed to choke out what had been done to her.

'They weren't these hunky, handsome guys that I thought they were going to be. They were old and they were stinky and I hated them. They wanted me to do everything with them, like suck them and let them pee on me and they always wanted to do it up my bottom. I started to think that I wasn't pretty enough to get the really handsome men and I wasn't worth anything. They treated me like a toilet, those men. I used to get the gawks all day from what they made me do. I had the taste of gip in my mouth from morning till night.

She looked up at Detective Dooley and let out a moan, but this time it was a moan of relief. 'Then *he* came in this morning. Robert. And I thought he was gentle and lovely. And then he said what would I do for him, and I said anything, you name it. And then he said, that's it, I'm a garda and I'm taking you out of here. I can't believe it!'

Katie hugged her and let her cry it all out. She looked up at Detective Dooley and mouthed the words, 'Well done you.' Then she looked out of her window at the Elysian building, where Michael Gerrety lived. She knew that there was plenty of difficult work ahead of her, and tedious hours to be spent in court, but she also knew that sometime in the future she would remember this day as one of the best days in her whole career.

Fifty

As Katie was about to leave her office that evening, her phone rang. She was inclined to leave it, but it went on ringing so she walked back to her desk and picked it up,

'Katie? It's Michael – Michael Dempsey, your tame historian.'

'Michael, how are you?'

'Well, I'm grand altogether, but embarrassed that I never really got back to you about the High Kings of Erin. I've seen on the news that you caught them, so you have my congratulations.'

'Did you find out anything more about them?'

'Nothing that would have helped you very much, except that they were *totally* ruthless and they murdered anybody who challenged them or stood in their way. It made no difference if it was their father or their first cousin or their closest friend – they did it with no compunction at all. They made the Islamic State look like amateurs.

'Fair play, though, they did have a habit of taking hostages. There was Niall of the Nine Hostages who controlled almost all of Ireland by abducting important people from other provinces and keeping them prisoner. He used to demand enormous ransoms for their release – either grain or gold or cattle.

'Then there was Finn Mac Cumhaill. He was one of Erin's greatest warriors, and another prolific hostage-taker. He did it mostly for the ransom, but if nobody was prepared to pay for his hostages he would think up all kinds of inventive ways to kill them, such as cutting open their stomachs and filling them with rotten apples, and then letting his pigs get at them. He reckoned that if their death was gruesome enough, people would be more inclined to stump up ransoms in the future.'

'That sounds horribly similar to our High Kings of Erin,' said Katie. 'Listen – maybe we should meet. This might give the prosecuting counsel some interesting background.'

'I'd like that. But perhaps it would be wiser not to do it over lunch. Some of the things the High Kings of Erin did would turn your stomach. Enough to put you off drusheen for ever.'

Michael Dempsey hesitated for so long that Katie thought that he might have put the phone down. Just as she was about to say '*Michael*?', though, he said, 'I saw on the TV news what happened to you – you know, that neighbour of yours acting like a human shield.'

'Yes, well,' said Katie. She couldn't help conjuring up a picture of David Kane standing in her porch, smiling with supreme self-confidence and holding up his bottle of Bollinger.

'The thing of it is, there's an interesting little story about Finn Mac Cumhaill,' said Michael Dempsey. 'It just struck me as kind of *resonant*, if you know what I mean.'

'Resonant?' said Katie. 'I'm not at all sure that I do. You mean that it rings a bell, like?'

'It can't be historically true, of course, but when Finn's wife Uime was pregnant with twin boys, a jealous rival of hers turned her into a she-dog. She was turned back into a human before she went into labour, but her twins were both born as hounds. It wasn't her fault, but Finn never forgave her, and constantly beat her and whipped her as a punishment. Even if they were dogs, though, he was devoted to his sons. He gave them the same care and respect as if they had been human, and that's why why Irish veterinarians regard him as something of a patron saint.'

'Sounds like your typical High King,' said Katie, even though the very word 'veterinarian' had given her a chilly creeping feeling down her back. 'Sounds like your typical man, in fact.'

'Ah, but there's a coda to it,' said Michael Dempsey. 'Whatever grievance Finn had against Uime, he saved her life. The jealous rival sent warriors to kill her, but he stepped in front of her and the arrow that had been intended to pierce her heart pierced his instead.'

'I don't really know why you told me that, Michael,' said Katie.

'I'm sorry, Katie. It wasn't my intention to upset you. I just thought it was a perfect example of how Irish history repeats itself, over and over. We learn from history that we do not learn from history.'

'Oh, the High Kings of Erin have taught me something all right,' Katie told him.

'Oh, yes? And what's that?'

'The more that somebody tells you that they can offer you, Michael, the less you're likely to get out of them. Maguire's Law of Unfulfilled Expectations.'

***

Three weeks passed. It grew dark at four o'clock in the afternoon and the rain was colder. There was still no trace of Acting Chief Superintendent Molloy nor Inspector Fennessy, although the Anglesea Street press office had managed to keep their unexplained disappearance out of the media.

Katie's days were taken up with prosecuting Lorcan Devitt for homicide, kidnap, extortion, assault and at least eight other crimes, including drug-dealing and car theft and threatening behaviour. Pat Whelan and Eoghan Carroll had not yet reappeared – neither had Pat's wife or Eoghan's parents – but Katie guessed that they were waiting in hiding until they were sure that Lorcan Devitt was convicted and locked up. If he was found guilty of kidnap, then there was hardly any possibility that they would be charged with assault against Malachi and Ezra.

She had also arrested and charged Michael Gerrety for sex with an underage girl and reckless endangerment, and she was waiting for that case to make its slow and convoluted way to court.

Although her investigations were making good progress, she had been feeling so bloated and tired that she was relieved when it seemed that she was starting her period at last. The spotting, however, lasted only two days, and her breasts were even more swollen.

On the last day of the month, she went into Boot's in Patrick Street and bought herself a pregnancy test kit. *I can't be pregnant,* she thought, *it's impossible. David swore to me that he'd had a vasectomy and he's the only man I've slept with since John left.*

When she returned home, she found a letter waiting for her on the mat. The hallway had been stripped of its wallpaper now, and the carpet shampooed, so that any trace of David had been erased for ever. She hung up her coat and opened the kitchen door so that Barney could come jumbling out, wagging his tail and sniffing and wuffing.

'Hello, Barns, you faithful long-suffering creature,' she said. 'What about some Applaws? Chicken and rice? Lamb? You name it.'

She poured him out some dry dog food and then she looked at the letter. She didn't recognise the handwriting but it had been posted in Cork. She opened it and found a single sheet of lined paper that looked as if it had been torn from a notebook.

'Dear Kathleen,

This is by way of an apology even though I realise that no apology for what I have done will ever make amends.

After Caitlin and I broke up I went through what you might describe as a crisis, both financially and mentally. I know that I am a good detective but I have always found the job highly stressful. First of all I took out my stress on Caitlin but after she left I turned to coke, and some other stuff besides.

Not only did I lose most of my savings when our marriage collapsed, I found myself in deep debt to several drug-dealers. I went to Bryan Molloy asking for advice and he told me that there was a way out of my situation, which was to help him with the High Kings of Erin.

I know how wrong it was, but I was not thinking straight at all, and so I agreed. The way he described the plan, it sounded as if nobody would get hurt and only public money would be diverted.

I cannot tell you how bad I felt when it all went wrong and Brenda McCracken was killed and then Nessa Goold. The trouble was that I could see no way of turning back. Whatever I admitted to, I had no way of breathing life back into them.

I know now how much I have let you down and everybody else at Anglesea Street. I can understand that you will never forgive me but that is the burden I have to bear.

By the time you read this anyway I will have gone to face the judgment which I deserve.

Thank you for being a wonderful person. There is no more that I can say that will make you feel any better about me.

Liam.'

Katie took the letter into the living room and switched on the lights. She sat down and read it again, with tears in her eyes and shaking hands. She tried Liam's number again on her iPhone but there was no answer, so she called the station and asked them to send a patrol car to Liam's house in Douglas to see if he was there.

'If he doesn't answer, break in.'

She waited for over two hours. She was already in bed when Sergeant Brennan rang her back, not sleeping but reading through some of the reports that she had been given that day. She had been hoping that verbatim interviews with a fifty-one-year-old accountant from Togher accused of petty money-laundering might send her to sleep.

'There was no response so we forced an entry,' said Sergeant Brennan. 'The property was empty. Nobody there. We secured the property again before we left.'

'Thank you, sergeant,' she said.

'You're not thinking he might have self-harmed, ma'am?'

'I don't know, sergeant. I very much hope not. It's hard to know what people are going to do when they feel like there's no way out.'

***

She slept badly, even though she was so tired, and at 5.17 in the morning, when it was still dark, she climbed out of bed and went to the bathroom. The Clearblue pregnancy kit was waiting beside the toilet. Her period was due now so this was the time to use it.

At 5.30 she climbed back into bed again. Had David really loved her, in spite of the way that he had behaved towards her? Was aggression and violence his way of demonstrating how much he cared? Had he lodged his complaint against her for no other reason than he wanted her back?

He had taken Aengus Duggan's bullets for her, after all, and sacrificed his own life saving hers. But now she could never ask him why.

His child would never be able to ask him why, either. His child that she had just discovered that she was carrying inside her.

***

She was drinking coffee in the kitchen the next morning, still wrapped in her dressing gown, when the doorbell chimed. Barney was alert at once, and ran along the hallway to the front door.

'Who is it?' she called out. 'If it's a parcel just leave it in the porch.'

'It's me,' said a man's voice. A very familiar man's voice.

Katie's heart almost stopped in mid-beat. She drew back the safety chain and opened the door and there he was, wearing a long white raincoat, tall and suntanned, with his dark curly hair much longer than when he had left her.

'Hello, Katie,' he smiled. He held out a bunch of red roses wrapped in cellophane, and said, 'Pretty crappy, I'm afraid, but they were the best they had at the gas station, and noplace else was open.'

'John,' she said, and that was all she could manage to say. Her mouth puckered, and tears streamed down her face.

'Hey – *hey*,' he said, and stepped into the hallway. She put her arms around him and held him as tightly as she could. She breathed in and he smelled just like John, the same woodsy smell, and she couldn't believe that he was really here and that she was hugging him.

He kissed the top of her crow's-nest hair – once, and then twice, and then again. 'I'm sorry I came so early. The plane came in from London at six. I had coffee in the airport to kill time but then I couldn't wait any longer.'

Katie said, 'It doesn't matter, darling. Honestly, it doesn't matter.'

'Listen,' he said, 'I know I should have called you. I should have called you but I didn't know what to say to you and I was afraid to.'

She looked at him with teardrops clinging to her eyelashes. 'For goodness' sake! What were you afraid of?'

'I know it sounds crazy, sweetheart, but I was afraid you might have found somebody else. You haven't found anybody else, have you?'